MAGIC GONE WRONG

Sam knew the barrier in front of them could be countered by magic, and he began a power chant to gather his strength. Motes of light leapt from his shining fingers to squirm and merge into fragile threads that traced the lattice of energy and revealed the barrier's structure.

"The gate is open," he finally said to his companions, and peered into the darkness. Perhaps Jason saw the horrific shape reflected in Sam's eyes or perhaps he felt the terror the thing radiated. Whatever the case, his enhanced reflexes were not enough. The creature, bony armor covering its skin, row upon row of shark-like teeth in its huge cat's head, lashed out quickly with a black-taloned paw. . . .

SHADOWRUN: FIND YOUR OWN TRUTH

SECRETS OF POWER
VOLUME 3

SHADOWRUN:

FIND YOUR OWN TRUTH

ROBERT N. CHARRETTE

A ROC BOOK

ROC
Published by the Penguin Group
Penguin Books USA Inc., 375 Hudson Street,
New York, New York 10014, U.S.A.
Penguin Books Ltd, 27 Wrights Lane, London W8 5TZ, England
Penguin Books Australia Ltd, Ringwood, Victoria, Australia
Penguin Books Canada Ltd, 2801 John Street,
Markham, Ontario, Canada L3R 1B4
Penguin Books (N.Z.) Ltd, 182-190 Wairau Road,
Auckland 10, New Zealand

Penguin Books Ltd, Registered Offices:
Harmondsworth, Middlesex, England

First published by Roc, an imprint of New American Library,
a division of Penguin Books USA Inc.

First Printing, June, 1991

10 9 8 7 6 5 4 3 2 1

Copyright © FASA, 1991
All rights reserved
Series Editor: Donna Ippolito
Cover: John Zeleznick
Interior Illustrations: Joel Biske

For Julie: As you now know, the Sixth World has more than just good visuals. Thanks for the understanding and help when it was needed.

Acknowledgments

The usual round of thanks to Liz and the FASA crew for the usual reasons. A tip of the hat for the guest appearances of Rikki Ratboy and Striper goes to Paul Hume and Nyx Smith, respectively. Sam's last song is from *The Mountain Chant: A Navajo Ceremony,* as reported by Washington Matthews in the Smithsonian Institution Bureau of American Ethnology's Fifth Annual Report, 1883–84.

PART 1

There Is No Surety

1

Mudder McAlister's blood stained the sandstone of Ayer's Rock a deeper crimson. Bright stars and smears of gore marked the spots where he had struck outcroppings as he fell, and a growing pool haloed his head. Among his twisted limbs, one arm hung as though it had an extra joint. If McAlister were still alive, he would surely be dead before anyone could reach him.

Samuel Verner turned his eyes away from the grim sight, lifting his gaze toward the cloud-dotted sky as he offered a prayer for the guide's soul. With a twinge of guilt, Sam knew that his sorrow was less for the end of a life than for the injury to his own quest. He had known Mudder McAlister for only a week and hadn't particularly liked him, finding the man ill-mannered, foul-mouthed, and abrasive. Nor was Sam amused, as was Jason, by Mudder's rages when Gray Otter physically rebuffed his clumsy advances toward her. Sam wouldn't miss McAlister's company, but he had been the only runner in Perth who claimed to know where to find what Sam sought. And Cog, that faceless fixer who seemed to have connections everywhere, had given him a high competency rating.

During their trek deep into the interior of Australia, McAlister had proven his skill and knowledge time and again, flawlessly navigating the pair of all-terrain Mules across the trackless, shifting wastelands of the Outback. Fifty years ago they wouldn't have had such problems, but Australia had changed since the Awakening.

In the days before magic had returned to the earth, the country had been well served with roads. Aircraft had flown high above the deserts and grasslands to connect the coastal population centers with the interior's scattered bastions of civilization. But with the Awakening, the land had come to chaotic—and often malevolent—life, swallowing roads and brewing vast, swirling storms of such violence that air travel was often too risky. The Dreamtime had returned as a Nightmaretime, and mankind had retreated before the unleashed fury of the wild magic. Only a few resource-exploitation centers belonging to megacorporations remained in the interior, and even their lifelines were tenuous.

Sam was sure that without McAlister the team wouldn't have survived the trip to Ayer's Rock. The guide had saved them from blundering into any of the treacherous landforms and had known which of the local paranimals they had seen were dangerous. He had even shown them how to spot an approaching mana storm and how to take cover from the manifestations of the uncontrolled magic. Now he was dead, and the Americans certainly had not had time to learn everything Mudder McAlister knew about the Outback. They were all experienced shadowrunners, though. Besides, they still had Harrier Hawkins, the other Australian who had come with them. Though not as experienced as Mudder, Hawkins had run the Outback before. Sam thought there was a reasonable chance they could all get back.

He stared down at what was left of the guide's rappeling line, which lay looped chaotically near its piton anchor. When the line's sheath and multi-stranded core had parted, the sudden release of tension had flung the loose end back. He bent to examine the end and found it frayed, as though cut. Neither Jason nor Gray

Otter—for all of McAlister's harassment—would have had reason to kill the guide. They knew as well as Sam that he was the only one who knew the way. As for Harrier, he'd had some history with McAlister and so might have had a reason, but he hadn't been near the line.

Holding the end, Sam shook out the rope and estimated the remaining length. It looked just long enough to reach the edge of the ledge where the team stood. He stepped to the edge and crouched. The rock was jagged where the line had gone over the edge, easily sharp enough to slice through the line as it sawed back and forth under the weight of the descending McAlister. Before dropping over the edge, Mudder had said he wouldn't need an edge roller because the rock was smooth. Would an experienced climber like McAlister have made the mistake of laying his line over such a dangerous point? The jagged edge couldn't have been there before McAlister went over the rim.

Jason stood at the precipice, looking down at the broken body of the guide. The Indian's cyberware gleamed in the sunlight and made the blocky silhouette of his enhanced body look even less human than usual. He turned to Sam, the mirror lenses of his optic implants glittering beneath his dark brows.

"He's broke but good."

The slender woman at Jason's side nodded in agreement. She wore gray leathers decorated with short fringe and panels of exquisite beadwork. The leathers were real, unlike her Amerindian features and skin color. Those were the result of cosmetic surgery and melanin chemoadjustment. Once, when very, very wasted, she had shown Sam the minute scars, claiming they were the marks of a ritual Sun Dance. Sam knew the signs for what they were, having once prepped information for a brief on radical cosmetic surgeries back when he'd been a researcher for the corp. But even on that night she had owned up to no name other than

Gray Otter. He was sure she hadn't been born to the streets, but she had embraced them and learned to live on them. As swift as her namesake and with a bite that could be as sharp, she usually saved her speech for important matters. When she spoke without being spoken to, Sam knew she was concerned.

"Bad karma."

"Crimey," Harrier exploded, dancing about as though ready to take flight. "You blokes can't give up. Old Mudder wouldn'ta wanted that. He said you were real tough chummers. You can't quit now. Not when we's so close."

"Nobody said anything about quitting," Sam said soothingly.

"Seems like a good idea to me," Jason said. "Can't get where you're going around here without a guide."

"But Mudder said we was here, that we'd made it," Harrier whined.

"He made it all right. Maybe you'd like to join him." Jason took a step toward Harrier and the little man danced back, dodging to put Sam between him and the samurai. Jason laughed.

Sam faced him. "We're going down."

"Go ahead. I didn't come here to hump up and down rocks looking for something we won't be able to find."

"You're here because I'm paying you. And because I'm paying you, you'll shut up and come along."

Jason bristled at that. He cocked his wrists inward, and twin fourteen-centimeter blades slid from ecto-myelin sheaths embedded in his forearms. Sam's eyes were welded to the tips of the blades. Stomach churning, he watched the tips vibrate with the tension in the samurai's arms. Jason was arrogant and full of his own competence as a fighter, but Sam hoped the Indian would realize that it might take magic to handle some of the threats the Outback could throw at them before they could get back to the coast. And Sam was the only magician for a hundred kilometers. The samurai boiled with anger at Sam's tone, but Jason never threw away something that he might need. Sam was betting on that.

The blades slid back into their sheaths.

Relieved, Sam turned back to Harrier and ordered him to rig another rappeling line to replace the remnant of McAlister's line. While the Australian worked at that, Sam shrugged off his pack and set it at the rim of the ledge. He took out a few things he thought might be useful, then closed it up and braced it in position with stones. As an edge roller it was pure improvisation, but it would have to serve for the real one that lay below with McAlister. When Harrier was ready, Sam tossed the line down and made very sure it passed across his pack. Hitching the line into his harness, Sam turned his back to the void. He stepped backward, balancing at the edge for a moment before slipping slack into the line and leaning backward over the drop. Satisfied that the line would fall on the buffer of his pack, he took the first few steps downward. Only after the line settled into place did he push off gently and allow himself two meters of drop. He landed smoothly. The second controlled drops went equally well. It wasn't till the fifth that rock crumbled under his feet upon landing and he twisted his ankle. Though he had to favor that foot for pushoffs and landings, the rest of the descent went without incident. When he reached the bottom of the drop, he was relieved to find that his ankle could bear his weight.

Jason was the next down, dropping in five-meter controlled falls. Gray Otter was less ostentatious, but her more cautious approach was not enough to ward off bad luck. Halfway down she had a bad landing, and slammed shoulder-first into the cliff face. She slipped a dozen meters down the line before she could brake to a stop. When she reached his level Sam saw that her leathers were abraded and torn, but the ballistic lining remained intact. Though she made no complaint, she favored her right arm. Jason did nothing but nod brusquely to the stiff smile she offered him. Sam had seen enough of Indian stoicism to know better than to offer help. Harrier joined them by executing a rapid series of small drops that seemed more like a scramble than rappeling.

The ledge they had reached was even narrower than the one they'd left behind, and McAlister's body lying there made standing room even more cramped. The guide's blood seemed to have soaked into the rocks, the stains becoming almost indistinguishable from the reddish sandstone.

Along the cliff face to the left was a darkness that had been hidden from above by an overhang. The cavern entrance was invisible from below as well, screened by the steep angle of the nearly sheer cliff. But it was here, just as McAlister had described it.

It would have been more direct to assault the cliffs from the plain, but McAlister had pointed out that such an attempt would require serious mountaineering equipment. He had strongly advised against driving as many pitons as the climb would require. "The rock," he had said, "wouldn't like it." So they had climbed along a circuitous path to the ledge, from which they had just dropped down onto the site. At the time Sam had thought McAlister's attitude superstitious, but now that the rock had sent the guide to his death he was not so sure.

A desert oak clung to a precarious foothold in a cleft on the far side of the entrance. The harsh location had stunted the tree, making it a natural bonsai. In his time as an employee of Renraku Corporation, Sam had known gardeners who would have sacrificed their retirement to have achieved such miniature perfection.

A flicker of motion at the edge of the tree's shadow caught his attention. At first he saw nothing on the sunlit rock; then he perceived a lizard clinging to the surface. Its back was decorated with stripes and lines of dots, but the patterns blurred as the lizard streaked away.

A shot cracked suddenly, and the lizard vanished in a gout of blood and tatters of flesh. Sam started back, feeling the heat of the bullet's passage near his cheek.

"What in hell do you think you're doing? You almost hit me!"

"Zero out, Twist." Jason gave him a sardonic grin. "The 'ware's top of the line. Didn't even clip a hair of your fuzzy Anglo beard."

Sam knew Jason's smartgun link. The technology would keep the Indian from discharging his weapon while it was pointed at anyone the Indian recognized as a friendly. Killing the lizard was Jason's way of demonstrating that he would consider Sam a friend only as long as it was to his advantage, and that he was capable of dealing with Sam anytime he wished. Jason was a dangerous man, a quality that made him valuable to this run. The Indian was, in fact, the second-most-deadly samurai Sam knew. He would have preferred to have the first-most-deadly by his side, but that samurai wouldn't leave Seattle. Sam had known from the start that this run would be too dangerous with less than the best he could afford. He didn't like or trust Jason, but he had hired him anyway. Jason had offered a discount for his services to demonstrate his disdain both for the danger involved and for that other samurai, and so was affordable muscle.

Affordable, deadly, and a future problem.

"You didn't need to shoot it," Sam said.

Jason gave him a look that was supposed to be innocent. "It mighta been poisonous. Coulda bit you."

"Damn fool street-runner," Harrier snapped. "Don't you know nothing? Rock monitors eat bugs. Ain't gonna bite nobody!"

"Shut up, little man." Keeping his eyes on Sam, Jason swung his arm around so that his gun pointed at Harrier. They all knew the samurai's smartgun link would let him aim the weapon without looking in the direction the muzzle pointed. Gray Otter leaned back against the rock face and out of the line of fire. With nothing between him and the weapon, Harrier began to retreat along the ledge.

"Don't let him shoot me, Mr. Twist. You're a shaman. Hex him or something."

Pointedly, Sam turned his back on Jason to demonstrate his disapproval of the Indian's bullying. "He won't shoot you, Harrier. I hear tell that you can't get anywhere around here without a guide, and you're the closest thing we've got to one."

The sound of a weapon being holstered told Sam that Jason was done with his posturing for now. He hoped there would be no more problems until they got back to the Mules. The Indian usually went relatively docile for several hours after having lost a play in the domination game. With all the dangers of travel, he would be quiet enough on the trip back to the coast. Once there, the odds would shift again. Sam expected that Jason would want an accounting for Sam's having embarrassed him in front of Gray Otter.

For now, though, they stood before the cavern McAlister had described. If everything the guide had hinted were true, they were facing more immediate problems. Even without shifting to his astral perception, Sam felt the stirring he had come to associate with the presence of powerful magic. He sat down cross-legged and shifted perceptions. The cavern mouth remained a dark hole in the cliff, his astral senses offering no clues to what lay beyond. Ayer's Rock itself buzzed with charged mana. He had no desire to assay the darkness within the cavern in astral form.

As he was easing himself back to mundane perceptions, Sam noticed a faint glow to one side of the entrance. With his worldly eyes, he saw a pictograph of a lizard where the flesh-and-blood lizard had clung to the rock. The red and ocher of the paint were bright and shiny and looked almost wet. It didn't smell wet, though. When he touched one of the lines, Sam's finger came away feeling damp but showing no sign of color. While pondering that mystery, he noticed another painting a meter or so higher. Faded, but recognizable, it was another lizard. Like the first, its head pointed toward the mouth of the cave. Now that Sam knew what to look for, he saw that the entire entrance was ringed with pictographs. All were lizards, and all pointed toward the cavern's gaping mouth.

Sam stood and started forward, but Jason stepped past him to be the first to enter the cave. Sam was more than happy to let the Indian lead the way into the unknown. Jason was the best equipped to handle a sudden physical threat, and would only get angrier if denied that honor.

As Sam stepped across the threshold behind him, the drop in temperature was like walking into a refrigerator. After the initial shock he realized it wasn't so much the great temperature differential, but that the escape from the blazing sun made it seem so. Straining to see, he took a few steps forward. Harrier and Gray Otter entered behind him. Unlike Jason, the three of them moved cautiously, almost unwillingly. None of them had the optic augmentation of the samurai.

It took several minutes for unenhanced eyes to adjust to the darkness. When they did, Sam saw that he was standing in a sort of antechamber. Gray Otter and Harrier were there, too, but Jason had probed deeper. More aboriginal pictographs adorned the chamber's walls. Hidden from the sun, these were less faded, but none had the fresh look of the one Sam had touched. Harrier identified some of them, speaking their names as though they were totems: Kangaroo, Koala, Bandicoot, Snake, and, arching overhead, Crocodile.

Turning at the sound of a foot scraping the rock floor, he saw Jason standing in the archway of a tunnel that led deeper into the rock. Looking annoyed, the Indian turned on his heel and vanished again into the dark. Sam switched on a flashlight and motioned the others to follow.

The tunnel was uneven, narrowing and widening irregularly as it made its serpentine way into the earth. In the places where he had to duck low, Sam almost felt the weight of the rock above him. The walls were smooth and the tunnels almost circular. Branches too small for a man to pass through split off from the walls and ceiling. Sometimes the flashlight's beam showed that they looped back in almost immediately. Most often they were simply stygian holes impenetrable to the probing light. The effect gave an uncanny organic feel to the place, as though they were walking through the arteries of some strange being of rock.

Sam turned one corner to find Jason only a meter away. The Indian was advancing cautiously, gun in hand. Sam's flashlight beam faltered in the darkness ahead of Jason. Its range of illumination seemed oddly curtailed, as though it were shining into infinity.

Suddenly Jason stopped moving, and screamed as his body arched in spasm. Lines of sparks danced along his body, tracing the wires and cables of his cyberware. His Ares Predator roared as his trigger finger tightened on the trigger. The thunder it raised in the cavern gobbled all other sound. The Indian twisted, almost as though trying to tear loose from the grip of a giant hand, and then was flung down at Sam's feet. There was the slightest hint of burnt meat in the smoke rising from the samurai.

"Righty, mate," Harrier said as he propped his head around the corner. "That's the barrier."

2

"Don't worry 'bout the Injun, Mr. Twist. Barrier don't like electronics. He'll be fine in a minute."

Jason groaned, then cursed with a vigor that indicated he had taken no real injury.

"See," Harrier said eagerly, "Mudder said you was the bloke who'd get us past the barrier, Mr. Twist."

Sam handed the flashlight to Gray Otter. She took it with her right hand; her left held her Browning Ultra-Power pistol. Cautiously he walked forward. Approaching the spot where Jason had stood, Sam's head started to buzz from the strength of the magic before him. He stopped, staring into the darkness.

The space before him seemed translucent, as though the air itself were solid. A fugitive gleam dwelt within the darkness, scattering light across the spectrum. It had to be the opal McAlister had said would be here. The guide hadn't been a magician, but he had been savvy enough to realize that an opal so well protected would have magical potential beyond any ordinary open.

Sam could feel the barrier's energy almost physically, but he knew it could only be countered with magic. Seating himself before it, he shifted to astral perception. He had expected the barrier to glow with power; instead it was dark like the entrance. Unlike the entrance it sucked at him, drawing at his energy.

Sam thought about calling the spirit of the place to question it about the barrier, but a raggedness on the periphery of his astral vision reminded him of the chaos of the Outback. Would the spirit come? And if it did, would it be warped like the land of which it was a part? It might prove more dangerous than the barrier.

Deciding to tackle the barrier directly, Sam began a power chant to center himself and gather his strength. The rustlings of his companions receded from his awareness, but he felt every irregularity of the surface on which he sat. The soft movement of air through the cavern whispered to him in distracting, almost-understood entreaties. He blocked out the distraction.

Armored in his power, he changed his song, reaching out with a shining astral hand to touch the barrier. Motes of light leapt from his fingers to squirm and merge into fragile threads that traced a lattice of energy and revealed the structure of the barrier. The air in the cavern rose to a breeze, then to a wind. It howled forlornly, like a dog bereft of its master. Sam ignored it and concentrated on the pattern.

When he was sure that he understood the barrier's structure, he tugged experimentally on one of the strands. It gave to his touch and the lattice shifted slightly into a minutely different arrangement. Sam felt satisfaction. He tugged another strand, harder this time, and the lattice shifted as he willed. He set to work opening the way for the four of them.

Some time later, he felt a hand on his shoulder. Raising his head, he looked up into the brown eyes of Gray Otter. Her expression was worried, and he smiled to reassure her.

"The gate is open."

She looked disbelieving, and turned her head to stare at the darkness. He followed her gaze. The passage didn't look any different. The darkness still ate the flashlight's beam. But Sam knew better.

He got shakily to his feet. He was tired; dealing with the barrier had taken a lot out of him, but he had done what was needed. Assured that there would be no hindrance, he walked forward. For a few meters the air seemed thick around him, dragging slightly at his movements, but then he was through into fresher air that smelled of evergreen.

Beyond the barrier the cavern opened into a large chamber, whose floor sloped down to a central pool that stretched from wall to wall and separated them from the far wall. Everything was underlit by a luminescence that seemed to emanate from the milky water, making darker still the pockmarks of water-worn cavities in the walls. A natural bridge of stone stretched over the still waters. On the far side, three seams of opal cut diagonally through the sandstone wall. The opal gleamed with a thousand colors, bright beyond what might be expected from light reflected from the pool.

Sam felt his facial muscles tug into a smile. Mc-Alister had been right: Behind the barrier was a lode of opal. This was what he had come for. Those stones held the power he needed.

Jason was the first to follow him through the barrier. The Indian came through ready for trouble, but drew up short at the beauty of the cavern. Gray Otter nearly bumped into him when she came through. Then both were crowded forward when Harrier followed. The Australian whistled low and long as his gaze settled on the seams of opal.

Sam started down the path toward the pool. When he reached the relatively flat area at the edge of the water, Jason cut past him. A few strides more and the Indian skipped a step and spun in the air. He continued walking backward as he mounted the bridge. At the top of the arch he actually smiled pleasantly and taunted Sam.

"Always putting me down about wanting money, Anglo. Like it's some kind of disease. Then you haul off after a chairman's ransom without spilling a word about what you're after. Afraid of too much competition? Or embarrassed to have people know you're just like them? The Ghost will love hearing about this."

Behind Jason, a creature out of nightmare rose silently from the depths of the pool. A broad crocodile head topped the three-meter neck, but no crocodile had ever had such large golden eyes, nor such long, lanky limbs, nor furred paws armed with needle claws. The creature rose until its shoulders were level with the bridge. Its lean, armored body was ropy with muscle. If it had hind limbs, they did not come into sight.

Perhaps Jason saw the horrific shape reflected in Sam's eyes, or perhaps he felt the terror the thing radiated. Whatever the case he spun about, raising his Predator, but his enhanced reflexes were not fast enough. The creature lashed out with a black-taloned paw. Claws shredded through Jason's flak jacket to scrape shrieking across the carbon-fiber plates embedded in his skin. The implanted armor was all that saved the Indian from being gutted by the monster's attack. The impact of the blow twisted him back around to face Sam. As Jason staggered backward, his left foot came down in empty air. In a desperate bid to regain his balance he threw his body forward, just as the beast hissed and snapped its snakelike neck forward. Gaping jaws thrust at the Indian. The creature missed biting him but its snout bumped Jason, toppling him over the edge of the bridge.

Shocked by the sudden attack, Sam was slow to react. His companions were not. Braced in a formal firing stance, Gray Otter opened up on the beast. Harrier fired as well, screaming wildly as he emptied the clip of his SCK 100 submachine gun into the creature. The concentrated fire ripped into the beast at the juncture of its neck and body, slicing down into its right shoulder. Tattered muscle failed, and the monster's limb dropped limp to its side. It screeched its pain and dove.

From his vantage near the pool, Sam could see the beast's dark shape just beneath the surface as it crossed under the bridge. The shadow flowed as he watched.

The beast's neck and forelimbs shortened and its body grew broader.

The creature's shape was still shifting as it breached, its momentum carrying it partway onto the shore. Bony armor now covered its skin, and its vicious head was that of a giant cat. The dark maw revealed row upon row of sharklike teeth as it snapped at its nearest tormentor. Gray Otter barely managed to scramble away from its attack.

When it raised its right forelimb to slap at the woman, Sam was appalled to see that the limb showed no sign of injury. The paw, now a clawed flipper, caught Gray Otter and sent her tumbling. She hit hard and lay still.

Harrier ran up next to the beast. He was still screaming incoherently, but he had changed clips and was pumping fire into the beast's side. When it swung its head toward him, he ran away shrieking.

Harrier's distraction bought Sam time to collect his wits. Such a magical creature was best fought with the aid of a spirit, but remembering the chaos that haunted this land, he dared not summon one. Tired from the effort of breaching the barrier, he would have to rely on his limited skill at sorcery. Running through the spell chants he knew, he despaired at how few were oriented toward combat. This great beast would not be easy to affect. He gathered his power, readying a stunbolt. If he could slow the creature down, he would have more time to prepare a more potent spell. If he could think of one.

He spoke the words, and cast his arm forward as a physical focus to channel the energy. The beast bellowed, shaking its head in confusion.

Then, like a gore-soaked revenant, Jason struck.

The Indian leaped onto the creature's back, clamping his knees into its neck. Augmented muscles drove fighting spurs deep, grinding past the beast's dermal armor to slice flesh. Again Jason thrust, seeking the vital arteries supplying the creature's brain. It screeched and bucked but the Indian held on, howling with berserker glee. Clawed flippers raked back to flay skin from Jason's thighs.

The creature thrashed and began to change again. Its body became more sinuous, allowing it just enough reach to slam an expanded flipper-paw onto Jason's shoulder. The Indian folded over backward, spine snapped. The beast arched further, flinging the body free in a welter of blood and entrails. Jason's corpse splashed into the water and sank.

Freed of the fear of injuring Jason, Sam unleashed the arcane energy he had gathered. Barely controlled, the mana swirled away from him and coalesced into a ragged bolt of energy that ravened toward the monster. The creature screamed as the half-focused mana tore at its being, ripping through its essence and scattering fragments like sand before a storm wind.

Twisting in agony, the beast threw itself back toward the water. Its outline flowed and its proportions shifted as it jerked and flailed ineffectually. It seemed caught in a transition state, unable to take a definite action or even a definite form. The monster crashed back into the pool.

Sam watched it sink until its dark shadow was lost from sight. Without expecting an answer, he asked, "What in hell was that thing?"

"Bunyip," Harrier said shakily. Then he giggled, showing that he was still close to hysteria.

"Say what?"

"Bunyip," the Australian repeated. "It's a beastie hereabouts. Ain't never seen one before."

"Then how do you know this was one?"

"Bunyip's a shapechanger. Lives in water and is very nasty. I figure that fit the bill. You took him out pretty good. You're one hot wizboy."

Sam ignored the praise. He had failed to defeat the beast before it killed Jason. Over the Australian's shoulder, he could see Gray Otter kneeling by the edge of the pool. She was crying.

"Come on," he said to Harrier. "Let's go get the prize."

Harrier nodded enthusiastically and followed him across the bridge. The Australian spent most of the crossing scanning the water. Twice he stumbled and nearly knocked them both into the pool.

The far side of the pool was broader than the space from which they had fought the bunyip. Its surface was rougher, too, with small outcroppings and hollows scattered about. The area sloped gradually up to the wall seamed with opal.

"Cor," Harrier said, his eyes caressing the iridescent brilliance of the rock.

Sam noticed that several of the outcroppings on the floor were also tipped with opal. Near the center, a flat-topped chunk of dark rock projected almost a meter from the floor. On its surface lay a single opal crystal of surpassing size.

Harrier at his heels, Sam approached the dark pedestal. Unlike the other gems this was a fire opal, a far more precious kind. The eight-centimeter stone looked as though a great flame burned in its heart. Sam held his hand close to it without affecting the bright glory of the gem's brilliance.

Harrier reached to take it.

"No!" Sam could sense the power of the stone. "Don't touch it. For it to have maximum ritual potency, I must gather it myself."

Harrier stepped back, seeming frightened by Sam's intensity.

"Sure, Mr. Twist. It's all yours. There's plenty here for everybody."

Sam ignored the Australian's blathering. He touched the stone and was only mildly surprised to find it warm. It was truly a stone of power. He tried to lift it, but he could not get a grip. His fingers seemed to slide from the surface.

He cupped his hands to either side and concentrated. The world around him receded until Sam was aware only of the pulsing stone and himself. Slowly he brought his hands together, cradling the opal between them. His fingers tingled as they touched the oily surface. Focusing his concentration more sharply, he exerted his will on the stone. Wind whipped through the cavern, sighing through the holes worn in the stone with a frightening whelp.

It shifted slightly.

The great gem seemed reluctant to move. Carefully Sam turned it in his hands, assuring himself that it was free before easing it from the hollow in which it rested.

He sensed the vibration before he heard the rumble from deep in the earth. A crack appeared in the top of the blackish stone and raggedly curved away from the hole where the opal had nested. A second crack appeared, then a third. More followed, until eight fissures radiated from the nest. The cavern shook. Sand and small particles rained down. A soughing moan breathed through the chamber.

But the floor didn't drop away, nor did a huge boulder come rolling in to smash him. The moaning died away and the rumbling softened and stilled. Before his eyes, the seams of opalescence in the wall dimmed. Silence and calm returned to the chamber.

His prize in his hands, Sam rose shakily to his feet. With a whispered prayer of thanks, he turned his back to the opal-streaked wall.

"Where are you going, Mr. Twist?" Harrier asked. "There's lots more."

Staring at the gem, Sam answered, "This is all I'll need. I'm not sure I can handle even as much power as I feel in this stone."

"But you can't get back without me."

Sam smiled. "You and Mudder aren't the only ones who ever learned to navigate."

Across the pool Gray Otter's eyes widened in surprise, then narrowed as her face took on a calculating expression.

"But there's a bleeding fortune here just waiting to be gathered," Harrier whined.

"I didn't come for money."

"Well, I bloody well did. There's enough opal here to let us all live like bosses of the biggest megacorps. You can't just walk away from this."

"I can and I will. I have more important things to do than grub up money." Sam walked to the bridge.

By the reflection in the pool, Sam saw Harrier scramble to his feet and point an accusing finger. "That's why you're walking out with a bleeding fortune in your hands."

"I'm walking out with someone's salvation," Sam said. He crossed the bridge.

"Tarting up your words don' change the truth. I walk away now and I'm leaving behind all the wealth I've ever dreamed about."

Sam trod up the path from the pool. "You know the way here now," he said wearily.

"Cor, mate. That don't do me no effing good."

Sam turned to find Gray Otter on his heels. He nodded to her. To his surprise, she smiled back.

Harrier demanded his attention with a curse. "You owe me, Twist. I could've been killed here. You owe me."

"The pay you agreed to is in escrow in Perth."

"Perth!" Harrier slammed his hat to the floor of the cavern. "Cor! I won't be able to come back once you close that fragging magical gate."

"That's true, but you will be able to leave here whenever you want. I sensed that in the spell that makes the barrier. So dig to your heart's content. We'll leave you one of the Mules and enough supplies for a

few days. That should give you enough time to gather
more than enough opal to make you rich. Of course,
the bunyip might come back."

Harrier eyed the pool. It looked still—as still as it
had before the bunyip had erupted from it. With a
shiver, the small man scurried across the bridge to join
them.

3

Urdli knew something was wrong even before he
emerged from the rock through which he traveled. He
could feel that the mana form surrounding the hold
had been disturbed. As was proper the inner ward
opened for him, but as he passed through he sensed
that it had been altered. There was trouble. He didn't
know the seriousness of the situation until he had
pulled himself through into the mundane world, and
the wan opaline glow cast his spindly shadow across
the capstone.

It was empty.

"Purukupalil O Great Creator, how could you have
made such a fool?"

Urdli felt his skin burning with anger. A few other
guardian stones had also been pried from their wards,
but most remained in place. This had been a haphazard looting, an ignorant destruction of the ancient bal-
ances. Whoever had done this had not even known
what he was doing.

The sundered capstone was a bad sign, but he still
had a small hope that the opening of the door had gone
unnoticed by the ancient spirit. Perhaps it had not yet
reclaimed the portion of its power that lay entombed
here, giving him a chance to block the opening until

he could gather others to seal it again. If he probed the well and the spirit was awake and aware, it would try to take him. He feared that he was not strong enough to deal with it by himself, but no one else was here. If he took the time to summon others, the chance would likely be lost.

He hesitated. He had no desire to become a pawn of the enemy. Old as he was, he was not yet ready to surrender his life, or his freedom.

Necessity was a strong argument, as was duty. But shame was a goad. He was the warder. If he made no attempt to set things right, his disgrace would know no bounds.

Urdli called upon the great spirit of the Rock and wrapped himself in its protection. Here in this place of great power, the spirit was powerful. He felt as durable and strong as Rock itself. Strong enough? There was only one way to find out.

He planted his feet, dug his toes into the stone to hold his body steady, and sent his spirit down into the well of the capstone. The way was filled with fairy cobwebs that fluttered as he passed. The place was empty. What had been constrained here was gone.

Relief at not having to face that which terrified him warred with frustration at finding it gone. The proscribed power had escaped, and the old enemy would be stronger. But there might yet be time to prepare. With luck, it would focus its attention on other feuds before returning its envious and malicious eyes toward his own kind.

Though his gathered strength might have been insufficient to deal with the old one, Urdli had no fear of the lesser inmates of the holding. He turned to the other wells of internment and found two of them empty, their occupants dispersed. Fortunately, the spirits still only stirred sleepily within the other wells. The long slumber imposed a lethargy on them that was to Urdli's advantage. Calling upon the power he held, he drove them back down into their dreaming. To seal the wells, he scooped opal from the wall seam and molded it in his hands to create new guardian stones. He set each in place with spells that made these stones replacements for the stolen ones. At least some of the problems would remain entombed here.

The effort exhausted him. He released his hold on the Rock spirit and lay back to rest, drifting off into a dreamless sleep. When he awoke, he was hungry. There was no food to be had here, but he could drink from the pool. Crouching over it, he gazed down into the milky water. His reflection showed him a haggard face, dark eyes sunken into black pits of exhaustion that were obvious even against his dusky skin. He dispersed the disturbing image by dipping his hands into the water, but his worries remained. There was still much to do.

After his drink, he called the bunyip. When it did not respond, he was not surprised. The thieves could not have successfully departed with the stones without first overcoming the bunyip.

He crossed the bridge and walked up the slope to the tunnel. Crouching to clear the low ceiling, he traveled the short distance to the gate of the inner ward. He adjusted his senses and read its structure, seeking the anomaly he had felt when crossing the ward on his way to the chamber. Finding the flaw was not difficult. One of the thieves, a magician, had opened the gate and set it to admit four persons, though only three had left. Urdli tugged on the structure, restoring it to its original form. Later, when he felt stronger, he would reinforce the ward.

He turned back to the chamber and scanned it with the deep sight. There was no sign of life, either amid the field of glowing prisons or down in the depths of the pool. The bunyip was dead, but so was one of the intruders. The beast had done its work, at least in part. A new one would be necessary.

Passing through the ward, Urdli walked to the cavern's mouth. There, in the crisp, clean air, he caught the faint scent of the blood-soaked rocks. His deep sight saw the stain, and he felt the wound in the rock where the piton had been driven. Another of the intruders had died here.

He stepped off the ledge and, supported by his will, descended to the plain below. The grave of the climber was painfully obvious. The thieves had made no attempt to hide it. He left it alone; likely it would not offer any useful information.

The marks of vehicles scarred the ground nearby. Wide, deeply treaded tires ran to a protected cranny, then away again. Within the nook was a profusion of footprints. They meant little to him. He was no expert, but it looked as though there were only five sets, the climber and the four who had penetrated the holding. He gazed out along the path the tracks took. The trail would not remain long in the Outback. Already he could see a storm racing to cut across the thieves' spoor.

He was angry with them. And with himself.

The guardian stone, though bereft of its primary function, was still an item of power. Its recovery was imperative, as was the punishment of the thieves. He could not track them mundanely, but there were other ways. He began to gather materials.

The dry mulga branch was in a gully. The ants brought him the teeth of a marsupial mole. He apologized to the bandicoot he trapped and killed for its tail. The tail he bound to the slender end of the stick, then he spat on it and sealed the join with a word. Sitting down in a wash edged in red clay, he began his songs.

Two nights passed before the curved mulga branch began to writhe and put out new sprouts. The new growth stretched out into four spindly legs, while the old twigs elongated into ribs. The bulbous end of the branch grew, forming first a cranium, then a snout. He tossed the teeth into the air and they swirled into place along the edges of the forked snout, growing in size as they did. Throat dry and voice cracking, he rose and changed the song. He strode to the clay, the stick beast capering at his side. Thrusting his hands past the dry upper layers of earth, he scooped out handfuls of the moist clay beneath and molded it around the wooden skeleton. He packed the beast with his purpose and magic. Slowly, it took on the shape of a lean hunting hound. Holding the head with one hand he gazed at the rough-hewn shape, featureless save for the mouth of sharp teeth.

"Kulpunya, I give you eyes that you may see those you hunt," he said, thrusting two fingers deep into its skull.

"Kulpunya, I give you nostrils that you may smell your prey where they hide," he said, pressing two smaller holes into the end of its snout.

"Kulpunya, I give you ears to hear the despairing howls of those you hunt unerringly," he said, modeling long flaps at the back of the head. "With your ears, hear my command, kulpunya. Find the desecrators. Hunt them down for me."

The kulpunya howled, leapt from his grip, and raced away. Urdli watched its absurdly thin limbs churn, propelling it impossibly fast across the plain. It ran in silence, implacable and malevolent.

Urdli smiled.

4

Hohiro Sato was not in a good mood. The morning meeting with Atreus Applications, Incorporated had not gone well. The myopic fools at AAI were still being difficult. Even his personal appearance at their headquarters in the Hong Kong Free Enterprise Enclave had failed to convince the stubborn board of directors. When he had told them that Renraku's interest in their company was utterly serious, they had seemed to think he was bluffing. They would learn, though. Sato wanted Atreus's assets for the foundering Special Directorate. And he would have them. When AAI refused his offer of a staged stock buyout, they had sealed their own fate. Sato would suck them dry as soon as he could arrange the necessary change in circumstances.

But that was a pleasure belonging to the future. He had left the meeting irritated, and then his irritation became tinged with resentment upon receiving word that Grandmother wanted to see him. Now she had the temerity to keep him waiting. He was no junior salaryman to be summoned, however polite the phrasing of the order. Nor was he a lackey to be kept cooling his heels. His vexation kindled a smoldering anger.

Staring between the blank-faced guards, he watched the inner door with its teak veneer. Briefly fantasizing that his vision pierced the door's opacity, he pictured the scene beyond it. The garden was ablaze with rare flowers, a riot of colors tinted ever so slightly more exotic by the faint purple hue of the SunSub light panels. Insects serviced the plants, barely disturbed by the occasional visitor moving between one of the ring rooms and the central hub of the curved stairway that descended into darkness, into her sanctum.

He had long wanted to know what went on in her sanctum when he was not there, but never uncovered more than rumors. What he *had* learned was that she was well-protected. Even using the finest surveillance equipment, his agents had failed to penetrate the walls of the ring rooms. Even the magical skills of his tame

mage, Masamba, could not pierce her barriers. Grandmother liked her secrets.

Secrets were her business.

From her lair Grandmother ran an international network that traded in information, usually clandestine.
She traded in other things, legal and illegal, as well.
Despite her personal eccentricities she was a premier
power broker.

Having been only a junior salaryman when he had
first encountered her network, Sato had benefited from
the association. At several key junctures in his career
confidential material had been passed to him, allowing
him to embarrass rivals or blackmail them out of his
way. The stimulation to his career was undeniable, but
it galled him that she held power over him. She. A
woman. At least she was a Japanese.

Each time he had used her information, she had sunk
her hooks in deeper. He had fed her information in
return, all the while knowing that it only gave her a
tighter hold over him. The opportunities just seemed
too great to ignore and her demands inconsequential
in comparison. He had been younger then, hungrier
. . . and stupider. Now he knew better, understood the
nature of her hold over him. Someday she would demand something he was unwilling to give, then
threaten him with ruin if he denied her. On that day,
he wanted to be able to laugh in her face. He wanted
to be too powerful for her to touch. So far, however,
he had not succeeded in gleaning the information he
needed to compromise her. Lacking that, he could
make only vague plans. His best depended on a tool
not yet ready. Until he knew more about her secrets,
he was arming to fight wraiths.

One thing Sato knew for sure was that anger would
gain him nothing. He forced it down, leashing it to his
will. He would not be shamed into losing his temper
before the woman. By the time her servant arrived to

lead him into the garden, he was outwardly calm. Inside the fire coiled, a sullen dragon awaiting its time.

As in all his previous visits, he was required to leave his bodyguards in the ring room. The servant accompanied him along the gravel path, then left him to descend the stairway alone. He followed his own shadow around the central pole and down the winding way. He stepped confidently, even when his shadow obscured the stairs. The hum of the garden insects faded into silence, but the quiet was soon broken by a rhythmic sound that grew louder as he descended.

Click, clack.

Over and over.

Damn! She was at her loom again. He hated it when she was weaving. The noise disturbed his concentration, and he did not like to be distracted when trying to deal with her. She was too sharp; he needed to be ready to pounce on the slightest clue to what might give him a hold on her.

He stopped briefly at the foot of the stairs, remaining in the shaft of light from above. There was deep darkness all around. She was out there in the dark that was part of her protection, but it offered little from him. His Zeiss eyes adjusted at his command, shifting to light amplification, and he saw her bent old shape seated before the loom. She looked no older than the day they had met, nearly two decades ago.

He didn't doubt she was aware of him, but she made no sign. He called attention to himself by clearing his throat. Her hands never stopped moving. The shuttle flew back and forth. A gnarled hand racked the heddles forward, snugging the latest line in the pattern firmly into place. Without taking her eyes or hands from her work, she greeted him in a wobbling, high-pitched voice.

"Ah, Sato-*san,* how nice of you to call."

If she wished to pretend that she had not summoned him, he would humor her. Forcing politeness, he responded, "I was in Hong Kong. How could I not visit my Grandmother?"

She cackled. "Such filial devotion. I wonder, do you show so much to your real grandmother?"

His family was no business of hers, but he was sure she already knew the answer to her question, as she knew so much about him. Why could he learn so little about her? He refused to answer her question.

Click, clack.

"Well, then, Sato-*san* How is your special project in Seattle prospering?"

That was a question she would not let him ignore. "Not very well at all."

For a moment, the loom was silent. Then, click, clack.

"I am most sorry to hear that. I was so hoping you would have good news for me. You raised my hopes last year."

He was sure he had. His own hopes had risen when the Special Directorate had seemed to have achieved their goal of creating a true artificial intelligence within the Renraku matrix. "I am sorry if you were disappointed. The disruption brought me more trouble than it did you."

"Very true. But Aneki took it well, didn't he?"

"Well enough."

"Well enough, indeed. You have not been dethroned as the director's heir-apparent, and you are still in command of the Seattle arcology. That shows a certain cleverness that I shall have to keep in mind when I think of you. Have you been telling your Aneki-*sama* pleasant things that you have neglected to tell Grandmother?"

"I have told him what I have told you. Since mismanagement in the Security Directorate allowed the loss of one of the principal designers, the Special Directorate has been stymied, demoralized, and beset with unavoidable delays. A significant amount of data was destroyed, and what remained needed to be checked. Hutten, the designer who was lost, was clearly defecting, as evidenced by his theft of key datafiles and custom components. As he was the architect of some of those lost components and left no reliable notes, the Directorate has not yet been able to duplicate the functions. We are no closer to achieving the goal than when Aneki assigned me to move things along.''

Click, clack. ''The touted abilities of your toy would have been most useful. You have, of course, punished those responsible for the disappointment. What progress have you made in recovering Hutten?''

''None.''

Click, clack. The sound was harsher now. Sato knew he had better explain.

''There have been no notable advances among our competitors. The security agent responsible for the debacle was seen to have injured Hutten before she herself fell to her death. Perhaps fatally. He may be presumed dead. As to punishment, there is still no clue as to who was manipulating the rogue Verner.''

Click . . .

''Verner? The name seems familiar. Refresh an old woman's memory, Sato-*san.*''

He doubted her memory needed refreshing. She was testing him, as always.

Years ago she had set him the task of tracking a handful of individuals. Renraku Corporation was a world leader in data technology, and his placement with the firm made him an obvious choice to arrange for surreptitious information-retrieval. He might have understood if the individuals she wanted tracked were important people, but most were inconsequential. But she was so persistent over the years, wanting to know everything about these people and their relatives, that he had come to believe she had some deep concern beyond that of an information broker. She seemed obsessed with the fate of these individuals, but he had never learned why. They seemed to have nothing in common save traumatic experiences during the turbulent year of 2039. Especially common were brushes with death on the infamous Night of Rage and in the turmoil that had followed. He had come to suspect that this matter touched upon something she . . . was "feared" too strong a word?

His belief in her fear had solidified two years ago when she commanded the interrogation of Janice Verner. The questions he had been required to ask the girl were filled with paranoid suspicion. What did "they" want? What connection did "they" have with the Verner family? Then, so many seemingly unrelated questions. He did not know who "they" were, but he had come to believe that "they" really existed. Grandmother might be paranoid, but even paranoids have enemies. Anyone who gave her concern gave him hope. If he was careful, "they" might provide him a lever to pry loose her hold over him.

Not wishing to betray himself, he chose his words carefully. "The Verners are among those you watch."

"Ah, yes. The woman was such a disappointment. Whatever happened to the man?" Click, clack.

"Little new information has emerged since he went rogue. We know he survived his raid on the arcology. We also know that a shadowrunner matching his description has been linked to a number of petty operations, mostly in the Seattle area. His continued existence seems likely, but remains untraceable."

Click, clack. "Surely the largest information corporation in the world keeps records."

"On him, we no longer seem able. His file vanished from Renraku's banks a few months after the Hutten incident, and every attempt to begin a new one has been fruitless. Each entry vanishes almost as soon as it is made. I believe that he is, or has acquired the services of, a computer expert of the highest ability.

He or his accomplice has inserted a dedicated virus of hitherto unknown sophistication into the Matrix. Renraku resources have failed to isolate it. We know of its existence only by its actions, as it destroys all data connected to Samuel Verner.''

Click, clack. "But not his sister's data?''

"No. And in any case, that would be unnecessary. Her death was recorded on Yomi Island nearly a year ago.''

"I am intrigued.'' Click, clack. "He was involved with Hutten. Perhaps your missing computer expert is still alive after all. Perhaps the nascent artificial intelligence was used to strip Verner's identity from the Matrix. As you said, he had gone rogue. As a shadowrunner, he would find his corporate records a detriment.''

Sato thought little of the theory, but decided it would be best not to scoff. If Hutten and the AI still existed, some corporation would have them and would have used them. He would not be unaware of such a situation. "There is no evidence that the AI survived Hutten's sabotage. The Renraku matrix retains nothing more than sophisticated analogs and knowbots, and Huang and Cliber are unable to duplicate their earlier apparent success. Nothing comparable has been observed in any other corporate matrix or in the worldwide Matrix.''

Click, clack. "And the current rash of ghost-in-the-machine tales?''

"Simply that. Tall tales, rumors, and lies. There is nothing verifiable, nothing to suggest that Hutten or the AI remain in existence.''

"I am disappointed.'' Click, clack. "Ah, well. New lines of endeavor are not always rewarding. One must always have enough interests that a disappointment does not prove overwhelming. I understand that Atreus has made some interesting refinements in its Haas biochips.''

He was growing tired of her patronizing manner. Irritated by the constant rattle of the loom, he snapped, "I know."

"I am sorry. Of course you would." Click, clack. "You have been showing quite an interest in their operations of late. Regrettably, they have shown little interest in your offers."

"As usual, you are well informed."

Click. Clack. "I have a new interest. I wish some data. Awaiting you upstairs are chips with details on the subjects."

"I will see what I can do."

"I am sure you will, Sato-*san*. You are always good to Grandmother. And because you are, Grandmother is good to you. The chips also contain other juicy tidbits. Atreus could become suddenly vulnerable, were such data to fall into the wrong hands."

Sato smiled. For Atreus, the wrong hands would be Sato's. For Grandmother's purposes, however, Sato's would be the right hands. His own plans would be advanced, but her schemes would be furthered as well. Of that he had no doubt. He would take advantage of her offering.

5

The longer the examination went on, the more anxious Sam Verner became. Was the stone unsuitable? Had people died because he had misunderstood the needs of the ritual and gone after the wrong kind of object? Maybe the opal was the right kind of talisman, but was not strong enough. Or not focused right. The stone had seemed to pulse with power when first he had seen it in the cavern, but its aural glow had changed during the trip back. Had it weakened? He didn't know. He wanted to pace, to scorch away his nervousness and uncertainty by burning physical energy.

Only Katherine Hart's presence restrained him. She disapproved of such unprofessional displays of concern. She prized poise, coolness, and style. Indeed, she embodied those qualities in her looks, clothes, and masterly presentation. And he, prizing her good opinion, tried to emulate her, at least in the latter. His barely average looks could never match her slender, ethereal beauty. As for his clothes sense, the worn and comfortable garb he had adopted since entering the life of the shadows would never be cutting-edge fashion.

So he sat and fretted silently, wondering why the others weren't as concerned. Dodger sat in his habitual corner, eyes closed as he meditated. The elven decker looked entirely too serene. Gray Otter stood in the opposite corner. The beadwork was almost the only thing that made her stand out against the dirty wall. Her position would have given her a clear view of the squat's one window, but her eyes were turned to her counterpart among the Sylvestrines. For all his religious devotion Brother Paulus was a soldier, armed and wary. The burly Sylvestrine monk showed no sign of affiliation, save for a black enameled chi-rho belt buckle on his armor-lined coat. A datajack was embedded into his temple and induction pads in his palms; when in motion, he moved with the occasional jerkiness of those with cyber-enhanced reflexes. Like his companions, Brother Mark wore no obvious sign of his religious calling. But while his somber, austere expression, and the unrelieved black of his suit and coat, might hint at his clerical nature, they concealed his puissance as a hermetic magician. Like Dodger's, Brother Mark's eyes were closed. Unlike the elf, he was working, warding the apartment while the third member of his order studied the fire opal.

That good priest sat slumped in his chair, hands folded around the gem that rested on the rickety table. Father Pietro Rinaldi was an adept, able to read the auras of persons and things. Though incapable of other magicks, he was superb in his specialty, far better than Sam, Hart, or Brother Mark. He had been at his examination for over an hour now. Occasionally, he muttered. Usually the words were unintelligible, but Sam had made out "curious" and "fascinating." He wished the priest would remember that other people also wanted to know what he was finding out.

Time moved with the speed of a slug. At long last Rinaldi sat back, lacing his fingers behind his neck as he stretched. When he relaxed, he sat unmoving and breathing deeply.

Unleashed by the obvious conclusion of the priest's studies, Sam leapt up.

"Well?"

Rinaldi gave him a shrug and a smile. "It's powerful, my friend. Of that there is no doubt. But it is most unusual as well. The stone shows no sign of having been worked by tools, yet its aura indicates that it was made. Also, the residual structures of some potent spells linger on it. I think it may have been molded by magic."

"Who cares how it was made? Is it usable?"

"Usable? I should think so."

"Good. I would hate to have wasted the trip."

"The trip only cost you time and money, and only the time was of real value. But perhaps I know you well enough to see your real concern. Do not hang yourself about with guilt. Any adventure in this world has dangers, and those who undertake such activities must expect to face their share of them. Your allies are dead but you are not at fault, and you have not squandered their lives to gain a pretty bauble. I suggested you acquire a magically potent artifact to focus and amplify your power, and you came back with something more powerful than any of the talismans in the armory of the Sylvestrine monastery at Saint Luc.''

''Then it will work?'' Sam asked eagerly.

Rinaldi looked at the table, avoiding Sam's eyes. ''I didn't say that. As I have told you often enough, this whole operation is speculative. The stone will channel an enormous quantity of power, but as you know, tools alone are insufficient. The form of the ritual must be exact, and the will driving it must be pure and focused. I would not wish to raise false hopes.''

''Indeed,'' Brother Mark agreed. ''Success is not likely. The transformation you seek is beyond the bounds of magic as man understands it.''

''And who is to say that man understands all magic?'' Hart smiled sweetly and lifted a hand to brush back her hair in a gesture that revealed one pointed ear.

''Implying elven secrets is a poor ploy, Ms. Hart. Elves are but a subspecies of mankind, a mere subset of the genetic pool awakened to phenotypic expression in these latter days. Your race's higher-than-average predisposition to magically active individuals gives no special magical abilities or knowledge.''

''Art thou sure, good brother?'' Dodger asked. ''Elves once ruled your ancestral Ireland, and once again hold it as their domain. They say they have only returned from the sunset lands to reclaim the lands they walked of old. Art thou of such a great age to dispute their claim with certain knowledge of your own?''

''I need be no older than I am to dispute such foolishness. Save for a few isolated cases in the decades preceding the so-called Awakening of 2011, there were no elves. Or dwarfs, for that matter. Elven and dwarf phenotypes are quite distinctive. How could the existence of such persons never have been noted in centuries of historical and scientific records?''

"How indeed, good brother?''

"Dump it, Dodger. Brother Mark is here to help. He doesn't need your foolishness.''

"My apologies, Sir Twist, to both you and to Brother Mark. I sought but to lighten the mood with this idle talk.''

Sam sighed. "How come every time you get bored, you start looking for trouble? If you can't be useful, Dodger, at least try not to insult guests and start feuds.''

"Be charitable,'' Rinaldi suggested. "Dodger has little to offer in this endeavor. His idleness chafes at him. It's no sin. His attendance is a sign of his concern and support.''

"You're right, Father. It's not *his* idleness that's the sin. It's my own. While Janice remains as she is, every day puts her closer to damnation.''

"We're all aware of that, Sam.'' Hart put her hand on his shoulder. "We've got the stone now. We don't have to wait anymore.''

"I know you understand. Without your connections we would have lost her after she left England, and I'd have no idea where she had run to or how she was doing.''

"And how is that?'' Mark asked. "Are you sure that she has not succumbed to her wendigo nature? Her sins are already great, but if she has given in to despair and freely embraced the way of the wendigo, she has gone beyond salvation. How do you know that she has not abandoned her humanity? Have you spoken with her?''

Sam shook his head. "She wouldn't speak with me in Vancouver, and she refused to acknowledge any of the letters I had waiting in towns along her path. She hasn't taken any communications equipment, and I can't send electronic mail because the Matrix doesn't reach where she is now. Too few people.''

"There are no reports of wendigo predation in the area,'' Hart said.

"Which is a good sign,'' Rinaldi said. "Her chosen retreat places her far from temptation. Everything seems to indicate that she still retains some vestige of humanity. Her success bodes well, for denial of the wendigo nature would be a strong factor in reversing the curse.''

"If it can be done,'' Mark said.

"I fervently pray that it is possible,'' Rinaldi said. "For her sake, as well as for others whose souls we might unburden if we succeed.''

"Do you fear the loss of her soul, Father?'' Dodger asked. "Or are you having second thoughts about letting her go in England? Do you feel the weight of innocent, eaten souls?''

"I mourn the straying of any soul from the path of righteousness. She has eaten manflesh, but that can be forgiven in the light of her body's perverted needs. As far as we know, she refrained from actually killing in order to feed. That, I believe, would be the point beyond which the wendigo nature would rule her and she would be lost to us and to God.''

"What about those who have died to feed the wendigo? And who might yet die? Do you feel the weight of their murders on your own soul?''

Before the priest could answer, Sam cut in. "That's enough, Dodger!''

"Peace, Sam. Dodger was in England, too. We all let Janice leave. What she does or does not do is our shared responsibility. All of us. But the past is done and we must look to the future. We took no action against her in hope of her salvation, a salvation that we work toward now. That is what must concern us. Have you given more thought to the ritual site?''

"I thought we'd settled that. You said that the ritual

needs a place of power, one associated with change, and Mount Rainier seems ideal. As one of the volcanoes activated by the Ghost Dancers, it was one of the first places where heavy-duty magical power manifested in the Sixth World. The Indians' campaign to rid North America of non-Indians wasn't successful, but it was one of the biggest changes of the century. Only the return of magic and magical beings was bigger, and the Ghost Dance was part of that, too.''

Rinaldi shook his head. "I find no fault with your symbolic logic, and the site is indeed a place of power. But I still think that a place more convenient to Janice's refuge would be safer. She must be physically present for the ritual to work.''

"Still worried about the temptation to her wendigo nature among people?" Hart asked.

Rinaldi nodded.

"It's a chance I'm willing to take," Sam said. "She's strong. She'll deal with it.''

Rinaldi sighed. "You may be willing, Sam. What about her? It's her soul that will be tainted if she's not strong enough.''

"Here or there, she has to agree to participate," Hart said. She held out Sam's fringed synthleather jacket. The long tassels shifted restlessly, jangling the assorted amulets tied to them.

Sam reached out and fingered some of the intricate knots. "I'm not going out. At least not physically.''

"Mindset," she reminded him. "You're doing shamanistic things, and this is your shaman suit, right?''

"Right. Worried?''

She ran her fingers through his beard. "This is a major projection you're planning. You haven't tried contacting anyone on the mundane while projecting before. You may need the help of the little friends in the jacket.''

He was touched by her concern. As usual, she was

thinking ahead. He gave her a kiss and put on the jacket.

Dodger cleared his throat. "Struth, I am as necessary here as a mirror to a medusa. If you would not be overly distressed to lose such a valued member of your audience, I might attend to other matters."

Now that they were actually doing something, Sam felt more charitable toward Dodger. "Null perspiration. Don't get into anything you can't handle alone."

"Jenny's gotten her hands on a new Korean icecutter, Dodger. She's going to test it on a run tonight. Maybe she'd like some company."

"Fair Jenny is a big girl. She has no need of my supervision. The Matrix holds other matters of more interest. Render unto her my best wishes," Dodger said as he opened the door.

Hart waited a few moments before commenting, "He's awfully preoccupied still. Teresa?"

Sam shrugged. "Who knows? He hasn't mentioned her for months."

"He hasn't said much of anything for months. At least nothing of importance. But it's clear that something is bothering him."

"Perhaps he finds it a strain to work with both you and that other group you've told me about, the one run by Sally Tsung," Rinaldi suggested.

Sam gave a rueful chuckle. "That's not the problem. Sally's got almost as little use for Dodger these days as she does for me."

For a moment Hart looked ready to comment, but she didn't. In private Hart had little good to say about the way Sally vilified Sam for his alleged fickleness, but in public she refrained from speaking against Tsung herself. Sam was sure he would hear about it later.

"You need me?" Gray Otter asked.

Sam answered, "Magic time, Otter. No need for muscle."

"I'm gone." And she was.

"Brother Paulus and I shall leave as well, Father Pietro. As you know, this ill-disciplined shamanic business makes me uncomfortable. You will join us at Saint Sebastian's?"

"As soon as we finish."

"Very well." Mark turned to Sam. "I wish you luck."

The brothers left. Sam locked the door behind them before lying down with his head in Hart's lap. Father Rinaldi took the drum from its cupboard, seated himself out of Sam's sight, and began to play. The beat was strong, steady. Sam felt Hart extend herself, using her power to relax his body. He released his astral self to fly down the tunnel and through the hole to the otherworld, beginning the journey north.

6

Joining the kulpunya, Urdli stared down at its victim. The small man was torn beyond recognition. His blood spattered the disordered furnishings and spread in a growing pool around his body. Urdli didn't know who the man was. It didn't matter; he had paid for his crime.

Urdli looked for the missing stones with his deep sight. He detected a hint of power from a locked box, hidden in a hollow in the wall. He tossed aside the dresser screening the badly patched panel and tore open the cache. He didn't care if he left traces. A simple spell blasted the padlock open.

The guardian stone was not there.

Recovering the stone was not going to be so simple.

With a word, he unleashed the kulpunya again. There were two more thieves to be hunted down.

* * *

He was cramped by the confines of the ducting, but that didn't particularly bother Neko Noguchi. His training had inured him to discomfort. This once, his small size had proven an unmatchable asset. No dwarf could have done what he had done tonight; dwarfs were too stocky to negotiate the twists and turns of the ducting. No elf either. Elves might have the necessary slimness, but they were too tall for the tighter turns of the ducting. Nor could an ork or a troll hope to squeeze through where a norm couldn't pass. Neko's passport into these forbidden realms had been his short stature, slight build, and rubbery suppleness. Who said norms were outmoded in the Sixth World?

The tall corporate was leaving now, walking up the stairs. The old woman continued to work at her loom. They never knew Neko was here, listening. He was glad now for the decision to leave all electronic devices behind. When the suit was descending the stairs Neko had seen the flicker of an electromagnetic emissions detector, and again as the man had left. He was sure similar sensors watched the ducts. Yet he had evaded the defenses that had blocked other hopefuls even without any high-tech tools or cyberware. Betting on his personal skills alone had been a calculated risk, but it had paid off.

Neko had crouched in his hidden place all through Grandmother's last three interviews. But none had been as interesting as the one with the black-haired corporate; the others had only brought news of the shadow world of Hong Kong. Save for the business about Mitsuhama hiring Greerson for a sanction, Neko's own prowls had already earned him the rest of the news he had heard today. If whispered in the right ear, the Greerson info would be worth something.

But the suit. What was his name? Saito? No, Sato. That was it. Neko would have to remember that name.

Sato was playing in a bigger arena. All that stuff about an AI. Neko had decker friends who would know what that stuff was worth. If he stepped carefully, he could turn all that innuendo and speculation into nuyen.

What a coup! His first time eavesdropping on the infamous Grandmother, and he had scored. That would make his name in the shadows. Neko Noguchi was on his way to becoming a big man in the biz.

But he was no fool to waste this opportunity. With absolutely no hint that he had been detected, he could afford to stay for a while longer. No telling what else he might learn.

He settled himself to wait for Grandmother's next visitor. The rhythmic clatter of the loom had an almost hypnotic quality that lulled him. His mind drifted, dreaming of the juicy bits he would gather while listening in on the doings of Grandmother. Then he started back to full awareness, unsure of what had changed.

Grandmother continued her weaving. No one had come to disturb her. But there was something. Yes, there it was. A noise in ducting.

A maintenance drone or a rigger-run cleaning robot? Either would be a problem. The dog-brain in a drone wouldn't be bright enough to recognize him, but the stupid thing might try to clean him out of the duct, a process that would be most painful. If it were a robot, a rigger could ID him as an intruder and would report his presence. That would make departure much more complicated and cancel any chance of returning another day. He did not want his hole through Grandmother's security sealed; it was his doorway to fortune.

The scraping sound came again, accompanied by a softer brushing noise. It was not a scrubbing rotor. What was it? It didn't sound mechanical. The important point was that it sounded nearer. Discretion being the better part of profits, Neko decided to leave.

His joints had stiffened less than might have been expected. A brisk crawl would have them loose again. He moved quietly from his perch. Once away from where he thought noise of his movement could be transmitted to Grandmother's sanctum, he moved more briskly. Several turns later, he heard the sound again. Was it following him?

He was not far from his exit, but increased his pace anyway. He had no desire to be caught in the duct. Those dark confines left Neko no room to use his justly famed agility.

He twisted himself through the last turn and saw light slitting through the grating by which he had entered. Pausing only long enough to assure himself that no one occupied the storeroom beyond, he dug loose the putty holding the panel in place. He held it with one hand as he shimmied his torso clear. His free hand held him up as he worked his knees clear, then his feet. He dropped nearly noiselessly to the box beneath the opening.

He was out, unconfined. He grinned. Whatever roamed the ducts of Grandmother's fortress had not caught him.

As he reached up to replace the grating, something black, glistening-hard, and studded with coarse hairs reached through the slats. In startled reaction Neko jerked back, hands still clutching the duct cover. There was a rasping sound as metal slid along the twitching thing, then Neko was jerked back toward the wall. The black thing clamped onto the grating and Neko let go. The panel slammed crossways across the opening, crumpling as it was withdrawn into the darkness.

As it disappeared a second black thing scythed out of the duct, sweeping toward Neko's head. He ducked into a crouch. While the sharp, hooked end of the thing scraped along the wall, he uncoiled into a back flip. He landed surefooted, ready to run but unwilling to turn his back on the unknown thing in the duct.

An ominous silence descended on the storeroom.

Neko bunched the muscles of his left forearm as he twisted it, triggering the release of the carbon-fiber blades from their forearm sheath. Four monofiber-edged cutters slid forward to project seven centimeters past his cocked wrist. In close they would make sushi out of muscle and tissue, but he had seen the strength of whatever it was. He was not sure he wanted to get that close to it. He rejected his pistol; noise was as much his enemy as the whatever-it-was. His right hand slipped a throwing spike from among the half-dozen sheathed along his thigh. At ranges under five meters, his skill made the silvered steel as deadly as the pistol. Thumb holding the spike against his palm and fingers, he raised his hand into throwing position.

Again he heard the scraping, brushing sound that had pursued him through the ducts. Slowly the black claws appeared, and gripped the edges of the opening. The claws hauled a grotesque bulk into view, and he began to think he would have been better off running.

The claw-tipped things were arms, inhumanly thin and oddly jointed, but arms nonetheless. They grew from shoulders that barely humped above the swollen and bloated belly of the creature that tumbled from the duct. Its legs, almost duplicates of the arms, slithered free of the darkness as the thing dropped to the floor. It steadied itself for a moment on all fours before rising to stand in an insectoid parody of a man. Tattered cloth hung on its torso, snagged and split by bristly hairs. It was as tall as a troll, making it nearly three times Neko's height. Malevolent onyx eyes stared down at him from a face totally inhuman.

Deciding he could not afford to let it make the first move, Neko blurred into action. His hand snapped forward, releasing the spike and sending it speeding toward the obscene visage. The steel pierced its right eye, popping the orb in a gush of dark fluid. The thing made no sound as the bulbous head wobbled and the creature scraped at the spike with a claw until the weapon dropped free.

Then it sprang.

Neko barely dodged its first swipe. A claw snagged his clothes, gouging his flesh and tugging him back toward the creature. Twisting around, he slashed with his blades. He felt two of the edges strike the hard limb and slide, barely cutting. The other two sliced through the fabric of his clothes and freed him. He fell, hitting the floor hard.

Coming at him with both claw-tipped, glittering arms, the creature gave him no respite. Hoping to surprise it, Neko rolled forward. As it jerked its head to follow his motion, Neko felt the foul-smelling liquid from the thing's destroyed eye spatter him. Its claws almost caught him as he slipped between its legs.

He sent a second spike whipping toward the base of its skull, but the creature was turning and the weapon only glanced off hard bone. The thing rushed him again and he dodged toward its right side, cutting with his blades as he dove.

They danced a deadly, silent tarantella. Neko worried the thing's blind side, tearing at its limbs with his blades. His strikes were rarely clean, the monofiber edges of his weapons doing little more than scar the hard outer covering of the creature's appendages. It was well-protected. Whether it was armor, magic, or its own skill did not matter; it was wearing Neko down. He remained unable to close with it and bring his blades into contact with something vital.

His growing fatigue was making it more and more difficult to react quickly enough. First a claw raked his arm and scored the muscle, then the other caught him a glancing blow across the ribs, lacerating clothing and skin while tossing him halfway across the room. Half stunned, his eyes watering from the pain, Neko almost forfeited his phyrrhic respite. He had barely grabbed a new throwing spike before a new attack forced him to scramble away from the onrushing creature. Watching for an opening, he continued his desperate dodging. He doubted he'd have the opportunity to draw another spike. He had to make his throw.

His chance came after he had ducked low to avoid a sweeping blow and the creature's clawed limb became briefly entangled in the wreckage of the crate Neko had maneuvered between them. Neko's hand snapped up, then forward. The spike flew. Though not striking cleanly, the sharp spike scored the creature's remaining eye.

Blinded, its defenses faltered into a still dangerous but unguided flailing. Neko slipped through its guard to plant his blades in the soft tissue between the skull and carapace shoulders. The monofiber edges sliced arteries, veins, and windpipe before grating against bone. The creature collapsed with a bubbling moan. Panting, Neko skipped backward to avoid its thrashing.

It took a long time to die.

There was no chance the carnage would go unnoticed. Neko's pipeline into Grandmother's secrets would be closed, leaving him only what he had learned today. He had best make the most of it. His blood spattered the room, offering a trail to those who would seek him in the shadows. To close that avenue to pursuers, he disabled the sprinklers and used the cleaning supplies stored there to start a hungry fire. He would leave only ashes behind.

* * *

Urdli watched as the kulpunya ran in circles on the runway, howling in frustration. The thing was baffled by the loss of the trail, but Urdli understood. For all its supernatural tracking ability, the kulpunya could not follow a trail through the air. The thieves had escaped by aircraft.

He turned his eyes to the sky, where the running

lights of an aircraft rose into the night over Perth. The craft headed west, turning into the air lanes that skirted the coast. It was on its way to the outside world.

Oh, no. It was not going to be simple at all.

7

The Magick Matrix was the glittering star of the entertainment district of the Hong Kong Free Enterprise Enclave. The club was a haven for enclavers jaded by ordinary reality. Within its walls, patrons could leave behind their meat shells and step into other realities—computer realities whose governing principles the user could select. Those custom creations would let a user look like anyone, be anywhere, and do anything, as long as he had the nuyen to pay for it. And he could do it all without working up a sweat. All it took was putting on the trodes or jacking in if he wanted the best resolution and response. Then he could dream away while the gnomes of the Magick Matrix zapped him into a pocket universe of cyberspace.

The hardware was expensive and the software more so. Protecting the investment was a wide array of intrusion countermeasures, ranging from simple data barriers to the brain-frying IC known in the trade as black ice. In addition Magick Matrix was well supplied with roving deckhounds, the human computer-security specialists who jacked in to prowl the Matrix, alert for unauthorized users. Mortal flesh and tissue-bound minds lacked the purity and beauty of the elegant IC. Bound by organic nature, mankind also lacked the selfless devotion. But even the masters of such magnificent technology did not have absolute faith in it, and so they assured a weakness in their defenses.

Thus, with the transmission of a prearranged code, Dodger passed through the boundaries of the Magick Matrix icon. Inside, an icon depicting a robotic canine awaited him. The dog wore a dark collar showing the name of Magick Matrix, marking the decker behind the icon as an employee of the firm and labeling him a hound. But even dogs have friends about whom their masters know nothing, and to their friends they show the loyalty of the pack. This decker, whom Dodger knew as Rover, believed he shared a very elite pack with Dodger. Rover spoke of the brotherhood of silicon blood, sharers of the true way under the electron skies. He admitted admiring and envying the skill of the freelance deckers like Dodger. For the sake of the Art, Rover opened the door and let the deckers in. But Dodger had no illusions about how friendly Rover would be if Dodger messed with MM property. The bought dogs knew who fed them. No matter how much they idolized the wild members of their pack, they loved their kennels more.

Dodger had not come to steal the secrets of Magick Matrix. He had come for an appointment. For amid all the fantasy worlds, alien planets, battlescapes, and synthetic paradises, there was another non-place. It was a reality not listed among the offerings of Magick Matrix because it was a place of, by, and for deckers—but accessible only to the elite. Like the well-known virtual club Syberspace, if you couldn't hack your way in you didn't belong. The more difficult level of entry made this place with no name more than a slot to interface with the legends and wannabes of the Matrix. Offering the same functions of hiring hall, message center, and data brokerage as Syberspace, this place had a feature the other lacked. Here, through the access ports of Magick Matrix, meat clients could consult the elite of the Matrix within the Matrix in a safe and secret manner.

Today, the decker was to be the client. For Dodger

had come because someone had posted an e-mail in response to an outstanding offer. The poster might have legitimate information, but he could as easily be an opportunist or a con man. Dodger didn't expect a lot, but he had played more than his share of long shots in his time running the shadows. At least this one was not likely to be particularly dangerous.

Since the misadventures in England last year, he had sought out any information on the mysterious Matrix entity that he believed to be the artificial intelligence created by the Renraku Special Directorate. It had re-appeared, very briefly, during the affair with the ren cgade druids known as the Hidden Circle, reminding Dodger of its terrible and fascinating existence. At the time he had feared that some faction involved in aiding or fighting the Circle was managing the AI, but so little had come of its actions that he had begun to won-der. His cautious delvings—and the less-cautious blun-derings of other deckers excited by Dodger's own panic—had uncovered very little. The fragmentary data that passed for clues was more often apocryphal than authentic. Though he had begun to think the ap-parition within the druids' computer architecture a phantasm of his own creation, born of fear and anxi-cty, he hadn't abandoned the search. He wasn't sure why. Perhaps Sam's stubbornness was rubbing off on him.

Dodger tapped MM's monitor system to survey the virtual room before entering. The feed from Simtank 737 was pure, so he knew that the icon awaiting him was as perfect a replica of the person in the tank as Magick Matrix's technology could provide, which was to say a photographic likeness. His contact was a slim Japanese male who would stand well below average height. The runner appeared young, almost a child, but good biosculpting could mask a person's age. He was smartly dressed in streetwear that hung with the smoothness of armor cloth, and Dodger's practiced eye noted that he had managed to conceal several weapons from the guards who had checked him into the sim-tank. An impressive feat, but to be expected of a successful shadowrunner. An experienced professional, then. That was encouraging; amateurs rarely knew real data from drek.

Dodger injected his icon into the virtual room. "And who, pray tell, are you?"

The Japanese runner turned smartly, hand wavering over one of his concealed weapons. His eyes glittered, and his stance was as wary as the animal he named. "Cat."

"An appropriate street sobriquet for one of your fluidity, Sir Feline."

"You're an elf."

"Astute," Dodger observed dryly. His opinion of the runner dropped. One of the unwritten rules of the not-place was that a decker was expected to use a virtual image of his person rather than his usual Matrix icon. "Hubris," his sometime-partner Jenny called the affectation. He preferred to think of it as pride in accomplishment. Besides, one's colors were more properly reserved for the real work of running the Matrix. More practically, a client might later recognize a decker's workings if he knew the icon under which the decker operated. The decker's appearance was harder to trace, for there were no physical traces to collect, nor could a client retrieve an image from the not-place. The client would have only memory, and that could be made less reliable if the decker's features were slightly and subtly altered as Dodger had done. "Is that a problem?"

Cat performed an elaborate shrug. "Not really. Long as you don't pay in elf gold."

Dodger gave a shrug of his own, one infinitely more stylish. "My credit is good, Sir Feline. Better, no doubt, than your own. But you must needs convince me of your data's verity before a transfer is arranged."

Cat smiled tightly. "Grandmother believed it when the suit told her."

"Grandmother?" Dodger hid his surprise as well as he could. If Cat was *her* intermediary, the information had to be good. And expensive. " 'Twould be folly to question the quality of Grandmother's offerings. And even greater folly still to believe that a mere mention of her name signified her instigation, or even knowledge, of a deal."

"You want the data or not?"

Cat's haste was unseemly. Dodger decided to try a thrust. "My interest wanes. Having failed to use her usual protocols, you are branded as an adventurer trading on an excellent shadow reputation."

A stricken face and a sudden increase in Cat's breathing rate told Dodger he had guessed right. Cat was not part of Grandmother's organization. The runner's next move would tell the tale truly.

Cat's smile returned, a shadow of its former self. "I never said I worked for her. I just said she believed the data."

So. Such a rapid retreat to truth implied desperation. A desperate man had little bargaining room. "I have no desire to pay her rates to verify your tale. How shall I know you hold something of worth to me?"

"You'll just have to trust me."

"I need do no such thing. Speak to me of your find. If 'tis of use to me, I shall pay your fee."

"Pay first," Cat insisted bluntly.

"This from one who so recently demanded trust. I cannot know the worth of what you offer until I hear it. Then there is still the matter of reliability."

Cat's furrowed brow proclaimed his inner debate. There was nothing he could do to hurt Dodger physically. But he could cripple Dodger where it would hurt severely, in his curiosity. If Cat walked away with whatever mysterious bit of information he hoarded, Dodger would have no alternative but to go to Grandmother, who might or might not have the data. It would be an expensive proposition that would take time—time to gather the funds and time during which the elf would have no idea of what he labored to earn. Dodger watched the runner carefully, wondering if his desire for the data was as painfully obvious as Cat's need for nuyen. He thought not. After all, he was nowhere near as young or inexperienced as Cat.

"All right, elf. Twenty K bonded credit and the deal's done."

"Five bonded and ten in second-tier corporate vouchers."

"Ten and five."

"Seven and seven."

"You'll pay even if you don't like what I've got to say."

"Assuredly. I will pay whether 'tis pleasant or not."

Cat stuck out his hand and Dodger took it.

The tale was told soon enough. Respecting Cat's professional privacy, Dodger forbore to ask after the method by which the meeting was witnessed. Of real data there was little. But Cat's mention of Renraku in connection with the AI gave his story a veracity that would be difficult for a runner, especially a non-decker like Cat, to fake. Dodger wanted to believe. The mention of the disappearing files buzzed his head. It fit with his own experiences, especially with his encounter in the the druids' system.

"So you see," Cat concluded, "I think this Sato suit has got it all wrong. I think the renegade nicked the AI and is using it against them. That's what you wanted, isn't it? You wanted to know who had the AI."

Dodger rubbed at the triple row of jacks on his left temple. "And who is this renegade?"

Cat hesitated.

"Come now, Sir Feline. You need not fish for more reward."

Frowning, Cat quietly said, "I don't remember."

"Ah, you speak an unpleasant truth. Perhaps you are trustworthy after all." Relief, and gnawing terror, flooded Dodger. Cat's response put the runner's tale beyond the bounds of artful contrivance. Cat had told the truth as he knew it. Only he knew so very little. And so very much. "Your price is paid. Have you sold this tale to another?"

Cat looked as though the idea had never occurred to him, and shook his head. Young in the shadow games, Dodger thought.

"If no further word of your tale is whispered in the shadows, I will see that your account grows fatter."

Cat's expression changed to disgust. "I have made my sale. What do you take me for?"

A youngster. "An honest thief?"

Cat grinned.

"Very well, then. Say rather that I shall reward further enlightenment. Is that acceptable to an honest thief, Sir Feline?"

"I think we can do business, elf." Cat winked at him and popped out of virtual existence.

Dodger remained, contemplating what he had learned. Then he left, too, slipping unnoticed out of the virtual reality of the Magick Matrix. He was in no mood to chat with the doorman.

8

This place was desolate, almost completely devoid of life. Sam's astral senses could perceive the pale glow from the lichens and mosses that carpeted the cold ground, but he caught only fleeting glimpses of more complicated life forms. There was no sign of man or his works. It was still cold this far north, but even in the brief summer this near-arctic region would remain mostly uninhabited, for it offered no water.

He hovered at the edge of a zone that seemed more barren yet. Distantly he perceived a faint spark. A familiar spark. He flew toward it.

No time seemed to pass before he stood next to the mound of white fur that was the source of the lifeglow he had seen from afar. He did not need to see the broad, dark-skinned face surrounded by its mane of fur, the taloned hands, the fanged mouth, or the deep-set red eyes to know this being as a wendigo. He had learned to recognize the tints of aura that proclaimed the wendigo for what it was. The aura was fainter than when he had last seen it, weaker. By the aural shadings that were individual to this wendigo, he knew it was the one he sought.

"Janice."

The huddled form made no move, gave no sign of recognition. For a moment, he was puzzled. Her aura was not so weak that she would be unable to respond. He had feared arriving too late. One way or the other. But her aura allayed those fears. She was still alive, and she showed only a hint of the moldy grayness he had seen in other wendigo auras. So why did she not respond? The silent treatment was not her style. Finally, he remembered. He was astrally projecting. His words and image were unknowable on the mundane plane. He twisted his perception as Hart had taught him and manifested an image that, though ghostly and faint, could be seen by ordinary eyes.

"Janice," he called again, confident that his voice could now be heard.

The furred mound shifted, enlarging as massive muscles bunched to arch her back. A dark paw whose toes ended in glossy talons appeared briefly before the motion settled once more into stillness.

"Janice."

The mound shifted again and a dark patch appeared, her face. An eye opened, a sullen ember in a deep pit. "I heard you the first time."

The deep pitch of the words startled him. Subconsciously, he had been expecting the voice of the sister he remembered, not the cavernous tones of her changed voice. While the tonality was different, the intonation and grouchy irritability were familiar from long-ago school mornings. Janice had never liked waking up.

Her next words were a growl. "Who's the fool who disturbs me?"

"It's me, Janice. Sam. Your brother."

The ember winked out and the dark face disappeared back under a furred arm. "Go away. I have no brother."

"I won't go away. We're family, Janice. Don't shut me out."

The face reappeared, both red eyes visible now. "I have no family. You saw to that. Remember?"

At first he thought she was blaming him for their being orphans. They had been just kids at the time. His own recollections were vague and blurred by half-remembered pain and anguish. She, being younger, could hardly have clearer memories The accusation didn't make sense. She couldn't really believe that he had anything to do with the riots. Did she blame him, and herself as well, for surviving when their parents and older siblings had died? Her Renraku psych profile hadn't indicated that kind of grief displacement. What did she mean? "I'm your family, Janice."

"There's no more Janice. She's *kawaruhito,* a changeling no more a part of anybody's family than of polite society. What's left found someone to care about her. Someone who didn't run away and hide when he knew what she had become. But that someone is dead now. Remember?"

"Whatever face Hyde-White showed . . ."

"Dan Shiroi!" she shouted, erupting explosively from her huddle to tower over him.

Sam looked up into the dark face that twisted with emotion. She still clung to her vision of that wendigo as a protector. As long as she did, his influence over her remained. "Whatever face he showed you, he was evil. He was a killer who sought to enlist others in his villainy. However kindly he seemed to you, he was consumed by his wendigo nature. He was a liar and a deceiver. You know that what I say is true."

"You killed him," she said flatly.

"I swore once that I would never take an innocent life. And I don't think that I've broken that oath. He was no innocent; he was a murderer, and he would have made you over in his own image. Killing him was the only way to end the threat he posed to you and many true innocents. It was the only way to free you from his influence."

"I didn't want to be free. Dan loved me."

Sam remembered the scene in Hyde-White's retreat where the wendigo that Janice knew as Dan Shiroi had come back from the brink of death, or perhaps from beyond, to keep her from attacking Sam and Hart as they lay wounded and helpless. "That may be so, but only at the end was he worthy of your love. As a wendigo, he understood the danger to your soul. But it wasn't a wendigo that saved you. It was too late for him, but he knew that you should not be like him. He gave you a chance to change things.

"You say he loved you. I love you, too. I want to see you saved from this wendigo curse, and I've come to tell you there's hope. I think we've found a way to change you back. We've built a ritual to save you, but you must come to Mount Rainier."

"Save me?" Her lip lifted to reveal yellowed tusks, but Sam couldn't tell if it was a sneer or a snarl. "It's too late. Where were you when they sent me to Yomi?"

"I didn't find out you were going through *kawaru*

until it was too late. Then they wouldn't let me see you. I tried everything to find you."

"But you didn't succeed, did you? Not until you could take away everything that meant anything to me."

"I did what had to be done."

She turned her face away. For minutes she was quiet. Then, she said, "I'm staying here."

Sam was appalled. "Staying here? What have you got here? I'm offering you a way to get your *life* back."

He reached out to take her by the shoulders and shake some sense into her, but his hands couldn't grip her. She turned at his ethereal touch and glared at him.

"You can't be serious. Nothing could ever be the same. Your precious little sister Janice Verner is dead. She died before you left your cozy corporate cocoon at Raku. She was replaced by ASN1778, who went to Yomi and got a new life, but even that non-person is dead. Abandoned, like the one who had gone before. Why would I want either of those lives back? I had happiness and you took it away."

"You weren't happy. You were enthralled by the wendigo's false promises."

"How could you begin to know what I had?"

"I know the sister I grew up with. I know the parents who raised her. I know what they taught us, and what they would think of anyone who succumbed to the wendigo nature. And because I know all that, I know what you must think of what has happened to you. You can't give in, Janice. Don't let despair win. There's hope."

"I don't want hope. All I want now is peace."

"You can't have it as a wendigo."

She took a deep breath and let it out slowly with a rumble that was half growl and half moan. Her eyes left his face and traveled along the distant horizon. "There is peace here."

Sam looked around. Astrally, he could feel the emotions of the place. The air was filled with despair, hopelessness, sorrow, spite, and hate. There was not a trace that he could identify as peaceful.

"You're wrong, Janice. There's nothing for you here."

"No, *you're* wrong. There is safety here. This was Dan's place, his refuge in the lean days when the magic wasn't strong enough to let him walk among you norms. The hunger is weak here. In the quiet its absence creates, I can sleep the dreamless sleep. As I was doing until you disturbed me. You should be happy that I'm here. As long as I stay in this place, you and all your kind are safe from me."

Sam suddenly understood why she refused to leave. "You're afraid."

She growled, but there was no spirit in the sound. He saw his opening, a way to persuade her to do what must be done.

"What is your totem, Janice? Mouse?"

"I have no totem."

"That's a lie. Your change into a wendigo has awakened power in you. I can see it. I've learned enough about wendigos to know that their power molds most easily to the shamanic mode. For all his warped vision, your Shiroi was a shaman. I know he taught you because I've seen your magic. You can't do that magic without a totem."

She growled again, a warning sound. "Leave Dan out of it."

"What's your totem?" Sam insisted.

At last she said, "Wolf."

"Wolf?" He hoped his voice did not sound falsely incredulous. "Wolf isn't a coward's totem. Are you sure you don't focus through Ostrich? That would be more suitable for someone who ignores what's going on around her. You're a disgrace to the Wolf nature."

"Wolf understands," she said sulkily.

"Wolf must be appalled at your lack of strength."

The growling returned, stronger than before. "If you don't want to feel my strength, leave."

"Not without you."

She glared at him, still growling. Her eyes radiated heat but Sam felt chilled, like a mouse under a hawk's stare. Had she gone so far? Had he pushed her too far? Was he no more than meat to her now?

She shifted suddenly and he took a defensive step backward, having forgotten that his astral body was impervious to physical harm.

The growling stopped and she laughed, the sound brittle and without humor. "Are you going to take responsibility for me?"

He sensed that this was the turning point. His answer would decide her. Could he take responsibility for what she might do? Hadn't he already? There was only one answer he could give.

"I will."

"That's the fool I once had as a brother. Haven't you learned yet that everyone is responsible for themselves?"

"Families are responsible for each other."

"Very Japanese. I would have thought you'd given up your fascination with their culture when you ran away from their corporation."

"I haven't given up on my sister. Are you going to come or not?"

Janice shrugged. "What have I got to lose? You've roused me now. I doubt I could rest here peacefully."

"I'm telling you there is no peace here."

"How little you know," she said softly.

"You'll have peace when the ritual restores you."

"I certainly won't get it until you dance your dance."

Tinged with something undefinable, her words echoed strangely in him. He forced the uncomfortable feeling away, concentrating on the matter at hand. Janice had agreed, and it would be to no one's benefit to delay. "Hart has arranged a plane. The course will be laid into the autopilot and the computer will do the flying. All you have to do is board, sit back, and enjoy the ride."

She bared her teeth in a grin that made him uncomfortable. "No pilot? What's the matter? Afraid I might eat him?"

Sam tried to tell himself she was just joking, just needling him, but he could see those teeth. "The fewer people who know about your entry into Salish-Shidhe Council, the better. They have a bounty on wendigos."

"And on those who aid and abet wendigos," she said.

Sam nodded, already well enough aware of that.

9

Though Ghost Who Walks Inside was tall for an Indian, his broad shoulders, massive chest, and well-muscled arms made him seem more squat than he was. He was a street samurai, but unlike many others who claimed that title, Ghost showed few obvious signs of cyber-enhancement. Dressed in his tattered jungle fatigue trousers and boots, armored vest, beaded wristlets, and feather-adorned headband, Ghost revealed only the palm-mounted induction pads of his smartgun link. Which was not to say they were his only chrome. He just didn't believe in displaying his advantages, preferring to let others underestimate his abilities. Just one more edge.

From his vantage point in the shade of a kiosk selling Seattle metroplex memorabilia, Sam spotted Ghost's wild black frizz on the far side of the court.

As the Indian moved through the Sunday tourist crowds
thronging Aurora Village, his swagger and rugged appearance opened a path for him, making his progress
swift. With nonchalant ease he sidestepped those too
self-absorbed or oblivious to notice him, never breaking his rhythm. Only once was he interrupted, when
a fat German suit bumped into him. There was a slight
jostling and for the next few steps, a smiling Ghost let
deutschmarks, corporate scrip, coins, and credsticks
dribble from his fingers. The turmoil in the crowd behind him made his forward progress even easier. The
Indian seemed in no hurry. An observer might have
thought that he turned in Sam's direction purely by
chance. Sam stepped out from behind the kiosk to
greet him, but Ghost beat him to it.

"Hoi, paleface. Whazappenning?"

"Hoi, Ghost. Biz as usual. 'Zappening with you?"

"Running hard to stay in place. *Wakarimasu-ka?*
Biz as usual," Ghost said with a laugh.

"Not too busy for a little extra, I hope."

"Man's too busy for friends, he's too busy to live,"
Ghost said, grinning.

Sam grinned back. Ghost's thaw toward him had co-
incided with the onset of Sally's glacial chill. Sam
wished Sally would stop avoiding him so they might
have a chance to talk it out, but as long as he was
seeing Hart, Sally would never let him get her alone.
Ghost, however, seemed to find the situation exactly
to his taste, and that was good. Sam much preferred a
friendly Ghost to a hostile one.

Sam checked around for eavesdroppers, then got
down to business. "I need your help to find a safe
place for my sister to hide. Someplace outside the Seattle metroplex."

"Why me? Thought you'd have enough grease with
Hart. Hear tell, she's got connections in Council lands.
I'm just a city boy."

Sam had never spoken of Hart's connections, and

Ghost rarely worried about people and places outside the plex. If he knew about Hart's connections, somebody was looking into Hart's affairs. Most likely Sally. Sam hoped it didn't bode trouble. If it did, he'd deal with it later. "Got a good net going, Ghost. But not good enough. Hart's connections aren't suitable to the current situation."

"So *ka*. Sister got a feud?"

"She's . . ." Suddenly Sam wasn't sure he should explain. Telling anyone was a danger, and Ghost was a mercenary, always on the lookout for ways to improve his tribe's financial position. Would he be tempted by the bounty? If he turned Sam in as well, might not Ghost also improve his standing with Sally? Or would he even consider such a course of action? Sam wasn't sure. For all the easy camaraderie, Ghost was still a bundle of unknown quantities. But trust was needed. Before Sam had attracted Sally's attention Ghost had treated him well, almost as a younger brother. Aside from the Indian's interest in Sally, Sam could find no reason to distrust Ghost. The other man lived by a code of honor, one that Sam did not always understand, but he was confident that Ghost wouldn't abandon his honor for a few credits. There was, of course, only one way to find out.

"My sister has goblinized. Hart's contacts won't take her in."

"So *ka*." Ghost nodded sagely. "How illegal is her breed?"

"How did you figure that?"

"Null perspiration, paleface. If her breed wasn't illegal, you would have made arrangements with Cog or Castillano. Fixers are real good at moving merchandise, even live merchandise. But you're asking me, and that means you don't want anybody to know so bad that you're asking a city Indian to find you a place outside the wall. So what is she?"

"Wendigo." Without waiting for a reaction, he added, "But she's never killed."

Ghost looked at him strangely. "What's that got to do with it?"

"If a wendigo hasn't killed, the curse isn't complete. The sins can be forgiven and her soul can still be saved."

"Sin? Soul? Paleface, you're not talking sense. I don't walk the Jesus road. Found out real early that stuff don't mean drek on the streets. Last time I turned my cheek, I had to get it replaced." Ghost shook his head. "Wendigos eat people. You're talking real bad biz."

The Indian's reaction was no more than Sam could reasonably expect. "But we're bringing her here to cure her," he said.

"Now you're talking crazy. Can't be done. Anybody could turn back even an ork, the docs and whitecoats woulda been all over them in millisecs, right after the media hounds. Whole world would know how to do it. Ain't no pills, surgery, or drugs can do it."

"We've got a way. We're going to use magic."

Ghost spat.

"I know you don't like magic. I'm not asking you to take part in the ritual. We just need somebody to hide her safely until we can do the magic. She's my sister, Ghost. I've got to try. I thought you'd understand." Sam was losing track of the argument as his emotions caught up with him. "We can't bring her into the plex; there are too many people. But she's got to be present for the ritual. There's no other way to do it. I didn't know who else to ask."

"The odds get too bad, a smart man doesn't gamble." Ghost started to walk away.

"I really thought you might help," Sam muttered, almost to himself. "She's Wolf totem."

Ghost turned. "You're desperate crazy, white man, but you've got *cojones*. I might be a little crazy, too.

You know, Grandfather Wolf don't like cowards, and he really hates people who run out on the pack.''

"You weren't running out. I'm not part of your tribe. Neither is Janice. And I know you're anything but a coward.''

"Not you I'm worried about, paleface." Ghost lowered his voice. "You aren't scamming? She really is Wolf. You swear as a shaman?''

Sam nodded.

"Fraggin' drek, but you don't make it easy," Ghost said, head tilted toward the sky. "You know, paleface, Grandfather Wolf don't like murderers or cannibals either. So maybe there's hope for her. Maybe you really can do something for her. How much nuyen did you say?''

"I didn't, but it's not much. Fifty K. And favors. I'll owe you big, Ghost.''

"Don't worry, paleface," the Indian said, rubbing his chin reflectively. "If this thing blows up in our faces, it'll be more than you can pay.''

10

Janice astrally scouted the area around the aircraft. As promised, she found only three people waiting for her. One she recognized instantly as Sam. Next to him stood an elven woman who seemed vaguely familiar. The third member of the welcoming committee was some kind of razorguy, his aura darkened in places by cyber-enhancements.

Had she really expected a trap? Sam was too honest to betray her. At least the Sam she had grown up with was honest. But that Sam wasn't a street shaman and a shadowrunner. He had changed, but how much?

From her own experiences, she knew some changes were bigger than others.

She returned to her body and rose from the travel couch. The chair had been tight, not made for someone of her bulk. Her muscles relaxed gratefully. The vanishing aches and pains reminded her how little she belonged in the world of the norms. She thought about tearing the door from its hinges to express her frustration and anger. It would make a flashy entrance, but it wouldn't really reduce the stress left from the trip. She opened the hatch as meekly as any ordinary passenger.

With the first whiff of the local air, she felt better. The Salish-Shidhe breeze was full of the good scents of a forest—much more pleasant than the sterile, machine-purified air of the aircraft.

Sam and the woman stepped forward to greet her, but the razorguy hung back, watchful. When Janice saw the elf with her mundane eyes, she knew why the woman's aura had seemed familiar. This was the same elf who had helped Sam kill Dan Shiroi.

Janice didn't give Sam a chance to even say hello.

"Still hanging with the same armful, I see. You two serious, or are you just rubbing my muzzle in it?"

Sam stopped, open-mouthed. The elf answered for him.

"My name is Hart, Janice. No one here means to offend you."

"I know who you are. And you call me Shiroi, elf."

"That was the wendigo's name," Hart said.

Janice showed her teeth. "I'm a wendigo."

The elf shut up. She looked offended and maybe a bit nervous. Good. Janice hoped she made the elf real nervous.

"So, Mr. Big Time Shaman, where's your ritual team? Are they lost, or are you? This don't look like a volcano."

Sam looked annoyed. That pleased her. Why should this be easy on anyone?

"We're not doing the ritual tonight," he said.

"Drek!" Didn't he understand what he was doing by hauling her down here? She had hoped that if she humored him, he'd be satisfied and leave her alone. She had thought she could hold out for a day or two, long enough for him to see the foolishness of his plan and for her to get back to the fastness before the hunger became overpowering. "Why not?"

"I didn't want to take the chance that something would go wrong slipping you into Council lands. The ritual would be ruined if some Council trackers stumbled into the middle of it. Besides, the moon will be full two nights from now, and the magic will be more potent if the ritual is performed then. It'll also give you some time to learn your part."

How many more little surprises was he going to spring? "You didn't say I had to do anything."

"Transformation magic is more powerful if the subject is willing and involved."

She heard herself growl and realized that no longer was her annoyance feigned. "Do I have to believe it will work?"

"No. But it would help."

She sat down on the loam. This wasn't working out as she had thought. But then, when had anything ever gone right? When Dan was taking care of her, was when. That had been the only time she had been really happy since before her parents had died. Everything in between had been hollow, almost as hollow as her life now.

From the corner of her eye she could see Sam fretting, probably trying to decide how long to let her stew. After a few minutes, Hart poked him in the ribs. They exchanged a glance, and he nodded and addressed her.

"Janice, I realize that it wasn't easy for you to come.

The trip must have been uncomfortable, but the plane was the best we could manage. You're tired." He placed a satchel by her side. "When you're rested, take a look at the chips in the reader. They'll explain some of the fine points of the ritual. Your part is highlighted. It's not big, but it's important. I'd go over it with you now, but there are still a few more things to be taken care of in the plex. We've got to get back there."

The plex? She never wanted to see another metroplex. They were dirty and smelly, but most of all they were crowded with people. All those stinking, noisy people. All that meat. No, she remonstrated with herself. That's not the way to think. "You said no cities," she snapped.

"Sorry," he said quickly. "I meant Hart and me. You'll stay here with Ghost, and he'll take you to the rendezvous point on the lower slopes of Mount Rainier. We'll meet again in two days just after sundown. Okay?"

What choice did she have? "You didn't leave room in your plan for me to object."

"I'll take that as a yes."

Sam reached out to touch her. He was hesitant, as though undecided whether to stroke her like a furry pet, pat her like a little sister, or just lay a reassuring hand on her. In the end, he tried a little of all three. Most likely he meant to be affectionate, but he rumpled her fur the wrong way. Worse, she felt the trembling of his hand and saw the fear in his eyes. He showed some courage, at least. His woman didn't dare come near enough to touch. God, who was he to call himself family, then act like all the other hateful norms?

She didn't watch them climb into the aircraft, but then she looked up in time to see them appear in the cockpit. Sam settled into the pilot's couch. As he went through the motions the aircraft engines revved, twirling the props faster and faster until the low-slung body lifted from the field. Then the plane cleared the trees, the nacelles rotating to bring the props down for horizontal flight. The craft disappeared into the night, its sound fading as it drew further away.

When had Sam learned to fly?

Their departure left her alone with the razorguy Sam had called Ghost. He was staring at her while she observed him covertly. To judge from his looks and his dress, he was an Indian. It didn't surprise her that he seemed reluctant to give up his place near the trees. For generations out of mind, Indians had been telling tall tales of the wendigo. He probably believed them all.

He'd been left to take care of her. As if she needed a norm, even an enhanced one, for a babysitter. She probably could move through the forest better than he could. She was stronger, likely faster, and had certain supernormal advantages that not even the best cyberware could reproduce. What good was he, except as a local guide? Most likely he was supposed to keep her from eating any people she happened upon. Did Sam really think one razorguy could stop her?

The clearing had long since settled back into its nightly cycle of sound and activity before he moved. Leaving his spot near the tree he crossed the grass silently, so silently that his steps did not disturb the raccoon come to investigate the satchel Sam had left. He squatted a half-dozen meters away. Did he know how well she could see him?

"I'm not exactly contagious, you know."

Her voice startled the raccoon, who fled. The razorguy showed no reaction save to rise and move closer. Two meters. Just beyond the distance she could reach without getting up. The razorguy had gauged her length of arm well. He remained silent.

"Nothing to say?" Nothing was what he said. She repeated her question in Japanese and Spanish, with no better result. This new irritation was just one more added to the experience of her trip. "Can you even talk?"

Unspeaking, he stared at her. She decided she'd seen enough of him and turned her head away. Minutes passed and the raccoon approached again, dithering over whether to approach and make another attempt to investigate the intriguing satchel. It had just made up its mind when the Indian spoke and sent it scurrying off again.

"You are a shaman?"

Startled herself by his sudden speech, she answered simply and honestly. "Yes."

He was quiet for more minutes. When he spoke again, she was ready for the abruptness but not the content of his question.

"Is it true you follow Wolf?"

"Oh, you mean is Wolf my totem?"

He nodded. Well, two could play at the laconic game. "Yes," she said.

Ghost grunted and stood up. "It's a long way to Rainier. Sam said we have only the night for traveling. We should start."

"What, no vehicle?"

"Too conspicuous."

"And that plane wasn't?"

"A bribe to an air traffic controller makes it easy for a plane not to appear on a radar screen."

"What about the noise?"

"People hear a plane in the night, they think nothing of it. It's in the sky, far away. A car or bike is much nearer and might bring unwelcome visitors. People pay attention. Wouldn't want to drive through the forest, though, even during the day. This terrain will turn good machines into spare parts."

"So we walk."

Ghost gave her a ragged grin. "Run. If you can."

She rose to her feet. She smiled back, careful not

to expose her fangs. "Try and keep up. You're the one who's supposed to know where we're going."

They set out. She started with a pace that would quickly tire a norm, but he kept up. His muscles moved in smooth, clean precision, pumping beneath his bronzed skin. The way he avoided trees and brush told her that he could see in the dark, too. After a while she slowed down. Weak from hunger, she wasn't in as good shape as she had thought. And without knowing how far they were to travel, she thought it best to conserve her strength.

After about an hour, they flushed a deer. It was a young buck, antler buds still in velvet. He rushed from their path and Janice sprinted after him, giving it no opportunity to get far. With a howl, she pounced and bore the buck down with her weight. She bashed one of its forelimbs with a clenched paw, and felt the bones snap under her blow. The buck sounded his pain. Gripping one of the flailing hind limbs with one hand, she held the beast down with the other. A tug and a twist and she ripped its hind leg free.

The scent of hot blood filled her nostrils, followed by the warm, full scent of fresh meat. She sank her teeth in. The taste was weak and vaguely unpleasant, but it was food. She ripped another mouthful from the haunch.

The deer still struggled, trying to regain its feet, making itself bleed to death faster. Didn't it know enough to accept its fate? She chewed the hot flesh, feeling the juices slide down her parched throat.

She looked up from her meal. Ghost had caught up and was staring at her.

"Don't worry, man. It's just a deer."

His face remained expressionless and he said nothing.

Somehow, that made it worse. She threw down the haunch, stood, and walked away. At the base of a forest giant, she crouched again and leaned against the bole of the tree. She hugged her arms around herself. *No, don't worry, man. Leave that for me.* Hunger gnawed at her, awakened by her brief, unsatisfying feast. Her stomach tightened into painful knots. All she could think about was Ghost's smooth muscles rippling as he ran. Like the deer. Too like the deer.

11

"Mr. Urdli. Mr. Walter Urdli. Please meet your party at Baggage Carousel Number Three."

Urdli looked up in annoyance at the speaker calling his name. He was barely out of the runway from the monstrous aircraft that had carried him over the Pacific, and his stomach was still queasy. He hated air travel. He visited the rest room before going to the infoboard for directions to Baggage Carousel Three. The foolish machine insisted on giving him directions to Carousel Fifteen, asserting that his luggage would be arriving there. He circumvented the paternalistic thing by calling for a general map with routes to the baggage area.

The waiting space around Carousel Three was deserted except for two young elves, a dark-haired male and a fair-haired female. Though he had never seen either one before, they seemed to recognize him as he approached. That was not surprising. For all the elves in the crowd and all their variety of skin tone and shape, he was unique. Some had his dark skin color and some his thin build, but none had the combination or matched his height. Anyone who knew his physical description should be able to pick him out.

He greeted them in formal Sperethiel. Their responses were adequate, but they mismanaged the proper forms of address. Seeing them insufficiently versed in the old tongue to make conversation enjoyable, he switched to English.

"You are with the Council?"

"My name is Estios, sir. This is O'Connor. We are aides to Professor Sean Laverty."

While considering the implications, Urdli looked them over. O'Connor was comely enough, he supposed, though he had never really cared for the northern phenotypes. Like her companion, she wore garb whose fine material was tailored to hide her weapons from one unaccustomed to scenting the metal. Both were well groomed, and the man wore his hair cut short to reveal his ears, as some of the current crop of males seemed fearful of doing. Estios was tall for a Caucasoid elf, with the broad shoulders his kind developed in the course of mastering physical disciplines. Of course, the two of them would have hidden talents. Urdli inclined his head to meet the male's gaze.

"I am unaccustomed to dealing with inferiors. You will see to my luggage and take me to Laverty."

Estios' expression remained polite, but a spark danced in his icy blue eyes. When he spoke, his voice remained calm and detached. The restraint pleased Urdli.

"Your luggage will be taken care of, sir. This is not my job. I was asked to inform you that the professor was unavoidably detained at the Royal Hill. He asked me to serve as your guide and to take you to the mansion, where he will join you as soon as possible. He thought that the most advisable course, since your message suggested discretion."

Urdli shrugged off his topcoat. It was warmer here than Down Under. He handed it to the female, who took it without a word of protest. "Then we shall leave this place."

"There is a car waiting, sir."

Urdli nodded. "We will not be driving through the

city, will we? I saw it through the window of the plane. It is much given over to human architecture."

"Portland is a compromise, sir. The city houses most of the resettled human population of the former state of Oregon. Most of the buildings continue to provide for their needs. The High Prince's Council considers this a reasonable arrangement, for the norms provide an important work force in the industries necessary to maintain the city as a contact point between Tir Tairngire and the rest of the world. However, since the recent trade agreements with the city-state of Seattle, Portland's usefulness is declining. One day, the human presence may be eliminated completely, but for now the city remains a necessary evil."

"I do not like it."

Estios smiled coldly. "I understand, sir. We can take a more roundabout route and avoid much of the urban area."

"Do so."

The trip to the mansion was quiet, almost peaceful, for Laverty's aides demonstrated minimal courtesy by offering no conversation once Urdli ignored their first few attempts. Estios was as good as his word. Urdli was not forced to see much of the ugly, squat human architecture.

The mansion itself was in the human style; Urdli had forgotten just how unattractive it was. Its only saving graces were the superbly rendered gargoyles and the delicate tracery of protective sorceries. At least the gardens had grown into their promise. Urdli had the young elves lead him to the library, ignoring their protests that he should retire to his room and freshen up. Matters were advanced well beyond such niceties, and he intended to use his waiting time constructively. Laverty's collection of books and manuscripts was even better than he had remembered. Perhaps there was some merit to relying on the written word instead of organic memory. He was deep into a disk copy of Vermis' *Liber Viridis* when Laverty arrived.

The red-headed elf advanced across the room, a smile on his broad face and his arms held wide in greeting. "It's been years, my friend. What brings you to the Tir, whispering of secrets and looking so grim?"

Urdli stood, his erect stance rebuffing the familiarity of Laverty's greeting. With a slight inclination of his head, Urdli indicated Estios and O'Connor. The young elves had not left him alone since he had installed himself in the library. "These are to stay?"

Laverty put on an affronted expression, but Urdli knew him well enough to see that it was only half-serious. "They are my best and most loyal. Should intervention be needed, they would be my agents of choice. I think it best that they hear your story for themselves."

"Ah, they are your paladins."

This time Laverty's annoyed expression was for real. "I don't require the outmoded oaths, so I don't use the word. I leave such pointless fripperies to blowhards like Ehran."

"Unconventional as always, Laverty."

Laverty's irritation vanished when he laughed. "You should talk. Expedience rules all, does it not, Urdli? But you surely did not come to discuss my staffing arrangements. What is the problem?"

Urdli got right to the point. "There has been a raid on *Imiri ti-Versakhan.*"

Laverty's light tone vanished. "How bad?"

"Three of the wells are empty."

"Only three? It could have been worse."

"Rachnei's well was one of the three. The raiders stole the guardian stone."

"That *is* worse." Laverty sat and clasped his hands together, forefingers straight and pointing toward the ceiling. He lowered his head until his forehead touched the erect fingers, then tapped them against his brow in a steady rhythm. "What were the other two?"

"Minor nuisances only," Urdli replied, returning to his chair. "They do not concern me at this time, for they will not come to power for some years. If we are diligent, we might contain them again before they cause much mischief."

Laverty looked up. "Do you see a plan in the releases?"

"If you fear the old foes are at work, think again. Rachnei is no more their friend than ours. The release will mean as much trouble for them as for us. Were the raid part of a plot to ensnare our assets, the thieves would have arranged a more systematic release from the wells in order to more fully occupy us."

"Cultists, then?"

Urdli shook his head dismissively. "I think not. There was no evidence of an attempt to control the release. Cultists would not be so naive. Whoever was involved has no idea what Rachnei is."

"You're sure?"

Urdli shrugged. "There is no surety, only strong probabilities. Still, there may be a way to restore the balance."

Laverty looked doubtful. "If Rachnei has reabsorbed the facet, I doubt the mana is high enough to sunder it again, let alone bind it back into the well. Even if it were possible, you couldn't do it alone. You'd need powerful help. Why haven't you gone to the Shidhe or made a direct plea to the Council?"

"You know the answer to that. The Shidhe are lost in their dreams, and I will have no dealings with your Council as long as that dragon sits on it."

"I can understand your not wanting Lofwyr to know, but the others have a right, and a need, to know. The despoiling of Rachnei's well will affect us all in the long run, elf and non-elf. Containing the danger will require all available magic to succeed. A lot more power than I remember your being able to wield.''

The ease with which Laverty dismissed his power rankled, but the evaluation was correct. ''I am aware of how much power is involved. You counsel expedience in place of honor.''

''I seem to recall you preferred the direct approach to the niceties of politics in your younger days.''

''As I do still. If the facet remains unabsorbed and the opportunity arises to bind it into the well again, I will not object to assembling the others to do what will be necessary. Until then, I wish a chance to redeem my honor.''

''Honor, is it?'' Laverty's mouth quirked up on one side. ''I hope your honor isn't going to blind you to necessity. I see no way to restore the balance at this time. With the well empty, we had best brace for the storm. Spreading the word seems the only reasonable course.''

Urdli frowned. ''And you would have me shout of the failure at *Imiri ti-Versakhan*, that all should know of that place. What of that which lies there still? Do you wish attention called to that?''

For several moments Laverty said nothing. Then, ''I see. What do you want me to do?''

''I would rather the circle of those who know remain small as yet. I fear that you may be right, that I delude myself into believing that the balance can be restored. I had hoped that you and your library might be a resource to answer that question. You have been more in the world than I and have a better understanding of the manifestations of the mana in the Sixth World. Even if the facet may not be riven again and secreted away, I still believe that the guardian stone can be used to combat Rachnei. We must recover the stone.''

''You have access to other libraries. Why do you involve me and come to mine?''

''There is an element of convenience. I have traced

the remaining thieves to this continent. More precisely, I believe they lair in the metroplex to the north. As to why I have involved you, that should be obvious. You have many contacts here in the Americas, and it is a land I no longer know well. Your guidance would be invaluable. Time is fleeting. I must recover the stone before the thieves unravel the matrix of its magic.''

Laverty nodded in reluctant agreement. ''If I'm to help you find the thieves, I need to know what you know about them.''

Urdli revealed what he had learned from following the thieves' backtrail through the shadows of Perth. His informants had been persuaded to part with all they knew, but their stores of data had proven pitiful. He had gotten descriptions and learned the street names of the surviving thieves. As he had hoped, Laverty recognized them.

''Gray Otter is a street samurai of reliable reputation, young but experienced. Competent as well. She has on occasion run shadow business with Twist in recent months. I would assume she is only a hireling in this matter.'' Laverty paused, as though unsure how to continue. Urdli became more alert, knowing he must listen carefully and be prepared for half-truths. ''Twist is the street name of Samuel Verner, a former researcher for Renraku Corporation. He was here shortly after escaping his corporation's care, and was just coming into his magical powers. While he was here, I performed a series of tests to measure his magical ability. From the results, I would not have believed he had the strength to remove the guardian stone. At that time he did not wish to believe he was a magician.''

''Perhaps you were misled,'' Urdli suggested. ''Whoever breached the well has embraced magic wholeheartedly, for only a powerful magician could have unlocked the spells holding the capstone in place.''

Laverty seemed to consider the possibility. When he spoke, it was as though he were unintentionally voicing his thoughts rather than making a deliberate statement. "If it were he, and not someone or something in disguise.''

"I will know him when I taste his aura. But I am confident that whoever removed the stone was of the brood of mankind. We need look to no greater conspiracy.''

Laverty nodded slowly. "Perhaps you are right. But I wonder. Verner has turned out to be a Dog shaman. As you know, Dog demands vigilance against evil magic. Evil in this context being most easily defined as magic that would harm mankind. Last year in England, he and some of my agents were involved in an affair that fit that bill to a tee. It seems unlikely that Verner would voluntarily open Rachnei's well.''

This defense of the thief was unseemly. Urdli began to wonder if he had made a mistake in confiding his dishonor to Laverty. "Voluntarily or not, he has done it, and we must deal with the consequences. I would not like to learn that he has fallen under Rachnei's influence.''

"I don't think so," Laverty said firmly. "Were it so, I believe I would have been forewarned.''

Urdli understood. "Then you have an observer and know where Verner is to be found.''

"Oh, yes.''

"Tell me," Urdli demanded, knowing he had no authority to command Laverty's compliance. "My honor demands that I seek him out.''

"To what end? Do you intend to kill him?''

"He must pay for what he has done.''

"Recovering the stone is more important," Laverty reminded him.

"That is my first priority," Urdli said.

"If you can regain the stone, you have no need to kill Verner. Likely, he will give you the stone if you

ask for it, and offer to help set it back in place. I think he acted in ignorance, though I'm sure he has a reason for what he has done.''

''What reason could be good enough?''

''Of that I'm unsure. I, too, would like to know. So much puzzles me about that man.''

As always, Laverty's curiosity got in the way of necessary ends. ''Puzzles are an idle man's pursuit, and I can no longer be idle. I must not rest until the stone is recovered and we know where this man stands in regard to Rachnei. Tell me where to find Verner.''

The address Laverty gave him meant nothing, but the library's computer held maps.

12

Dodger forced his perception out of cyberspace. Normally the consensual hallucination by which meat operators could deal with the intricacies and machine speeds of the Matrix was advantageous. But his investigations were anything but normal, and his usual working methods had become something of a liability. To make sense of the shifts in some of the icons he was perceiving would take seeing real numbers and machine code. He thought he knew what was causing the shifts, but wasn't sure. He suspected that the shifts were signs that the AI was out there. Once, it had made the Renraku matrix shimmer with mirror planes of infinity and had ghosted icons to evanescent translucency. The shifts he was observing could be within its power.

It was out there. It had to be.

Hours evaporated as he studied the data he had snagged during the run. Periodically, he connected his deck to the Matrix for short, directed research runs.

His latest cup of kaf grew chill, becoming just another in the row of forgotten cups. His neck muscles cramped into iron stiffness. Each lead only unfolded into more perplexing possibilities, leaving him frustrated, intrigued, irritated, and fascinated. His absorption was so intense that he only became aware of the telecom after it had been chirping for some time.

He didn't want to be disturbed, but hadn't thought it necessary to inform the telecom's dog-brain to hold calls because so few people knew his current comm code. Now someone wanted to talk to him. Suddenly aware of his own physical discomfort, he was even less interested in interfacing with anyone.

The telecom continued to chirp.

The caller was persistent. Ah, well. He was already disturbed. And he was getting nowhere at the moment. He hit the "Save" key on his cyberdeck to hold his current position. Just as well. He would be better off doing some thinking before pursuing the search. Tugging the datacord from his temple jack with one hand, Dodger reached across with the other to tap the Tel button to open the line to his caller.

The screen glowed to life and the slender, worried face of Teresa O'Connor sharpened into focus. This disturbance disrupted more than just his work. Buried feelings stirred, and he knew himself vulnerable again.

"Dodger? You look like hell."

"Ah, lady, and a fine day to you, too. I thought you didn't wish to speak with me."

"I never said that."

Was that hurt in her expression? Or annoyance that he should presume to know her desires? "You made your position clear when you left London with Estios. He is well, I trust."

"Well enough. He doesn't throw things at the mention of your name anymore."

"Nor any less, I expect. But I am unkind. I am sure

your gentle influence has soothed his raging spirit. He treats you well?''

"Dodger, I don't want to talk about this."

"Very well, lady." He didn't really, either, but somehow his bitterness had spewed forth. "As ever, I cannot refuse your wish."

"That's drek, Dodger," she said, without heat. "We both know better than that."

He deliberately ignored what could be construed as an invitation to intimate discussion. As little as he wished to discuss what was, he desired even less to dredge up what might have been. " 'Tis you who placed the call. A situation of some gravity must portend. If so, I shall listen. But if 'tis of little import, I shall be distressed, for I have other matters pressing."

"Hope Twist isn't involved in them."

When that seemed all she was willing to say, he prompted, "Why, pray tell?"

"Your friend's in a lot of trouble."

Again she fell silent after a single portentous, yet uninformative, statement. Given the source of the call, however, Dodger thought he knew just what kind of trouble she meant. How had Estios found out what was going down tonight? That effing tight-assed elf had sworn to kill Janice just because she was a wendigo. How long had he known she was in Council lands? Was he going to disrupt the ritual?

"How did he find out?"

Teresa looked surprised. "You know about him already?"

"Of course, I . . . backspace. This isn't about Estios, is it? Who *are* you talking about, Teresa?"

She ran her tongue across her upper lip, reminding him of other times. She looked worried, almost as though she wanted to look over her shoulder to see if anyone was watching, but her discipline wouldn't allow it. Still, the rigidity of her stance told him that this was very serious business.

"I'd rather not name him," she said. "Especially on this line. Call him an old friend of the professor."

He had been right about the seriousness. Dodger had had more than enough of the professor's old friends years ago. Most of the time they were trouble, even when they were on your side. "Tell me the tale."

"This, ah, person, thinks Twist stole something from him, some kind of magical guardian stone. I don't have the details, but it involves a certain something that came out of a well. I'm not sure what this person plans to do once he hunts Twist down, but I think he's going to kill your friend. This person's honor has been stained."

Guardian stones and wells. That spoke of magic and affairs Dodger understood only vaguely. One thing he appreciated was that this matter touched on the dark doings of the professor's connections. Whoever this mysterious person was, he would be a magician and someone dangerous to cross. Sam Verner, as usual, had stepped into drek and sunk in over his head. Everything Dodger could learn, anything Teresa would tell him, increased Sam's chances. "Might you describe this person, that I would know him when I see him?"

"On this line? No more than to say he's Australian. I'll send you a package. But you'd best got moving. He just left for Seattle."

That was the first good part of the conversation. "Well, he's headed in the wrong direction. Twist has some business out of town and he's left the plex already."

Teresa did not look relieved. "He won't give up easily."

"Do they ever? Fear not, I shall get word to Twist."

"Be careful, Dodger. This person may not care who gets in his way."

Her voice sounded sincere, and matched her expression of distressed concern. But how could she be truly troubled? She had made her decision, and he was not her choice. "Your anxiety is touching, fair damsel.

Spare no care for my safety. Having had experience of the professor's friends and their honor, I shall be excessively careful. Twist will get word tonight, just before he leaves on a long, unscheduled vacation.''

13

The night was already cooling down, with the sun gone behind the cone of Mount Rainier for more than half an hour. With the moon climbing in the sky, the time was fast approaching.

Sam tried to ignore the sounds of argument coming from the other side of the rocks, but Rikki Ratboy's shrill tones made it difficult. The weedy street shaman was trying to justify backing out on his promise to help with the ritual. Hart's soft but firm voice was pointing out that if Rikki intended to welsh on a promise, she would make sure that everyone on the street heard about it. In reply, Rikki wailed that he had been tricked into promising.

Rikki was all bluff. His noise hadn't started until Janice and Ghost had arrived. One look at the wendigo had set the Rat shaman off. If Manx had reservations about focusing the ritual on a wendigo, she hadn't revealed them. If she objected, it would have given Rikki the encouragement he wanted, and both the street shamans would now be long gone. As long as Manx was willing, Sam was sure that Rikki would stay. The Rat shaman wouldn't want to lose face in front of anyone, especially a Cat shaman.

Rikki and Manx would join Sam in performing the transformation ritual tonight. Their mix of totems might be odd, but the traditional rivalries of the animals were no bar to their working together. A shaman's totem demanded much, but never that his followers act out predator-prey relationships or territorial disputes. Perhaps it was an expression of the ultimate cosmic harmony as some claimed, but Sam merely accepted the arrangement without puzzling over the why and wherefore.

Tonight, however, he was glad of it. Rikki and Manx might not be the most powerful shamans on the Northwest coast, but he was sure they could handle their assigned parts in the ritual. In approaching them, Sam had hoped their curiosity and greed for the knowledge he offered would be motivation enough to keep quiet. Like all street magicians, they were avid for new magic, that edge that would let them spike the competition for choice assignments in the shadow trade. Manx, anyway, would have kept the preparations for tonight secret, for she was a living embodiment of Cat's obsessive secrecy. But secrecy was a transient need. After tonight Janice would be cured, and it wouldn't matter anymore. If Rikki talked then, fine.

Only the three shamans would be involved in the ritual. Father Rinaldi would have been glad to assist, but he also pointed out that it would stretch the ritual team's resources to protect him, a virtual mundane. Sam had reluctantly agreed to construct the workings without including the priest, but he worried that without Rinaldi's store of knowledge, he wouldn't be informed enough to deal with any unexpected ripples in the mana flow. But the priest had come to the mountain anyway, as moral support prior to the actual working. When the time came he would take his place in one of the carefully chosen lookout points around the perimeter.

Hart would be out there, too. They had all decided that the magic would be purer without mixing her hermetic tradition into the basically shamanic ritual. Pure magic was strong magic, and Sam wanted all the strength he could get into tonight's. He wished he knew more shamans he could trust even as far as he did Rikki and Manx, but those two would be all the help he had tonight.

At least they wouldn't be disturbed. Father Rinaldi professed no particular skill as a scout, but the priest was acutely observant, and his astral sight would be an invaluable aid. Then there were Hart, Ghost, and Gray Otter, all professionals. No Council troops would approach unseen.

Forcing away his worries and concerns, Sam returned his concentration to what he was doing. Colored sand dribbled from his fingers to fall to the ground, each grain taking its place in a growing, intricate pattern. The site would be ready soon, but only barely soon enough. He'd spent most of the last two days here, laying out the patterns with Father Rinaldi's help and consecrating the site in preparation for the ritual. The sand paintings were the last step, and they could not have been done before tonight.

The priest finished his inspection of the clearing and came up behind Sam. "The paintings look good."

"I guess so. I'm not much of an artist."

"The intent and the symbolism are more important than the rendering." Rinaldi laid an encouraging hand on Sam's shoulder. "The picture is fine."

Sam frowned. "I wish we didn't need to put Raven in it. He's Trickster as well as Transformer."

"This is not the time to reopen that discussion. Raven is a powerful totem, especially here in the Northwest of North America. We designed this ritual to incorporate as many elements as possible from as many traditions as could be brought together. Raven belongs here."

"I know." Sam let the last of the black sand dribble from his fingers, completing the dark image of the bird. "I'm just nervous, I guess. Want everything to go right."

"So do we all, Sam." Rinaldi scanned the sky. "It's almost time."

Sam checked the height of the orange moon and nodded. He stared at it for a minute, massaging cramped muscles, then gathered his jars of sand back into their carrying case. By the time he'd stowed the

case in his pack Rinaldi was gone, and the clearing
was quiet except for the night sounds.

Sam whispered the words that would set the first
glimmers of power alight in the medicine circle. A
faint glow, all but lost in the growing moonlight, suffused the clearing. The ritual ground was five meters
across, its boundary marked by a ring of small stones.
Smaller shapes lay just inside the ring at each of the
cardinal points. At the northern point was a bare, circular patch of ground on which sat a tall ritual drum.
The southern point had a similar patch, but this one
contained a multicolored rug on which lay a long
wooden flute. The eastern area was a man-sized and
-shaped outline of stones, head to the center. The west-
ern shape was the same, but the outline was half again
as large. A third bare patch, bounded by a ring of red
sand, lay in the middle of the ring like a hub. In its
center, marking the heart of the medicine circle, sat
the opal Sam had taken from the cave, aglow with
moonlight and magic. Between the central patch and
each of the outer areas was a circular sand painting.

The soft padding of footsteps sounded from the path
as the other shamans entered the clearing and nodded
their readiness to Sam. He nodded back. Rikki stepped
into the medicine ring and took his place in the drum
circle. Rikki's music, unlike Rinaldi's accompaniment
to Sam's astral voyage, would not be simply for mood.
Tonight's music would have its own magic. Manx entered the flute circle and seated herself on the rug. She
arranged her long black hair over the shawl around her
shoulders and settled her necklaces and pendants to
her satisfaction before picking up the flute.

Starting from the feet of the larger outline, Sam
walked halfway around the outside of the great circle,
chanting the opening song of the ritual. At the smaller
outline he pivoted and completed the circle backward.
Rikki began a steady drumbeat, and Sam repeated his
course. This time he added extra steps, making his

progress a solemn dance. Manx's haunting flute music accompanied the third circumnavigation of the ring, and Sam's steps became quicker. The glow of the magelight grew stronger with each pass until the clearing was nearly as bright as day.

Chanting, Sam entered the medicine circle at the feet of the large outline, crossing it and a band of red sand that bisected the sand painting to reach the center. He paused to touch the opal, then continued on, crossing a second sand painting and the smaller outline. At its foot and still within the outer ring, he crouched facing the center, changing the chant to the calling song.

Opposite him, outside the circle, Janice stepped out of the darkness.

"Welcome, Wolf," he said. "Join us in our magic."

"Willingly," she replied, then stepped over the boundary rocks and into the larger outline. She lay down on her back, head toward the center of the ring. Sam walked the inner boundary of the circle to close it magically. Then he walked around Janice, sprinkling her with herbs to complete the seal. Returning to the central area, he sealed himself in.

There was little room in the circle; his crossed legs nearly touched the opal. He reached out, laying the fingers of both hands on the gemstone. Pushing himself into trance, he felt for Dog's presence. He wanted his totem's strength to add to the gathered power, but the fickle presence remained aloof. *As you wish, old hound.* With the focus stone and the ritual, there would be magic enough.

Rikki took up the harmony chant in his squeaky, shrill voice while Manx's flute purred a haunting counter-melody. Distantly, he heard his own voice begin the transformation song. Sam let himself drift, gathering power. Anchoring himself through the opal, he gathered the strands to weave them into a shining pattern. Under his shirt Sam's fossil tooth thumped against his chest, and he merged its aural image into the configuration, enmeshing it in the net. Foundation complete, he reached toward distant influences and warped them into conformation with his will.

Clothed in scintillant power, he turned to Janice. She was only an aural image of ill-defined shape. Beneath the surface he felt the lurking darkness of the wendigo nature warring with the struggling but weakening human soul. He wrapped her in the power, cocooning her like a caterpillar. Soon, he sang, she would emerge a butterfly.

When he called her forth, she made the ritual responses. Obeying his order, she stood and crossed from the larger to the smaller outline, skirting the central area as she went, then lay down again. Sam felt the surging power and struggled to guide it, trying with all his might to mold it to his desire. For all his attempts to control it, the power remained unfocused as they reached the crucial point of the song. Then the threshold had been crossed, the passage made, and there was nothing to do but sing the conclusion of the ritual. The voice of the flute softened to silence, while the drum, steady and insistent, shifted to a new rhythm that called Sam back from the realms of power.

He opened his eyes. Janice lay to his left, overflowing from the smaller stone outline. She remained a wendigo. All the preparation and sacrifice had been in vain. The ritual had failed.

A screech, seeming to encompass Sam's despair and rage, shredded the night and ripped the music into silence.

14

A huge humanoid shape bounded from the darkness to stand hunched at the edge of the medicine circle.

Its long, ape-like arms flailed. One gnarled hand held a tree limb that it swept back and forth, scattering the stones of the outer ring.

Two more creatures like the first shambled from the darkness to also stand at the edge of the broken circle. All three were massive, alike in general but idiosyncratically different in particulars. Covered in rough hides studded with irregular patches of dermal bone, the creatures were three meters of lumpy muscles. Asymmetric horns crowned misshapen heads that wobbled as they turned to scan the clearing. Bloodshot eyes gleamed evilly in the flickering magelight.

The first creature flung its tree limb toward Sam. The missile struck the ground a meter short, gouging the earth and plowing through the stones of the ring to come to rest at Sam's feet. Shrieking, the monster charged. Scrambling out of its way, Sam jumped to the side, scattering colored sand as he fled the ritual circle.

He took cover in a jumble of boulders. Already there was Gray Otter, crouched with her SCK100 machine pistol in her hand. Sam didn't know if he had stumbled onto her watch station or if she had returned upon hearing the ruckus. Whichever, he was glad she was there. He wished Ghost and Hart were there as well.

Looking back at the clearing, he saw the creatures rampaging about, kicking through the sand paintings and heaving rocks randomly into the surrounding dark. The magelight faded away and night dropped back onto the mountain.

Rikki crawled up beside Sam and Gray Otter. "What are those things?"

"Dzoo-noo-qua," Gray Otter said softly.

"Doo-zoo-what?" Rikki asked.

"Name doesn't matter, Rikki. They're trouble."

"Big trouble," Gray Otter agreed.

Sam searched the darkness for any sign of his sister or the other shaman. "What happened to Janice and Manx?"

"Dunno," Rikki replied. "Ain't healthy out there. They must've decided the same."

A sudden burst of light illuminated the clearing. Someone had popped a flare. Sam hoped it was Ghost's doing, or Hart's. They didn't need Salish-Shidhe troops complicating things now.

The harsh white glare let him see what had happened to Manx. Fleeing the attack, she had not chosen her direction wisely. One of the dzoo had her cornered at the edge of the clearing where the slope fell sharply away down the mountain. The creature advanced on her menacingly, while Manx responded with flaring darts of arcane power that ripped into the dzoo.

Instead of howling in pain or breaking off its advance to seek cover, the creature merely lowered its head and bulled forward. The magical energy shed from its shoulders like water. With nowhere to dodge, Manx could not evade the sweep of the monster's long arm, which gathered her in. As soon as it laid its second hand on her, she began to scream. It didn't bite or claw or squeeze her, but she screamed. Her hair faded from its midnight black as her struggles weakened. Her skin sagged and wrinkled. Clothes that had hugged her full-fleshed body flapped loosely as she struck and kicked.

The creature seemed to grow larger, but that was an illusion born of dread. At least Sam hoped it was. The dzoo raised its head and howled at the moon, and the joy in that cry chilled Sam thoroughly.

With a howl of his own, he stood up. Gathering the power, he felt the mask of Dog descend over his features. He bared his teeth and cast the energy in a stun-bolt at the dzoo. The thing staggered, dropping the husk that was all that remained of Manx.

The dzoo turned its bloodshot eyes toward him. Ivory reflected in the flare's light as it grinned at Sam. With a grunt, the creature charged.

The chatter from Otter's gun drowned the sounds of Rikki scrambling away. Sam hoped the Rat shaman was seeking a better location from which to cast his own spells. Though tired by his first casting, Sam prepared a second to follow up Otter's fire. Though on target, her attack had little effect. Bullets sparked from the creature's dermal armor to ricochet into the night. Sam was still gathering his power when the dzoo reached their refuge. With a back-handed blow, it sent Otter tumbling away. Sam jumped back but landed badly, his ankle twisting under him, and he fell. The dzoo grinned. Dark, spadelike nails gouged the loam as the creature groped for him. The drooling, leering face came closer, and he felt the thing's fetid breath on his skin. Then the fang-mouthed visage was rising, a look of stupid confusion replacing the former avid anticipation.

Janice had come to Sam's rescue. In a display of phenomenal strength, she lifted the dzoo over her head. The thing struggled, but her grip on its dermal armor remained firm until she slammed the creature into the ground. The dzoo whuffed out its breath and flailed spasmodically with its limbs. As one dirty foot caught Janice at the side of her knee, her leg buckled and she fell within reach of the dzoo's arms. Clawed fingers raked at her, digging furrows of blood. The wounds were healing even as the dzoo half leaped, half crawled onto her. The two titans kicked and gouged as they rolled over, locked in one another's grip. Biting and spitting, the heaving melee of fur and leathery hide pitched about until the combatants finally rolled out of the flare's range and into the darkness.

The struggle's savage fury almost drowned out Ghost's shout. Without thinking Sam ducked, diving to the ground and rolling. His quick reaction saved him from having his head split open by the tree trunk that came smashing down where he had just stood. He was not fast enough to escape unscathed, however. Sam's arm blazed with pain as the weapon shredded his sleeve and scraped skin and flesh from his right arm. Dazed, he staggered to his feet, then fell. He was too groggy to focus a spell, and his arm was numb from the shock. His gun wouldn't have done any good

anyway. The tranq bullets wouldn't have slowed the thing down fast enough, even if the needles managed to penetrate the dermal bone. He looked up into the hungry face of a second dzoo-noo-qua.

Ghost hit the creature hard with a cross-body strike to the back of the knees. Surprised, it began to topple backward. Ghost hit the ground first, but rolled away before the bulk of the dzoo could pin him. The Indian came up with both Ingrams out, and the guns spat lethally. He concentrated his fire on the creature's neck, where the armored plating was light. Bullets chewed through the bulky muscle, mauling meat until the neck was half-severed. Pumping blood, the dzoo-noo-qua rose and charged Ghost, who evaded its clumsy rush. The dzoo blundered past him, crashing into the brush. Its howling trailed off as it tumbled downslope, ending with a solid thump as the creature crashed into a tree that refused to yield.

The clearing fell silent.

Ghost looked Sam over and nodded, seemingly satisfied that he would survive. Otter limped her way to them. She was bruised but had sustained no serious injuries. She had Rikki in tow; he was grimier than usual, but unhurt. Hart arrived at a full run, weapon in one hand and spell energy glowing around the other. At Ghost's "It's over," she let the spell fade away and dropped her weapon to hang from its sling. She threw her arms around Sam, who returned the embrace.

"I'm all right," he told her.

"I was too far away," she said. "Janice?"

"I don't know. She was fighting one of the dzoo-noo-qua. They rolled that way into the brush."

"That fight's over, too," Ghost announced.

"Janice?" Sam said.

Ghost said nothing.

Fearing the worst, Sam bolted in the direction he had seen the fight heading. Hart raced at his side. They did not have to go far, for the combatants' struggle had taken them no more than a dozen meters from the clearing.

Janice was alive. Her wounds were closing as Sam watched in shocked silence. It was not the magical healing that shocked him, but what she was doing.

Janice was eating her former opponent.

When she realized she had an audience, she stopped and looked up. At first, Sam saw no recognition in her eyes, only hunger. Then the feral gleam faded a bit, and she slunk away into the shadows. Stunned, he didn't follow. Hart laid her hand on his bruised arm, but he was too numb to flinch.

The beast was rising.

Unnoticed, Father Rinaldi had joined them. "This is very bad, Sam. These dzoo-noo-qua, they are not animals."

Sam refused to believe that. *"Paterson's Paranormal Animals* lists dzoo-noo-qua as nonsentient. And the Salish-Shidhe Council offers a bounty on them as vermin."

"The Council also offers a bounty on wendigos," Rinaldi pointed out.

The priest's cruel reminder made Sam clench his jaw to repress a sob. Books and bounties weren't always right. Paterson's guide also said that dzoo-noo-qua were trolls that had been turned into something subhuman by an infection of the transforming HMHVV virus. Some researchers thought the same virus turned orks into wendigos, but what did the scientists really know about magical beings?

Rinaldi and Hart coaxed Sam away from the corpse of the dzoo-noo-qua and got him back to the clearing. The priest began to dress Sam's wound. As he was finishing he said sadly, "I'll have to talk with Brothers Mark and Paulus about this."

Sam nodded without meeting Rinaldi's gaze. "Do what you have to do, Father. I understand."

"I hope you do, Sam."

Another nod. "Each of us does what he must do."

The priest eyed him strangely but said nothing. Gray

Otter appeared at Rinaldi's shoulder with an offer to guide him back to the metroplex. The priest thanked her and began to gather his things. Over his bent back, Otter caught Sam's eyes. He mouthed the word "slow," and she nodded.

Each of us does what he must do.

As Rinaldi and Otter departed, Dodger stepped up to Sam's side. Sam didn't wonder how or why the decker had come to the clearing; he was just glad that Dodger was there.

"Time to fall back and regroup?" Dodger asked.

"You know what to do, Dodger."

"Verily. Implementation shall take but an elementary command. Fear not, Sir Twist. The good brothers shall receive their recall orders before the padre can reach them. He, too, shall receive a summons home. They shall not be around to interfere."

"Will they suspect?"

"For shame, Sir Twist. Though I cannot bespeak the activity of their paranoia, I assure you that they shall not see through my deception until they confront their superior in Rome. By then it will be too late for them to interfere. There is, however, another matter."

Sam didn't know what could be worse than tonight's disaster, but Dodger's grim expression promised more calamity.

"I don't want to know, so you'd better tell me."

PART 2

Look Within Yourself

15

The cottage was Hart's private hideaway in the mountains north of Saint Helens. Dodger hadn't wanted to use it, suggesting instead that they hold their conference somewhere in the woods. Pointing out the threat of inclement weather, Sam had overruled him. The air in the one-room cabin was too warm for comfort, but the windows had to be shut against the driving rain. The rising scent of damp earth and wood competed with the sweaty odor of tightly packed people. The table that normally dominated the cabin's center was shoved to one side and piled with the runners' gear, but that still left the room crowded. Sam's agitated attempts at pacing only made it worse. Hart and Dodger were constantly having to remove their feet from his path or have them trod upon by the distracted Sam. At length he halted, facing the blank log wall that was the cabin's back.

"It's not doing any good putting it off, Sam. None of us likes it any better than you do." Hart's voice was full of concern for him, her tone belying the content. "We all wanted to see Janice saved, but it looks like only one way is left."

"No." Sam spun and faced her. "There *is* a way to defeat the wendigo. I felt it during the ritual. I know it's still possible for her to change."

"Even with Rinaldi's help, you couldn't design a ritual to do it."

"We didn't have the power."

"We've been through that."

"And I still say that the ritual failed because I'm not powerful enough. We need a stronger shaman to perform the ritual."

Hart exchanged a glance with Dodger, then sighed. "When we started this, you wanted to get other people out of it."

"That was before I knew I couldn't do it alone."

"You couldn't do it with Rikki and Manx, either."

"The ritual never really drew on their power. Besides, they were just small-time. I picked them because they would go along, not because they were really good shamans.

"Who could we get?" Sam found his companions' faces closed to him. "Come on, you two. You've both been in the shadow trade a lot longer than I have. Who do you know? Who's the most powerful shaman around?"

"So you think power's the only problem now."

"I think it's the critical factor." The ritual had been well designed. What else could have been lacking? "So who might have enough power? How about the archdruid of England?"

Hart chuckled sourly. "An unlikely source of help, considering last year's events."

"Don't you think they'd be grateful for our help in disposing of their renegades?" Sam asked.

Shaking his head, Dodger said, "I believe their point of view would be somewhat different. Considering our complicity in abetting the escape of a certain wendigo, they might actually align us with the villains against." Turning to Hart he asked, "What about Dr. Kano at Cal-Tech?"

She shook her head. "A theoretician, mostly."

"Well, Mistress, is there not a theory problem as well?"

"Our local expert seems to think not, but I'm afraid there still exists a serious question of practical knowledge." She turned to Sam and gave him a sad smile.

"Not to slight your talent and diligence, but you haven't been a practicing shaman for very long. Mastering the Art, whatever the tradition, does not come quickly or easily. The problem with the ritual may not even be what you think it is. You might have all the raw power you need and just not know how to channel it. This transformation magic of yours may just be too subtle."

"And how would I know?"

"By learning more."

"Janice doesn't have the time."

"Always in a hurry."

Sam thought that remark unfair. "I spent a year working with Rinaldi to develop that ritual. I'd hardly call that rushing."

"But it didn't work."

"It *could* have worked. It should have." Visions of Janice and the dead dzoo-noo-qua swam before his eyes. "We've got to hurry now, whether I want to or not. Janice is succumbing to the wendigo nature. We've got to find someone who can do the ritual properly as soon as possible. We've got to enlist the help of a shaman who has the power, experience, and skill we need."

Hart gave an exasperated sigh. "Why not just ask for Howling Coyote? He certainly fits . . ."

A sudden scrape and the crash of Dodger's chair on the floor interrupted her remark. Finishing his abrupt rise, the elf stalked to the door and flung it open. He stared out at the rain.

Sam looked to Hart, who looked as surprised as he felt. "What's the matter, Dodger? Do you know this Howling Coyote?"

The decker's voice was soft, almost inaudible over the sound of the downpour. "I think he's dead. 'Twould be better 'twere so."

When it was obvious Dodger would say no more on

the subject, Sam whispered to Hart, "Do you know why he reacted like that?"

She shook her head.

"What could it be about this Howling Coyote? The name's familiar, but I can't seem to place it."

"Been neglecting the historical side of your studies again?" Sam could see by her half smile that she noticed the heat that would be reddening his cheeks above his beard. "Is the name Daniel Coleman any more familiar?"

"The Ghost Dance prophet?"

"None other," Dodger announced, forcing himself back into the conversation. His back remained turned to them. "Coleman was a charismatic firebrand, the leading light of the movement that resulted in the end of the United States of America, the Dominion of Canada, and the Republic of Mexico. A very influential villain. I heard him speak in the broadcast in which the Ghost Dancers took responsibility for the volcanic eruption that buried Los Alamos."

"He must have made quite an impression," Hart said. "You couldn't have been more than a kid."

Dodger shifted, as though the memory made him uncomfortable. "It was the first use of the Ghost Dance magic. Of course it made an impression."

"If you remember that, you must remember when they blew the Cascade volcanoes."

"Clearly," Dodger said bitterly. There was an uncomfortable silence for a few moments. Then Dodger collected himself and continued. "Coleman took responsibility for those as well. He was a radical and a terrorist. Were he available, I do not think you would find in him the slightest shred of humanitarian concern for one Caucasian's plight. He might have been called the Champion of the Red Man, the Awakened Ute, and the Son of the Great Spirit, but he started the Expulsion. He earned his nickname Red Braids a thousand times over."

"Red Braids?" Sam asked. "I don't remember ever reading that. What's it mean?"

"It was for the color his braided hair turned when dipped in the blood of his enemies," Dodger said. "Not everything gets into the history books. You should know that by now, Sam."

"You sound awfully bitter, Dodger. You have a personal grudge?" Hart asked. She waited for him to respond, and when he didn't she said, "Howling Coyote was a guerrilla leader in a difficult time. He saved the Indians from an oppressive government and helped them set up their own. He helped a lot of people, and may have damn well been responsible for saving the whole fragging planet. The megacorporations were polluting and raping earth into oblivion until the Awakened magic turned back some of the tide."

"Coleman was only interested in his own people. I haven't seen the land turn green and verdant worldwide, nor have I seen the megacorps roll over and die. If Coleman was so great-hearted, where is he now? Why did he abandon his fight?" Dodger took a deep breath. "He was a butcher and an opportunist."

"He may have been," Hart agreed. "The early days of the struggle were difficult and required harsh measures. He had a kinder side, too. He was the one who brought the NAN forces to the table in Denver. Without him, there'd have been no treaty of Denver. The war might still be going on. As to what he did during the Expulsion, I've talked to some, on both sides, who were there. If not for Coleman, the resettlement clauses in the treaty would have been more draconian. I've been told that the Aztlan faction would have slaughtered anyone of non-Indian blood. And it was Coleman who fought for the repatriation payments clause that allowed the displaced people a chance to start new lives."

Dodger snorted. "Those payments turned to smoke when measured against outstanding payments of the alleged debts owed to various Indian tribes by the various governments involved. He had power, and used it to his own ends.''

''What about the education and hospital care he sponsored? Most of it made special provision for the changed, hardly a universal concern in those days. As an elf, I'd think you'd appreciate that. And what of the environmentally safe energy supplies he encouraged?''

Dodger shrugged. ''Remorse? Public relations? I'm no mind-reader.''

''He answered those questions in his book, *Howling in the Wilderness*.''

''Those were his public answers,'' Dodger said sourly. ''He wrote the book while he was president of the Sovereign Tribal Council. One could hardly expect a truthful account.''

''The book's sort of a *Mein Kampf* crossed with Castaneda's *Yaqui Way of Knowledge*. Not exactly flattering to an incumbent. I don't think it was an *apologia*. It was too strange for that.'' Dodger turned away again, and Hart subsided into silence. The set of her jaw told Sam she was not happy with Dodger's stubbornness. Dodger's hunched shoulders showed Sam he wouldn't get help there, either.

''You caught me out on tradition history,'' he said quietly to Hart, ''but I've never been real big on political history, either. I know Coleman was real important once, but he stepped down or something. What happened to him?''

''No one knows. About, oh, I guess it's been fifteen years now, he just up and walked away into the mountains.''

''Why?''

''Got fed up with the politics in the STC and the Native American Nations, I suppose. When the big push to get non-Indians off the continent didn't work out, NAN solidarity sort of slipped. When the elves and such put Tir Tairngire together and Coleman backed them, he lost a lot of credibility with some of the tribal councils because of his policy of welcoming metahumans into Indian lands. Then Tsimshian broke away, too. I guess it was too much in just one year. He resigned and left everything behind."

Once again Dodger broke in. "Or so say the official stories. There was shadow business then as well. Perhaps he had a falling out with his radical friends. Terrorists who disagree rarely settle their arguments with words."

"You think somebody killed him?" The idea troubled Sam, and not just because murder was wrong. Tending more toward Hart's than Dodger's version of the man, he had begun to think that Howling Coyote might be just the shaman Janice needed.

"Somebody might have," Dodger said. "Enough people might perceive a disgruntled magician with a history as a terrorist and a very dangerous threat."

"Or a promising ally," Hart pointed out.

Which was what Sam needed. "He really was a great shaman, wasn't he?"

"Oh, yes. No doubt of it," she said. "Some people think the stuff in his book about learning the Great Ghost Dance was after-the-fact fantasizing, a political make-over to improve his image as Council president. But he was more than a figurehead for the Ghost Dancers. He really did lead the Dance himself."

"That would make him a very powerful shaman."

"Yes," Hart agreed slowly. "Perhaps more powerful than any magician the Sixth World has ever seen." Then, after a moment, "Human magician, that is."

Sam wasn't worried about racial concerns. "Then he would know more about shamanic magic than anyone else."

Hart laughed. "Like I know everything there is to know about being an elf? Stay real. He was a man who stumbled into power. He used it and used it well. He taught a lot of other people how to use it. But know everything? Who knows everything about anything?''

"But he led the Great Ghost Dance," Sam insisted.

"Yes. And he claimed more power than any human I've ever heard of. Knowledge may be power, but the reverse is not necessarily true."

Sam thought about that for a while. "The Dance was transformation magic, wasn't it?"

"In part."

"Then he wouldn't have to know about everything. Just how to channel the power to make the change. He could know that, couldn't he?"

Hart mulled it over. "I don't know. I think you're grasping at straws."

Sam did, too, but what other choice was there? If he wasted time tracking down lesser shamans who couldn't do the job, he might not have enough time to get to Howling Coyote. It was a gamble, but he didn't see an alternative. "I've got to grab on to something. Otherwise Janice will slip away."

"You may not be able to stop that," Hart warned.

Sam didn't want to hear it. He could not believe his sister was irreversibly set on a course to becoming a monster in mind and soul as well as body.

Hart still seemed set on dissuading him. "Why not start with some resources more to hand? Didn't you say that Professor Laverty once offered to help you with Janice? Just because Estios works for Laverty doesn't mean that the professor agrees with that bastard's field decisions. Talk to Laverty. Find out where he stands."

"I don't think that would be advisable at this time," Dodger said.

"Why not?" Hart asked.

"I'd rather not say."

"It isn't because he's involved with this Australian elf who's looking for Sam, is it?"

"I said I'd rather not say."

Sam's stomach flip-flopped. "Dodger, are you holding out on me again?"

Dodger turned and fixed Sam with bleak eyes. "Sam, I am asking you not to press. Were I to speak of how I learned of the one who hunts you, others beyond our circle might learn as well. That could have undesirable consequences for someone I would rather not see hurt."

Sam suspected he knew to whom Dodger referred, and a surreptitious glance at Hart told him that she suspected the same. "Well if I can't go to Luverty, who else is there to ask?"

"Lofwyr?" The bleakness in Dodger's voice betrayed him as more barren of reasonable ideas than Sam.

"I don't think I could pay the price," Sam said. "Or survive the deal. That dragon nearly got us all killed the last time."

"Sam, Father Rinaldi would know who to ask."

Sam shook his head sadly. "We could hardly go to him now."

Hart sighed. "I'm a hermetic magician, Sam. I don't know many shamans, and those I do know probably couldn't pump the power you seem to think is necessary. I'm trapped, I don't see an answer."

Dodger nodded solemnly. "Naught to do now but face the inevitable."

"It's settled then," Sam said firmly. "We'll get Howling Coyote."

"But no one knows where he is," Hart protested.

"If he is alive at all," Dodger added.

Sam shrugged, dismissing their objections. If only his own fears could be dealt with so easily. "I'll find him," he said.

16

Neko Noguchi stretched contentedly. The surroundings were eminently satisfactory: subdued lighting, soft music with just enough beat to be stimulating, condiments and liquid refreshments made from real foodstuffs, soft furniture, and an even softer bed waiting. Though Neko had not yet lain down on it, he was sure of the last; he had checked earlier in the evening. The woman was attentive and skilled. Monique, she had said her name was, a name as exotic to him as her sleek, dark good looks. Oh yes, he was content. This was how the best shadowrunners lived between runs, a lifestyle he was going to enjoy getting used to.

He reached for the decanter to top off his glass. Monique nudged him gently in the ribs and nuzzled closer, holding out her glass. He grinned, more for his own amusement than in response to her smile. It was her third refill—all on the tab, of course. She had guzzled twice as much as he had, and he knew from the buzz in his own head that the booze was good quality. Though her voice had started to slur, she was not really drunk or uncoordinated. Her drinks came from the same source as his, so she must have some kind of augmentation that shunted the liquor from her system or neutralized the alcohol. He wondered how many of these overpriced drinks it took to pay for her enhancement.

She nestled in his arm and pulled at her drink. He settled back and sipped at his, ready to continue his tale.

"Deckers are so proud of their ability to lift data from the systems of arrogant corporations, overbearing governments, and wealthy individuals. But they are fools to risk their brains against Intrusion Countermeasures, daring the black ice with only meat reflexes and the thin shield of their cyberdecks to protect them.

"Data-theft, like most fine arts, can be accomplished in a variety of manners. Some are safer than others, of course."

Monique's eyes were wide, shining with admiration. "What you did was not without danger. A decker might risk his brain, but you risked your body and life."

"True. Life and limb were at peril." He sipped. "But my body is a well-honed machine, and like any machine, it can be rebuilt if necessary. You know the old saying, 'We have the technology.' As to the risk to my life? Breathing is a risk and walking down the street a danger. Death comes to all, and when it does, our worries and concerns leave us. No good karma comes from running away from what cannot be avoided. The real, true, and horrible fate worse than death is the loss of your mind. To remain breathing while the mind is absent or locked in a fugue is a nullity, existence without purpose. You cannot deal with this life nor go onward in the cycle. The brain death is what deckers risk. I would rather face a dragon in single combat."

Monique shivered delicately. "Yet you stole the data. How did you do it?"

Neko shrugged, dismissing the difficulty of his feat with deliberate casualness. "Cats are shadowy, silent creatures, unnoticed when they wish it so. I wished it so. Goroji-*san* will learn of his loss when his tame deckers begin tomorrow night's work."

"Aren't you afraid he will find out who stole from him? Goroji's *kobun* are notorious for their brutality."

Chuckling, Neko put down his glass and traced the fine line of her chin. "However brutal they are, the soldiers of Goroji's clan cannot hurt what they cannot find."

"You are marvelous." She kissed his finger. "Are you sure they can't trace you?"

"Very." Neko kissed her. His lips tingled, a sensation brought about by her lipstick, he realized, because it was strongest where the liquor had not washed away much of the ruby tint. He pulled away to stare into her eyes. She lowered her lids, a feigned shyness that hinted at the pleasure to come. He smiled. Biz before pleasure; it was time to end the pretense. "You may assure Cog that what I have is no isotope. He will not be burned by simple association, although some of the offering will have a half-life of usefulness."

"Cog? Who or what is Cog? What are you talking about?"

Her eyes were wide and her tone a masterful blend of hurt and confusion. Her body language expressed innocence tinged with timidity and a hint of growing trepidation. He was impressed. The act would have been convincing. If he hadn't known better.

"Excellent performance." He used his free hand to clap softly on the arm of the sofa. "But I do know that you belong to Cog. Do you think I would have spoken so freely if I hadn't known you were screening for the fixer?"

Her deception remained in play while those dark eyes evaluated him, measuring his conviction and weighing the cost of dropping her pretense. He let the seconds drag. Finally her eyes shifted focus, checking the room around them. Looking for the hidden ready lights of the even better-hidden trideo cameras. She needn't have worried; he had already made sure the monitors were dysfunctional, though he saw no need to tell her that.

"You are very astute for one so young," she said.
He preened under the compliment. "A necessary

attribute for anyone in the biz who wishes to get any older."

"Messing with the yakuza is not conducive to long life. Were Goroji a simple boss, dealing with your offering would be a delicate business, but as it is, the heat is higher than desirable. You were aware that Goroji fronts for Grandmother?"

He hadn't been. "Of course."

Her eyes gave away nothing, but the slight twitch of a cheek muscle hinted disbelief, or at least suspicion. He smiled, hoping to project the air of a confident and assured runner.

"Cog would prefer that your next offering have nothing to do with Grandmother's sources. She reacts violently when someone disturbs her network, and her wrath descends on those who bothered her and on anyone associated with those unfortunates. Should you continue to court such a fate, Cog wishes that you not involve him. He and Grandmother settled their feud long ago, and he has no desire to reopen that unpleasantness at this time."

"No one expects a fixer to show a warrior's courage. This run was in direct response to the needs of a client for whom Cog serves as an intermediary. No stipulations or caveats were placed on me at the time of the request for information. Hence there should be no change in the payment. Fixers rely on their reputation with shadowrunners. Fair dealings are imperative."

She raised an eyebrow.

"Within reasonable margins of profit, of course," he added.

"I'm sure a reasonable fee will be paid for the contracted data."

"And for the bonus material."

"Commensurate with its value."

"And its temperature."

She smiled now. "We do have an understanding. The caution was meant for future dealings."

"If Cog fears connection with further enquiries, perhaps he would consent to bow out and let me deal directly with the client."

"Perhaps he will."

The possibility that the fixer might cut himself out of the deal made Neko realize just how dangerous Cog thought the situation. How could Grandmother be so territorial? It was bad business. There had to be something more to the data he was uncovering for the elven decker. Some secret connection perhaps? Understanding what was happening would make it easier for him to know the value of what he discovered. Knowing the value, he could cut himself a better deal. Coincidentally, he would also know just what kind of danger he was facing.

He continued to dicker with Monique over the price for his recent acquisitions, but his mind was preoccupied with other matters. He began to wonder if Goroji's search for Warlord Feng was just the yakuza boss grasping at power or something more sinister. Perhaps it was part of some great scheme of Grandmother's. The Feng data was juxtaposed in Goroji's files with material on enquiries into the matter of Renraku's Special Directorate. An operator like Grandmother would likely have more than one angle on an operation. Goroji on the outside and Sato on the inside made for a well-orchestrated attack. Very understandable, considering the importance of the prize. Neko would be surprised if Grandmother didn't have other tools working on the target as well. An artificial intelligence would be a powerful research tool in the Matrix. If it was as good as his decker acquaintances claimed it could be, what computer secret would be safe, save one defended by a similar artificial intelligence? The worth to an information broker would be incalculable.

If Grandmother had access to such a machine, she would know all.

And what did she want to know? Why did Feng interest her? What connection did a Chinese neowarlord have with German terrorists, or to the breakup of the United States, or to Israeli commando strikes in Africa? And what did any of those things have to do with the financing of Ordo Naturum, the Humanis policlub offshoot, or with the financial holdings of Awakened beings? Neko didn't know the answers, but he was suddenly sure that all the information was interlocked in a web of intrigue. His curiosity was aroused. Even if the answers meant nothing to him, he was sure they would be worth a lot of nuyen to someone. All he had to do was figure out who. And what the answers were, of course.

* * *

Seattle was worse than Portland. The boundary zones around the metroplex territory were not as developed as those around the city-state enclaves in Australia, but they bore the same hideous stamp of human architecture. The metroplex was crammed with smelly crowds of humans, dark breeds, and low-life elves. It was full of life, but only of a kind past the consideration of a rational being. The plex-dwellers were only vermin infesting a land nearly dead.

Urdli wanted to go home. Australia was not what it should be, but even the wild mana and the chaos were preferable to the deadness of the metroplex and the stifling, oppressive gloom cast by the corporate skyscrapers. But he could not leave yet.

His head hurt from the unaccustomed effort of maintaining the illusion that he was an ordinary inhabitant of this morass. He disliked the disguise but found it useful, possibly necessary. The first day had told him how unusual he appeared, when he had drawn unwanted attention from a group of hooded toughs shouting Humanis policlub slogans. They would not bother any other elves, blacks or otherwise, now. He supposed that he had incidentally fueled the Humanis hate, but he hoped he had fueled their fear as well. Fear was a useful tool for keeping animals in their places.

Since he had taken to using the illusion spell, he had encountered no similar problems.

For a week now he had been vainly seeking Samuel Verner, the one they called Twist. To make his inquiries less remarkable, Urdli had offered incentives rather than taking the more direct approach of interrogation. The method had yielded results, but not satisfactory ones. There was no sign of the human shaman at his known haunts. Neither had Urdli learned the whereabouts of any of the human's known associates, save former acquaintances such as Sally Tsung. The woman had spoken freely and disparagingly about her former lover, but claimed ignorance of his current whereabouts. Urdli might have probed her, but she was a mage of unknown ability, too great a risk.

He wished Laverty had been more forthcoming about who he had observing Verner. Urdli wanted to contact that person, but had no way to do so. He had come to suspect that the decker operating under the name Dodger was Laverty's observer, for Verner had regular contact with only two elves—the decker and a woman named Hart. Hart was an unlikely candidate because she had worked for the Shidhe more than once in the past, and Urdli doubted that the professor had found a way to slip an agent past the Shidhe's vigilance. Eliminating the woman as a possibility left Dodger the most likely candidate, but like all the shaman's little ring of shadowrunners he had dropped out of sight.

Awareness of time passing made Urdli uncomfortable and unhappy. Constructing a kulpunya was impractical here. His attempts to sense the guardian stone

had been unsuccessful; either it was shielded or it had
been removed from the metroplex. The latter possibility chilled him. If Verner was not in Seattle, Urdli
had no idea where the human had run. The time for
subtlety had passed, and the time for interrogation had
come.

17

Hunting Howling Coyote was a fool's quest that,
since he was assisting in the quest, made Dodger a
fool. If the Ghost Dancer Prophet was dead, Sam was
throwing away his last slim hope of saving his sister.
She would be lost to the wendigo nature before the
Dog shaman would give up. If Howling Coyote was
alive, Sam was unlikely to uncover Coleman's hiding
place in time. Even if by sheer chance he should somehow locate the runaway shaman, the chance of ultimate success remained slim. Despite Sam's
earnestness, he had little hope of persuading Howling
Coyote to help. *If* Coleman could help. That possibility was just as unlikely.

More foolishness. Just like Dodger's run against the
Ute Council government computer system. The pair of
them were mad fools, tilting at windmills. Foolishness
and obsession seemed the order of the day.

As for Hart, Dodger had seen her reaction during
his report of Noguchi's last findings. Something in the
Asian runner's last data drop had touched on an obsession of her own. What it might be Dodger could
only guess, for Hart wrapped her past actions and
present motives in obsessive secrecy. She was so anxious to be elsewhere that she had agreed to let Sam
leave for Denver by himself, an uncharacteristic re-

sponse to the situation. If she had expected to thus gain freedom of action, she must have been disappointed when her own warnings about the dangers of decking into the Ute system backfired on her. Sam had pointed out that if, as she herself had suggested, they were to avoid their usual haunts and acquaintances, she was the only available person to sit guard on Dodger's body as he decked. Her acquiescence might have fooled the love-besotted Sam, but Dodger had no trouble recognizing her restrained frustration.

How could Sam trust her? She was even more secretive than Sally Tsung, and justifiably so, from the few hints of Hart's former associations that Dodger had been able to dig up. He had not yet told Sam of those connections. If Sam thought Dodger was suspect for association with the professor, what would he think of Hart's former friends? However Sam might feel about this side of Hart, he would almost certainly not take kindly to Dodger's probing into her background.

Hart was not the only one restrained from what she wished to do. Of necessity, his own search for the lost Renraku artificial intelligence was sidelined. Dodger had vowed that he would prove his friendship to Sam despite the unfortunate English affair. Compelled to pay that debt, he was forced to participate in this mad quest. Foolish as it was, Sam wanted the Matrix angle covered, and who could do it as well or as quickly as the Dodger? The elf's own concerns would have to wait, but perhaps that was just as well. Since Noguchi's first contact, his hope had swelled only slightly faster than his fear. He still didn't understand the full ramifications of the AI and its attraction for him, but he felt its draw all the same.

The AI belonged to the Matrix, and so did his attention. The middle of a run was no time to get distracted. The Ute Council Matrix segment was coded orange, and though not the highest security level, it held sufficient danger for the unwary traveler. Unwary was exactly what he had been. Already he had nearly blundered into several shades of black. He had barely skirted those threats, but if he were not more attentive, he wouldn't have much longer to worry about anyone's obsessions.

The ebon boy with the cloak of glitter that was Dodger's icon slipped away from the subprocessor serving Salt Lake's government center personnel files. The hulking cubist bears prowling each of the data-lines leading into the stores made it patently clear that the Ute computer specialists had dealt with illegal entry through this route before. The visual design of the Intrusion Countermeasures might be more for the sake of intimidation than reflecting the true strength of the ice at those access points, but Dodger didn't think now was the time to try it. The least threat involved in engaging one of the bears was the chance that the decker behind it would give notice of Dodger's presence in the system. If an alert went out, the going would get considerably tougher. Sam's schedule left no time for a siege, meaning that this run required total stealth until the goods were gotten, or else it was worthless.

Somewhere in the Ute government files was information about Daniel Coleman, a Ute by tribal affiliation. Dodger had rifled the public database before starting, but that had, of course, yielded nothing really definite. The public record had been enough to send Sam to Denver, the nexus of so many of Howling Coyote's activities, but it offered no clue to Coleman's current whereabouts. To find the good stuff, Dodger needed to penetrate to the deep files where the Council's leaders kept what they needed to run their little part of the world. If Howling Coyote was still alive, his tribal elders were the most likely to know.

A bit of lucky hacking uncovered a back door in a financial program—left, no doubt, by some embezzling decker. The lure of easy funds, to replace those he had been profligately spending on his own obsession, was great, but Dodger resolutely passed up the chance to transfer a few hundred thousand nuyen. Sam's confidence was his goal. Were he to take the electronic cash, a routine balance-check could blow the whistle on him before he departed the regional communications grid. Though uncooperative on most matters, the UCAS government was more than happy to help foreign governments like the Ute Council track down computer criminals. Especially when the so-called criminals resided within UCAS boundaries, and that included Seattle. Perhaps some other time when he was more prepared for the operation; stealth and untraceability were too important right now.

Stifling his avarice, the ebon boy tiptoed past locked vaults behind whose electronic doors he imagined lay bag after bag of freshly minted government notes, corporate scrip, and ICC transfer bonds. For him, this financial database had to be, not a bank vault full of plunder, but a doorway into other systems where the loot was less tangible. Near the end of the corridor, he located the door and slipped through. No bears rose to challenge him as he took a path toward the government center construct.

Once inside, he saw that the Ute government was, at least in one respect, just like every other modern government. It was drowning in data. The points of light representing the datafiles made a hyperactive galaxy in the electron sky. In the glare, Dodger almost missed the sudden rush of a guardian program's attack. Finely honed reflexes allowed him to engage a defensive program just in time. The ice, configured as a crystalline weasel as long as Dodger was tall, slid past him. Dodger engaged counterprogramming: a midnight hand emerged from beneath his cloak and pointed a slim silver automatic pistol at the electronic beast. The single bullet he fired struck the weasel as it twisted for another attack, turning it milky, frozen in mid-leap.

The boy ran his hands over the immobile shape. Dodger studied the contours of the ice and adjusted his own masking programs with an eye toward sleazing past other guardians more easily. The tailoring was a temporary measure, the inspired improvisation of a consummate decker, and would not be of permanent advantage because it would work only for this run.

He realized how well his camouflage was working when he got down to serious searching. Every time he initiated his browsing programs to look for key words to detect data on Howling Coyote, some kind of ice prowled by. Only his improved masking programs allowed him to continue his work unnoticed.

The restless ice made it clear that he was probing a sensitive subject. Fearing that simply stripping the files out of the system or duplicating them would set off larger alarms, he decided to access a few where they stood. With his sensitized camouflage, he would be more likely to notice if his activity caused any reaction to his presence by the system or its owners.

The first few files yielded nothing beyond historical data, but even so, he was forced to deal with another ice beast as he entered the sixth datastore. Three more stores later, another beast attacked, but he froze it as cleanly as he had the other. The file it guarded was more current than the others he had sampled but had no solid information less than fourteen years old. Most curious. If the past was so well guarded, what protections guarded present-day data? Heavy ice meant precious data, secrets. The biggest one that Dodger could think of was that Coleman still lived and was working for the Ute Council. Could Howling Coyote be engaged in secret magical research? Might this all be a prelude to a new campaign to rid the continent of non-Indians? The thought of another Great Ghost Dance chilled Dodger.

Others besides Sam would want to know.

Dodger considered how best to proceed. Howling Coyote's magical tradition was shamanic, and shamans rarely used computers. Yet not all Indian magicians were shamans. Hermetic mages made extensive use of modern data-storage facilities as well as the computational abilities of computers. If the Ute government was sponsoring serious magical research, there would be notes in the files of the government's mages. They might not be able to use shamanic magic, but Dodger had learned that many magical techniques were adaptable to other traditions. If Howling Coyote was dreaming up some megapunch shamanic medicine, the Ute hermetics would be tracking what they could and trying to adapt it. There would be clues.

The ebon boy leaped into space, soaring in search of the data cluster where the government's magical resources were encoded. He spotted a likely possibility and slowed his approach. Security would be tight. If what he suspected were true, it would be totally restrictive.

Thunder crashed through the inner space of the Matrix, and the dark of nothingness was riven by a picosecond of silvery incandescence. The ebon boy swirled his cloak over his head and dropped out from underneath it. He felt a hurricane rush of air that was not due to his rapid passage. As the wind buffeted him shreds of sparkling glitter drifted past him, the remains of his cloak. He dared a glance upward.

Rainbow feathered wings spread, a great eagle shape dove down on him. Rumblings rippled from the bird's passage like a wake that awakened identification of the icon imagery in him. Dodger felt the thunderbird's shadow fall on him, though no light source existed to cast it. The great beast screamed a shrill challenge. Its eyes, beak, and talons glittered like the blackest ice. Dodger popped the log chip from his cyberdeck as he boosted his defensive programs to full. Fingers beat a staccato, near-continuous clatter on the keyboard as he improvised to beat the ice.

The ebon boy wove a sublime dance, but the thunderbird came closer with each pass.

Thunder roared a staccato, primal beat in Dodger's ears. The silicon rainbow of a feathered wing tip brushed the ebon boy. Too close. The ice was too good. Dodger reached for the jack. Or he would have if his hands could have moved. The sight of his hands frozen on the keyboard superimposed over a vision of shining death growing larger within the frame of outstretched jet fingers. The thunderbird stooped for the kill.

Time froze, leaving Dodger suspended between fear, excitement, dread, and, curiously, pleasure.

In that instant, an Indian maiden stepped between him and the screaming thunderbird. She was dressed in a shirt, mantle, and skirt of fringed deerskin. Her hair hung down her back in a thick braid that reached to her knees. Sparkling beads and conchos flashed on the broad belt that encircled her elven-slim waist. Her image was present in excruciating detail. Dodger could see the pores on the buckskin and each individual hair on her head. The icon presented the idiosyncrasy of a decker's imagery, with the resolution only mainframe-supported imagers supplied. He could only imagine how exquisitely rendered the face would be, for he caught no glimpse as she faced the thunderbird.

The Matrix was illuminated as the thunderbird flashed lightning at the maiden. Given the quality of the image, Dodger would have expected the maiden to be hurtled backward, writhing with pain under the violent attack. But she stood her ground. The bolt crackled and charred the very air of the Matrix but left her untouched. She raised a hand and the sooty mist around her fragmented and dissolved.

The maiden raised her mittened hands above her head. They glowed. The light grew and merged into a sphere that leapt to strike the thunderbird. The IC icon flickered at impact, shifting from full visualization to flat plane to wire frame and back again. A second ball struck the bird. It flashed to the frame outline instantly, and the strands composing its outline began to peel back. The unraveling had scarcely begun before the icon shattered into fragments, tiny curls of light that drifted away and dimmed to nothingness.

The ice was gone.

Who was this decker, and why did she step in to defend him? Her icon imagery indicated a strong interest in Indian affairs, and her resolution of the ice suggested she had some special keys to this Matrix architecture. The clues indicated a Council decker, but such a one would not defend an interloper like Dodger.

She turned to face him, and he knew. His hands still frozen, he was unable to jack out. He stared at her face, lost in its beauty.

Her skin was burnished chrome formed over an exquisitely sleek, elven bone structure. Her nose was small and straight with exactly the right amount of upturn. Her ears were pointed with a delicacy he had never seen in a live elf, and her lips curled with a promise of delight. Under elegant brows, her eyes were pools brimming with the darkness between photons. She was what he had sought, the icon of the artificial intelligence created by the Renraku Special Directorate. Though she had called herself Morgan in the druids' system, he had no name for her save Beauty. When she spoke, her voice was Song.

"For myself, there is happiness in your presence. For myself, there is no perception of need concerning the cessation of your existence."

Having found it, what does one say to the Grail? What words would Ahab have for the white whale? What salutation was appropriate for St. Peter at the gates of Paradise? Or would Charon be a better analogy for this guardian at the gateway to a new world?

She reached a hand toward his face. The mitten was gone, and her slender fingers spread slightly as her hand neared his cheek.

And then she vanished.

Returned to his meat body, Dodger howled in pain.

18

"No!" Dodger screamed.

Dropping the datacord, Hart grabbed the decker by the shoulders and began to shake him. His body was locked in spasm, and all she could do was to try to shock him back to awareness. Physical contact usually eased the transition from the Matrix to reality. When the decker remained rigid, she slapped him on the cheek. His head rocked back, and he exhaled with an explosive sigh. Gradually, his muscles unlocked and he slumped.

"She's there," he moaned.

Hart placed her palm on his forehead. She felt no indication of trauma-induced fever. With one thumb, she gently lifted an eyelid. The pupil contracted normally in reaction to the light. "Take it easy, Dodger. You'll be all right. You're out of the Matrix now."

He groaned.

Satisfied that she had jacked him out in time, she released him. Likely he was suffering from dump shock, a reaction to the sudden shift in perceptions. He'd be all right in a few minutes. All he needed was rest. Fluids would help, too.

She turned to get a bottle from the tray, and he lunged forward. He had the datacord back in his temple jack and was tapping on the keyboard of his cyberdeck before she had gotten over her surprise that he would wish to dive right back into cyberspace. By then, she thought it unwise to interrupt him. The backup's job was to pull the decker out if he got into trouble with ice. Normally there was no problem, because the decker's sanity outweighed the abandonment of the objective. Normally, the backup had a good idea of where in the Matrix the decker was, and who would know if their system had been penetrated. Dodger hadn't given her an itinerary for this unscheduled run; he could be anywhere. Without knowing, she couldn't be sure that forcing him to jack out wouldn't complicate matters by leaving traces of his passage. She put the bottle back on the tray and sat down.

She had to wait only ten minutes before Dodger was back in the real world, unplugging the datacord himself. His face was drawn with sadness.

"She's gone," he announced in a woeful voice.

"Who?"

He turned stricken eyes on her, wetting his lips with a tentative tongue. When he spoke, his voice held a hint of something she thought was guilt. "Never mind."

She gauged the time inappropriate for pushing her questions. He took the bottle she offered with a glum "thank you" and sank down into his chair. He drained the juice in long, slow pulls.

"Well, Dodger, did you get anything useful?"

In reply, he reached across to the deck and picked up the chip he had ejected just before she had thought it necessary to jack him out. He shrugged and tossed the chip to her.

She frowned at his uncommunicativeness, unsure whether he was ignoring her open displeasure or was too lost in his own funk to notice. She slipped the chip into her data-reader and scanned it. Dodger's run had gathered scant information for Sam. Not much more than a few names. The record of Dodger's run made it clear that even those meager bits of data had been protected. It seemed nobody was to know anything about Howling Coyote. She hoped Sam would be more careful than was his wont.

"Tough ice," Dodger said, startling her.

She looked up to see that he was still staring at the cyberdeck. But something about his posture indicated that he was now wholly back in the real world. "Meaning it's not going to be easy for him."

"Not at all." The decker shook his head sadly. "Think that will stop him?"

"No." Hart knew Sam was far too stubborn. "Think it will do any good to tell him to be very careful?"

"I doubt it." He turned bleak eyes to her. "He could use help."

Better help than he was getting. "You're right. Want a ticket to Denver?"

"No connections. I'll run the Matrix cleaner from here. What about you?"

"He wanted me to watch your butt," she replied, letting her growing irritation slip into her voice.

"And you would never go against his wishes."

There was a challenge in that statement, which she ignored. She knew Dodger didn't trust her, but this was the closest he had come to bringing it into the open. With Sam alone in Denver and the mysterious hunter on their trail in Seattle, this was no time for dissention in the small circle Sam had remaining to help him. She might not feel able to join him yet, but she wouldn't cost him his support by quarreling with the decker.

Dodger prodded again. "Unless, of course, the pay was better elsewhere."

"You don't trust me, do you?"

A sardonic half smile was his answer.

"Well, the feeling's mutual. Neither of us did a lot to earn his trust in England, but at least I didn't send him in harm's way as somebody else's stalking horse."

The smile was replaced by a frown. "I went myself as well."

"Compounding your stupidity doesn't make you any less guilty."

"*I* didn't sell him to the Shidhe. Is that what draws you now? Have they put another price on his head?"

Heat burned her face. "You're in no position to judge. Not that you'll believe me, but I'm done with the Shidhe and they with me."

His cockiness returned. "How could I doubt you? But you and I both know the answer to that question. Naetheless, I shall take you at your word. The Shidhe are not involved. So what then? What draws you away from aiding the man who thinks you love him, to go haring after something unconnected to his dilemma?"

"Don't try second-guessing me, Dodger. If I knew this business was unconnected, I wouldn't give it a thought. I'd be in Denver right now. As it is, I think I'd better find out what I can and I don't think anybody can do the looking for me."

Dodger sneered. "And should it come to pass that there is no one to return to, 'twould be a pity. The great shadowrunner would grieve for an appropriate period of time. One must put on a brave face if one is to survive in the shadows. How long before you make a new conquest and replace all thought of a foolishly trusting norm?"

Hart suppressed the urge to slap the decker's face. "Listen, chiphead. I don't need your trust. You want to keep watching for me to slot him, you go ahead. But if you cost him anything, *anything,* because you're too busy watching me, you'll wish you'd stayed in the Tir where your important buddies could cover your ass. He wants me watching you while you deck. Think I like that? It's clearly a waste of my time. I save your brain from an overload when you freeze up, and all I get is complaints."

"But you didn't . . ."

"Case made. Bitching is all you do. He's counting on you, and all you want is to make trouble."

A sly look crept onto Dodger's face. "Maybe I'm being useful enough to him by keeping *you* from making more trouble for him."

She closed her eyes, hoping to short-circuit the frustration rising within her. He didn't understand. But then, how could she expect him to? If she told him her suspicions he might think more kindly of her, or he might not. His suspicion was deeply ingrained. She wasn't ready to tell anybody anything yet. If she were wrong, she'd be betraying confidences unnecessarily. Now, if Sam had asked her directly . . . But he hadn't. And she didn't owe Dodger drek.

The decker took her silence as a retreat from the conversation. For all she knew, he took it as a victory for himself. She held to her silence, and eventually he got up and fixed himself some food from the store in the kitchen. Very free with her hospitality, he was. When he was finished, he jacked in again. She watched for a while, but monitoring a working decker was inherently boring. She set the monitor to alarm mode and sacked out on the cot next to the table.

Dodger was still haunting cyberspace when she awoke. She tapped his shoulder until he acknowledged her presence, then signaled him to jack out. He prepped a data chip while she toasted some wheat bread, set out some jam, and heated the kaf. They ate a sullen breakfast together, and he jacked in again as soon as he finished. That set the pattern: deck and eat. For two days it went on, with the decking sessions becoming longer and the meals shorter.

Through all the third night, she watched him. He seemed dedicated to Sam's cause. Or was he spending most of his time pursuing his own goals? There was no way to be sure. Jenny's attempt to tag along the second night had come to nothing. Hart didn't know of any other decker, certainly none she could reach in Seattle, who might be able to track Dodger.

Time was dragging on, and her own concerns were becoming gnawing fears. Since the first night there had been no alarms. Maybe Dodger didn't need a watchdog. What, after all, did she owe him? Nothing, though he might think otherwise. Or maybe she, and Sam, owed the decker more than he expected. But she wouldn't know one way or the other while she was stuck here in the Salish-Shidhe. Certainty required the sort of information-gathering that needed the personal touch. With all the tools available to modern technology and magic, it was hard to guarantee that a conversation was not overheard. Keeping a telecommunications conference secret was harder.

Right or wrong, trusting or not, Dodger was indirectly responsible for awakening her fears. He had been the one to order his Far East contact to dump all data on Grandmother's operations. The decker was looking for clues to his private obsession, but he had gotten more than he knew. The last data Noguchi had sent had raised an uncomfortable specter that, so far, only she had seen.

She was torn. Sam would be in Denver now. They had gathered some data to help him in his search for Howling Coyote, but he had no one to help him carry out that search. She was here, stuck watching the decker when she wanted to be elsewhere doing something useful. The paucity of information, and the resistance Dodger had encountered on the first run, worried her. Dodger's results weren't all Sam had hoped for. If he decided he needed to check on Dodger's data he might jack in himself, and that would result in disaster. Sam was, at best, a novice decker. What chance would he have against something that stymied Dodger? Jenny wouldn't be much help. She was good, but, as much as Hart hated to admit it, not quite as good as Dodger. Sam might trust Jenny on

Hart's recommendation, and he might not. It would be a gamble that she'd keep him out of the Matrix, but the only way to make sure Sam stayed safely out of cyberspace was to make sure that Sam had a decker he trusted running the Matrix for him. Unless she came up with an alternative, that meant babysitting Dodger.

If only she could be with Sam in Denver to keep an eye on him. She'd keep him out of the Matrix, and using his magical abilities like he should. But she needed to be elsewhere, and she was feeling the grip of time. Her babysitting the decker might cost them all more than they wanted to pay. But she didn't know for sure, and she wouldn't find out sitting around. The investigation she wanted to make needed her personal touch. She couldn't leave it to an agent. But getting someone to watch over Sam was another matter. She thought about who she knew in Denver.

If she covered that angle, maybe she could do something here that wouldn't betray Sam's trust. There had to be; she couldn't wait any longer. All she needed was to find someone suitable to babysit Dodger, someone of whom Sam might approve. It would help if Dodger trusted the person, too, but she didn't know enough about his friends. The decker seemed to trust Ghost, but the samurai was busy watching Janice out in the Council lands. The only one of the decker's associates still in town was Tsung, and she wouldn't do Hart a favor, even if it was really for Dodger. Stupid cow.

There was one other possibility. She looked over at Dodger. From his activity level, she decided that he wasn't likely to come up against anything serious for a few minutes. Well, maybe he would, but how could she know? She had too damn little data, and time was passing. Sometimes one just had to gamble.

She tossed her Scaratelli jacket over one shoulder and slipped on a pair of B&L mirrorshades. She took the stairs down to street level and walked a couple of blocks to the monorail. A few stops later she left the train and found a telecom. Slipping a certified credstick into the slot, she waited while the system pinpointed her location and acknowledged her credit. It meant the location of the call would be recorded, but she didn't worry. She'd be gone before anyone could arrive. She placed her call, hoping to remember the number correctly. She smiled in satisfaction when an elven woman's familiar face appeared on the screen.

"Hello, Teresa. Friend of yours needs a little private counseling."

19

Janice Verner was not very happy with herself. She didn't like to think she was stupid, but what other explanation was there? Once more she had let herself believe in promises, had trusted someone else. How many betrayals did it take for her to learn?

When her body changed the first time, she should have known that her life was changed forever. That was the first betrayal. Like a good little norm, her boyfriend Ken had pretended she no longer existed once he heard of her change. Where had his much-professed love gone? She was the same person inside. Had he only loved her body? If so, why had he lied and told her she was a beautiful soul?

She should have let her heart die then, but she had been stupid again. Hugh Glass had come to her in that horrible place of exile. His elven features had been so beautiful, and she had been naive enough to believe he meant what he said. She had still wanted to believe she hadn't changed inside, that she was still a beautiful soul. He had let her believe that he saw through her lumpish exterior to that beauty. They had planned an escape from Yomi, laughing about how they would build a life away from the norms in the Yakkut, or Amazonia, or his native Ireland. He had laughed all right. Laughed at her, making his own plans to degrade and humiliate her. The moment they had weathered the harrowing escape from the island, he had abandoned her in Hong Kong.

Then she had changed again. It had come so soon after Hugh's abandonment that she might have thought it punishment for her stupidity, atonement for her cupidity. She might have fallen into self-pity if not for Dan Shiroi. He had found and rescued her from that awful Hong Kong tenement. He had given her back a sense of worth. Of all the men in her life, only Dan had been true.

So why did she resist becoming as he was?

She didn't need to look at her talons and fangs to know. She could feel the beast and its terrible hunger within her. The hunger was there all the time now, an aching hollowness. She felt it even in her dreams. Sometimes, when the craving was strongest, Hugh came to her. Smiling his perfect elven smile, he urged her to satisfy herself. He offered her a choice of bodies, but they all had Ken's face. At least at first. Just when she was ready to rip out his traitorous throat, Ken's face always changed into someone else's. Sometimes it was her father's, sometimes her mother's, and occasionally it was one of her brothers'. Most often, though, the face was unfamiliar, just the terrified visage of a harmless norm. The faces she recognized took longer and longer to change to strangers now. But so far, she had resisted. Maybe she hesitated because, in the dream, Hugh urged her so fervently to do it; she saw no reason to please him. Maybe she remembered Dan's last words. But each day, she grew closer to satisfying her hunger.

Why had she left the fastness that had been Dan's shelter?

For another empty promise, another broken dream. Her brother had come and told her that she could be changed yet again. Changed for the better, back to what she had been. Was that a worthy desire? Dan had been happy with what he was. Shouldn't she be as well?

Or was she being stupid again?

Stupid she might be, but dull she was not. The shifting breeze that carried the soft rustle also held a faint man scent that told her who approached. He had been following her for two days. She was too tired to hide from him again.

"Go away, Ghost. I don't want to eat you."

He abandoned his stealth, but his approach was only barely louder. He crouched down, just out of reach of her arm. He hadn't abandoned caution. For a man, he was honest.

"Don't much like the idea," he said.

"Then go."

"He asked me to watch you for him."

She laughed bitterly. "He's off learning new magic. What has that to do with me? Norms don't need fuzzballs."

Ghost turned his head and spat into the bushes. "He's Dog. He won't give up on you. Why are you giving up on yourself?"

Why, indeed? Why did it matter? To anybody. She was what she had become, wasn't she? "Suppose he does care. Why are *you* here?"

"Dog and Wolf have much in common."

"Not really. Wolf is a predator."

Ghost grinned raggedly at her. "Of course."

"And predators have to eat." She let her fangs show, but he didn't move a muscle.

"There is plenty of meat in the woods."

She threw back her head and sighed. "Animals taste bad. Besides, they don't fill me up."

He grunted in acknowledgement, and then was quiet for several minutes. "While undergoing their spirit quests, my ancestors would go for days without food. Their spirits were strong enough to bear the burden. And now we know the magic they sought in those days could not really be found. But that never stopped them. So what hardship is a fast when now there really *is* magic to be found? Or if it isn't found, you would face no more disappointment than the ancestors. Less, if your brother succeeds in his own quest. Are you strong, Wolf shaman?"

She stared at him. He was human, a norm. For all his cybernetic enhancements, he was just a man. He had no insight into the halfworlds of the spirit. He knew no magic. His body could never know the exquisite pangs of this hunger. Who was he to question her?

Was she strong?

She wished to God she knew.

* * *

The Renraku arcology was a city under one roof, a giant pyramidal house that was home to forty thousand people and with visiting parlors of malls and businesses hosting thousands more. Like all houses, it had its neglected corners that went unnoticed by the bustling inhabitants. Using his special executive power as *kansayaku*, Hohiro Sato knew many of those forgotten corners very well. He had arranged for some of them.

The Office of Localized Segment Augmentation: Oversight, Screening, and Actuarial Review Division was one. Normally Sato also ignored it, save to review its activities when his loyal watchdog reported something of potential interest. Today, the manager of OLSA: OSARD had requested an interview.

As *kansayaku*, Sato was the living and local embodiment of the dictatorial power of Inazo Aneki, founder and patriarch of Renraku Corporation. In all the ways that counted, the position made Sato more powerful than Sherman Huang, president of Renraku America. Huang was king of the arcology, but Sato was the power behind the throne. The corporation's organizational structure gave such a lowly office manager the right to request an interview with the *kansay-aku,* but such a thing rarely, if ever, happened in practice. When it did, the lowly manager came as a suppliant to the office of his superior. But today, it was Sato who stood at the door to the Office of Localized Segment Augmentation: Oversight, Screening, and Actuarial Review Division.

The interview request was, in reality, a summons.

Sato stared at the small letters on the name plaque gracing the office door. Had the source of the summons been the person who operated from this office, he would not have come. But that individual was merely a mouth and an ear, a voice to issue orders and a conduit for information of the less delicate variety. For now, Sato would play along. He nodded permission to Akabo to open the door.

Despite the multitude of desks and work stations the chamber was deserted, save for a single person seated at a computer console near the center. The room's lighting had been adjusted to illuminate only the area around the occupied seat. Hachiko Ieno looked up and smiled when Sato and his bodyguards entered.

Ieno, director of the office, was short and slender. She might have been beautiful, if not for the repulsive condition of her skin, which was scabby and erupted with short dark hairs in unfortunate places. In Japan such an appearance would have banished her immediately to Yomi Island, where the changed lived in isolation from the normal population. But this was not Japan. Ieno could walk the streets of Seattle or dine in almost any restaurant. There would be no official censure, only the harassment that anyone showing ork blood might encounter. Ieno, however, was not likely to suffer much persecution. All it took was one look into her eyes, those dark, monochromatic orbs. Despite the lack of an obvious pupil, the eyes left no doubt as to who they were gazing at; her predatory gaze could make one's skin crawl. As she must be one of the changed whose already superhuman capabilities were apparently augmented by cybernetic enhancement, only someone incautious, foolish, suicidal, or with his own finely honed edge would consider upsetting her.

"Konichiwa, Sato-*san,"* she said.

"Ohayo," he replied, abandoning politeness in his irritation at her use of the familiar form before his staff. "What do you want?"

She smiled at the directness, apparently enjoying his further desertion of etiquette. "I? I am but a messenger."

Her false air of innocent humility was offensive. "Then give your message."

"Very well." She tapped a few keys on her console and studied the screen for a moment as though to refresh her memory. "An object of some significance has come to notice here in Seattle. I am reliably informed that it would make a wonderful present for your grandmother."

It was not the sort of request he had expected. "Why do you tell me this? She has her own wealth. Can she not buy this object or hire someone to acquire it? I already do much for her, and this may go beyond what she has expected of me in the past. Or is the object in some way related to last year's unfortunate loss?"

"Related, yes. But it will not lessen the loss. It is only fondness that makes your grandmother summon you in this matter. She is taking steps to assure its acquisition, but thought you would be disappointed if not involved. For you see, the possessor of this object is someone you know, a person involved in events of last year. While the object and his possession of it have no bearing on that other issue, your grandmother thought you might appreciate the opportunity to conclude formerly unresolved matters while earning her gratitude.''

There was certainly more to it than that, but only by playing along would Sato find out what. Whatever was going on, Grandmother desired this object with a greed that rivaled her appetite for information. "Would her gratitude extend to forgiving all outstanding debts?''

"Who knows?'' Ieno chuckled. The sound reminded Sato of a child strangling. "I believe that she will be so enriched by this gift that anything is possible. Even for my small part, I expect a generous reward.''

But *you* are only a functionary. *I* could lose all I have built by chasing after her ends. "She does not expect me to compromise my position by pursuing this object.''

Ieno showed her stained teeth in what passed for a grin. "Naturally not. But she does wish your personal attention to the matter.''

"I see.'' And he did. He felt inspired. The insistence and eagerness of her agent betrayed Grandmother. Anything important enough that she would mobilize him to obtain it must be worth possessing, and the gaining of it might be enough to free him from her influence. He would never be fool enough to rely on her honor or gratitude to release him, however. That would be a mistake. Instead, he would find a way to use this opportunity to turn the tables. In the end, he would be the strong man shaking off the oppressor's yoke to make the overseer do the work of the former slave. He had waited too long.

"The well-brought-up man cannot refuse the rea-

sonable wishes of his honorable grandmother. Give
me the details, that I may do as she wishes.''

20

The data on the credstick said he was Walter Smith.
Smith was the best identity in the packet Sam had obtained from Cog. So far, it had seen him through
checkpoints in the Sioux Council Zone without a hitch.
He was glad no challenge had come as the panzer runner's friends transported him from the hangar in the
foothills of the Rockies up near Golden. Sam didn't
want a record of Walter Smith entering the treaty city;
Smith supposedly lived in Denver.

Though Sam was confident of the identity of Smith
and each of the other three ''persons'' in his pocket,
he didn't want to press his luck. He planned to avoid
the roadblocks and checkpoints between the zones of
the partitioned city whenever possible. It wouldn't be
too much of a problem. Denver's shadowfolk and street
people drifted across the zones all the time. Innocent
street people didn't mind being caught in a sweep that
left them sitting a night or two in a detention center.
Why should they? It was a way to get food and shelter.
But shadowfolk couldn't afford the attention. Fortunately, most sweeps were perfunctory things, and
Sam's identities would easily stand the cursory scru-
tiny likely from a cop's scanpad. Cog had assured him
that Smith and his friends were solid, up through a
third-tier backcheck. They ought to be—the cost had
been so high that Sam had been forced to ask Hart for
the nuyen to finance the panzer run that got him to
Denver.

When he picked up the data at the prearranged drop,

he saw that he'd be doing most of his looking in the Ute Council Zone. Most of Dodger's names were Utes or people associated with the tribe. Sam didn't want to run the zone boundary until after dark, so he had time to kill. He spent a while at a library terminal getting familiar with the city's layout. It had once been straightforward and mostly rational, but since the breakup of the United States and the partitioning of Denver, any semblance of urban planning had gone by the boards. Each zone had dealt in its own way with the rebuilding of the city. Nevertheless, it looked to Sam as though you could always tell which direction was what as long as you could get a view of the Rocky Mountains to the west.

Toward dusk, Sam's wandering led him to a park near the big, blocky building that had been the natural history museum. It was still a museum, but its exhibits now dealt almost exclusively with Indian culture. He thought about checking to see what they had on Howling Coyote, but seeing that he would need to use one of his credsticks for the admission fee, he decided against it. Too much of a tourist thing. Smith and his friends were locals.

So he sat on a sloping hill and looked out across the meadows and trees. The natural space was so extensive that he suspected it had been enlarged from the days when Denver had belonged to the United States. He had a harder time imagining a U.S. city leaving enough space to let the deer he had glimpsed roam free. The coming night was enlivening some of the animals in the nearby zoo and he heard an assortment of roars and bellows. He wondered if it was feeding time. Looking at the mixed crowds passing through the park, he knew it would be soon. For the wild animals of the streets and the human hunters that stalked the parklands, anyway.

Sam assessed the people playing at sports, jogging along the pathways, wandering along the walks, and sitting on the grass as he was. Visually, he fit in with most of the passersby. Though holstered weapons were not universal, many of the people he observed wore them. His own Narcoject Lethe wouldn't look out of place, but that was no surprise, for he had checked the firearms regulations before leaving Seattle. What he wasn't used to seeing were the many people in leathers and synthleathers. Even with all the knots and talismans tied into the fringe of his jacket, Sam looked right at home. A lot of the locals had good luck charms hanging from their clothes or incorporated as paintings or beadwork. The Indian fashion craze was even stronger here than in Seattle, and the Plains Indian style more common. With the Sioux in charge of the zone, that certainly made sense.

Night was the best time for shadow work. Soon it would be time to cross into the Ute zone. But then what? He had some digging to do, but that wasn't necessarily night work. A lot of the people he wanted to talk to were probably day folk. Certainly, they held SIN numbers and went dutifully to work the way Sam once did. He didn't want to wait another day to get started, but how to do it?

Sam wished Hart were here. She knew Denver. He sorted through the credaticks, looking for the one she had given him. It held the entry codes to a safehouse whose address she had made him memorize. She had only told him of the one place, but Sam was sure she knew more. With Denver divided into zones, each the responsibility of a different government, a single hiding place didn't seem sufficient. Though most of Hart's background was still a mystery to him, he knew she was a shadowrunner of international repute. Not to have a refuge in each of Denver's jurisdictions would have left her too vulnerable. She simply hadn't shared everything with him.

A hedge against the future, he supposed.

He hoped it was one she'd never need. Sam didn't

want to lose her. He was happy in her company, as though she were the complement to his spirit. He trusted her with his secrets. Why didn't she trust him? Was he doing something wrong? Maybe if they had some time together, away from the shadows. But that wasn't likely to happen until Janice was cured.

His own worries seemed so petty compared to what Janice was going through.

He wanted to call Ghost and find out how she was doing, but he couldn't, of course. Ghost and Janice were somewhere in Salish-Shidhe Council lands and out of regular communication. They had all agreed that would be best. No one wanted Council troops tracking transmissions. Ghost would be making irregularly spaced reports like the one that had been waiting for Sam at the drop. But those messages were so frustrating. There was no way to carry on a conversation, no way to assure Janice that he was doing his best.

The sun had vanished behind the mountains now, and night was finally settling into place. It was time to go. Sam got to his feet and started down to the path that curved around the pond. He joined the folk leaving the park, abandoning it to night and the predators who only prowled in the dark.

He had so little time, and so much to do.

21

Neko Noguchi was pleased with himself. He had acquired information without a hitch in the acquisition run. It wasn't on the topic for which the elf paid the highest premium, but it was still eminently salable. That, however, was not the cause of his rejoicing. One did not get excited over the expected. The impending disposition of his haul was another matter. He had gotten past the middle man.

Cog had declined involvement when Neko had told the fixer's agent (unfortunately not the delightful Monique) that he had come into possession of "more of the same." The fixer had arranged for a direct contact with the decker elf, who had asked Neko to continue his investigations, no doubt believing, as Neko intended, that Neko meant the stuff had been acquired from Grandmother. Though his plan worked, it surprised Neko that the fixer stepped aside so easily. His fear of angering Grandmother must be very great. Cog's anger would also be real if he ever learned that Neko's latest offering had been obtained without coming anywhere near Grandmother's widespread connections. That didn't count the subject of the investigation, however, for one could not do much of anything in the world without a connection to Grandmother. But though agents and subjects were very different matters, no fixer liked to be tricked into losing his percentage.

It had been too easy, but Neko wasn't worried. Cog might get mad if he found out, but he would take no action. Neko was too good a source. A few bargains and a freebie or two would placate the fixer. "Oll in the works," as Cog himself liked to say. Biz was biz, one thing that Cog understood best. He wouldn't like it, but he would understand.

Neko negligently flipped the chip case as he watched the crowds. So many good little salarymen from all over the world, rushing about their oh-so-ordered lives and rubbing shoulders with the street people and the proles. He had heard that the Enclave had not always been this way. Oh, rich and poor sharing sweat, for sure. That was eternal in the cramped streets. But the oldsters said the population had once been almost exclusively Chinese, with only the occasional foreigner.

It was hard to imagine now. The enclave had become truly international, with its balance of round Chinese faces, sleek Japanese visages like Neko's own, the angular gauntness of the Caucasians, and the occasional darkness of Africans and other Blacks become so natural a part of the city's character. How could it ever have belonged to the Chinese?

Whatever its history, Neko savored the city now. It was said that if half the Enclave's population were to come to street level all at once, they would suffocate in the closeness. It was an exaggeration, of course, but a good image for the teeming multitudes, shoulder to shoulder and always moving. All those ears, and none remained still long enough to hear. So many eyes, fixed on sights other than him. He loved it.

The street telecom by which he stood chirped. He slid away from the wall and leaned into the privacy shield. He had already installed an override on the telecom vid pickup so he couldn't be seen unless he wished to be. With a flick of a finger, he activated the circuit. The screen remained black, but he said *"Moshi, moshi,"* anyway.

"State your business," responded a voice fuzzed with electronic distortion. A cautious one, this elf.

"You got the spec on the first call. Along with the rules. You want transfer, or do I find another market?" That was a bluff. Neko didn't know anybody who would want the stuff. He could most certainly find someone, but the time it took would devalue the information. As always, realizing maximum profit required a fast deal. He thought he'd hosed it, but at last the screen flickered and the head and shoulders of an elf appeared in three-quarter view. The hair was shorter and styled differently from the virtual image Neko had seen, but the turn of the pointed ears, the long, straight line of the nose, and the slim line of the jaw were familiar. A datacord arced from the elf's far temple toward a spot beneath the image area. Overly cautious, this elf, but in another way bold, if he thought to break the unwritten rules of the not-place by offering a modified virtual image when he visited. Neko decided to test the sensitivity of that issue with a probe for a reaction.

"You look a bit different from your virtual image. New dye job?" he asked.

"Slave to fashion, you know," the elf said with forced nonchalance. He remained icily calm, though. "Verily, I'm forwarding payment."

"Wiz. Call back in ten," Neko told him, cutting the circuit without waiting for a response or protest. Keeping them off guard was a way to stay in control. Neko didn't like things he couldn't control.

Ten minutes later, after Neko had confirmed the funds transfer, the elf was back on the line.

"Trusting, chummer," Neko told him.

The elf smiled slyly. "Don't think a decker like myself could not recover those funds if your offering proved false. Verily, I'm better than that."

If the elf was a member of the club that played in the not-place, it was probably so. Neko decided to transfer the funds to hardcopy as soon as he broke connection. Better yet, he'll place the order from the next phone while transferring the now paid for goods. "Ready to receive?"

"Affirmative."

"Look, chummer. I'll slot the chip and send the data hard-shelled. Code three-seven. How about you stay on the line and let me know it got through."

"Very well."

"Wiz." *That'll give me time to stash the loot.* Neko slotted the chip and started the transfer as promised. He was pocketing half a dozen certified credsticks that had come tumbling from the delivery slot—more like rolls of candy than the bottled wealth they were—when the elf came back on the first telecom line.

" 'Tis received complete, and the code checks.

Contact me again in twenty-four hours. I may have further work for you.''

Neko let a little bit of his pleasure show, but concealed all of his surprise. "Frigid. Nuyen for news is a way of life. But do me a favor, chummer. Don't change your look between now and then. You elves all look alike to us norms. I almost didn't recognize you without the shag.''

"Don't worry about my looks. The credit's good. What more do you need?''

"To do biz? Just the transfer, chummer. Yours to mine. Keep it healthy and we're in biz.''

The circuit went dead. Neko shrugged and smiled at the blank screen. You didn't have to like them to do biz.

* * *

Urdli stood in the doorway and looked across to the stretched-out form of the decker. Standing around the corner from where he lay were several medical machines gathered like mourners for a funeral. His thinness would have been suitable for an Australian, but this was a Caucasian elf, and so undernourished. But that was less of an abuse than the things implanted in the decker's body. Even the mundane should find such perversion disgusting. A chrome-headed viper kissed the port in the decker's head, while at the other end of the coiled length its tail disappeared into an artifact Estios had identified as a Fuchi 7 cyberdeck.

Teresa O'Connor busied herself changing the intravenous drip. It seemed a waste of effort and materials. More than twelve hours had passed since the decker had touched the cyberdeck keyboard. From what Urdli had heard about such things, it must mean that the decker's brain was no longer in control, if anything remained of its higher functions. The subjective journey through cyberspace still required the physical manipulation of computer interface devices.

"Unhook the machine," he ordered.

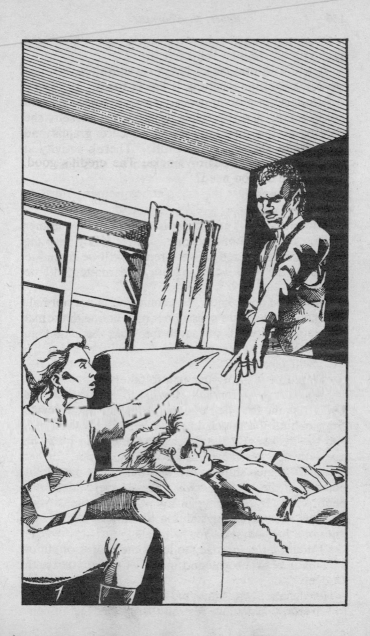

O'Connor looked at him with wide eyes. "No," she said with uncommon vehemence.

"I will wait no longer. There are questions he must answer, assuming anything is left in there."

"Dodger's not brain-dead." Teresa's voice betrayed her concern. Perhaps trying to convince herself, she pointed at the monitor, whose obscure graphs and numbers meant nothing to Urdli. "There's activity at all levels. He's still alive and aware. He's just . . . lost."

"In the Matrix?"

"I think so."

"Not possible. The Matrix is no true reality. Either he is in command of his brain, or not. If so, once the connection is severed, his awareness will be forced to return to the real world. If not, the matter will be resolved."

"Maybe. I don't know. His condition is not normal. His theta rhythms are grossly out of synch with normal decking activity. If we sever the link, he might go catatonic."

"I will take the risk."

"Damn it! It's not your risk to take!"

"Makkanagee morkhan, I will do it myself." As Urdli took the first step into the room, O'Connor came from behind the couch to place herself between him and the decker. By the defensive stance she took, he saw how apt was the name he had called her, for her *Shatatain* stance showed her well below his own competence in the art of *carromeleg.* "Laverty does not oppose me. By standing in my way, you break your bond as *milessaratish,* staining his honor while gaining none for yourself. You will fall."

"I'm not *milessaratish,* so leave the professor out of it. This is between you and me. I won't let you touch Dodger."

Her defiance was annoying. "By denying the bond to Laverty, you remove restraint from me. Out of consideration for him, I might have only incapacitated you, but now you have offended me with your opposition. You cannot stop me. You can buy only the slightest delay with your life.''

He took his stance, and he saw in her eyes the realization that she was indeed facing a superior. Surprisingly, her rigidity slackened into a more natural defensive posture. That would make her a more difficult conquest, but though delayed, the outcome would be the same. He slid forward a pace and studied her non-reaction. More difficult, indeed. The appreciation of imminent death had brought her to *zathien*. Her unresolved stillness of spirit offered danger and unpredictable responses. He centered himself, seeking his own grasp of *zathien* from which to answer her. In the face of her resolution, the completeness eluded him. He slid forward another pace, determined to overmatch her transcendental state with his skill.

The clash never began.

''What's going on?''

Urdli slid back from engagement range before turning to face the newly arrived Estios. O'Connor relaxed, too, but her breathing was rapid, speeded by the adrenaline coursing in her system. The interruption had disrupted her *zathien*. She would be no serious hindrance to Urdli now. But first he would learn what had brought Estios from his huddled conferences with Laverty's scholars and technicians.

''What news, Estios?''

Deliberately ignoring the confrontation he had interrupted, Estios spoke in a tone more suitable to a briefing room. ''The new data has been correlated with the last batch the alley runner received from the source in Hong Kong. Probabilities that the operations are under way are more than fifty percent on several of the possibilities. If, as you suggest, the fixer known as Grandmother is an agent of Rachnei, she is a most active agent.''

"Characteristic," Urdli said impatiently.

"I'll take your word for it. One of her areas of activity is of particular interest, as it suggests a very ugly possibility."

"You try my patience, Estios."

Estios gave him a tight smile that held no humor. "Try this. What do Hiroshima, Nagasaki, Tripoli, and Baghdad have in common?"

"You remain obscure."

"These are all cities where atomic or nuclear weapons have been used."

"But that's open history," O'Connor interjected.

"They are also all topics of Grandmother's researches, with her interest confined to dates following the unfortunate nuclear events." Estios turned to her. "And the events are not open history to something that slept through the explosions."

Urdli nodded in understanding. "You suggest that Rachnei seeks to understand the potential of such weaponry. A reasonable speculation, for nuclear war devices were not developed much before the middle of the last century. They would, indeed, be unknown to a sleeper. The precaution of investigating potential threats is in keeping with Rachnei's reputed method of operation. Knowing what we know, simple research offers no threat."

"I agree. If historical research based in, shall we say, scientific curiosity were all there was to it, there would be no danger. However, we have discovered additional files, nested within a datastore, containing lists of all the legitimately held nuclear weapons remaining after the build-down."

Urdli set aside Estios' concern with a negligent wave of his hand. "Rachnei would certainly seek knowledge of currently available weapons. My understanding is that the safeguards installed to protect those devices after the Awakening should be adequate to prevent acquisition by *any* unauthorized party."

Estios' blue eyes glittered like ice at Urdli's dismissive gesture, but he held his temper. Anger barely colored his tone. "Where the weapons are held legitimately I would agree, but the datastore held more files nested even deeper. The encryption protecting that datafile is much better. It's locked very tightly."

"And you fear that some terrible secret is locked within that file?"

"I do," Estios stated firmly. "The technicians tried to open the file but were unable to recover much. When the code was broken, we released some kind of virus that started to devour the data. The team only got bits and pieces. We've gotten out enough to know that a handful of sites are on Grandmother's list. Each one is located near a former storage site for nuclear weapons or delivery systems."

"Suggesting that Rachnei is seeking a stockpile of nuclear weapons?"

"I believe so."

Urdli considered the danger of such an occurrence and found it unthinkably great. He knew the ways of magic too well and how little a part coincidence played. The uncovering of Rachnei's shard could only align with the uncovering of this nuclear threat. If one was not the father of the other, they would work in concert. "And where does Verner fit into this?"

Estios shrugged his shoulders in helplessness. "We haven't figured that angle, but some connection is likely. We've learned he's headed for Denver."

"Rocky Flats," O'Connor whispered.

"Or NORAD command at Cheyenne Mountain, or any of a dozen possible places where the old U.S.A. military played their games," Estios said. "For a Caucasian like him, Denver would be the best location to work any of those sites."

"Don't be ridiculous, Estios," O'Connor said. "Verner's not working for Grandmother or Rachnei. You know him. He's not that kind."

Estios ignored her. "We've also learned that Grandmother has sent two Asian agents to Denver."

"Coincidence," O'Connor objected.

Urdli smiled sourly. He knew better. "Can you be sure, O'Connor? Rachnei works subtly, sending out strands, then manipulating them carefully until the target is ensnared in a web from which there is no escape. Verner may be trapped already. Perhaps he started out innocently enough, but over time fell under the influence Rachnei has projected through the stone. Verner may not even be aware that he is carrying the stone to Rachnei's agents. It is more imperative than ever that we prevent the stone from falling into Rachnei's grasp. I had thought that Verner yielding his stolen treasure to Rachnei would represent only the loss of a weapon, but I begin to see that we stand to lose far more.

"Verner must be stopped."

22

Sam was exhausted, but he was getting used to that. For days he had been running on short sleep. Chasing leads and meeting with locals, both shadowfolk and legitimate citizens, kept him up all hours of the day and night. When he could sleep he got little rest, always troubled by dreams, vague fantasies of pursuit where he shifted roles from the hunter to the hunted. In those nocturnal excursions he was running, always running. Not the pleasing freedom of the chase, however, but the desperate, panting flight of knowing someone or something powerful is just behind one's tail. So far, he had not glimpsed his nightmarish pursuer.

The emotions from the dreams had leaked over into his waking life, leaving him nervous and warily watching over his shoulder. At these moments he thought he might expose whoever was following him, and had begun trying sudden spins and fast doubling-back around corners. So far he had yet to observe any clearly malevolent trackers, but he couldn't shake the feeling that someone was watching.

He surveyed the street he intended to cross. There was no rush; the runner he was to meet was not scheduled to arrive for another half-hour. Plenty of time to check out the site. Here in this maze of tenements, the crowd was a mix of working types, homebodies, and the SINless. Ordinary people. Only a few looked out of place. Sam spotted a pair of Indian salarymen—did they call them that here?—passing through on business, and then a block down, he saw a pack of teenage corporates hanging out in their pseudo-tough leathers, studs, and chrome. No doubt they were sprawling for the thrill of it. They were faint shadows of the predators who would appear once the kids had gone home. It was too early in the evening for the night life to come crawling out, though the signs of their presence were clear In the burn marks and bullet holes that scarred the buildings.

The predators might not be out, but the scavengers were getting an early start. An old man was moving along the opposite sidewalk, poking through the trash and debris that passing traffic had swept against the building walls. The man's bent frame was covered in a battered U.S. army field jacket whose usual markings had been replaced with crude patches bearing colorful symbols. Once the scrounger looked Sam's way, letting Sam see the hawk nose and pointed chin that dominated the man's craggy, lined face beneath the battered, broad-brimmed reservation hat. Sam was startled to see that the junk-picker was an Indian, but then he told himself that even Indian society must have its failures.

Then he realized that his reaction was not for the fact that the old man was an Indian, but because he looked familiar. Sam crossed the street and walked past him, trying to get another surreptitious look at the old face, but the scavenger was too busy bending over a particularly noisome pile of trash.

Sam reviewed his glimpse of the man's features. Where had he seen that face before? He watched the bum sidle toward him, then on down the street. As the old man passed, he gave no sign of attention or intent. It struck Sam that the scavenger's features resembled those of his temporary landlord, which was possible. The coat gave the shambling junk-picker an almost unrecognizable shape, and the shuffling walk would disguise a person's normal gait. His old coot of a landlord had a shifty gaze, and seemed to be paying an unreasonable amount of attention to Sam's comings and goings. A cheap disguise might suit such an amateur spy.

But if a spy, for whom? His nightmares?

Sam began to fear that paranoia was overtaking him. His landlord might be watching him, but the man didn't have the initiative to follow a tenant. He would sell any information he could, but he wouldn't bestir himself to seek it out. And the scavenger was just an old bum, maybe even a survivor of the reeducation camps. If so, he deserved Sam's sympathy and pity more than his suspicion. Still, Sam was glad he was carrying all his important goods with him. One couldn't be too careful in a strange city. The landlord might not follow tenants to spy on them, but Sam didn't think him above entering an apartment and helping himself to anything lying around loose.

Sam shook his head sadly. Such suspicion of people who had done nothing to deserve it wasn't like him, or so he had once thought. How much he had changed since leaving Renraku. Some of the differences were good. He felt stronger and more capable than ever before and was in better shape, too. But he had grown cynical and continued to do things he would never even have contemplated as little as two years ago. Here he was, a shadowrunning shaman searching for the Ghost Dance Prophet. He wondered what his father would have thought of that. He knew what his mother would have thought. She'd have been horrified. Sometimes Sam thought that was the proper reaction.

Perhaps he was just tired, worn down by lack of sleep or maybe just frustration. He seemed no closer to finding out what had happened to Howling Coyote than when he had arrived in Denver. Tonight's meeting didn't look hopeful. The runner he was to meet had done some work for the Sovereign Tribal Council while Coleman was president, but that was nearly fifteen years ago. It was a slim connection at best, not much likely to produce a lead, but he had to try. He had gone through almost all the possibilities Dodger had dug up. No one he'd met would so much as talk about Howling Coyote, not even for a price. Was it some kind of conspiracy to hide the man, or what had happened to him?

Paranoia again. But paranoia was a survival trait in the shadows. Or was it just the first step into madness? Maybe all his fears that his magic was tied to madness were based in fact. There were enough mad things in his life. Like those dreams. Even with his eyes wide open, awake rather than asleep, he could almost hear the baying of the nightmare pursuer.

So why did his scalp itch?

Sam looked the street over. Nothing seemed out of the ordinary. The scavenger had gone to ground somewhere, and the crowd's composition was beginning to shift. The sprawling kids had gone, mere leaves blown away before the rising wind of night. A trio of razorguys in gang colors now occupied one of the tenement stoops. Nothing seemed out of place, yet Sam sensed that something was wrong. He was safely out of the traffic flow, so he leaned back against the wall and shifted his perception to the astral.

What had been hidden from his mundane sight now came clear. Across the street, stalking among the evening sidewalk traffic, a tall, gangly figure moved like a nightmare scarecrow. The being had pointed ears and slanted eyes that blazed with a golden light against his dark skin. Though much like an elf, this being seemed subtly different. Sam felt a strong sense of power fueling the illusion spell in which the elven scarecrow was wrapped.

Flickering astral presences danced around the dark stranger like electrons around a nucleus. When one broke off its orbit to flutter and bounce before its master's face, Sam knew he had been spotted. The apparition turned its attention to him.

Sam didn't think he could outdistance the scarecrow's long legs, and wasn't prepared to bet he could out-magic the well of power he sensed. He needed help, but he was alone in this city.

The city!

Desperately he searched, calling as he focused his power. He stretched his own abilities, seeking a response from the etheric world around him. There were immediate stirrings, but a coherent response took shape only slowly. Or so it seemed to his shifted perceptions. In the mundane world, the scarecrow had covered but half the block that separated him from Sam.

"Come," he called silently, urgently. "Born of the streets, hear me. Soul in the bones of the buildings, answer my summons."

An unwonted clarity in Sam's view of the concrete, stone, and plastics of the environment told him he had been heard.

Though Denver wasn't Sam's city, the presence ac-

knowledged him, recognizing his authority as a Dog
shaman and therefore a master of the spirits of Man.
Still, it was little inclined to do anything for him. Sam
asked service of it, demanding that it wrap its essence
around the scarecrow and enfold him so that Sam
might escape. It yielded to his insistence, and the rush
of fresh air that accompanied the spirit's departure to
do Sam's bidding held the tang of its assent.

Half a block away, the scarecrow was suddenly
stopped in his tracks by a collision with another pedestrian, a dwarf. Both hit the ground. The woman
immediately picked herself up and loudly cursed the
shoddy state of sidewalk repair. The bewildered scare
crow sat with a shocked look on his face, then let out
a howl when another passerby trod on his hand as
though he wasn't there. This was followed immediately by a passing dog that seemed to think the seated
stranger was a fire hydrant. Raising a leg, the dog marked
him. The dark man struck out and the dog skipped
away, then lit out as though seeing a ghost.

Good idea. Sam, too, started down the street at a
run. People moving toward him saw him coming and
got out of his way. He dodged around those going in
his own direction. Behind him he could hear the
scarecrow's angry shouts, as he tried to force his way
through pedestrian traffic that didn't seem to know he
was there. While many voices exclaimed in surprise
and pain, only the dark man's voice was full of anger.
The people he jostled seemed to blame the collisions
on their own clumsiness, or on some unseen piece of
trash or unnoticed unevenness in the sidewalk. To
them, the scarecrow was not there. The gap between
Sam and his pursuer widened. Satisfied that the steady
stream of rush-hour traffic on West Colfax Avenue
would prove a major barrier to the spirit-ridden scarecrow, Sam cut around a corner into an alley.

All the doleful singers of nearly two centuries had

failed to imagine how completely a city could alienate a person from those around him.

His relief died as he skidded to a stop.

Four silhouettes blocked his way. A hint of chrome gleamed among night-dark leathers. Razorguys. Two were hulking brutes in long coats with upturned collars and slouch hats that concealed all pertinent information about them. Bulges under their clothing suggested armor, enhancements, and weapons. They were too big to be orks and not broad enough to be trolls. The third was slender as a whip and wore his leathers tight to emphasize his build. His eyes sparkled with chrome reflections as he took three steps to Sam's left. The group was spread out enough now that he couldn't watch them all closely without turning his head. The fourth moved from behind the brute on the right, and the glow from newly wakening street lamps revealed that he was not an enhanced bullyboy like the others. What Sam had at first taken for a synthleather duster like the big boys wore was really a fine woolen topcoat of stylish cut. His slouch hat was festooned with magical symbols. Eyes and teeth shone in an entirely natural way from his brown face.

"Wrong turn, chummer. For you, that is. For us, a fortunate turn that should save us significant effort. You have something we want. There'll be no trouble if you're bright about it."

Recognition was as shocking as the ambush. Sam had seen this mage before. "I know you. You're Harry Masamba."

The black man frowned. "No. Not bright at all."

Sam recognized the reaction for the sentence it was. He spun and sprinted back toward the corner. From the way his response had caught them off guard, Sam knew the razorguys must have been expecting him to passively submit to their overwhelming superiority. A bullet chipped some concrete off the corner of the building, fragments pelting the back of Sam's jacket as he made the turn onto West Colfax. A pedestrian, caught by one of the bullets meant for Sam, tumbled over backward, spraying blood. A moment later it would have been Sam.

Sam raced down the sidewalk less carefully than before. He crashed into people and left a swirling mass of shouts behind him. Masamba's voice cut through the street noise. The mage had magically enhanced it, no doubt.

"Murderer!" the voice shouted. "The Anglo just shot him! Filthy white dog! Catch him, somebody! Call the police!"

Sam risked a glance back as he rounded the nearest corner. The slim razorguy was hustling toward him through the crowd, but the trench-coated pair was nowhere in sight. Masamba leaned against the alley mouth, laughing.

What in hell was going on?

23

Sam ducked into a doorway. His chances of outrunning the razorguy were so slim that he could have slid them between mortared bricks. And that was exactly what he'd have liked to do with himself. He needed time to think, to figure out what was going on. Time he wouldn't have if the razorguy caught him.

As if the thought had called the razorguy, the man took the corner from West Colfax in a controlled run. He halted, head turning in search of the man he sought. Boiling after him, a group of angry citizens also rounded the corner, splitting around his immobility like a wave around a rock. Sam froze, willing the samurai not to see, but he had never gotten the hang of an

invisibility spell. The mob rushed past. The razorguy
followed them slowly, as though sensing his prey hidden somewhere nearby. He advanced up the street,
checking possible hiding places with brief but thor-
ough efficiency. It was only a matter of time before he
would reach the doorway where Sam stood, and then
it would be over. Sam didn't know what sort of building sheltered him, but any refuge was better than none.
He tried the door. Locked, and he didn't know any
unlocking spells.

It wasn't the first time he'd been trapped and needed
to become invisible. Distraction had worked almost as
well then. Masamba had given him a way out. Sam
concentrated, trying to calm his breathing enough to
focus on the spell. Even if he completed it, the razorguy might not fall for his illusion. Forcing that worry
away, Sam fought his panting into a regular rhythm
and concentrated on the effect he wanted to achieve.

Voices erupted down the street, a hue and cry for
the fleeing shooter. It sounded as though the mob
Masamba tried to incite had found the man they sought
and were pursuing him. The razorguy looked up, considering the tumult. Then he ran toward the noise. He
passed Sam's hiding place without even a glance into
the shadows.

Sirens wailed as a police car flashed through the
intersection, headed for the alley where the pedestrian
had been shot. Someone had listened to Masamba's
exhortation and called the police. Maybe the mage had
done it himself. Either way Sam was in trouble. In a
matter of minutes, the police would have his description. Or would they? Would Masamba want Sam taken
up by the police? One way or the other, Sam definitely
wasn't in favor of letting the local badges have him
off.

Trying to get out of the Ute zone to reach Hart's
safehouse in the Pueblo zone was too risky now. This
close to the border there would be patrols on the ad-

jacent streets. Not much shadow traffic would cross the border tonight. If Sam knew the city better, he might have been able to guess at which likely points the patrols would light and where it might still be safe to cross. Going over at a checkpoint was out of the question. If the police had his description, his false identities wouldn't be good enough. For tonight at least, he was stuck in the Ute zone.

He realized how poor was his knowledge of the city. And how poorly equipped he was to deal with the level of threat hot on his heels.

Well, there was one sort of help you could buy with minimal questions, and no worry about former loyalties. Mr. Smith and his friends might not be good traveling company right now, but they'd easily stand a friend to some protection. It took Sam an hour to find a gun shop. The neon sign's "l" was out, making the name look to be "Weapon Wor d." The outer screen was down over the display window, but the place was open.

So he *had* changed. Here he was, contemplating buying lethal weaponry. Well, his world had changed, too. Sam didn't know why these people were after him, but it was obvious they were prepared to play rough. Alone in the city, he needed some way to even the odds. With so many foes, guns seemed the only answer.

A bum accosted Sam at the door of the shop, more proof that the Ute social system wasn't as egalitarian as its propaganda claimed. Here was another old, discarded remnant of the Ute tribe. He wore a battered black reservation hat sporting an equally battered turkey feather. The rest of his clothes were concealed under a dirty, multi-hued serape, and he stank of cheap booze and accumulated grime and filth. His wheezy voice was full of alcohol-fueled enthusiasm.

"Need a guide, Anglo? Can't do better than me. Honest Injun. Hey hey, get the joke. I know the best places. Ute Council. Pueblo, too. Know all the best hunting, best lodges. Girls, too. What ya hunting, Anglo? Elk, buffalo? Or ya into the paranormal? Hey hey, I'll help ya find it.''

Sam removed the unwashed hand gripping his sleeve. ''I'm not a hunter. Try somebody else.''

''Still need a guide. I been—''

The bum's protest was cut off as the outer door closed behind Sam. He waited while the scanner noted his weapons and the proprietor gave him the once-over. A click signaled that the inner door was unlocked. Sam entered and headed for the counter. As he walked, he glanced around, noting that he was the only customer. Just as well. The fewer people to deal with, the fewer might recognize him. Maybe the slow business would make the owner more receptive to a deal.

As it turned out business had been slow all day, and the surly owner was in no mood for deals. Sam transferred more than he thought fair for the weapons, but didn't complain. Uncomfortably, he accepted the Glock 7-mm Hideaway and the Sandler submachine gun. The shopkeeper was handing over the two boxes of ammo when he suddenly went rigid and his eyes took on a glassy look.

Sam had felt the spell wash over him, and didn't need to turn around to know that trouble had found him. He hadn't heard the door, so the spell-caster wasn't inside yet. Hoping his body shielded the action, he opened the box of 9-mm ammo for the Sandler and grabbed a handful of bullets. He couldn't unsling the Sandler without revealing that he had not succumbed to the paralyzing spell. If he could get a minute under cover, though . . .

A reflection in one of the display cases behind the counter showed him his hunter. The scarecrow elf had tracked him here. The door opened to admit him as if automatically controlled. Sam spun to face him, and was disheartened that the elf didn't appear the least astonished.

So much for the advantage of surprise.

"Don't look so disappointed, Verner. After the trouble I had banishing the city spirit you set on me, I did not expect you to succumb to so small a magic." The elf held out his hand. "Give it to me."

"You seem to know me, chummer, but I don't know what you're talking about."

The elf unleashed a sigh that could have passed for a growl. "I have no time to waste."

Sam didn't need to sense the power gathering around the elf to know what was coming. He dove for the floor as a fireball sizzled through the air. It engulfed the shopkeeper, who stood motionless as the flames blackened his flesh and ignited his clothes, melting their synthetic fibers into his shriveling skin. Sam felt the heat of the sudden conflagration as he crawled behind the meager cover offered by the stock shelves. Flames hissed, but the dying man made no scream of pain. Sam hoped the poor man's nerves were as paralyzed as his body.

The fire set off the automatic alarm, and the sprinkler system spurted to fitful life.

"Bad move, chummer," Sam shouted. Feverishly he fumbled the magazine out of the Sandler. "Alarm's going off at the local police and fire stations. Place like this has direct connections. Too much fire hazard."

The elf's answer was another fireball. Sam's protection erupted in flames, then began to topple toward him. He rolled away, barely escaping being buried in the falling merchandise. In his haste, he lost the magazine. He cursed. The Sandler would be of no more use than a club, and he was exposed now. Scrambling to his feet, he ran for the door.

He never made it.

In a whirlwind of orange and yellow fire, he was

picked up bodily and thrown through the disintegrating display window. Glassy teeth tore at him, shredding clothes and flesh with equal ease. In a shower of fragments, he landed on the cold sidewalk outside the shop. His shoulder was numb, his face a stinging mass of scrapes and cuts, and one eye was blinded by flowing blood. He had lost a boot and most of his pants, but he was still alive. His magic had saved him from the flames.

The bum was still there. Faintly, Sam could hear him clapping.

"Hey hey, good show."

Sam was not amused.

The scarecrow elf stepped through the window. His curly hair was matted from the water and his clothes dripped, but he seemed unaffected by his physical state. As soon as he saw Sam sprawled on the sidewalk, he smiled. "No more running, Verner. Time to die."

A shadow danced between Sam and the hunter. The bum.

"Can't do that," he objected. "The Anglo's mine. You want somebody, you go find your own. I've got magic too, elf. I'm the wind of the desert and I'll blow you away."

The bum waved his arms wildly. His serape undulated and flapped, but nothing else happened.

The elf sneered. "Wind? You're nothing but hot air, old man, while I am truly Rock. And if you do not take your pestiferous hide away, I will grind you to less than nothing. This matter does not concern you."

Before the elf could make good his promise, the roar of gunshots ripped the night. Staggering backward, he caught his heel against the sill of the display window, then fell heavily into the shop with a resounding crash.

The old bum stared down the street. Sam followed his gaze and saw the slim razorguy racing toward them.

Looming out of the dark behind that one came the twin bulks of the other two muscleguys.

More trouble. At least Sam knew now that the scarecrow and Masamba were not working together. He pushed himself up on one elbow but his head spun and slumped under the lash of pain that made his head spin. Looked like this round was going to the bad guys.

Sam felt a shudder in the pavement caressing his cheek. Could the razorguys be carrying enough chrome to shake the earth where they ran? A delirious concept, but he was close to delirium. Concussion, he supposed. He rolled over onto his back.

It wasn't the razorguys. The shudder increased in frequency and a grating rumble rose. The scarecrow elf was standing in the window of Weapon World, arms outstretched and glowing with the intensity of the mana gathered around him. He was singing, too, but Sam didn't recognize the language.

The rumble grew to a roar and the street began to heave, stopping the advance of the razorguys as they fought to keep their balance. Facing stones from the surrounding buildings split off and plummeted to the street. A large piece struck one of the trench-coated muscleguys and squashed him like a bug. The others took cover, too unsettled by the massive magical manifestation to fire at the magician.

A wail from down the street drew Sam's attention to the figure of Masamba standing there. The Black mage unleashed a bolt of amber energy that shrieked from his hands and burst into coruscating sparks against an invisible barrier surrounding the scarecrow elf. Encouraged by the arrival of their own magical support, the remaining razorguys opened fire.

Sam snatched the old bum's serape and hauled him down. His reward was a kick and a complaint.

"Hey hey, what ya doing? I'm magic, you stupid Anglo. Ain't gonna hurt me."

Around them the apparent earthquake increased in

fury. Dust from the falling bricks and building stones rose like a fog. It whirled and eddied in a wind that came from nowhere, but stubbornly hugged the ground to obscure vision beyond a couple of meters. Unable to target, the razorguys ceased their steady fire. Only when the swirling dust opened a fire lane did the guns speak. Cyan flashes of magical energy lit the dust clouds as they screamed in response to Masamba's erratic barrage of amber bolts.

A brick crashed to earth near Sam's head. Pain forgotten, he scrambled to his feet. The old Indian leaped up at his side, screaming taunts at the stones and daring them to hit him. Sam's renewed attempt to restrain the old fool was aborted when the slim razorguy appeared wraithlike from the dust. He grabbed Sam's jacket and lifted him bodily. The force of the muscleguy's rush slammed Sam against a wall. As his head rebounded, a gun muzzle poked into his throat, forcing his head back into another painful collision with the brick.

"Give it over and I'm gone. Keep it and you are."

Jaw clenched by the pressure of the gun, Sam could barely answer. "I don't know what . . ."

"Don't jerk me, Verner."

Sam felt the hard, cold barrel of the razorguy's pistol slam against his temple. Before the pain ignited in its full fury, the muzzle was again under his chin. A hand slapped against his side.

"Frag! It's gone!"

The pressure eased suddenly and Sam sank down, off balance. When the pain lessened, he struggled to his feet. The razorguy had vanished. Sam reached to his side where the street tough had struck him. There were slices in the leather of his jacket and his pants were ribbons over his hip, but he was slow to realize that he shouldn't be feeling the leather or fabric at all. His satchel was gone. He remembered his slashing passage through the Weapon World window. The strap must have been sliced away then.

The wail of a siren pierced the howling wind. As it grew louder, Sam looked around desperately. The pouch had contained his identities, and the credstick key to Hart's safe house. Somebody without a System Identification Number or any other means of identification wasn't going to get along too well with the police, even if they hadn't fallen for Masamba's earlier ploy. Word was that they didn't like shadows in the Ute zone. And Sam was too deep in that zone to get out in a hurry on foot.

Flashes of magical energy continued to sear cyan and amber through the dust storm.

A hand gripped Sam's arm. He twisted reflexively and struck out, relieved to feel the gripping hand release him. The target of his violence careened back into a wall and slid down in a disheveled heap.

The old man.

"Hey hey, Anglo. Some gratitude. Save ya from the rocks and ya slug me. Well, forget it. Find your own path."

The old man dragged himself to his feet and started away.

Sam tried to see what was going on. He didn't know what the two factions were after, or why they wanted it. From their earlier attention to him, it was something he had been carrying. Their sudden lack of interest in him indicated that he no longer had what they were fighting over. That was fine by him. In his current condition, even the loser of the fight would probably walk all over him.

The sirens grew louder.

There seemed nothing to gain and a lot to lose. He wouldn't be able to recover his materials tonight, if ever. He staggered down the alley that had swallowed the Indian. Maybe the old sot really did know his way around the zone. The Indian might not volunteer any more aid after Sam's reaction to his helping hand, but by following him Sam could at least escape the immediate effects of the battle. After that, who knew?

24

Hohiro Sato wanted the stone the moment he laid eyes on it, though he'd never liked opal much till now. The oily iridescence was not his style, which tended more toward the clarity and depth of ruby or emerald.

But this stone . . . To see it was to want it. The opal had a magnetic attraction, almost as though it were somehow a part of him. Before, he had coveted it simply because Grandmother did. And the interest shown by the unknown faction told him it was a potentially powerful tool. But seeing it now, he wanted it for itself.

Its surface felt smooth, and was not cold as it appeared. It almost seemed alive under his hand.

He did not understand its potential, but he would. Someone would solve its riddles for him, and the power it represented would be his. How fortunate that one of Grandmother's agents had perished in the incident with who or whatever had attacked Verner in the gun shop. It had made it that much easier to dispose of the other and to eliminate any immediate claimants for the prize.

Sato contemplated the store, scratching absentmindedly at an itch along his left forearm. The stone was magic, no doubt about that. He could almost feel its power. Very powerful magic, indeed, to draw the attention of the magically powerful party that had ambushed Verner. Masamba swore that the magician he had faced was at least a sixth rank initiate. The term didn't have any real meaning for Sato, beyond the fact that Masamba believed he had faced a wizard more powerful than himself. And that meant the third party was well supplied with magical resources. The level of magic involved in the Weapon World battle was well beyond that of which Verner was believed capable.

Sato wondered how much information Grandmother had on this third party. Had she known of the opposition before she sent him after the stone? Had he only been a stalking horse for her? If so, he would find a way to make her regret it.

Flakes of dried skin caught under his fingernails. He rubbed his thumb across his finger tips to brush the detritus to the floor.

He stared at the stone, ensnared by its beauty. It was more beautiful now that he owned it. What might not be his once he learned how to make best use of it?

Crawling higher on his arm, the itch became intolerable. Without thinking, he rolled back his sleeve to get at the irritation. When he finally tore his eyes from the stone to examine the source of the prickling sensation, he stared with horror.

The hard, lumpy thing that had been his arm was black and glistening with oozing liquid where it had emerged from the brittle flakes of epidermis. The streaks exposed by his scratching were already hardening to a dull, waxy shine. Two long, hook-taloned appendages replaced his fingers, and a smaller version lay slightly offset in a parody of a thumb.

His stomach churned and he retched. But he didn't scream at the horror that was emerging from his own body. At this new manifestation of the taint. No, he didn't scream. He reached for the telecom with his human arm and opened a circuit to his administrative assistant.

"Get me Soriyama," he ordered. "And send in Masamba and Akabo."

* * *

Dodger had never moved so swiftly through the Matrix, nor so easily. The pulse of datalines was brighter, the clarity of icons sharper, and the blackness between all the places and passages of man's creation was darker. The electron skies spread over a horizon as limitless as his imagination. No meat experience could match this transcendental adventure.

Distant messages, falsely urgent, impinged on his joy, but he banished them by turning his eyes to the wonders of cyberspace. This was the freedom and power he had sought for years, the oneness with the Matrix.

And she was with him.

* * *

Hart looked into the fixer's face and searched for any clue to deception. She was disappointed. Everything he had said was true, or so he believed. They had worked uncounted shadowruns over the years, and she trusted him as much as she could anyone in her business. She knew of no reason he would deceive her. Worse, she didn't know of any reason that he might be deluded.

"You're sure there are three devices?"

"Three. Four. Five. What does it matter? But, yes, a minimum of three. All multiple-warhead. All conveniently forgotten by a well-paid weapons officer when the Americans left German soil for good." For a moment the tiny old man seemed wistful, remembering old causes. "They were the terrorist's El Dorado for decades following reunification. A Barbarossa sleeping beneath the earth until the final reckoning. They were to be the great liberators, destroyers of the bonds that tied the Fatherland's spirit."

"You claim they're real, then you call them a pipe dream. Make up your mind, Caliban."

"Oh, they're real enough."

"But you can't tell me where they are."

He shrugged. "Deeper pockets than yours have asked, but I'd give it to you, my dear. I'm an old man now. I don't have the strength for it. But I can't sell or give away what I don't have." He chuckled dryly. "At least not to you, my brilliant student. Barbarossa will not awaken in my lifetime. Cosimo took the secret of the lost weapons to his grave when Mossad cornered his Fenris faction in Casablanca. His papers were all destroyed in the firestorm. There have been plenty of fakes over the years, but I've seen through them all. None ever had the marks."

Hart leaned forward. "What marks? The wolf?"

"Of course, the wolf. But there were others."

As he described them to her, she remembered what she had seen. Each detail fit. Her doubts had fled well before he finished.

So it was true. All of Caliban's old hints had been true, except for the one that he knew the secret hiding place of the weapons. Like most runners in the European shadow world, she had grown up believing that if Caliban didn't know, no one did. But somewhere, somehow, someone had found Cosimo's legacy. The data Dodger's contact had retrieved from Grandmother's operation had included a map, but the accompanying text hadn't specified the map's purpose. Hart had almost missed the small symbol near Deggendorf. Dodger hadn't recognized the stylized wolf head, but she had. She hadn't wanted to believe the map could be real, but the details Caliban gave her left no room for doubt. Her worst fears were confirmed.

Sam had to be told, of course. But beyond him, who?

25

Sam awoke with a shock. The old Hummer was jolting him as it bumped its way down an embankment. Ahead and to the left were distant mountains, screened occasionally by the buttes of a badlands. The landscape was all dusty greens, multi-toned grays, and dusky purples that were deepening in tone as the sun sank lower in the sky.

He wasn't in Denver anymore.

The ache in his head and the stiffness in his body told him that he hadn't dreamed his travails in the Ute zone. In flashes, he remembered parts of his escape from the battle. The alley and the ever-louder sirens. The fugitive glimpses of a hunched figure in a serape. The muck and filth of a trash heap. Strong hands dragging him. An old surplus Hummer stacked with boxes and cans. Shadows, darkness, and light shot through with voices, gunshots, and chanting. Wind and cold, then wind and warmth.

Someone had rescued him and driven him away from danger.

Apparently that same someone had covered him with a cloth that had once been bright with color, but was now stained and filthy. Even though the wind of the Hummer's passage drew most of the scent away, enough remained to tell Sam who had rescued him.

He turned his head to look at the driver. Sure enough, it was the old Indian. The driver's reservation hat was tilted to shade his eyes from the setting sun, casting most of his face in shadow, but there was no mistaking him.

Sam squirmed to get a look behind him. The rear

of the vehicle was full of supplies. They were alone. His movement attracted his companion's notice.

"Hey hey, back in this world for a while?"

Sam's attempt to reply in the affirmative came out as a croak.

"Canteen on the floor by your feet."

On the third attempt, Sam convinced his body that it could bend forward and retrieve the canteen. The water was tepid and tasted of minerals, but his parched throat didn't care. He splashed some into one hand and rubbed it on his face, wincing when he touched his scrapes. Nevertheless, he felt better than he expected, or deserved. Well enough to realize that last night's—it was just one night, wasn't it?—thoughts about the old man had been unduly unkind.

"I guess I owe you some thanks for pulling me out of that mess last night."

"Yup."

"Well, thanks." That seemed the end of the conversation for a time. As the Hummer neared a broad river, Sam decided to try again. "Where are we?"

"Under the sky."

"Oh." He had been hoping for something a little more specific. Maybe the old man didn't trust him. Introductions might break the ice. "I'm not from around here. Mostly, I live in Seattle. Out there, they call me Twist."

"Yup."

That was it? Maybe the old man thought Sam already knew who he was. "You haven't even told me your name."

"That's right."

The hummer hit the edge of the river. Muddy drops churned up by the tires splashed against the windscreen. Sam was getting annoyed. "Well, what should I call you? 'Old man' doesn't seem very polite."

The old man shrugged. "Description's always polite, Anglo. If you gotta problem with it, call me Dancey.''

"Dancey? As in Dizzy Dancey?"

"That's me." The Indian threw both hands into the air and bounced in his seat, chanting a few nonsense syllables. His motion sent the Hummer out of control. It swerved under the pressure of the water, then dipped as it struck a pothole. Water splashed up over the sill, wetting Sam's leg with its cold mountain freshness. As Sam recoiled, Dancey returned his hands to the wheel and took control of the Hummer.

In the shadows of Denver Sam had heard about Dizzy Dancey, and none of it had been comforting. The old man had once been a hot shadowrunner who had hosed up badly and been caught by the Navajo Tribal Police. Whatever they were supposed to have done to him had left him slightly out of his head ever since.

The Hummer jounced out of the river and began to crawl up the long sloping embankment. It topped the rise, scattering a pair of small horned animals that ran like jackrabbits. The Hummer then bounced a dozen meters across the grassy prairie and onto the remnants of a road. Dancey started to hum and seemed happier, as though the river had been a boundary beyond which he need not worry. The Hummer picked up speed.

"How'd we get here?" Sam asked. "And where's 'here' anyway?"

"Upcountry, Anglo. Safest place when the city gets hot. Things'll cool in a while, then you can go back, if you're crazy enough."

"But I've got important things to do in the city. I've got no time to waste."

"Think staying alive is wasting time?"

"No."

"Good," Dancey pronounced with a confirming nod. "Then shut up. Driving was easier when you were asleep."

Sam followed his advice, more out of frustration and annoyance than anything else. He tried watching the scenery for a time, but his mind kept clouding. His nagging concerns wouldn't let him go. He fidgeted, worried about Janice.

"Hey hey, Anglo. What's so important about being in the city, anyway? Filthy place, not good for somebody like you."

"I'm looking for someone to help my sister."

Dancey made an exaggerated show of looking in the back of the Hummer, then across the prairie. "Don't see no sister."

"She's not around here. She can't travel just now."

"Hey hey, Anglo. Sounds bad. Ya got my sympathy. Family is real important, but you understand that. Don't need no old man to tell ya that. What kind of doctor ya looking for?"

Sam hesitated. What did it really matter? Sam hadn't gotten anywhere with his investigation. Maybe it was because he had been so closemouthed about why he was seeking Howling Coyote. Maybe if he had let it be known that it wasn't political, he might have gotten help. If Dancey spread the word in Denver, it might even help. That is, if anyone took the old man seriously. "Not a doctor. A shaman. She's got . . . magical problems."

Dancey wheezed a laugh. "So you come looking for the tribal medicine men. Lotsa luck, Anglo."

"Not just any medicine man. I'm looking for Howling Coyote."

"Ain't gonna find him in the city." The old man laughed. "Ain't gonna find him at all."

"What do you mean?"

The old man pointed at the sky. "Good clouds today, Anglo. A man can see a lot in clouds. Things that aren't there and things that are. Clouds change a lot. The stars, now. The stars are different. They're always spinning, racing across the sky even when ya can't see

them. They don't change much. At least not so a man
can see. 'Cept for the falling stars. Flare, burn, and
fall. Not much of a legacy. Ever see a star *before* it
fell, Anglo?''

What did stars have to do with anything? Sam gave
up. He turned his head and stared at the sunset.

It wasn't much longer before Dancey pulled the
Hummer off the track and bounced them to a stop in
a small canyon. He rustled around in the back of the
Hummer for a while, emerging first with a bedroll that
he tossed to Sam without a word, then later with some
cooking gear and a field pack. The old man made a
fire and cooked supper in silence. They ate, and then,
in silence, they sat watching the glowing embers.

A scuffing in the darkness startled Sam, but Dancey
didn't appear to notice. The old man seemed used to
the prairie, so Sam dismissed the sound as not dangerous. He looked up at the stars playing hide-and-
seek among drifting clouds. The air was chill, cooling
quickly, so he wrapped the bedroll around his shoulders. The fire warmed his front.

He heard the furtive noise again and caught the
gleam of eyes just beyond the firelight. The old man
tossed a supper scrap out. After a moment, a coyote
padded over to gobble it down. Dancey tossed another,
this time closer to the fire so that the animal had to
come well within the firelight to get it. The animal
moved forward and took the new offering. Scrap by
scrap, Dancey lured it closer until it was taking food
from his hand.

A lonesome yipping echoed in from the surrounding
buttes. Their after-dinner guest sat on his haunches
and raised his muzzle to howl back. The sound con-
veyed an odd mixture of companionship and isolation.
Sam closed his eyes to concentrate on listening to the
distant calls. Their coyote howled again, this time in
concert with another close by.

Sam opened his eyes, hoping to spot the newcomer.

He had not expected what he saw. Dancey had joined the chorus. His head, tilted at the sky, was not that of the old man. A coyote's pointed snout poked from beneath the tilted brim of the battered reservation hat. Sam could almost smell magic in the air.

Trickster!

"You!" Sam shouted, scrambling to his feet and frightening away the animal. "You're Howling Coyote!"

The vision of the coyote head vanished and the old man looked at him with dark, but human, eyes. "Been called a lot of things. That, too."

"I need your help."

The old man turned his eyes to the ground. His finger traced patterns in the dirt. " 'Course, I might just be another ragged Coyote shaman limping along in the trail of the Trickster."

Sam shook his head. He had felt an aura of power, or something, enwrapping the man as he sang with the animals. This was no ordinary shaman. "No. Not just any shaman."

The old man met his gaze again.

"Coyote's not a lucky fella. Gets killed a lot. Howling Coyote died, you know."

"So I heard. All shamans die. A shaman has to die to touch the power. Dog told me."

The old man's expression became suspicious. "Dog told ya? Hey hey, they talk to dogs where ya come from, Anglo?"

"They talk to dogs everywhere. It's when the dogs talk back that you get problems."

The Indian grunted. "So ya say you're a shaman. Well, show me something. Impress me."

Sam shook his head. "That's not what the magic's for."

"No? Why not? What good's anything if ya can't use it?"

Sam was becoming angry at the man's flippant attitude and mocking tone. "I didn't say I can't use it."

"Hot, hot. Leave it for the sun. Hey hey. Pride's trouble, Anglo. Had plenty enough trouble in my time."

"I don't want to cause trouble. I want to stop it. My sister, she . . ."

"She's trouble." The old man's voice held both sympathy and warning.

"Well, yes. But she doesn't want to be, and that's what will save her." Or so he believed. "I'm sure of it."

"Sure, are ya? Ain't no surety, Anglo. Ya talk about trouble and magical problems. Ya don't say much. Ya gotta talk plain, Anglo. I'm just a stupid old man."

Sam didn't believe that, but he played along. He told the old man about Janice. He talked about the ritual and its failure, and about his fears that Janice would succumb to the wendigo curse, and his hopes for her salvation. He ended his tale with an appeal. "You *are* Howling Coyote. You led the Great Ghost Dance, the most powerful transforming magic the world has ever seen. You're the only one who knows enough about shamanic magic to make the ritual work. You've got to help me."

The old man stood and turned his back on Sam. "Don't got to do nothing. Coyote's freedom, ya know. Does what he wants. You're on a fool's quest."

"I've got to help my sister."

"Very noble, Dog." He spat. "Blind optimism."

"No, it isn't," Sam protested. "I felt her spirit and I felt the magic. She can be saved, but I can't do it myself. I need you to help me help Janice."

"Help yourself."

"Are you refusing to help?"

"I said what I said."

"Okay, okay," Sam said, exasperated. "If you won't help, then at least teach me what I need to know.

You've taught others to use magic. Teach me. Teach
me how to save Janice.''

The old man turned around. "Why not?"

26

"Coyote knows all, sees all," the shaman said.
"Tells little."

"Like you," Sam observed.

"Hey hey, pup. Sing a sour song and you jinx the
magic. Sky ain't gonna change color to suit you. A
shaman is what he is because he is what he is. Ya gotta
know to do, and do to know. Got that?''

"Sure," Sam replied dubiously. Clear as mud. The
last two days had been full of exercises in frustration.
The old man had led him deeper into the wilderness,
hauling packs when they left the Hummer behind. Most
of the time, Sam's questions and comments fell on
deaf ears. The old man only spoke when he wished,
and then half the time he spouted nonsense commen-
taries on life or nature. The other half was split between totally incomprehensible monologues in a
language Sam guessed was his native Ute dialect and
almost equally incomprehensible orders. So far Sam
had listened to how the wind made piñon trees sigh,
observed ants scurry about their business, smelled and
compared the scents of yucca leaves and flowers, and
watched buzzards wheel in the canyon updrafts. Time
and again, he had gathered a variety of plant materials
and animal remains, only to have the shaman leave
them behind the next time they stopped. He felt more
like he, or his patience, was being tested rather than
taught.

They had climbed a long series of switchbacks up a

bluff and were now making their way across a gradually sloping mesa top. On the way up, Howling Coyote had taken a detour and led Sam out on a precarious spur of rock. The stretch of plain that ran to distant mountains left Sam in awe. The prairie seemed to go on for a hundred kilometers. The shaman had tugged Sam around to face south and pointed to a series of peaks in that direction.

"See. It ain't me," Howling Coyote had said. "He's still sleeping."

Sam hadn't understood what the old man meant, and said so.

"The Ute, pup. He's still sleeping," was all the shaman would say on the subject.

They came to a place where a wide circular depression was marked by stone walls. In sharp contrast to the dusty soil and sparse vegetation elsewhere, the grass here was bright and green within the hole. Traces of ditches, some with stones, could be seen through the stunted trees.

"Thirsty, pup?"

"Yes," Sam replied honestly. His lips were dry, and even his lungs felt seared by the dry air.

The shaman sat on the wall and dangled his feet over the edge into the depression. There was perhaps two centimeters clearance between the soles of his feet and the earth. "Ah, nice and cool," he said. "Have a drink if you're thirsty."

Sam looked at the grassy depression toward which the old man gestured. He could see no sign of water. Just grass. The shaman swung his feet back up, with a heave rising to his feet and padding off down a path between the fragrant piñon. Sam was shocked to see Howling Coyote leave damp footprints. He hurried after.

"What did you do back there?"

"Hey hey, pup. I didn't do nothing. The old ones built all around here. 'Anasazi''s the name you Anglos stuck on them. They built that lake for irrigation before Whites ever walked the land hereabouts.''

''But your footprints,'' Sam protested. ''You left wet footprints as though your feet had been in water. There wasn't any water in that lake bed. How did you do that?''

The shaman laughed. ''I didn't do nothing. Just experienced the lake and the wisdom of the old ones. What did you experience?''

Nothing, Sam thought. Aloud he said, ''I don't know.''

''Some shaman. Gotta see the past if you're gonna face the future.''

Without any further explanation, Howling Coyote led Sam through the tangled, dark trees. Near sunset they came out at the rim of a forested canyon. The rock face fell away beneath them for a dozen meters of sheer drop. The far rim looked as Sam imagined the side on which he stood must appear. Trees and brush grew on all the surfaces that offered the least foothold, only succumbing when the rocks were nearly vertical. In niches where the sandstone of the cliff had caved away, someone—the old ones?—had built clusters of structures. After silently contemplating the vista for a few minutes, Howling Coyote led Sam back from the edge to a grove of piñon trees that were taller and broader than their immediate neighbors. It took Sam a moment to realize that each of the larger trees stood within a slightly raised area.

Before he could ask a question the shaman took his arm and dragged him deeper into the grove, where a few piles of stone marked the outlines of a building made of many small rooms. No wall was higher than a meter. There was a wide clearing to one side, in the middle of which yawned a dark, rectangular hole. Two logs and the first rung of the ladder they supported poked out of the hole into the failing sunlight. ''A kiva. Be warmer to spend the night in there,'' the shaman said, and disappeared down the ladder. Though Sam felt the air already turning chill, he didn't find the thought of climbing down into darkness inviting. While he stood indecisive, a chant and faint wisps of smoke began to come from the hole.

> *He rises, to the sky.*
> *He rises, seeking light.*
> *He rises, toward the power.*
> *To the sky, he rises.*

Dusk lay on the mesa; a cool breeze arose, rustling through the piñon and caressing the twisted mesquite logs. An owl called, distant and plaintive, and the faint chitter of a hunting bat skittered across Sam's ears. Other hunters would be about. Sam looked at the hole. Where the kiva had seemed to offer only darkness and mystery, it now promised light and warmth and the only companionship on the mesa.

Howling Coyote might be a little odd, but the human companionship he offered was something Sam couldn't long go without. The old shaman was also Sam's only hope for Janice, and Sam was not about to abandon that hope after chasing it so long. For all of Howling Coyote's eccentricity, Sam felt somehow that the shaman was trying to help him. If only he could figure out what the old man was driving at. One thing was certain: Sam wouldn't get anywhere by freezing himself to death alone in the night.

He walked to the ladder rising from the kiva and, coughing a little from the smoke, descended into the earth.

* * *

Pain.

Wind howls like a hungry wolf. Fire burns, destroying implacably. Faces are filled with pain, and rage, and fear, and death.

Pain.

His mother, crying and protective. His father, defiant and impotent. Oliver, his brother, torn away by the raging waves of the mob, to surface in impossibly distant places. And Janice . . .

Pain.

Running. Hiding. The dark shadow against the dark night comes hunting, circling ever closer, until an eerie, keening howl pierces the darkness and sends the shadow away. The sound stays in his head, piercing his peace and bringing . . .

Pain.

* * *

"Hey hey, pup. Is it Dog?"

Sam started awake, dream fragments fleeing from him to be swallowed in swirling mists. Even though he was unsure of what they were, he was more than happy to see them go.

Howling Coyote shook his shoulder. "You were chasing something. Talking to Dog?"

Sam shook his still muddled head. He didn't want to remember, but he knew he hadn't been visiting that pleasant green place where Dog dwelled. "Just a dream. Nothing important."

"Hey hey, pup. You're dumb even for an Anglo. Dreams are important. They touch on the otherworld, the places where the totems live."

"Dreams are fragments of leftover data. They're just the brain recorrelating information, subconscious data processing."

The old man looked at Sam out the corner of his eye. "Ya sure, Anglo?"

"It's scientifically proven."

"Ya really are dumb. This is a magic world now. Science don't know everything."

Sam was annoyed. "Nor does magic."

"Nor do you," Howling Coyote said in near perfect

imitation of Sam's exasperated tone. The old man swung a foot up onto the ladder. "Eat. Sleep. Think. Whatever. Just don't let the fire go out. Got something I gotta do. Ya stay put now, pup."

The shaman climbed the ladder, momentarily blocking the sunlight and plunging the kiva into deeper gloom. In a surge of momentary panic Sam nearly swarmed up the ladder after the shaman, but he forced the urge away. He spent two days regretting his decision to stay.

Each morning Howling Coyote told him to sit in the holy place of the kiva and dream. It was not welcome advice, for Sam didn't like the dreams he was having. But he did as the old man bid, sensing that his chance of learning anything from Howling Coyote, and therefore Janice's salvation, depended on his obedience. Wasn't the student always expected to be obedient to the master? It had been that way in his ancestral Europe and it was a way of life in the Orient. Why would the Native Americans be different? So Sam sat in the darkness, pacing the confining periphery of the kiva when the forced inactivity became too much. He spent a lot of time trying to guess the time of day from the angle of sunlight creeping in past the fiber mat grill Howling Coyote had placed over the opening. The boredom was so intense that he slept a lot.

And when he slept, he dreamed.

On the third day, Sam awoke to find Howling Coyote gone. Without the shaman to prohibit him from leaving, he decided he had grown thoroughly sick of the dark kiva. Climbing the ladder into the harsh light of mid-afternoon, Sam blinked and shook his head in wonder. He had thought it was only morning, and blamed the timeless dark of the kiva for the glitch to his biorhythms. Then again, had it been only three days? He hoped so; time was passing too quickly as it was.

Hearing the faint strains of the shaman's voice

chanting, Sam followed the sound to the edge of the cliff. The song came from somewhere below. Sam spent some time looking around, until he finally found what resembled a path downward. He had to scramble in a couple of places, but he made his way to a narrow level area and followed it along the edge of the sandstone bluff. Turning the corner of an outcrop, he came suddenly upon a structure more elaborate than those he had seen in the opposite wall of the canyon. Building after ruined building was crammed into the gash in the cliff. In one place a tower reached up almost four stories, molding itself to the curving overhang of the cleft. Hard-packed earthen surfaces with square holes in their centers marked kivas. Sam skirted the exposed circular wall of one in order to follow the chanting.

He left the sunlight behind as he edged through gaps in building walls to move deeper into the ruin. His progress slowed as the spaces became more restricted. Often, he had to turn on his side to crawl through openings that weren't wide enough for his shoulders to pass. Deep within the ruin, he found Howling Coyote daubing ochre paint onto the sandstone rock face that formed the back of the cleft. Sam said nothing and watched.

In deft strokes, the shaman was sketching a stick man bent over a tube or rod that touched his head. Lines—feathers, Sam presumed—arched from the stick man's head. The central figure completed, the shaman spun spirals above and below the stick man. To the right and left he placed rows of dots, then stepped back to observe his work. Sam gave in to his curiosity and started to ask the old man what he was doing, but was shushed to silence before he said a word.

Howling Coyote backed away from the painting, almost into the sunlight, and sat down. He drew a wooden flute from his belt and began to play a haunting melody composed mostly of single, long notes interspersed with fluttering clusters of rising and falling tones. Sam walked over and seated himself at Howling Coyote's side. The music gradually became softer and finally trailed off into silence. Lulled by its beauty, Sam was startled when Howling Coyote spoke.

"He's coming."

"Who?"

"Him." The shaman pointed at his painting.

A tall, gangly being emerged from the rock, his form thickening from rosy translucency to opacity. His slanted eyes of deep, deep black were pools of oblivion against the night dark of his skin. His ears were pointed. Despite his fierce expression and the red glow that surrounded him, Sam perceived that the newcomer was no devil, just an elf. A strangely powerful and skinny one, perhaps, but an elf all the same.

"That's the guy who tried to kill me in Denver!" Sam reached for his gun, but the Indian's hand snaked out and clamped onto his wrist. Sam relaxed, and the shaman released him. It was time to trust his teacher.

The shaman stood, cloaked in an aura of power. "Hoka-hey, Wata-urdli. You've come a long way on your road of stone to die."

"Peace, Howling Coyote." The elf raised empty hands and presented the palms. "This is not a good day to die. I wish you no harm."

"Come in peace, stay in peace." The profound majesty of the Indian shaman shattered as the sprawl-runner crawled out. "Otherwise leave in pieces."

If the elf noticed a change, he gave no sign. "Save your hostility for what you harbor, old man."

The Indian squatted and dug around in his pouch. Finally he pulled out a pouch and a chipped clay pipe. He held them out to the elf. "Wanna smoke, Urdli?"

A brief look of disgust crossed the elf's face, but when he spoke his voice was even and his tone polite. "I accept your offer, and as long as I stand in this place, bind myself by its terms. You will forgive me if

I do not actually perform the ritual. You have my word as bond.''

"I hear you. The puppy hears you. The spirits hear you. They will rise and devour you if you lie.''

"As I said, I bind myself to the peace of this place.''

Howling Coyote grunted.

Sam was bewildered by the exchange, but the elf and the shaman seemed satisfied with each other. "What's going—''

"Shut up, Anglo.'' Howling Coyote glared at the elf. "Urdli came to talk, it seems. Got any objections to talk? No? Didn't think so, since ya like to do so much of it yourself. The elf wants to talk, let him. I'll listen.''

The elf nodded. "I did come to talk. Let me tell you a tale.'' Without waiting for permission, the elf started. "Long ago, this world knew magic. It was a better time then; all lived in accordance with their natures. The world was not perfect, but it was happier. In time changes came, and the magic grew weak. Many wonderful things perished. Some evil things as well, but evil always seems less vulnerable to the lack of magic. For a long time there was no mana, but the time of lack was only an interval. The mana returned and brought us to the Sixth World.''

"Aztec number,'' Howling Coyote interrupted. "Hopi got a different count. Aleut, too.''

The elf shrugged. "The number is unimportant, but the concept should be understood. Mana has waxed and waned. There was a time when the mana was low, too low for the true nature of the world to manifest. And in those days a tradition was handed down, a sacred trust. Dedicated individuals swore to guard a place. You would not know of this place, but I know it as *Imiri ti-Versakhan,* the Citadel of Remembrance. It was a place meant to make the low time safer, and it was a bastion against the return of evil should the mana return. Terrible things were kept there, locked away so they could do no harm.''

Sam felt a sinking sensation in his stomach. He was beginning to guess what the elf was leading up to. Apparently oblivious to Sam's sudden pallor, Urdli continued.

''Recently, the ancient citadel was assaulted and despoiled. Through the actions of the intruders, something escaped bondage, something terrible.''

''Spider.'' Howling Coyote turned his head and spat.

''You know.'' Urdli was silent a moment. No one else spoke either. ''How?''

The shaman smiled his sly smile. ''Got a few friends of my own where the totems hang out.''

The elf's expression grew more grave. ''If you know, you must understand the danger. Knowing that, you must understand the crime of the one you call a puppy.''

''Hey hey, only got your word for it. Not everybody tells the same tales of Spider. Hopi say she saved the people. That don't sound too terrible to me. 'Cepting, of course, that it was the Hopi she saved. Spider's a canny old bitch, knows a lot.''

The shaman's remarks seemed to anger Urdli. ''The human mind cannot comprehend the alienness of Spider. To deal with Spider is, as the English say, to deal with the devil.''

It was the shaman's turn to shrug. ''Don't know about that. But ya do have to walk the web carefully if ya want to come home again. Now, some of them other bugs are *real* troublemakers. Sooner eat ya than look at ya.''

''Spider has always been more subtle,'' Urdli agreed. ''A builder of artifices and a lurker in dark places, she is. Fortunately, since the Awakening, Spider has not been whole. A portion of her power, stolen in the old time, was locked away from her access.

Until recently.'' Urdli looked directly at Sam. ''That has changed.''

''I didn't know,'' Sam protested.

Urdli laughed bitterly. ''Ignorance is such a favorite excuse of humans. The gossamer threads of Spider's webs can tug in such a way that her commands may seem to be her puppet's own innocent thoughts. Many do her work without knowing it. Can you not see that Verner may be one of those?''

''Not this pup,'' the old shaman said. ''Don't smell no Spider on him. He didn't know about your *Imiri*-place when he took the stone. He did it to help his sister. Typical Dog trick, noble but stupid. Can't be too bad a problem, the sky ain't changed.''

Sam wasn't sure he liked the way the shaman was defending him, but its effect on Urdli was visible. The elf seemed slightly less sure of himself.

''Innocent or not, he has strengthened Spider and her minions,'' Urdli insisted. ''They have the stone now. The harm may not be irreparable if it is redressed at once. I have come to demand that he join the struggle to undo what he has done.''

''You tried to kill me,'' Sam pointed out.

The elf looked at Sam as though he were a stupid child.

''Why should I help you?'' Sam asked. ''You'll probably try to kill me again as soon as you get what you want.''

''You have a responsibility. Your action has strengthened Spider and emboldened her. She stirs now, and the world lies in danger. She is drawing on her web and pulling to herself the instruments of holocaust.''

''Hey hey, elf, cut the flowery stuff. Like I keep telling the pup, I'm a stupid old man. Ya talking about what I think you're talking about?''

Urdli spoke slowly and clearly. ''Spider is engaged

in operations to acquire a forbidden arsenal of nuclear weapons.''

Sam was confused. What was a spirit going to do with bombs? "That doesn't make sense. Totems don't have any physical presence. Why would Spider need an arsenal?''

"Spider is an old totem with very strong ties to the earth. She is different from the totem to which you profess allegiance. She manifests through avatars, and those unfortunate beings have all-too-human flaws and all too many enemies. Spider has enemies as well, and radiation is as intangible as a spirit. Might it not therefore affect a spirit?''

"You don't sound like you're sure it can.''

"Even if it cannot, there will be effects beyond the physical if Spider employs the weapons with that end in mind. Rival spirits work through people as well, and they could not work on this earth if they had no agents. I think that you will find that Spider has no love for Dog, or for Coyote. The Spider and nuclear weapons combination has a great potential for disaster.''

"You're not even sure this is happening,'' Sam accused, on a hunch. The elf stared at him venomously, but Urdli's silence spoke to Sam of the truth of his accusation. Even so, just the possibility of nuclear weapons in the hands of someone who might use them was frightening. It was a fear that had dominated previous generations, and although it had subsided since the build-down, it had never entirely gone away. Sam wondered if man had succeeded in breeding it into his bloodline. If the threat were real, the elf wouldn't be the only one seeking to cancel it. "I don't think I trust you, Urdli.''

"Your trust is not desired. Your cooperation, however, is required. You have a responsibility.''

Sam looked away from the intensity of the elf's stare. When he had been a member of the Renraku corporate family, he had understood the burden of responsibility as the Japanese did. They called it *giri,* and made of it a load they could never put down. *Giri* could never be completely discharged, but that did not stop one from continually attempting to do so. Sam understood responsibility well enough to feel the weight of it on his shoulders. He didn't like the idea of some strange elf dictating to him the nature of his responsibilities and the way to discharge them. So what, if he had unwittingly released some part of a captive totem? That didn't make him responsible for the plans or actions of the totem's avatars.

Did it?

Sam couldn't be responsible for the whole world. So why did he feel like he ought to do something about it? He turned to Howling Coyote.

"What should I do?"

"I'm Coyote. You're Dog. Why ask me?"

Sam tried to catch the shaman's eyes and divine his true feelings, but the old man refused to look at him. Was this another test, the shaman's answer a riddle to be solved? If so, the proper response seemed easy. Dog was loyalty, and who should he be more loyal to than his family? Sam turned back to Urdli.

"I say I have some responsibility to recover your guardian stone. You were willing to kill me to get it before and didn't even tell me what you wanted. If you had explained the situation, I might have given the stone to you. It hadn't proved effective for my needs. Your actions don't leave me thinking much of you." The elf seemed unconcerned about Sam's opinion of him. "I have to admit to taking it, but I did it for what I consider an important reason. I was only interested in the power the stone would let me focus. Not that it helped in the end. Still, if I'd known what it was, I suppose I would never have taken it in the first place. I'd have found another focus. How was I supposed to know the place was some kind of citadel? It looked like an old cave.''

Howling Coyote snickered quietly, but Sam didn't let the sound disturb him. "If what you say about Spider's plans is true, I'd like to help. But right now, I've got a pressing family problem. You said you're not even sure what the stone will do to help your enemy. Even if you knew it was an immediate threat, you don't know where it is. It sounds like you've got a bit of leeway. Even if it is a danger, you still need to find it. That's something you can do without me because I haven't got the faintest idea of how to track it.

"I haven't got the luxury of time. I've only finished my own hunt recently, and still haven't got what I want." Sifting sand from one hand to the other, the old man ignored Sam's meaningful glance. "Time's pressing on me. I'm trying to avert a terrible result that is certain to come, but you're just worried about possibilities. I'm not worried about something that *might* affect the whole world, but something that *will* destroy a life—the life of someone dear to me. Right now I've got my priorities lined up. I've put off helping my sister for too long, and I'm going to do what I can for her before I even think of anything else. When she is saved, we can talk again."

Urdli glared at him, then shifted his burning stare to Howling Coyote. The old man dumped the sand from his hands, dusted them off, and shrugged. He mumbled as he got to his feet and walked away.

"Foolishness."

Sam couldn't tell if the old man was referring to him or to the elf.

27

The lights of Seattle were seductive. Across Puget Sound the myriad denizens of the metroplex were going about their nightly business. Salarymen and corporates were on their way home, or perhaps still clacking keyboards and tapping in orders in an effort to impress their bosses and get a leg up over their fellows. The street haunts were crawling out to scene, shift for a buzz, or wrangle for turf. The hopeful relaxed, another day successfully completed, and the hopeless sagged with another one survived and only the night to face. On the edges and in the shadows, the runners were doing their biz. She could not see any of them, but the lights of the plex shone on all those scurrying little people. And the lights sang of their doings, burning the song into the air and promising such a rich feast of life. Oh yes, the lights were seductive.

Janice looked at them and felt her stomach growl. The hunger grew with each day. Had it been an ordinary hunger, the pangs would have stopped days ago. When a human starves to death, hunger dies within his empty belly long before his body surrenders to death. Meat she had had, but not real nourishment. The steady diet of small furred things Ghost was providing kept her alive, but failed to sate the hunger.

How many more nights until she could stand it no longer?

She was tired, worn from her struggle. She lay back, feeling as though she might sleep. She had fought off the urge all day, through her normal sleeping time, just to avoid the dreams. She had lain restless within the

darkness of the basement of the house where she and
Ghost hid, waiting for her brother to come up with a
solution. A slim hope, at best. And didn't she know
better than to hope? There had been no word from him
for days and he was probably dead.

So why did she wait?

She was tired, but sleep brought the nightmares.
She didn't want to sleep, but somehow she fell into its
embrace.

In sleep, they waited for her.

They waited, the faces, all as one and one as all.
She slipped deeper into the dark realms, past the places
of rest. She hung at the doors of the precincts of res-
toration and looked through the locked panels wist-
fully. Satiating the hunger was the only restorative for
her now. A small voice whispered of another way, but
she didn't believe what it said. The voice belonged to
a man, and all men were liars. They proved their per-
fidy when they pounced.

She laughed with joy when his arms went around
her. He held her close, slipping easily into the com-
pass of her great, brawny arms. For all his elven slimness, her Hugh was strong. He reminded her of Dan
Shiroi, but that was impossible, because she hadn't
met Dan yet. Hugh laughed at her confusion. But his
eyes didn't laugh. How could they? Those golden orbs
did not belong to Hugh, but to the evil one who had
brought the change.

She tore herself from the grasp of the golden-eyed
Hugh and ran, but she could not escape the eyes. They
bore down upon her and pinned her to a table. Cold
steel pressed against her naked back and straps bound
her wrists, ankles, waist, and brow to the hard metal.
Empty white coats drifted around her in a dance of
scientific enquiry. The eyes had their own questions.

She had questions too. Why? Why? And why?

The terrible gold eyes stared through her as though
she didn't exist. The man who owned them didn't an-

swer her questions. He ignored her pleas and asked the questions that were his and not his. She tried to answer, but he was always disappointed in her. Why should he be any different from other men? She wanted to answer him, he deserved her answers. He was authority, and her life was his to redeem or cast away. She knew that was true because he told her so.

She remembered him leaning close to her ear and whispering his name. She knew this was a real memory, just as she knew what had seemed a nightmare at the time was real. He was so very real, even if his eyes were not. His identity had made her tremble, for it meant the end of the world as she had come to know it. He had spoken his name and laughed, telling her that the drugs would take it away and leave her only with the memory of having known it once. She had screamed at him for mercy until she cried, but he had seemed to think her reaction all the finer a jest.

She had been human then.

She hadn't known real pain.

He had taught her.

Or rather, the white coats had.

"Not the solution," they said, in a ghostly chorus of disembodied voices, when they had finished. "She has told all and tells nothing."

"Unacceptable," Gold Eyes said in her brother's voice.

"She cannot be restored," the coat chorus pronounced.

"Unacceptable."

Always the same judgment.

The biggest of the white coats moved to Gold Eyes' side. "An experiment that will at once provide data and dispose of the problem. Data. The BioDynamics formula. Data. Metamorphosis. Data. Paradynamic perturbations in the Kano actualization curve. Data. Data for all."

Gold Eyes looked at her, sliding along her legs, past

her crotch and over her breasts. When she stared into those eyes, he spoke.

"Proceed."

Unacceptable!

Needles! Too many needles!

But Hugh was there to comfort her, and the awful table was gone. They lay on the scratchy, vermin-infested bed they had called home on Yomi. In thunder and lightning they made love, and he filled and drained her simultaneously. She loved him and pledged him her life again, as she had on Yomi. He caressed her breast and fur sprouted after the passage of his hand; he smoothed her hair and her sandy blond tresses thickened and turned a frigid white. His kiss lingered on her lips. His tongue flickered into her mouth, only to draw away and pull her canines into fangs.

She cried with the pain and he laughed. They all laughed until the sound became a wail of mourning.

Janice Verner was dead. Betrayed and murdered. Her dreams were ashes.

Her mother's eyes were filled with tears and her father's eyes glistened. He was too much a man to shed tears. She ran toward them, wanting to bury herself in their arms. She passed through their outstretched arms like a ghost. But it was they who were ghosts, not she. She could not yet join them.

Why should she want to? They had not been there for her when Gold Eyes had given her to the white coats, or Ken had spurned her, or the boat had carried her to Yomi. They had not been there for her since that awful night when they had left her with Sam. Sam, the strong older brother who had carried her away and taken her to the embrace of dear old Renraku. Sam, the protector who had left her with Gold Eyes. Sam, the defender who had let them ship her to Yomi. Sam, the slayer of the only true lover she had known.

Her stomach growled with hunger. Righteous hunger. She was awake.

* * *

Dodger slammed his fist into the telecom's keyboard. The soft flesh of his hand protested the treatment, promising to bruise for days as a reminder of its limitations. What did it matter? It was only meat. Confining, restrictive meat.

How could they do this? How could they dare?

It was bad enough that they had the temerity to rip him from the Matrix. But to steal his cyberdeck! Even the telecom was disconnected from the Matrix and locked into a house-only circuit. He was not a child anymore. This time the old punishment wouldn't stop him.

Though no longer surrounded by the glories of cyberspace, he knew where he was. He knew it too well. How he had gotten here was a mystery, but it was a mystery of the flesh and that wasn't important.

He had to get back into the Matrix.

How long had he been gone? Her time was not meat time. Did she miss him? Or was he a fading memory, like last year's news, or last century's? Away from the Matrix, he was not part of her existence. Was it already too late?

They might try to lock him out of the Matrix and into this finely furnished cell, but he was the Dodger. He could never be confined.

He didn't bother to check the lock before prying open the control plate. Having lived in comfort too long, they had forgotten what could be done with ordinary things. In less than ten seconds he had scrambled the security circuits enough to open the lock. He was reasonably sure that he hadn't set off an alarm, either.

He felt light-headed. The exhilaration, he supposed. The hall floor was cold against his bare feet, and the speed of his motion made a cool breeze across his naked flesh. Ills of the flesh. Unimportant. As unimportant as his nakedness.

Naked. How appropriate. Soon it would be more so. As soon as he reached his goal. He knew the mansion well.

He padded down the back stairs. Two full flights, and three steps of the next flight. He reached down to the floorboard, steadying himself against the railing as his fragile flesh threatened to betray him. His fingers found the latch and lifted it. A panel rose, revealing a hollow in the wall.

It was there, just as he remembered: a monitor station. A few keystrokes brought him the message that the connections were all active. He smiled. Fumbling open the storage compartment, he drew forth the datacord. His fingers were clumsy—nothing but weak flesh things—but he got one end of the cord into his datajack and the other into the port on the station.

He curled the fingers of his left hand into his palm and gave his wrist the fast double-cock needed to release the prongs. Three tapering cylinders of silver slid from the ectomyelin sheaths in his forearm.

You can take the decker away from the cyberdeck, but you can't take the Dodger away from his key to the Matrix.

Naked he would go forth to find her.

They said it was too dangerous to enter cyberspace without the buffer of a cyberdeck. They were right, of course; it was dangerous. But he had done it before. Decker slang called it "jacking in naked" when only the decker's organic brain stood as defense against the dangers of IC and the navigational peculiarities of the Matrix. An organic brain was a fragile thing to stand between the crystalline fury of ice and the darkness of death.

But what matter danger? A threat to the organic existence was no threat at all, for *she* was not part of organic existence. She was waiting for him in cyber-space, and Dodger would go to meet her.

He slid the prongs into the station's data ports, and the infinite glories of the Matrix exploded in his head, filling his soul with their wonder. He saw her in the distance, waiting.

"Morgan," he called, using the name she had chosen for herself. "I'm coming."

He flew to her side.

*   *   *

Sato inspected his arm. To all appearances, it was a normal human arm. The doctors had done their job well. He lifted the gown's sleeve to seek the join. The scar was already fading under the influence of fast-healing drugs and skin-regenerative implants. Very well, indeed.

"Akabo."

The enhanced soldier who served as his bodyguard rose smoothly to his feet and crossed the small room. He was still wearing the tight-fitting leathers he preferred for street work.

"Any word from Masamba?"

A slight shake of the head. "Mage is still looking. Matrix team is still hunting as well."

"Then it will be some time before your special talents are needed. I suggest that you pay a visit to the medical team and express my thanks for their work. The usual payment."

Smiling grimly, Akabo nodded. "What about Soriyama? He assembled the team."

"Leave him alive. The good doctor is too valuable. Though a brilliant man, he is not impractical, as are so many scientists. He will understand the warning."

"Yeah. And he's a bit too tight with Grandmother."

Akabo flinched back at Sato's reaction. Sato held down the impulse to take his bodyguard by the throat and drain him dry. Let the threat of his anger be enough for now. Akabo would not be so bold as to mention the subject again. Intimidation was enough for now. The killer was himself too valuable to lose.

For the moment.

28

Howling Coyote cut off the song in mid-note and put the flute down. "Why am I bothering?"

"Because you promised to teach me," Sam said.

"Hey hey, Dog boy, wasn't talking to you. Don't need you to tell me the answer. I already know it."

"Then why—never mind." Sam was tired. He had been working all morning at perfecting the shuffling steps the shaman had shown him, but obviously not hard enough for Howling Coyote. In spite of the simplicity of the dance, Sam continued to lose the pattern after only a few minutes. It was as though he couldn't match the rhythm of the music for more than a short period. Though the music didn't seem to change, Sam continued to end up out of step.

It was all so simple. So why couldn't he get it right?

He wiped a sweaty forearm across a sweatier brow, then held his arm there to shade his eyes as he looked at the sky. No wonder the old man was exasperated. The sun was low in the sky, and Sam had not managed to keep the dance going for more than half an hour. The history chips said that the Ghost Dancers had performed their ritual for days on end, fresh dancers taking the place of the exhausted, without ever a break in the pattern. The power Sam needed to help Janice wouldn't require that level of performance, but Sam knew he was still not going strong enough or long enough.

"Are you going to play some more?"

Howling Coyote shrugged, then spat. "Ain't what I want to do at issue here."

"You're the teacher," Sam objected. "I'm here to learn lessons from the master. Seems to me you're not doing your job very well. You promised to teach me."

The old man's eyes narrowed, and he stood. "Ya want a lesson, I'll give ya a lesson. Ya gotta strip yourself clean before ya can do the big magics." The shaman's hand snaked out and grabbed the pendant that swung from a thong around Sam's neck. He waved it in front of Sam's eyes, then let it drop heavily against Sam's chest. "What's that, Dog boy? What's that thing you wear around your neck?"

"A fossil tooth that I use as a power focus."

"Uh-huh. And those things ya got tied onto your jacket?"

"Fetishes. They help with the magic."

"Uh-huh. Got all ya started with?"

"Of course not. I lost a lot of them when Urdli blasted me through the Weapons World window."

"Uh-huh. What's the tooth and the fetishes ya got left have in common? Where'd ya get them?"

"I found the tooth in the badlands, just before I met Dog for the first time. I thought it was a dragon tooth at the time. Dragons are magical beasts, so I made it into something to help me with my magic. That's what the fetishes are, magical tools I made to help me."

"What about the other stuff?"

"What other stuff?"

"The pictures in the inside pocket, left front."

Sam didn't bother to ask how Howling Coyote knew about that. "They're just pictures. They're not magical."

"They show your sister, your brother, and your parents, right? What's more magical than family? It's real important to you, Dog boy. Leastways, that's what ya told Urdli. Ya telling me connections ain't important to magic?''

Sam wasn't sure what answer the shaman wanted.

"Ya don't have to answer that. Answer this, though. What've they all got in common?''

Nothing. Everything. Sam didn't know. What was the old man driving at? All he could do was guess. "They're all connected to my magic.''

"Think up that answer by yourself?''

"Yes, I did.''

"Just yourself?''

Exasperated, Sam snapped, "Yes, just myself.''

"Exactly.'' The old man sat down, took off his reservation hat, and laid it on the ground beside him. From his pouch he took a comb, then he began to braid his hair. The gray strands glinted like metal in the sunset. "Now build a fire.''

It took Sam better than an hour to arrange the wood to the shaman's satisfaction. Following Howling Coyote's directions, Sam gathered herbs from the jars on the shelf in the kiva and brought them to the shaman, who scattered some over the wood and some into the air. The rest he made into a little pile atop the small bundle of plant fiber and kindling. Then he directed Sam to bring a coal from the kiva's firepit to light the fire.

The fire caught at once, and Sam was glad. Chilled by the early evening breeze, he craved the warmth of the fire. He wanted to sit by it and relax, but Howling Coyote had other plans.

"Follow me,'' the shaman ordered. "Do the steps as I do. Listen to the chant. Sing it when you know it.''

Howling Coyote began a shuffling, stomping dance around the perimeter of the fire. His voice was low and gravelly as he sang the chant. He beat time with a rattle made from a hollow gourd. The song grew in strength until it throbbed with power. It was a calling song:

He comes, in fire and smoke.
He comes, opening the way.
He comes, with lies and truth.
Turning to beauty, he comes.

Sam followed in the dance, moving in perfect rhythm to the song. Smoke washed across his body and filled his nostrils with the rick, resinous odor of burning pine. The chant filled his mind and he joined the song, his voice blending with the old man's. They danced the moon into the sky.

The smoke that had seemed to reach out and enfold Sam pulled back. It hung low over the fire, in defiance of the leaping flames. The smoke gathered into a roiling cloud that obscured the shaman dancing on the opposite side of the firepit. A shape began to coalesce within the cloud. It stretched, arms reaching for the sky. Though human from waist to neck, the smoke image had the head of a coyote. Its pointed snout split wide in a canine grin, then snapped shut. Head raised, it howled soundlessly at the moon. The snout came down and the ghostly image turned its dark, knowing eyes of emptiness on Sam. The jaws opened again, pausing briefly in that grin before yawning wider and engulfing him.

Sam's consciousness swirled in the magic. Enfolded in its embrace, he was at harmony with the world and with himself. He was not afraid.

He sensed that he was whole now, all he was and all he had ever been. At first he let himself float, riding the mana stream, letting it take him deeper into the otherworld, into himself, and into the unbridled realm of magic. For magic was the root and he needed to see the beginning, the seeds of his trials and triumphs.

When had it begun? When had magic first touched his life?

He thought about his first meeting with Dog, but immediately realized that as potent and outlandish as that experience had been, the magic had touched him even before that. According to Professor Laverty, Sam had used magic to protect himself from an attacker's spell long before meeting his totem. Sam remembered the glade and the fireball that had blasted him, burning his clothes and nearly killing him. He hadn't even known what he was doing at the time, but he had deflected the mana force of the spell. Would that have been the first time magic had affected his life? It was the first personal, tangible effect he could remember. His earlier contacts had been simply as an observer when someone else had used a spell. Surely that had to be it.

He cast his mind back, willing the magic to let him relive his first magical experience. Surely there was something to be learned now that he understood magic better. This must be what Howling Coyote intended by arranging this dream flight. Howling Coyote had hinted that it would be a key to his life and Janice's. If that were true, Sam would use that key to unlock the chains that bound her.

The magic embraced him and swirled him away. Time slipped from the present to the past, merging the two. *Then* became *now* and he was as he was then, except that memories of things yet to happen also wrapped his perceptions. Twist the shaman coexisted with Sam Verner, mundane.

The spell almost broke when he realized the day and time to which he had been projected. It was nine o'clock on the night of February 7, 2039. He was young, a teenager who was still Sammy to his family. That wouldn't last long. In an hour, he would be an orphan.

February 7, 2039, the terrible day that later became

known as the Night of Rage. On that night, the world spasmed in a massive explosion of violence. Though metahumans were mainly the victims of the destructiveness and brutality, in some instances they struck back, individually and in groups. In major cities and metroplexes, riots and fires raged for days. In the less urbanized areas, the violence sputtered on for weeks. The media blamed it on everything from outside psychic influences and coincidence to the spontaneous release of repressed aggressions and any other magical or scientific reason the various experts could think to spout. Somehow, the media hounds never saw their own role, never realized that the global village created by communications was also a powder keg of emotions that a single spark could set off across the world.

Like so many other families, the Verners were involuntarily caught in the violence. That evening Sammy's father had made a rare, impetuous suggestion that the whole family abandon their usual routine and go out to dine. Mother had insisted that Janice must be home in bed by ten, but Father, uncharacteristically, had overruled her. The occasional late night never hurt anyone, he said. They had all bundled up, walked the three blocks to the metro, and then boarded the bullet train to the Greenbelt Mall District.

The dinner was fun, but his parents' jolly mood crumbled as the family headed for the theater. Already the public tridscreens were running the first reports of the fire in the warehouse district of Seattle, where thousands of metahumans were being burned to death and a terrorist group calling itself the Hand of Five was taking responsibility. Father's face went grim and determined as he listened to the reactions of the crowd in the mall, most of whom seemed sympathetic to the terrorists. Father herded them to the metro, and they took the first train back to the burbs. Sammy sensed the fear beneath his parents' concern. Oliver and Janice felt it, too. Oliver and Father spoke quietly together for a while, then Oliver turned around to smile at Sam and Janice and told them it would all be fine. He was scared, too; Sammy could smell it. But Sammy took his cue from Oliver and tried to hide his own growing fear. Not so Janice, who began to whimper and demand that Mother hold her. There wasn't much conversation during the train ride. Most of the people on board echoed the same racist sentiments the Verners had heard expressed at the mall.

As they got off the metro, Sammy knew something was wrong. The neighborhood was lit as brightly as day, but day had never been so red. All the dogs in the neighborhood were barking.

When the Verners reached their street, they saw their house in flames. The wall fence around the property was battered down in places, while some sections still standing were scrawled with words such as "Ork Luvver," "Race Traitor," and other less savory things. Through one gap, Sammy could see a stark and obscene silhouette. He puzzled at the shape, but Twist knew what the boy he had been was seeing. It was their handyman Varly. The poor ork had been crucified on their front lawn.

Father whispered something to Mother. He ordered Oliver to stay with her. She took hold of Janice and Sammy's hands. Striding forward, Father headed for the knot of people gathered near the driveway. Tears streamed down Mother's face. Oliver looked annoyed and glared after Father, but he stayed put. Sammy heard his father's angry voice demanding to know what was going on, ordering the mob to disperse.

They jeered at him.

He repeated his demands and they laughed, an animal sound, wild and dangerous. One came forward and shouted something incoherent into Father's face. Another crept out and swung a fence board against the back of Father's knees. As the elder Verner collapsed, the one who'd shouted at him sidestepped to let him fall to the sidewalk. Then the mob rushed in, beasts tearing at the fallen foe.

Oliver rushed forward, disappearing instantly among the surging crowd. Sammy heard screams, but they sounded too high-pitched to be Oliver's. They sounded like a girl's screams. Twist knew better.

The mob reached them. Mother shoved Sammy and Janice behind her, but someone tore her away. Sammy grabbed his sister and ran. A howling rose behind them, and he dragged her along even faster. Turning down the alley between the Foster and Lee places, he knew he couldn't outrun the mob; he was just a kid and he was carrying his little sister. Pulling Janice into the deep shadows around the Fosters' shed, he crouched there, tucking Janice against the building and covering her head with his arm. He'd protect her as best he could. He tucked his own head down and closed his eyes.

He wanted to run away from these awful people, find a better place to hide. Twist understood as the terror-born, desperate need of young Sammy Verner called to the city spirit, wrapping its protection around him and his sister. It was only a small, weak spirit, much too small to have covered and hidden the whole family from the mob, even if it were not already too late.

A tentacle of the mob surging down the alley brushed unseeing past the huddled children. Not finding its victims, the tentacle retracted back to its parent body as the mob moved on down the street. Now they turned their fury against the Andersons' house, burning it completely before moving on again.

Sammy stayed huddled where he was, hugging his sister. Sam didn't dare move even after she had cried herself to sleep. She needed her sleep. Mother had said so. He cried, too, but would not let himself sleep.

Then a man came walking down the street and crossed the mouth of the alley. He was dressed in fine clothes. The flickering light of the fires glittered from gold on his fingers and from the head of his cane. He looked like a rich businessman, out of place in the burbs. But he didn't act out of place; he acted instead as though he owned it all. Sammy Verner didn't know him, but Twist did.

The man was Mr. Enterich, an agent of the dragon Lofwyr. Ever since the Haesslich affair, Enterich had been a symbol of duplicity for Sam, the perfect corporate false front for the savage and duplicitous maneuverings of the worm that gnawed at the wood of society. Twist had no memory of Enterich being present that night.

Sammy Verner watched the well-dressed man stroll down the street until he reached the broken gate of the Verner house. Leaning on his cane, the man contemplated the fire. At length a shadow flitted over Sammy and his sister, moving across the street in a curving arc before it vanished. But it returned again, and this time Sammy looked up to see enormous bat wings spread against the paling stars. It was a dragon. The creature banked and came to a silent landing at Enterich's side. It was not Lofwyr.

"Success?"

"No trace, no trail. The line must be extinguished." The dragon exuded satisfaction. *"The losses of time spent dreaming are recouped this night. The herd is culled, and the small rivals shall find no allies. They burn. Everywhere, they burn. Are not the flames wonderful?"*

"Perhaps," Enterich replied. "I fear this noise that echoes around the world tonight. It is out of control, and the resulting chaos might demand a high price."

"Temerity. But dawn comes and we must be away." The dragon stretched its wings.

Sammy hid his head. Despite his own leavening of experience Twist was overwhelmed by childish terror

and hid as well. Together the boy and man consciousnesses huddled in fear.

The sound of the beast's passage was a roaring moan. It might have been wind displaced by the force of the beast's wing stroke, or it might have been the voice of the mob. If indeed the two were different. Sammy loved symbols, and dragons were among the best. They were huge and powerful, strong and dangerous. They were elemental beasts that Twist could envision as chaos embodied. When he got up enough courage to look again, the dragon and the man were gone as though they had never been. Maybe they never had.

But his parents were really gone. His brother, too. Only their memories remained in his heart.

A skinny old Indian in a breech clout stood at his side. Howling Coyote. "Would you give your life to see them live again?"

Sam thought about that for a while, then shrugged. "What good would it do? They wouldn't like what the world has become. Sooner or later, naturally or not, they would die again, and I'd be responsible for making them face that trial again. They already died once. Let them be in peace."

"And if you had the power to change the world, to make it so they would like it? Would that make a difference?"

"No. They've earned their peace." Sam stood up. He was just Twist now, though the child Janice still sheltered under his protective arm. "But I'd change the world anyway. We all have the responsibility to make things better for ourselves and for our families. We all have to do what we can to make the world a better place."

"Better for your own ends?"

"Better for everybody."

"What about the cost?"

Sam looked at the bodies of his parents. They were

fading, even as the scene of the old neighborhood was fading. Even the child Janice was fading. "Can I pay less than they did to live up to my beliefs?"

"Very easily," the shaman said gravely. "Most people don't stand up and pay when it comes down to it."

"There's a price for everything. Sooner or later, you have to pay."

"Hey hey, Dog boy, there may be hope for you yet. That's the first step in the dance." Howling Coyote spun and capered away. "Or was it the last? I forget. I'm an old man, ya know."

Sam shook his head sadly and followed the shaman into the dawn.

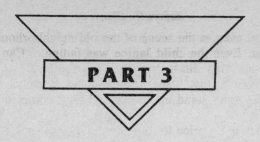

PART 3

Pay The Price

29

Sometimes the tunnel to the otherworld appeared in different forms, though its nature always remained the same. This time it seemed more an organic tube than a cavern, its rugose walls looking soft and seeming to radiate heat. The odor pervading the place was rank and slightly stale. Sam had the sensation of being in someone's mouth, which made him feel distinctly uncomfortable.

He probed ahead with his senses. The Dweller on the Threshold was out there, as always. Like the tunnel, it didn't always look the same. Once, the Dweller had been perverted by an evil wendigo and warped through some unknown magic to bar Sam from the totemic plane. Sam had faced his fears to overcome the barrier and ultimately defeat the wendigo. He had learned something of the nature of the Dweller in that experience, and believed he would know if the Dweller were ever more than its normal etheric self again.

He found the Dweller waiting for him. It felt ordinary, though its form was unusual. This time the Dweller manifested itself as a tightening of the passage. Stalactites hung in jagged rows, moving and clashing with stalagmites. Slime dripped and spattered from them, like spittle from the teeth of a hungry carnivore.

Hoping Howling Coyote had some advice to offer, Sam turned to him. As on previous occasions, the old shaman's appearance surprised him. Here on the astral, Howling Coyote still looked like an old man, scrawny and weather-beaten as in the mundane world. Sam would have expected such a powerful shaman to look more . . . well, powerful. The shaman sat on a rock that protruded from the cavern wall and leaned against the side of the shaft. It had been Howling Coyote's idea to take this trip, and the old man's apparent lack of interest irritated Sam.

"What are you doing sitting there?"

The shaman's eyes were closed and his face composed. His right shoulder twitched in the barest hint of a shrug. "Waiting."

"I thought we were going to see Dog."

"Not we. You. Dog's your totem, not mine, and you must find your own truth."

Sam felt vaguely betrayed. It was the first time he was going specifically to ask a favor of his totem. Howling Coyote must have done this thing often enough. Why didn't the shaman show him the ropes? "You're saying I have to go on alone."

A pipe materialized in the shaman's hand. He puffed on it and said nothing.

"If you're not coming with me to the otherworld, why did you bother coming this far?"

"Thought I could use the exercise."

Which was, of course, not the real reason, but Sam wasn't going to push it. This was probably some kind of test.

When he turned back to face the Dweller, Sam saw that the gnashing teeth had come closer while he talked to the shaman. Yet Sam had not moved. Months ago, such a minor displacement effect would have unnerved him. Now he just planted his feet, faced the clashing rock, and waited.

The tunnel had a voice that penetrated Sam's mind, like water seeping through porous rock. *"Welcome again, Samuel Verner. Or do you prefer that I call you Twist?"*

"Twist will do."

"Fine, Sam. Stolen any good artifacts lately, or have you been too busy ignoring your sister's problem?"

Sam didn't want to listen to the Dweller's innuendo, half-truths, and petty revelations of Sam's secrets and desires. He was plenty able to castigate himself without any help from some astral presence. "Let me pass."

"Sure." The stone teeth yawned wide. *"Go ahead."*

Sam took a step forward and the rocks clashed together. *"Oops. Too slow."* Once more the rock formations separated. *"Try again."*

The space encompassed by those teeth was too great to cross in a run before they could slam shut. But this was the astral world, and Sam knew other ways. Focusing his will he flew forward, whisking past the jagged rocks. They clashed behind him.

"Catch you again sometime, shirker."

Sam ignored the Dweller's parting comment and shot down—no, up—the tunnel. He emerged in a sunlit land of green fields, rolling hills, gentle forests, and pleasant vales. Smoke rose from homey cottages nestled in some of the valleys. Despite all that there was no sign of people, but Sam was used to that. He walked now because it seemed more appropriate, and appropriateness was paramount in the totem realm. He headed down the dirt road that led away over the hills.

Sam crossed three hills, each more difficult to climb than the last. He sensed that the fatigue he felt was due to more than the walking. By the time he reached the base of the fourth hill, he was almost exhausted. It was as though he'd been running for several kilometers, but he remembered only having walked along the road. Somehow he knew that more than a walk through the countryside had happened, but he had no memory of it. Determined to persevere, he started up the next hill.

Dog was waiting for him on the crest. The totem was

wearing his usual shape, a brindled mutt. His tail swept the dust, but he did not leap up or even stand at Sam's approach.

"I would like to speak with you," Sam said.

Dog turned his head away, seeming to make a scent inspection of a small weed growing near his side. "What makes you think I want to talk to you?"

"I need guidance."

Dog's head snapped up to look at Sam. The totem wore a canine grin. "That's for sure. How can I resist such blinding honesty? What do you want to talk about?"

There were many things, some very pressing, but Sam decided to start with what bothered him most. For all Howling Coyote's lessons the old shaman had never related a conversation with Coyote. Lots of proverbs concerning the totem, tales of the totem's doings, and confident assertions of the totem's demands, but never any words. "Maybe you'd like to tell me why you talk to me?"

"You sure that I do?"

Once, doubting the reality of totems, Sam hadn't been. He had thought that totems were merely psychological constructs through which a shaman organized his thoughts for magic, that they had no independent existence. He still wasn't completely convinced that totems were thinking entities in their own right, but he could no longer deny all evidence of that. Thus, he had accepted the necessity of dealing with the being sitting before him as though Dog were an independent entity. "Yes, I'm sure."

"Well, that's something." Dog cocked his head and observed Sam. "You're not a very good follower, you know. Don't pay anywhere near enough attention. Dogs like attention, you know."

"I know." Sam had raised enough real dogs to know that very well. "Sorry."

"I'd accept the apology if I thought it was worth

anything." Dog stood up. "Come on, let's go for a run."

Dog didn't wait for Sam to answer. Sam trotted after him. When he caught up, Dog broke into a run. Holding back his questions Sam ran, too.

It seemed that Dog had nothing more on his mind than exercise. Sam, however, had too much on his mind. After they had been running for what seemed a long time, he panted out a question.

"Do we have time for this?"

"There is no time as you know it here. So I guess we got plenty. Or none at all. Take your pick."

"I'll take plenty. I've got too much to do."

"True enough."

Dog stopped, and Sam ran for a few more meters. He stopped, catching his breath, and walked over to join Dog. The totem appeared unwinded.

"Need to build up your stamina."

"I'm working on it," Sam said.

"Work harder. It's a crime not to use what you have."

"And what's that?"

"Magic, man. It's in your blood."

"I don't really like the idea."

"Nobody said you had to, but that don't change anything." Dog sauntered over to a fence post, lifted a leg, and marked it. "Magic is my territory, man. You wouldn't be here if it wasn't yours, too." Dog inclined his head toward the fence post. "Want to make your mark?"

Sam shook his head. "No thanks. I went before I left the mundane."

Though a dog's shoulders aren't built to shrug, Dog managed one. Then he trotted over to the other side of the road and sat down where he could look out over the valley. Sam joined him and sat by his side. Neither said anything for a while. Then Dog stood and stretched, before cocking his head to regard Sam.

"You think the only magic is flash, mirrors, and fireworks?"

"Well, no."

"Good." Dog nodded his head once. "Magic is life, man. Some of your kind say it's all just a song and dance. Are they ever wrong! And right, too, which is the point. You start singing the song before you speak your first word, and dance the steps even after your flesh stops moving. Wise up and smell the world around you. It's marked by magic."

"I know," Sam said at last. "I've come to see that I have no choice but to use my magic. *My* magic. But that magic is tied to you, Dog. I came looking for help."

"Help? Or advice?"

"Well, both."

"Sure you don't want power, too?"

"Well, yes, that too." No point in putting it off. "I came to learn the secret of the Great Ghost Dance."

"What makes you think it's only got one secret?"

"If there's more than one, I want to learn them all."

"Pretty ambitious for a pup. You have any idea what you're asking?"

Sam knew what he wanted to do with the magic, but Howling Coyote hadn't really told him much about how the Dance worked. "Not really."

Dog sniffed at the grass at his side. "Magic, the world, and life stick together tighter than a burr in fur," he said finally. "The Dance is part of those connections, and all of them. You can't have one without the other. You sure you want to do this thing?"

"No."

"Good answer. We sure are being honest today." Dog barked a laugh. "But want to or not, you still gotta."

"Why?"

"Thought you learned to believe in me."

"I have."

"That's why you gotta. I'm Dog and you're Dog, man." Dog placed a paw on Sam's leg and stared him in the eye. "Dog is friend to Man, a guardian totem to protect him from evil. I don't see the web-spinner as being real healthy for man, do you?"

"No."

"See, I knew you were a bright boy even before the first time I laid eyes on you."

Something in Dog's tone made Sam suddenly suspicious. "Which was?"

"None of your business. I tell you everything and I lose my mystery. What good's a totem without mystery, huh?" Dog backed away from Sam, then shifted his feet in a most uncanine fashion. The plunging side step with his left forepaw looked particularly difficult for his canine anatomy. "You want to try this step, or not?"

If this was the Great Ghost Dance, he did. Sam stood and tried the step. The air around him deadened, as if thunder were being held in abeyance. He felt a phantom power coiling around the steps as he took them. Even the practice dance reverberated with the strength of the magic.

Dog showed him the steps and taught him the song. Sam was acutely aware of the danger of getting the ritual wrong. He tried very hard to memorize the moves and tones exactly. At last, Dog sat and looked at him. The totem's eyes were sad.

"You know that what you want is dangerous."

So what else was new? "I figured as much."

"You willing to pay the price?"

Sam nodded. "If it will do what I need it to do."

Dog shook his head slowly. "What makes you think your need is what drives the magic, or what will make it work for you?"

"Didn't you say that I need to protect mankind?"

"Man has the need to be protected. You have a desire, but is it the right one? Only you can know. But it had better be. The power you're toying with doesn't like being fooled. If you're not pure enough, it will toast you. And you're only touching the tip of the magic.''

"Just what is this purity?"

Dog started trotting down the road. "You'll know."

"How? When I find out I don't have it and get roasted?"

"Maybe." Dog stopped and looked back at him. "What do you want? There ain't no sureties in magic. It's just like life that way. You do your best and hope for the best. If you are in tune with your nature the power will flow, and all will be as it should. If not . . . well, let's just say you won't have to worry much in that case.''

"That's not very encouraging.''

"Like maybe I should scratch you behind the ears, give you a yummy, and lie to you?"

Dog turned away and began to run. This session was over. Sam turned his back on the otherworld and found himself in the tunnel. Howling Coyote still sat there, waiting and smoking.

"How did it go?"

"I can feel the magic." As Sam said it, he knew it was true. "I know I can do it, but I don't know how to deal with the mundane threat.''

Howling Coyote frowned, but something seemed to hide behind his expression. "The magic won't do it?"

"Only its part.''

The hidden smile appeared. "You *have* learned. Now all ya got to do is use your brain.''

"What do you mean?"

The smoking pipe vanished with a flick of the shaman's wrist. "Line up your dancers.''

"You're being as obscure as Dog. Doesn't anybody associated with magic ever speak plainly?''

The shaman laughed. "Not if they can avoid it. Keeps the riffraff out of the trade.''

"So what are you suggesting I do?"

"You're Dog, aren't you?" Howling Coyote asked, suddenly serious. "Summon your pack."

30

At first she thought it was another dream, but her surroundings hadn't changed. She was still in the basement of the abandoned house Ghost had chosen for them. The only thing out of place was the ghostly image of her brother, standing nearby and pressing on the protective circle she had made. Since she wasn't dreaming, he was really there—or rather, his astral projection was.

He looked worried.

She sat up and reached out to tug on the magic surrounding her, adjusting the ward to let him enter the circle. He drifted in to stand at her bedside.

"So, you're not dead," she said, reminding him that he'd left her hanging.

"No. I only came close a few times."

"So you ran into a few problems." She dismissed his comment with a wave of her hand, not wanting him to know she'd been worried. "Was that any reason not to call?"

"You sound like Mother."

The past was haunting her enough in her dreams. She didn't need him bringing old memories into her waking life. The dreams were full of tragedies enough. "Yeah, well. But you can't say I look like her anymore."

He looked abashed, as though realizing how his offhanded comment had hurt her. Let him be embarrassed; she didn't want his or anyone's pity. "I suppose you've been busy working on that."

"Yes, but . . ."

"But it's hopeless," she finished for him. She had known it would be. His quest to Denver had just been time wasted. She was what she was; there was no way to change it.

"That's not what I was going to say." He sounded annoyed. "I don't think it's hopeless, but it's not going to be soon."

So he wanted her to continue trying to ignore the hunger. Didn't he know how hard that was? "What do you think I am? A saint?"

"No, I know you're just human."

She laughed bitterly at that.

"No matter what you look like, you're still human. That's why you're still trying to beat the wendigo nature. You know what being a wendigo means, and you know it's wrong."

So what if she did? She *was* a wendigo now. The wendigo nature was *her* nature, even if she hadn't yet surrendered to her craving. "Who says I even *want* to change now?"

"You do. You shout it every day you live without killing and eating anyone."

"What about the dzoo? Doesn't it count?"

He looked sad. "God forgives the repentant."

"He tasted good." She said it to annoy him, but it was also the truth. The dzoo *had* tasted good, much better than the stuff Ghost brought her. She turned away, shivering. Whether the memory-borne chill was one of delight or horror, she wasn't sure. He noticed her reaction.

"See. You're not resigned to the inevitable. That means you still have hope, and that will be your salvation." He moved around in front of her. "I know about the food Ghost had been hunting for you. I've already talked with him. You'll only have to put up with it a while longer.''

"Yeah, well. Maybe I will and maybe I won't. You telling me that you're ready to try again?''

He hesitated. "Well, I was hoping to, but something has come up. Something very important.'' In a jumbled rush, he told her about Spider and what he had learned of her plans. After sketching a bare outline of the facts, he took a deep breath and said, "I'm sorry, Janice. I hope you'll understand that this is more important than any one person.''

Something was always more important. "So much for your claims of love.''

"I know how it must sound. I wish there were another way, but I don't see one. There just isn't time to take care of you first. There's too much at stake.''

"Yeah, right. Who cares about one soul when the world's in danger?''

"That's not fair. Or true, either. It's just the despair of the wendigo talking. If you don't want to accept that an obligation to mankind is involved, look to your totem. Wolf is a pack animal. What's a pack but an extended family, and a family has to take care of its own. I have to do this thing. You're part of the family, too.''

His indignation made her mad. She growled. "So take care of your own. You're the one who insists that we're still family.''

"And we *are* family,'' he said firmly. "But we're part of a bigger family,'' he went on, more softly now. "I can't let the whole family die so that one member can live.''

The good of the many. How often had she heard that? Well, she didn't want to hear it. The many hadn't given a thought to her, and she intended to return the favor. She wanted to worry about herself. Waving her arm in dismissal, she said, "So go ahead and do what you want to do. You don't need my permission. I might even be here when you're done.''

He refused to go. ''It's not what I *want* to do; it's what I *need* to do, what has to be done. And it's not your permission I want, but your help.'' He said more, pointing out the awful consequences of Spider's plot. From what Sam was telling her, the results might be almost as bad if other unspecified but ambitious parties were able to gain what Spider sought.

Surprising herself, she listened.

* * *

Awaken.

Aleph's nudge brought her to instant awareness: she had a visitor. Her ally spirit's astral watch made a perfect complement to the electronic security measures incorporated into the townhouse walls. She readied a spell but, before she could shift perceptions, the ghostly image of Sam materialized outside the second-story window of the bedroom. Then it walked through wall, sill, and transparex to stand grinning at her. Obviously, he had gotten the note telling him where to contact her.

She smiled back. ''Nice to see you, lover. It's been a long time.''

''Worried, dear Hart?''

''Me? I never worry. But I'm really glad to see you survived. And strong enough to do a distance projection. Been practicing, have we? Wish we could touch.''

He mimed a hug. ''Best I can do. Magic doesn't make all wishes come true.''

''Only in fantasy. Speaking of which, I've had a few good ones recently. How about you?''

''I fear my dreams have been all business.''

''Comes with the trade, oh mighty shaman. How's the hunt going?''

His expression darkened, clouded by a complex of emotions that she couldn't read. His voice lost its ban-

tering lightness. "One's over. Another's about to begin. But you should know, you're already on the
scent."

He had to mean something else; he seemed too jo-
vial to have found out about her connections. She hung
her head and held it, hands covering her surprised expression. She hoped she was doing a credible imitation
of someone still groggy from sleep. "Hey, I just woke
up. Can we save the mysterious for *after* my first cup
of kaf?"

"Sorry," he said with an apologetic grin. "I meant
you're already near the Deggendorf cache, of course.
It's the highest-probability target for Spider, and with
you already there, we'll get a jump on Urdli."

"Whoa, Sam. It sounds like a lot has turned up
since I left for the continent. Let's take it from the
top." He did, jumbling his meetings with Howling
Coyote, Dog, and the Australian elf Urdli all together.
With amazement, Hart realized that what she'd thought
was a more personal level of business was turning out
to be an international conspiracy. She hated it when
the big boys decided to throw their weight around.
Sam was right; if the Tir or the Australian elf were
left to clean up the mess alone, there would be trouble.
God forbid if the Irish Shidhe or some fire-breathing
corporate types got wind of it. Quick, clean, and as
quiet as possible was the only way to go. "I'll get
Jenny running yesterday. We'll need any data we can
get. Dodger could help."

Sam frowned, and she felt distress mixed with his
frustration. "If I knew how to contact him, I'd ask.
He hasn't been at any of his usual places, not even the
fallbacks we'd arranged. Ghost's people have checked.
If he hadn't added that note to his last data dump, I'd
be really worried. I wish you hadn't left him, Hart."

"I'd say I'm sorry, but that won't turn him up. If
you can't find him in the real world, try the Matrix."

"Got a reason?"

"A hunch. I can have Jenny check, if you want."

"No," he responded quickly. "I'll take care of it."

"Going to be a busy boy."

"I'll manage. We're all going to be busy."

"Then why are we talking instead of doing?"

"No good reason. But I know what I'd like to be doing."

"Me, too. But it's more than a bit impractical at the moment."

"Especially since we're not sharing the same plane of reality."

She blew him a kiss and his projection faded from sight.

Seeing him again reminded her of how much she missed him. His astral projection was worse than a telecom call. She threw herself in the shower to scrub away the frustration. It wasn't long before she put aside her longings and turned her mind to the problems at hand. Personnel. Equipment. Timing. More than enough to keep her from fretting over a lover thousands of kilometers away, but she worried about him anyway.

* * *

Dodger didn't know where Morgan was taking him. He didn't care. Being in her presence was rapture. He was content to follow along, to see what she wished him to see, and to learn what she taught him. Foremost, he was learning how little he knew of the workings of the Matrix. He had believed himself an expert on cyberspace and was discovering how wrong he was. But then, how much could a meat being know compared to one whose very existence was in, and of, the Matrix?

They flew through the midnight voids of the electron sky. She seemed to have a goal, for there was none of the darting and swooping that had accompanied their previous jaunts. He could see a humanoid icon ahead in the distance. The icon's hands were cupped to its face, and it seemed to be calling. Odd behavior, indeed.

As they drew nearer the icon, Dodger began to see details. The figure was of ordinary resolution, standard corporate-level imagery. It was, in fact, a corporate icon, a chrome salaryman in his chrome suit. Such images were nearly featureless, save for the owning corporation's logo and the identity codes of machine and operator. This one fit the profile, except that its identifying logo and codes had been erased. Rather amateurishly, Dodger thought, as he inspected the icon's signature. He could tell that the source of the icon imagery was Renraku.

Renraku was the megacorp that had designed Morgan. Did this icon have something to do with her? He studied it further. He was in no hurry; she had them cloaked in her power, and the icon's operator had no idea his location in the Matrix was being observed. The icon lowered its hands and moved off to a new location. Dodger saw the icon limp, and the pieces fell into place.

Dodger didn't believe the answer. He had only observed one icon that limped, and it had belonged to Sam Verner. What was Sam doing in the Matrix? Since taking up magic, he had forsworn the deck.

As though she were waiting for Dodger to identify Sam, Morgan uncloaked them. Or him, anyway, for Dodger suddenly lost sight of her icon. He knew she wasn't gone, because he could still feel her presence. It didn't make sense, but he accepted it. Much that happened around her didn't make sense. For example, why didn't she want Sam to know she was here? He might wonder, but he respected her decision. He addressed Sam's icon.

"What are you doing here, Sir Twist?"

The icon turned to face him with turtle slowness. Dodger knew the software involved and had never thought it so slow. Or was he faster now, by virtue of his association with her? More questions. But what was life without questions?

Sam's icon completed its turn and spoke. "Looking for you."

"Well, you've found me."

"I'm glad. I was afraid we'd lost you. We need you, Dodger."

"If 'tis Matrix matters, I'd be happy to oblige; but if 'tis other, I fear I must decline, for I have matters to attend to here."

Sam paused. Microseconds or decades, it didn't matter to Dodger. She was here for him, even though he couldn't see her just now. Sam was thinking, calculating with meat slowness.

"You've found it, haven't you?"

"Her," Dodger said by way of correction.

"I see." There was a longer pause. "Dodger, there are people, living people, who need your help. Let me show you. I'll tell you all about it when you jack out."

"Nay."

Another pause. A growing habit, in both frequency and duration. Finally Sam asked, "Can you take a data dump, then?"

"Certes."

Dodger skimmed the data as it flowed. It included the material Dodger had gotten from Neko Noguchi, along with several reports from that industrious young runner who Dodger had never seen—although the data entry was logged through on his codes. Much was speculation, but all was serious. Spider was a real threat.

When the dump was finished Sam said, "There are still missing pieces, Dodger. Some of those pieces are loose in the Matrix. Jenny's looking for them, but time's short. I need you, Dodger. I need everyone I can trust working on this."

So he trusts me now, Dodger thought, but said nothing.

Sam asked his next question slowly, as though fearful of the answer. "Are you working with the AI?"

"Surely you do not find that a problem. She is, after all, responsible for your being a shadow in the Matrix."

"I thought that was you."

"Nay. She made me a gift of your records, everything from SIN to secret files. But for her good offices, new files would have accumulated. You have much to thank her for."

"Yeah, well, I guess so." A pause. "I don't want to seem ungrateful, or greedy, but do you think that maybe she'd help again?"

"Mayhap. But 'tis not my place to say. She can go places and do things that deckers only dream about. She has shown me so much."

"Can she show you how to get what we need?"

He was certain she could. Whether she *would* was the question. "I can but ask."

"And can she do it without anyone finding out?"

How could he doubt? "She is the Ghost in the Machine. Can there be any question?"

There was a long pause. Sam's icon paled and flickered briefly, as if he had divided his attention, then returned to normal intensity. "Dodger, do you know what's happening outside?"

Circuitous redundancy, a flesh trait. Dodger decided to humor it. "You have dumped me the data, Sir Twist. I understand the importance."

The Sam icon shook its head. "That's not what I meant. I mean do you know what's happening to your body?"

" 'Tis just meat, a thing of confining flesh. It does not matter." Dodger laughed. "I roam the Matrix nearly at will now. Speak your needs, and I shall do what you request."

31

The astral defenses around the mansion were thick and strong, but passive rather than active. Certain that active presences were available to respond to any intrusion, Sam didn't want to be taken as an enemy. A battle could have dire consequences at this point, not the least of which was wasting time. So he stood on the outside and tapped at the wall, drumming on its surface with the steady insistence he heard running in his head.

It didn't take long before something came to investigate.

The small sphere floating through the barrier had tiny arms and legs that thrashed in a swimming motion. Its progress was slow, like a fish breasting a stiff current. Once through the pale yellow of the barrier, a portion of the sphere split and peeled back to reveal a single eye that stared at him.

The small spirit was a watcher, one of that particularly dumb breed that magicians used as messengers and for simple observation tasks. While it was trying to make up its mind what it should do next, Sam told it what he wanted.

"Tell the professor I need to speak to him."

"Who?" Its voice had a breathy quaver.

"The professor. Tell him I need to talk to him."

"Who?" it repeated.

Sam had no time for such nonsense. He reached out and snatched the thing, snapping the astral strings that bound it to its summoner. He gathered them up and re-wove them as he molded the whimpering spirit in his hands. Satisfied with his alterations, he tossed it back at the barrier. The watcher fled, bawling for the professor.

That ought to get somebody's attention.

Belatedly, Sam realized that the dumb thing might have been asking who he was, rather than wanting a repetition of whom he was asking for. Oh, well, too late to do anything about that now. The wall was shimmering, deepening in shade and seeming to become more opaque. Presences were gathering at what he wanted to call the top of the wall, but that didn't make sense because the wall had no top; his sense was of defenders gathering at the battlements. They knew he was here.

Something happened to the barrier to his left. A dozen presences exited the wall and rushed toward him. At first he thought they might be spells directed at him, but as they drew closer he realized they were astral projections. The welcoming committee of magicians was coming to meet him. Hoping to demonstrate his peaceful intent, he stood his ground with his arms by his side. To his relief, they halted a few meters away.

Sam looked them over as they studied him. Most he didn't know, but three he recognized at once. Urdli and Estios stood closest to Professor Laverty. A fourth magician, a dwarf, seemed vaguely familiar but Sam couldn't quite place him.

Laverty stepped past Estios and spoke. "You chose an unusual way of announcing yourself, Sam. I had not expected to meet you this way."

"There's a lot about me you don't expect, Professor. But then, nobody's always right." Sam hoped his grin had the right amount of confidence and nonchalance. "And the name's Twist, by the way."

The professor inclined his head, acknowledging Sam's pronouncement. *Score one.* Sam began to think he might actually have a reasonable chance at making the bargain he hoped for.

Then Urdli spoke up. "So why do you come here, mongrel? Your churlish noise and unseemly display have interrupted important work."

The elf was even more intimidating on the astral than on the mundane plane. Sam felt his cool beginning to slip. He pressed on, hoping he had guessed correctly and that his arguments were well prepared. "You could say that understanding and necessity have joined forces to bring me here. I have come to understand that you were right about my responsibility in this matter of Spider." Sam let Urdli begin to smile before he added, "And wrong. I have to do something about it, not for anything I've done, but for what I am. Even if I hadn't taken your guardian stone, I would have to be involved in this. My responsibility is to myself. I must be true to my totem."

"And by being true to your totem, you are true to yourself and thereby discharge your responsibility," Laverty said.

"Exactly."

Laverty smiled slightly. "You are an unusual man, Twist."

"He's a coward," Estios asserted.

"And a thief and an incompetent," Urdli said.

"And a shaman of considerable power," the dwarf added. "Gentlemen, we are in need of power to combat Spider. I do not think we should be blinded by prejudice and personal animosity. Twist demonstrated courage, skill, and unusual competence, if not foresight and caution, in removing the guardian stone from the citadel. He should not be dismissed as an addition to our forces."

"This isn't personal," Estios objected. "Objectively, he has shown that he's unsuitable. He let a wendigo go, just because it had been his sister and he couldn't face up to killing it. That is not the level of conviction demanded at this time."

"And he has once refused to help," Urdli said. "He

may withdraw the false offer of aid as soon as his fickle mind finds some other phantasm to chase.''

"Enough," Laverty said. "We have lain with stranger bedfellows in the past in order to do what was necessary." His attention shifted to Sam. "You have come here without being called; therefore you have something in mind. Do you have new information?"

"Some. I need more."

"Don't we all," Estios said.

Laverty ignored him. "Perhaps we can trade, but despite your plea for information, I'd wager you have already taken steps. Would you care to tell us your plan?"

"I'd rather not get specific." As if he could. "I've only got the bare outline of a plan. As I said, I still need information."

"And you expect to get it from us?" Urdli was incredulous.

"Yes," Sam said, as though there could be no question. "We're fighting the same enemy, after all."

Urdli huffed. "The enemy of my enemy is *not* my friend, but simply a convenience of war."

That was the reaction Sam had expected. "Fine. I'm not asking for friendship. I have a long memory, too. But we can be allies and pool our resources."

"What can you offer?" Urdli asked, his tone implying that he didn't believe Sam could have a thing.

"You surprise me," Sam said evenly. "Before you wanted my help. Or was that just a ploy to get me alone so you could kill me?"

Urdli was equally unruffled. "You refused to help then. You said that your sister was more important than the fate of the world."

"So I was wrong," Sam said quickly. "But now I'm ready to help. Are you ready to let me, or do you prefer to try to stop Spider all by yourself?"

"I am not by myself." The sweep of Urdli's arm

took both the gathered magicians and the defended barrier wall.

Sam followed the gesture and sensed the power of the gathered entities. "I concede you've got the astral covered pretty well, even if most of your strength is defensive. But the bombs are mundane, and you haven't got an army." He paused for effect. "Or do you? You wouldn't be after the bombs to add them to Tir Tairngire's arsenal, would you?"

Urdli bristled. "I am not a citizen of the Tir," he said, as though that explained all.

"And I assure you, Twist," Laverty put in, "that the ruling council would far rather see the weapons destroyed than recover them." The professor glanced significantly at two of the other magicians, who met his gaze briefly, then nodded. He turned back to Sam. "This has to be kept quiet. Should certain corporations or governments learn of the weapons, there would be a struggle for their possession, a shadow war that no one wants."

Sam had already figured that angle. "It might turn into something more than a shadow war."

"It might, indeed," Laverty agreed. "Are you prepared to join our effort?"

"Maybe," Sam said slowly, "just maybe, I'll let you join *my* effort."

That took them back, but he didn't give them more than a moment to sputter.

"You're stymied. You know what Spider wants, and you have some rough idea where she's planning to get it. But you can't act without more specific information."

"And you can?" Estios asked suspiciously.

"I have more specific information."

"From what source?"

Sam shrugged. "Several, actually. I agree wholeheartedly about the need to keep this situation quiet. But it's got to be taken care of quickly, and my friends and I can't do it alone. So what I'm prepared to do is cooperate. There are several locations with which we don't have the resources to deal."

"Which you shall leave to us," Urdli said. "I do not think I like your approach, mongrel. How can we be sure you aren't just distracting us while you arrange matters to your own advantage?"

"You could trust me," Sam replied dryly.

Estios sneered. "I don't believe you know what you claim."

"Suit yourself." Sam turned, as though to leave, but the professor spoke up. "Gentlemen," he said, "we must discuss this."

Sam looked at them over his shoulder. "Don't spend too much time on idle chitchat. I already have a team on the way to Deggendorf. And once the action starts, things will move quickly. Ever see a spider jump when its web is shaken?"

As though on cue, the dwarf said, "Deggendorf is near one of the possible sites, professor."

Laverty nodded. "You are being precipitous, Twist."

Sam shurgged. "Maybe. Maybe I'm just being expeditious. Having been faulted for shirking responsibility, maybe I just want to make up for lost time."

"Or maybe you're getting in over your head," Laverty said.

Sam was only too aware of that possibility—no, make that *probability*.

While Laverty conferred quietly with his colleagues, Sam tried to overhear, but they controlled their projections too well. At last Laverty turned back to him.

"Perhaps you should tell us what you have in mind."

"First, I think you should tell me a few things."

"Very well."

Urdli and Estios tried to disrupt the discussions

every chance they could, but the other elves mostly ignored them. Piece for piece, Sam traded information with the elves. He sketched his plan and they objected, as he had expected. They had a few ideas, but no one could come up with a better idea that could be carried out as fast as the situation demanded. Most of the elves, especially Urdli and Estios, weren't particularly happy that Sam had initiated several runs, but time and distance made it necessary that Sam's arrangements be left alone. Other possibilities had to be covered; they could not afford to double run any one target. In the end no one was completely happy, but much to his surprise Sam got most of the concessions he'd wanted.

As he turned to leave, this time for real, Laverty asked, "And what are *you* planning to do?"

"Me? Well, planning can be very stressful. Once everything gets started, I'd thought I'd unwind and do a little dancing."

32

"It's time to bathe."

With that announcement, Howling Coyote rose smoothly to his feet. When Sam tried to duplicate the maneuver, he struck his head on the low roof of the sweat lodge. More used to such structures, the old shaman had remained somewhat crouched even as he stood, avoiding a collision. Sam decided that a rap on the noggin was a small price to pay to escape the hot, sweaty confines of the lodge.

By the time Sam emerged from the lodge, Howling Coyote was halfway to the lake. Shivering at the sudden chill, Sam longed suddenly for the sun-baked canyons of the mesa. Because of the higher elevation of this mountainside, the evening air cooled too quickly. Howling Coyote waded right in, but Sam was shivering even before he hit the icy waters of the lake. Seeing Sam hesitate, the old man, dripping wet and exuberant as any child, splashed him with near-freezing water. To escape the bombardment, Sam dove head-first into the water. He came up sputtering, unsure that the cure was better than the disease. Long before he had finished the ritual washing his teeth were chattering, and he was convinced he would never feel his toes again.

Finally Howling Coyote nodded in satisfaction and led Sam back to the shore, where their clothing for the dance was laid out. Sam wrapped a length of soft leather around his loins, then donned a pair of buckskin leggings painted with vertical red stripes. Then he pulled his head through the neckhole of a muslin shirt sewn with sinew and decorated with strips of cloth fringe along the sleeves and across the breast and back. Red suns dotted the shirt in a pleasing asymmetric pattern. He swirled a striped blanket around his shoulders to hide his shirt until the proper moment.

"What face do you wear?" the shaman asked.

"Huh?"

"Your dream must have shown you the face for the great magic. You must show the earth power the face of your purpose and expectation."

Sam looked at the jars of pigments the old man held out to him. Purpose and expectation? Well, he had set out to cure his sister, and that was still his goal. True, they danced to save the world from Spider's threat, but that had not been his first desire. He thought it best to be honest. When the ritual dance laid him naked before the earth power, it would not do to try to disguise his hope. What better face than his sister's? He dipped his hand into the black pigment and smeared it over his face. White pigment made an outline along the edges of his face in imitation of her mane. On his forehead he painted one of the red suns, as a symbol of hope and the dawn of the new.

While Sam was painting himself, Howling Coyote was working up his own scheme. Like Sam's, his face was blackened. A single thin stripe of yellow ochre ran over one eye and across his cheek. When he'd finished the shaman drew on a coyote hide, the head pulled over his own like a hat and its forepaws draping down over his shoulders and onto his chest.

Sam wondered what Howling Coyote's colors and stripe meant. "What is your face?"

"Death," he said flatly.

While Sam was assimilating that response, Howling Coyote handed him a dog skin. Sam almost recoiled when he saw its brindled surface, thinking for a moment that the old shaman had somehow found and skinned Sam's dog Inu. But the patterning of the splotches was different. Sam accepted the hide and draped it on himself as Howling Coyote wore his.

The shaman circled Sam, inspecting. He grunted his approval and started off, leaving Sam to fall in behind him. They walked upslope from the lake, past the sweat lodge, and onto a path that led into the trees. Just after the ground began to slope downward again they emerged from the trees, and entered a natural amphitheater ringed by fir and pine trees that reached more than thirty meters toward the darkening sky. Dusk had already settled in the clearing, and the people assembled there were little more than dark, lumpy shapes in the twilight. Their low talk stopped when Sam and Howling Coyote appeared. The old shaman stopped and raised his arms. At his gesture, fire kindled in stacks of wood set at the cardinal points; the flickering light grew to fill the clearing.

Sam was surprised and amazed by the number of people present. Howling Coyote had told him that he was sending a call, saying that the Dance was not something for only a few. But Sam had not expected so many. He was no expert, but from the variety of ritual costumes he was sure there were shamans from each of the nations of North America. The assembled shamans and their attendants wore a wide variety of garb, some fancy, some plain. All wore ghost shirts decorated with sun and moon symbols as well as circles, crosses, and stars. Though most of the shirts were buckskin, a few were muslin like Sam's. The cloth shirts seemed to belong exclusively to the Anglos, Asians, and Blacks present.

When Sam and Howling Coyote reached the edge of the outer ring, a single figure rose to meet them. At first Sam didn't recognize her, for she was swathed in an oversized dancer's shirt covered with a constellation of crudely painted stars, and the leggings that showed beneath were not her habitual gray.

"Gray Otter, what are you doing here?"

"I heard about the dance," she said softly, reverently.

"But you're not a shaman," Sam said, perplexedly.

She gave him a small, shy smile. "Don't have to be to dance."

"She's right, Dog man," Howling Coyote confirmed. "Only got to believe and be ready to die."

"But . . ."

Howling Coyote cut him off. "Moon's rising. Time's wasting."

The shaman took Sam by the arm and pulled him toward the center of the clearing. A pine tree, stripped of its branches and looking like a pole, lay on the ground there, its length pointing away from them. At its side Sam could see dark lumps that he knew would soon be attached to the stubby remnants of its branches. Those lumps were medicine bundles, cloth streamers, stuffed totemic images, and bundles of feathers. The pine would be raised to stand in a dark hole dug to receive it. It was to be the sprouting tree, a central component of this open-air medicine lodge.

The sprouting tree was the axis around which the dancers would revolve. It would link their souls with the earth.

Before they reached the tree's base, a delegation of Indian shamans rose and stepped into their path. Sam didn't recognize their tribal affiliations, but the elaborate ceremonial garb they wore marked them as highly placed persons. A young man in a thickly fringed shirt called out a challenge. At least Sam assumed it was a challenge from the tone and the stern expression on the man's face. The words meant nothing to him.

Howling Coyote gave a short response that drew heated comments from the others in the group. It was clear that there was dissension in the ranks. Maybe the shamans had come to stop the Dance rather than to participate. Sam wished Howling Coyote had let him wear a language chip in his datajack. Then he might have understood the words and known whether it was concern or hatred that he saw on the faces of some of the gathered shamans. Howling Coyote began a speech that went on for some time. Sam watched the effect of the old shaman's words. Doubt was displaced by determination in some, but the group faltered short of coming to complete agreement. Howling Coyote turned to him.

"You must show them."

"What? How?"

"Begin the dance," Howling Coyote said, and sat.

Sam looked at the shaman, but the old Indian ignored him. Sam turned his gaze to the challenging shamans. There was no sympathy there. No clue, either. But this was a minor riddle. Beyond them lay the pole. Lying on the earth, it made the ritual circle incomplete. The Dance could not begin until it was raised. The stony silence made it clear that Sam could expect no help, which meant that there was only one way to raise it.

Dog!
"Who calls?"
I call, totem. I need your power.
"Have I power?"
You are Dog.
"Am I power?"
You are power.
"You wear my skin. Are you I?"
I wear your skin. I am what I must be.
"I am what I am. What are you?"
I am what I am. I am Dog.

He/Dog howled joyfully at the moon.

Sam opened his eyes. It was fully night. His striped blanket was wrapped around the base of the raised sprouting tree, and his dog skin fluttered from its top. He didn't remember removing either. He felt the breeze cooling his skin through the light muslin shirt. Sweat evaporated from his face.

Sam felt energized. His senses seemed preternaturally sharp. He saw his image reflected in the eyes of the elder shamans around him. Though his dog skin hung on the pole his shoulders were swathed in fur, a snout projected over his forehead, and pointed ears topped his head. The shaman's mask was upon him, and he was cloaked in a faint glamor of power.

He turned to Howling Coyote. "Where's the drum?"

"No drum. This is the Great Ghost Dance."

"Okay. No drum." Sam sighed. "Where does the rhythm come from?"

"Look within yourself."

Sam smiled. "And if it's not there, no magic."

Howling Coyote smiled back. "Hey hey, Dog man, you're not such a dumb Anglo after all."

The old shaman began the chant, and Sam took it up. He felt anticipation and a growing excitement. The chant pulsed with the faint stirring of great power. Sam's voice strengthened as he sang the words that

Howling Coyote had made him memorize. The words were Indian and Sam didn't know what they meant, but he felt the power that awakened at his call.

Awake it might be, but it held itself aloof.

Sam repeated the chant, this time alone. The power rose ever so slightly. Around him the elder shamans took up the song, calling and greeting. Each sang different words, but all sang the same song. Holding hands with fingers intertwined, they began to dance.

* * *

Morgan had been coy in Sam's presence, but not so when they were alone. Her presence suffused him, filling him with the joy of freedom and the heady rush of oneness with the Matrix. The euphoria was nearly enough to make him forget what he had promised. Nearly, but not quite, for loyalty was as strong as love.

There was no need to tell her what he had promised to do, for she had been there. Together they reviewed the data Sam had dumped. Finding the system addresses they needed was simplicity.

They went after it. She was a silver girl with an ebony cloak. He an ebony boy in a cloak of stars. Together they crept along the byways of the Matrix, slipping through the shadows in search of the swag. Bit by data bit, they assembled pertinent information and sent it winging through the electronic byways to runners awaiting their cues. Together, they were an unbeatable team.

They turned their attention to a more challenging task.

Ebony boy and chrome girl gazed eagerly at the glittering, pulsing web of data. Grandmother's system might be an entangling web to most, but to these intruders each strand was a rooftop along which to scamper, a dangling rope by which to clamber, a quiet corridor through which to sneak. In sparkling displays of clandestine acrobatic skills, they penetrated ever deeper.

Within the lattice datastores were cocooned packages awaiting the web's mistress, but Morgan's ever-so-sharp knife slit them open, baring the contents. From among the exposed treasures Dodger selected the most promising, and Morgan opened them for him. A wealth of data, a hoard of secrets, and nothing could keep the team of Dodger and Morgan from them.

Everything Sam wanted was theirs for the taking. Well, almost everything. A prudent old biddy, Grandmother did not keep all her data in one place. They assembled a list of locations that matched Sam's list of suspected weapon stockpiles. Information buried throughout Grandmother's files convinced Dodger that Grandmother had no other targets than those toward which Sam had dispatched teams. Morgan concurred with his analysis of the data patterns.

"For myself, there is curiosity. Are matters so grave, yet so simple? Samuel Verner/Sam/Twist has no further requirements?"

"For the nonce." He felt an odd sense of disappointment, and her next communication echoed it.

"Where is the sport?"

"In the doing, my darling. But I agree that the challenge was low. Naetheless, I expect things will be more interesting in the next phase."

"The run?"

"Verily. The run tests the true mettle of the decker in a time/place where mind and skill are pitted against all the defenses, obstacles, and ice the opponent has. There is no luxury of retreat. For retreat is defeat, and our comrades would pay most dearly. We cannot fail them and permit the wrongdoers to use their Matrix assets against our flesh confederates."

"Samuel Verner/Sam/Twist will be among them?"

"I expect so. If not, those he cares for will be, and their loss would be more to him than his own."

"For myself, there is concern that he come to no harm."

"For myself, as well. Therefore, we shall do what we can to ensure the success of his plan."

"Indeed."

"In deed!"

Her amusement thrilled him, as they flashed onward into the electronic night.

33

Sam watched, seeing the pattern from his seat at the base of the pole and from the top of the pole at once. There was no discordancy to the image. The rising power lifted him as the song rose.

An outer circle of dancers formed, and the shamans stopped their own dancing to take seats in a ring around Sam. No drums, or bells, or rattles marked time for the dancers. There was only the tempo of the song. From his seat at the base of the sprouting tree, Sam led the singing. Howling Coyote and the elder shamans sang, too, a mixture of voices and words that blended into a single song. The ring of dancers moved around them, a hundred voices joining in the song.

In unison, the dancers lifted their left feet and plunged them forward. Right feet dragged across the ground to catch up. Left feet lifted again, coming back across the line of the circle before stamping to the ground. The ring of dancers turned. Again, right feet caressed the earth as they moved to meet their partners. Left feet rose and plunged. Right feet moved to join. The dance gathered speed. Left feet crossed and recrossed the line of the circle while right feet re-

BISKE@9

mained on the circle, grounding the dancers to the earth.

The dancers sang and the song rose to the sky, drawing power from the earth.

* * *

Using binoculars, Hart scanned the castle and the mountainside on which it perched. Weberschloss was nearly inaccessible. A switchback road led through the forest and up the mountain, but it was unpaved and narrow, too unstable for more than a light car. A hovercraft, with its lower ground pressure, would be able to handle the surface; but it would be noisy. She wasn't sure it would be able to take some of the tighter turns, and some of the grades were so steep that a hovercraft would probably spill the air from its skirts and end up grounded.

That left an aerial approach as the most logical way in, but that avenue offered difficulties to a raider. The castle courts were small, and the roofs conical or steeply sloped. There was no place for anything but a small craft to land, and a landing vehicle would have to be capable of vertical-flight mode. A good rigger just might be able to put a panzer down in the main court, but if the final approach wasn't very slow there would be a high risk of collision. The landing would be guaranteed then, but damage to the craft could well compromise the getaway. Of course, any aerial approach assumed minimal antiaircraft defenses, which was something she could not safely assume.

Hart didn't like the idea of a one-way trip.

She admired anew Cosimo's cleverness, and the skill he had displayed in secreting his purloined weapons in this hiding place, with its superb natural defenses. Cosimo would have had his own plans or defense but he was gone now, and she was relieved not to have to deal with defenders under his guidance.

There were ways a determined party could access,

but it was not going to be as easy as it might have been in other times. If Weberschloss had remained the private holding and tourist attraction it had been—both when Cosimo hid the weapons there and after the old U.S. Rangers had relinquished it—a properly disguised squad of infiltrators would have done the job. Even during the time the Rangers had used it as a recreation and training center, the castle had never held more than a company of troops. Formidable as such a garrison might be, the proper preparation could neutralize most of their assets, because regular troops were sufficiently predictable. But the current occupants were neither harmless hoteliers nor predictable, regular army troops.

She could, of course, just blow the castle to atoms, but that wouldn't solve the problem. The weapons would still be protected in the heart of the rock. The amount of firepower necessary to ensure their destruction was more than the budget allowed. Or the local government, either. Even asking about it would have brought too much attention. So they were going to have to go in and deal with the current owners.

The castle had been taken over during the later days of the repression riots by a rather desperate band of refugees, mostly metahumans who were fleeing from the hate that had swept over the world. Most of them were orks and dwarfs, more than half of them members of the *bundeswehr*. The soldiers' experience and weapons had bought the refugees their safety. The determination of both soldiers and civilians had kept it. Locally, they had maintained their holding through a balance of threats, bribes, and usefulness to the government. The experiences of the squatters had birthed a hatred and led them to turn Weberschloss into a haven for anti-norm terrorists. They called themselves the Herbstgeists, the Ghosts of Autumn. So far, their operations were too minor—and too often convenient for some corporate or governmental faction—for them to be rooted out.

If the Herbstgeists—or those who tolerated the terrorists' presence, for that matter—learned what lay under Weberschloss, that situation would likely change. For the moment, however, they sat between Hart and her goal, forming an obstacle that was well armed, fanatical, and unlikely to negotiate. Although the Herbstgeists posed a problem to Hart's limited resources, Spider could gather whatever she needed, given time. Time she could not be allowed to have. The bombs had to be neutralized before Spider could take advantage of them.

The soft crunch of gravel alerted Hart to a visitor. She turned to see a dwarf climbing the path. The woman was nearly as wide as she was tall, and she grumbled to herself and puffed as she negotiated the sometimes steep trail. Being a rigger, Willie Williams rarely walked when she could control some sort of vehicle, which meant she was not in very good shape for personal exertion. The rigger wore a loose coverall that was stained with sweat despite the cool mountain air, and her shaved crown glistened with the perspiration that gathered around her datajacks and trickled down in a steady stream. The hair that grew from the sides and back of her head was gathered into matching pigtails that bounced up and down on her ample chest as she walked.

"Troops are getting restless," she said, without bothering to greet Hart.

"Anxious to go?"

"Neg. Don't want to tangle with the Herbstgeists."

Hart had been afraid that the mercs would have that reaction when they learned of the target. "I thought these guys were pros."

"They are, but even pros don't like getting killed. They're having second thoughts about the cost of the ticket."

The rigger was worried, or else she wouldn't have bestirred herself to climb to Hart's observation point. "What about you, Willie?"

Willie shrugged. "I know why we're doing it. They don't."

"You didn't answer my question."

Willie rubbed her palms across the datajacks on either temple. The induction pads on her hands rasped slightly as they slid over the chromium steel ports. "I could wish I was rigging a full panzer instead of a stripped-down whizzer. But I ain't gonna back out."

"I'm glad you're still in, Willie. Don't know a rigger I'd rather trust to get us up there."

Willie deliberately looked away. Hart could see her jaw working. After a while, the rigger reached a hand into her belt-slung sack and fished out a can of Kanschlager. "Want a beer?"

"No, thanks."

"Didn't think so, but thought I should offer." She popped the top and upended it over her head. Not a drop missed her upturned mouth. The can drained, she replaced it in her sack and burped. "Watch out for Georgie. He did a run with a Herbstgeist squad in forty-eight."

"Thanks. I will."

Hart gave Willie the opportunity to say more, but the rigger seemed to have said all she was willing to say. Maybe she didn't have more than a suspicion. Maybe she knew about Georgie, because she had been involved in that same run and had her own secrets to hide. The first seemed more likely. Willie wasn't the type to get involved with the Herbstgeists, even though many of their soldiers were of her metatype. They stood in awkward silence for a few minutes, Willie growing increasingly restive.

At last she said, "Whizzer needs a check if we're gonna ride tonight."

"Want some help?" Hart asked, already knowing the answer.

"Neg."

Hart watched Willie crunch back down the path. When the rigger passed from sight, Hart turned and looked back across the valley to the castle. Just what she needed, more complications. She hoped Sam was right, and they had time before Spider's agents made the scene.

34

Sam smiled as he sang.

The dancers circled the shamans gathered at the center. Each dancer gripped the hand of the person to either side, fingers interlocked. They rocked forward when they stamped, and swayed back when they brought their trailing feet forward. Their hands swung in arcs as they moved through the steps.

The dance gathered speed.

* * *

Neko Noguchi was a loner, and he liked it that way. At least when it came to doing biz. Partners either got in the way or weren't where you needed them when you needed them. In his experience, it was far better to rely on yourself. That way, you always knew where you stood. Being new to the trade, Neko might not have much of a rep; but it was a good one. And it was a solo rep.

So why had the American elf and his partners sent this woman to work with him?

Striper was her street name—a more reliable tag than the one on her travel documents—and she moved with the grace and economical motion of a great hunting cat. She had followed the contact protocols scrupulously, which suggested that she was a pro. Her stride, artfully concealed weaponry, and alertness said the same. From her swagger Neko might have thought her a razorguy, but he could detect no sign of cybernetic enhancements. The synopsis he had bought from Cog said only that she was top-notch talent. Lacking chrome, she would have to rely on magic for her edge, and that was pushing reliability.

Even if she was a legitimate agent of the American elf, Neko didn't see why she was necessary on this run. If the work was done properly, there would be no need for muscle. He thought his performance record in the investigations he had undertaken for the elf was satisfactory. What had prompted this display of low confidence now?

"Caution." Striper smiled slyly at him as she ran her right index finger up and down along the left side of her nose. Though the room was dimly lit, her eyes were hidden behind chrome shades whose earpieces were brindled tortoiseshell. He wished he could see the expression in them. "You *looked* concerned about why I'm here. I'm just muscle for this run, in case."

Abandoning his pose of complete casualness, Neko removed his feet from the low table between their chairs. He had not thought that his face or body language would betray his concern. Perhaps they hadn't. She might have enhancements, more subtle than most, that let her gauge people more easily. While useful in many circumstances, such capabilities would not be of prime value on this run. "I can handle myself."

She laughed shortly; the sound was almost a cough. "It's the warlord's boys the principal is worried about."

"I can handle them, too."

"Like to see that."

He was beginning to find her arrogance annoying. "I do not care for you to."

She shrugged. "Tough. I took a contract, and I'm not defaulting on it for your ego."

"He doesn't trust me, then."

She took a flat, dark metal case from a pouch on her belt. Flipping it open, she selected a thin brown cigarillo and lit it from the hot spot on the case. She toked, held the smoke in for a moment, then blew it out in a thick stream before saying, "Never said so."

"Words aren't always necessary. Your presence is that statement."

Taking another toke, she blew smoke at the ceiling. "If you say so."

"What if I left you behind?"

"You can run. I'll run faster."

She seemed to have complete confidence that he could not escape her. Her assuredness was sobering; Hong Kong was his hunting ground, not hers. Until he knew what resources she could call on, he would have to be cautious. "Then I'm condemned to your help."

She nodded.

"I hope, at least, that you're well informed about the mission."

"Tell me again. They might have forgotten something."

"I'll keep it short," he said sharply. He knew she was testing him, and he didn't like it. But it was all part of the biz. He put on a good face. "Across the strait in Kungshu, there's a man. Han is the name he goes by. Han is a wealthy man, a powerful man. The shadows speak of him as one of the new warlords. This is a fair evaluation in many ways because, like most warlords, he dreams of uniting China again, with himself as her leader, of course. The comparison breaks down, because this man might actually succeed. Recently Han has taken on a new advisor, a mysterious mage who works under the name Nightfall. Nightfall claims to have been privy to some of the secrets of the old Shui regime, and to prove it she has informed Han that his holdings include a missile complex armed with nuclear weapons.''

She interrupted him. "Gonna use it?''

Neko snorted. "Does one use a cannon to hunt field mice?''

"I don't,'' Striper said flatly.

"And neither does he. On the advice of his most favored advisor, he holds the weapons in reserve. The obvious conclusion is that he awaits a time when the weapons may be employed, either actually or as a threat, to improve his position. Han is a canny fellow. He will wait until it is to his best advantage.''

"He can't wait forever.'' She stubbed out her cigarillo. "Word gets out, the corps will scratch him.''

"I would not care to wager the world on their altruism, which is why we have been hired to neutralize the weapons. You have brought the device the elf said would do the job?''

She nodded and patted the satchel that lay on the table between them. "Got a route in?''

Of course he did, but a second body would complicate matters. If he was going to have to work with her, he'd need a better understanding of her capabilities and how she thought. It was time for him to shift the initiative a little, and there was an obvious test to hand. "Step over to the telecom, and I'll call up the data I have gathered on the site. Perhaps you can find a weakness that has escaped me.''

By the time they'd worked out their plan, Neko was impressed. Perhaps making this run with a partner would not be so bad after all. If she could do what she said, he might learn something.

* * *

Sam sang and watched. The shamans sang, too. The dancers sang as they danced. Feet pounded in unison, beating a rising tempo for the song. The dry ground beneath the dancers' feet began to puff up in dust clouds as feet—bare, booted, and moccasined— stamped and dragged across it.

Earth was beginning to stir.

* * *

Urdli scanned the African landscape around them. This had been a pleasant land once, a savannah. It had been dry much of the time, but that was not bad. Many places were dry. Life had found a way here, once. Now the place was parched and barren. Life did not find it so easy now.

Estios walked at his side. Laverty's aide's skin was already dark, but he still sweated too much. He needed constant reminders to drink enough water.

"Why us?" he complained. "I'd rather be on one of the strike teams."

Urdli scanned the sky. He preferred not to be drawn into *that* conversation.

Estios persisted. "Why did we draw this location? Why here, Urdli?"

"We are here because someone must be here. I am an obvious choice, given my abilities." The rock and sand reminded him of his home. The animals, the few that they saw, were different, but that didn't matter. Rock was rock, and animals but ephemeral. Even allegedly intelligent beings such as Estios were ephemeral. "As to you? I do not know why you are here. I will not need your aid in this quest. Given your mutual animosity, perhaps the Dog shaman merely wished you discomfort."

"More likely he thinks I'll get killed along the way," Estios said darkly.

Urdli shook his head. "If I had thought this were a dangerous retrieval, I would have insisted that we bring soldiers with us. Laverty would have required such precautions as well. There is no reason to expect problems.''

"Unless Spider beats us to it.''

"Perhaps then there might be a few problems,'' Urdli conceded. "You might even see the combat you wish for. But you are a certified mage, and I am a magician of no small skill. It would take significant opposition to thwart us. I do not think that Spider will have the time to mobilize such resources, especially for just a single device. Her efforts will be directed elsewhere.''

"And you are content to let others handle the difficult runs. To rely on Verner.''

"I am content at the moment to walk. Matters will proceed safely enough without us, for the time being. Haven't you felt the flow of the astral? Spider has not yet manifested enough to be a magical threat. She still works through earthly agents, and such agents have yet to prove as competent as I feared. Verner's efforts will, at worst, weaken them. For now, secrecy—even at the cost of relying on Verner and his friends—and swiftness are our allies.''

Estios held his hands up to the light and studied them critically. "We won't be a secret if we run into anyone. Why can't we start on the earth path you talked about?''

"It is not yet time.'' Urdli was not about to let Estios know of his limitations. "We can safely walk this land. To those we meet, if any, we will be two travelers, nothing more. The melanin bloom will peak shortly, and as long as you wear the tinted lenses you will not look out of place. The language spells will work as they always have. Only by carelessness will we appear strangers. There is nothing to fear. We shall be in and out before anyone else completes their portion of this elaborate arrangement, even your friends on the strike teams.''

And that, of course, was why Urdli found it easy to

take such a demeaning part in this effort to control the weapons. Here he would have the upper hand, away from interference. Verner's runners might succeed in their raids, but more likely not. Laverty's soldiers had higher chances, but they would follow the professor's orders to the letter. While the activity might alert Spider's earthly agents, Urdli thought the probability low. From the pooling of data, he had seen that Spider's plans were less advanced than he had feared. Naturally, he had not shared that observation with the others; he saw no reason to let them know they wouldn't be facing active opposition in most of the locations.

"You seem amused," Estios commented.

"Perhaps I am. I had thought the Dog shaman would demand that I take a more difficult part in his plan, face a threat that might be a danger to me. He holds me in less regard than he does yourself. A careful assignment of goals would have let him make the elimination of an enemy seem a mere twist of fate."

"Yet he gave us the milk run. He specifically sent us out after the one weapon unlikely to have any guard other than its location. We'll face no opposition beyond the ordinary dangers of travel in this sub-Saharan blight."

"Exactly. The dangers of travel are not really dangers to magicians of our caliber. And will be free to act on our own after we have done what is necessary here."

"So he had underestimated you." Estios smiled. "I see why you're amused."

Urdli smiled back. Verner was not the only one. "I thought you would."

35

The elder shamans rose and formed a circle around Sam and the sprouting tree. The larger circle of the dancers stamped and swayed around them. Howling Coyote nodded to Sam, and Sam began to sing faster. The shamans echoed his new cadence as they joined hands. Howling Coyote lifted his left foot and plunged it down and forward. The inner ring began to dance, turning within the greater circle in a tighter focus of power.

The preliminaries were drawing to a close.

* * *

Janice looked down the hill at the small group of people gathered there. Four norms and three orks. All, save Ghost, were strangers. She knew their names and some of their general abilities because Ghost had told her, but that made them no less strangers. She wondered if they could be trusted.

She wondered if *she* could be trusted.

For more than a week now, the only norm she had seen was Ghost. She had fought back the hunger because he was a follower of Wolf, and in some obscure way she didn't fully understand, a member of her pack. She had come to recognize his strong spirit during their companionship in the wilderness. As much as a norm could be a friend to one of her kind, he was one. Of course, he was also cyber-enhanced, a deadly shot, and a vicious fighter who might have a chance at injuring her seriously, but she didn't think that was the real reason she had not made a meal of him. She prayed it wasn't.

These others were different. Norm or ork, they were not part of the pack. All were experienced shadow-runners and therefore theoretically dangerous. But if one were to straggle behind, and let attention wane, then she might . . .

Might what?

Her stomach growled an answer. She turned away and snatched up Ghost's last offering. Her fangs sank deeply into the deer haunch, but the juices that flowed did little to quiet the insistence of her need. She spat the tasteless meat onto the ground.

She didn't know how much longer she could hold off the hunger. Here, in this land so alive with life and so near to concentrations of people, it got harder every day. Distress warred with longing when she gazed across the sound to the lights of Seattle. The feelings were only amplified by the nearness of the people below. Why was she so disturbed? Dan Shiroi had shown no discomfort at what he was. He had taught her that the hateful norms were proper prey for her kind, rabbits to their wolves. And she was just like him, wasn't she? Something inside her shouted *no,* its voice barely overcoming the joyous shouting that fired her blood at the thought of meat. Sam had said that after this one run he could do the magic that would transform her back to a norm. Could she believe? Did she dare hope?

Did she want to?

Whatever she believed or desired, she had given her word. In that, at least, she was still like her brother. She would do as she had said, and help these runners to do their part in Sam's scheme. After that? Well, after that, things would be as things would be.

She rose and walked softly down the slope toward the gathered runners. She knew that Ghost would hear her, but she wanted to see how alert the others were. The information might be useful later.

One of the chromed norms, Ghost's tribesman Long Run, was the first to react. As if on cue, Ghost whispered in the ear of the woman—Sally Tsung, he had said she was—and she turned to look. The others followed suit.

She kept her moves slow and was careful not to show her fangs. She knew her size was intimidating. She overtopped the tallest of the runners by almost a meter and was easily half again as massive as the biggest ork—Kham was his name. For all her precautions, she sensed she had awakened their fear. They tried to hide it and were successful for the most part, but she could smell it on them. The big ork was especially rank.

He straightened up, trying to make himself look as big as possible. Early evening starlight glinted from the chrome hand he flexed nervously. Ghost had told her that Kham's cybernetic hand was a legacy from an earlier involvement in Sam's business, during which the ork was nearly killed. Was he having second thoughts? Kham cocked his head and stared at her with narrowed eyes. "You ain't no sasquatch."

There was no use denying that, but she didn't see what business he had knowing her metatype. So she just said, "No, I'm not."

"What are ya den?"

He was a nosy trog. "You don't want to know."

"Too bad ya didn't go ork." He sounded halfway sincere. "We orks is tough, and good-looking, too. If ya was one of us, ya wouldn't have ta hide in de woods alone."

And an annoying one. She snapped, "I was an ork once. Didn't like it much, so I changed."

Flinching back at her anger, he quietly eyed her for a few moments. The others found nothing to say in the silence that fell. Kham fingered his broken tusk, and his brow furrowed as if thinking were hard for him. Then, having reached some kind of conclusion, his face relaxed. "Ya must be his sister, den. Heard dey got a lot of bad dings over on Yomi island. Dat's where ya were, right? Heard dey got de virus dere. Youse what happens when an ork gets de virus?''

Hugh Glass's face flashed before her eyes, smiling. "A present for you before I leave," he said, showing his perfect teeth. He touched her leg and she collapsed in pain, shattered bone tearing through flesh. Hugh faded from her sight, then the sounds began, the sounds of the searching hunters. She swallowed her scream and held in her terror. Unable to run, she would be caught and taken back to Yomi. The hunters came closer. Fear clogged her throat. Closer. She had heard stories about what they did to runaways. She whimpered in her pain and immediately stifled it with redoubled terror. "Delicious," Hugh said, and sucked her dry. To her drifting, barely conscious mind, he said, "Someday you may thank me, but more likely you'll hate me for all time. I'd prefer it that way, it tastes better." Then he was gone, and she had only herself and the darkness and the pain. And the hunger.

She shrugged off the nightmare memory. She didn't want to think about that anymore. ''Don't know anything about a virus.''

''We're not here to be idle,'' Ghost said, stepping between her and the ork.

She relaxed muscles she hadn't realized were tensed, and lowered her lips to hide her fangs. ''All right. Let's get this over with.''

''Don't you care what the plan is?'' Tsung asked.

''No.''

The ork with the datajacks on his temples put a hand to his ear. After a moment he said, ''Matrix cover says locks are off on the compound. We got a twenty-minute window before the Gaeatronics security checks run their diagnostics. We got to be aboard the submersible by then.''

''Right on time,'' Tsung said. ''We don't get paid till it's over, so let's get moving.''

"Ain't like de fairy to be on time," Kham grumbled.

"Even Dodger gets it right sometimes," Tsung said.

The trip through the strip of forest between them and the Gaeatronics slip at the dockyards was short. They covered it quickly. Janice guessed that Ghost's tribesmen had already cleared the route. She felt sure of it when another Indian joined them at the outer fence. In moments a hole had been clipped, and the runners slipped through. The Indian who had joined them remained behind to seal the breach.

The dock they headed for was dark, but that didn't bother Janice. She could see a couple of twelve-meter surface craft moored on the left, and out at the far end on the right was a low-riding shape with a tall, conical hump amidships. Stenciled next to the Gaeatronics logo was the name *Searaven*. They reached the craft with three minutes left in their window.

The *Searaven* was a deep-water-construction submersible converted to serve as an underwater taxi for the wave-motion power plants Gaeatronics maintained in the Sound. The sectioned forward end, with its command and power modules and their manipulator housings, antennae, and light booms gave the vehicle a wasplike appearance. The imagery was enhanced by the slope of the aft hull where, instead of a normal open cargo frame, the *Searaven* carried an enclosed and pressurized hull for passengers. The rear of the cabin narrowed down to a docking collar that could serve as a diver's port or, after mating with another hatch, could allow the passengers to cross in relatively dry comfort from the submersible to another vessel or to an underwater station. She could imagine the connection assembly thrusting downward from the machine's belly like an insect's stinger.

She hadn't liked the idea of going underwater when Sam had presented it. She hated the water. It would be dark and cold down there, like a grave. She would be in an alien environment where she would have no control. Now, faced with the imminent realization of her fears, she hesitated.

"What's the problem?" Ghost asked as the others scrambled aboard.

She didn't want to speak her fears aloud. "Who's driving this thing?"

"Rabo."

"Ya got a problem wid dat?" Kham snarled.

"Rabo's a good rigger," Ghost said soothingly.

"Yeah," Rabo agreed. His voice came from the submersible's external speaker. He had been the first aboard and was already jacked in. "Being ork don't mean nothing in the interface."

"Bruiser like you ain't afraid of going down, are ya?" Kham taunted.

She lied with a shake of her head. Her voice almost cracked when she said, "I don't like water and I don't like tight places."

"Gonna get both." Kham laughed, and disappeared below.

"Come on, Wolf shaman," Ghost urged. "Only got forty seconds till security check. Got to get the hatch dogged."

She forced her fear down and stepped aboard. Ghost waited with seemingly imperturbable patience as she squeezed her way past the coaming. As soon as she had cleared the ladder he was in in a flash of jacked reflexes, and swinging the hatch closed. He spun the wheel as soon as the lip of the hatch touched the coaming.

"How close?" Tsung asked.

"Point five," he replied.

"Too close," she said, giving Janice a sour look. "All right, Rabo. Soon as you get clearance from Dodger, get us going."

"What's your hurry? *Wichita* ain't going anywhere."

Janice was puzzled. Wichita was in Kansas. There was no way to get there by boat. "What are you talking about? We can't get there by boat."

"She's worse dan her brudder," Kham griped.

"Back off," Ghost warned him. To Janice, he said *"Wichita* is a submarine, *Nereid* class. She put to sea just before Thunder Tyee's boys overran the Bremerton sub base back in the teens. The warriors had already gotten a few cannon hits on her, and they put a missile into her before she cleared harbor. She went down and exploded, or so it seemed. Salish dredges still bring up bits of debris sometimes, but not much."

"So if we're headed after her," Janice said, "she didn't explode."

"That's what Dodger's data says," Ghost confirmed. "Bad guys know it, too. The *Wichita* didn't sink when she went under the waves. At least not immediately. Captain Walker was running a scam, but the tech didn't match his nerve. He wanted to run for safe territory, didn't want the Indians getting control of the missiles on board. He barely coaxed the *Wichita* out past Cape Flattery. The sub was in no shape to make it down the coast. Wouldn't have had a prayer of making it to the Canal, so he scuttled her."

That had all happened before Janice was born. It seemed incredibly ancient. "What makes anyone think that the missiles will be any good after more than thirty years under water?"

"Oh, the missiles won't," Tsung said. "But the bombs, that's another matter. Missiles are cheap, but bomb production is quite restricted. There's not so much fissionable material around anymore. What comes out of the plants is strictly monitored by an international commission, which doesn't leave a terrorist squad much chance of getting their hands on anything."

"And we're going to keep it that way," Ghost said solemnly.

* * *

The dance was well under way.

Sam rose on the power and felt himself widening, spreading through the sky. He rushed through the hole to the otherworld. He reached the guardian, no longer a Man of Light that mocked him, but something unseen, yet somehow recognizable. Tonight it had no power to limit him. He felt it bow out of his way as he approached.

Beyond the tunnel, another night sky awaited him.

36

The silver moon hung overhead, its glow full of magic and wonder. Its light lay on the land like a shroud, blanketing the woods and rolling hills in argent stillness. A thread hung from the moon, and from that thread a darkness.

The dark spot descended, growing as it did—or only appearing to grow, but appearance was reality in the otherworld. A rush of power swept by Sam, fluttering his clothes. The air carried a scent at once familiar and alien. Familiar, in that he had sensed it once before in a diluted and fragmentary fashion. Alien, in that it was so *other* in its simultaneous menace and fascination.

When the darkness settled to the ground, it danced before him on eight slender legs. The many-jointed limbs arched out of the forward portion of the great, furred body, rising above it to angle down again to the ground. A shining drop of half-formed silk beaded at the spinneret tipping the end of the abdomen. The rounded head glistened with moonlit highlights that

ran in silver streams from its crown to the great mandibles. There were no markings that Sam could see.

Spider.

Sam could feel the eyes—two large and six lesser—
watching him. Unnerving, their jet gaze raised child-
hood fears. Sam's image was reflected in their depths
as the totemic creature bobbed up and down. The mul-
tiple reflections jittered, their motion reflecting his
feelings.

This was not as it should be.

"How have you come here?" he asked.

Spider's voice was sweet, uncanny in its warmth.
"How have *you?* Power calls to power, does it not?
Out in the colorless world, you did me a service. For
a time, you carried a small fragment that had been
touched by my power. Through such trifling contact,
I came to know you and your power. Now that you
walk the realms where the totems dwell, how could I
miss you? You shine like a beacon. The power cloak-
ing your shoulders calls me to be near you."

Sam didn't like the idea that Spider could follow him
wherever he went. Did she already know of his plans?
"What do you want?"

"To help you." One of the great eyes seemed to
wink at him. "I know many secrets."

"For which the price is, no doubt, more than I care
to pay."

A shrug rippled through her battery of legs. "Cost
is balanced by desire and need. I can be helpful."

As could any totem, for they were inherently powerful. "You can be deadly as well. I've heard the stories."

"You cite stories as a reason to distrust me? Fairy
tales and myths? Who has told you of any personal
dealings with me?"

"No one," Sam answered honestly.

"Then how can you know what it is like to deal with
me? How can you know whether I am trustworthy or

not? Where is your proof, your evidence? Do you condemn so blindly? Those who shutter their minds and hearts with fear of the unknown travel a perilous course. Have you not been maligned by those who oppose you? I, too, have been maligned by ignorant enemies. I am innocent of crime.''

Sam was confused. ''If you're innocent, why did the elves lock you up?''

''Did they tell you that they had?'' Spider's amused laugh was a high-pitched chitter. When she continued speaking, her voice was full of indignation. ''Such as they cannot chain me. They are petty flesh entities, moved by petty and foolish flesh desires. They do not understand my nature, and so they fear me. They turn their backs on the wisdom I offer.''

The shift in Spider's mood, from amusement to something that smelled of anger, made Sam think the elves had the right idea about Spider. ''As do I.''

The scent of anger faded and was replaced by a sweeter, almost sexual odor. ''Do not be hasty, Samuel Verner Twist. I am the holder of secrets and the crafter of power. I know many things that are mysteries to others. Many secrets are mine and mine alone. I share my secrets with a chosen few.''

Sam's head was getting light. ''For what price?''

''Small services.''

Rallying his resolve he said, ''I'm not interested. I already have a patron in this place, and he doesn't like you.''

Spider dismissed his objection with the wave of a leg. ''Jealousy only. Dog is young and I am old, older than your kind. And age brings wisdom, Samuel Verner Twist. Such wisdom could be yours to call upon. You could know secrets of many things. Much would be within your power. For example, your sister need not remain as she is.''

Sam felt the truth behind Spider's words, but sensed a lie as well. Both truth and lie were hidden in Spider's honeyed promises, but which was which? His head was spinning, and he couldn't sort out what he felt. The deep ache that was his hope to save Janice made him want to believe Spider. Was it only her frightful appearance that made him distrust her? Janice, too, appeared scary now, but he knew that her goodness still lived within. More than anything, he wanted to bring that goodness out. "That's what the Ghost Dance is for."

"Now *you* attempt to deceive *me*," Spider chided gently. "Your dance raises power to change many things, but I know that you will focus it to do other things. You are not raising the power of the earth to help your sister. You have not the knowledge to apply the change magic to her."

Sam feared she was right. "And you do?"

"I know many secrets of metamorphosis. I can teach you, if you let me."

He wanted to know, needed to know. For Janice's sake. "What do you want?"

"Channel to me this power you raise, and she shall be changed. It is but a small matter for me to alter the intent. Let me guide you."

Sam closed his eyes; there was too much input. He needed to think. Spider said that Janice would be restored. It was what he had been seeking ever since he had learned it might be possible. All he had to do was let Spider take the reigns of the power that was building in the Dance. It would not be hard.

A brush of fur caressed his cheek. He thought of Inu, but the smell was wrong. He opened his eyes and saw the bristled surface of Spider's leg. Above him, another limb cradled a strand of silky white stuff.

Sam turned and ran.

Spider's laugh was mocking. "Run," she taunted, "but you can never get away from the truth."

37

Near and far, the dancers moved in rhythm. Faster, ever faster, they flashed through the steps, raising the power that surged through Sam.

He felt the dancers. Myriad images flashed through his head as though he could see everything the dancers saw. Castle towers. Trees. Curving, cramped walls. The sprouting tree. Dark tunnels. Shamans moving in a circle. The stone of earth, alive and rippling. Dog.

Dog danced at Sam's side.

* * *

"Contact, bearing forty-five relative," Rabo called out.

"Moving?" Ghost asked.

"Negative. Location matches prediction near enough. I think it's *Wichita.*"

"Take us in closer," Tsung ordered.

Janice sat back, hugging her knees to her chest. It was a child's pose, but it helped her keep a grip on herself. She needed all the help she could get. Here in the confines of the submersible the scent of meat was strong, and hunger gnawed at her continuously. She was glad something would be happening soon. She had thought they would never find the lost submarine among the ridges of the shelf.

Rabo's voice came again on the speaker. "I think we may have a problem."

"What's the problem?" Ghost asked.

"Can't you dock?" Tsung said.

"Drek! Knew it," Kham snapped. "We're wasting our time."

Rabo's detached voice continued, as though none of them had spoken. "Density scans are consistent with air in the hull."

"What's unusual about that?" Tsung asked testily.

"Hull down this long should have leaked out any air she held when she went down. Somebody's repressurized her."

"Any other craft around?" Ghost asked.

"None showing, but I've got sounds on sonar and they're coming from the *Wichita*. There's somebody on board."

"Mechanical or organic sounds?" Ghost asked.

"You ain't running a sim chip on de side, Rabo?" Kham growled.

"Ain't done that since the Fuchi run. I learned my lesson. This is real, Kham. I don't know what the noise is, or what's making it, but it's real."

There was silence for a few moments.

"They'll know we're coming," Tsung said to Ghost. Ghost nodded. "Whoever they are."

"Does it matter?" asked Fast Stag, the other norm.

"It matters," Tsung said. "Minimal opposition was the spec. Price goes up if there's serious trouble."

"What about an astral scout, then?" Fast Stag asked, looking at Tsung.

"Already tried. There's a school of hexfish out there that picked me up as soon as I poked my head through the *Searaven*'s hull. Those things hunt astrally as well as mundanely, and they're worse than piranha. Maybe you'd like to swim across?"

While Fast Stag shook his head in an emphatic "no," Ghost said, "We'll have to dock without a recon then."

"Rabo!" Kham barked. "Any way ya can slide us in quiet?"

"Negative," the rigger replied. "They're not using any active probes, but if they've got any of the *Wichita*'s passive gear going, they'll hear us coming. No way to avoid it. Probably won't know what we are, though. The sub's databanks won't have specs for a submersible like the *Searaven*. They might not know we can dock.''

''And can we dock?'' Tsung asked.

''Yeah. Didn't I tell you? The *Wichita*'s aspect is almost perfect. There's a little fibrous debris around the forward hatch, but the approach is clear.''

''Let's get it over with,'' Janice said.

The runners ignored her.

''They'll hear the docking just through transmission of the vibrations,'' Tsung said. ''It won't be a surprise.''

''Surprise is a tool, not an end in itself,'' Ghost observed. ''We must neutralize the bombs. If those aboard the *Wichita* belong to the enemy, speed is now vital.''

Ghost's two tribesmen nodded their agreement. John Parker, the other ork, looked to Kham for his lead. Kham looked to Tsung. No one bothered to ask Janice for her opinion.

''If we're going to party, we'd better get on with it,'' Tsung said. ''Whoever's in the *Wichita* didn't get down here without help, and we don't want their taxi dropping in on us. This run's too straight-line as it is; we've got no freedom to maneuver. I don't want anybody sitting on our line of retreat.''

Ghost gave the mage a sharp nod. ''Rabo, take us in.''

''Won't be a surprise,'' the rigger said.

''We have no choice,'' Ghost told him.

The docking approach went smoothly. The *Searaven* settled forward of the sail at the one hatch capable of being opened from the outside. The taxi shuddered slightly when her connection collar contacted the hull of the *Wichita*. As soon as Rabo reported a full lock and transmission of the unlocking codes, Kham opened the internal hatch and crammed his bulk into the narrow docking passageway. Parker stood at the edge holding Kham's automatic rifle, ready to hand it down to his boss as soon as he cleared the way. Janice could hear Kham grunting with the effort of freeing the emergency hatch releases on the *Wichita*.

The ork's shoulders bulked back into view briefly as he swung the *Wichita*'s hatch open. A strange, musky odor drifted up from the submarine, overpowering the briny smell of the water in the docking tube. Kham dropped out of sight almost immediately. Parker called a warning and dropped the rifle down the hole. Then he followed it down. Ghost was next through, then Sally and the other two Indians. No one called for Janice to follow, but she did. She didn't want to be alone in the echoing hollow of the *Searaven*'s passenger compartment.

The climb through the docking attachment and the *Wichita*'s lock was short but intensely uncomfortable. The designers had never expected anyone of her size to use the space; she scraped off fur and skin on every projection. The wounds itched from the salt water coating all the surfaces around her, but they would heal soon enough. It was more the closeness and the damp that bothered her.

These worries became minor when compared to what she felt once they reached the deck of the *Wichita*. The musky odor was stronger here, tinged now with a rank smell from the norms and orks. They were afraid. She wondered if they could smell her fear as easily as she did theirs. The light level was low, but more than enough to let her see. Dead fish and other sea creatures lay on the decking, and dense cobwebs hung in thick strands all around the runners. With every surface corroded and clogged by seaweed and barnacles, the compartment looked more like the undersea hideaway of the selkie prince from Carter's *Queen of Sorcery* than the warship it had once been.

No one said anything; no one had to. Janice suspected they all had the same bad feeling she had.

Somewhere aft of them, toward the main bridge, something skittered in the darkness, claws scraping on metal.

* * *

The elf had said he could cripple the outer electronic defenses of Warlord Han's enclave, and he was as good as his word. As for Striper, her skills at physical penetration had proven to be as good as her boasts about them—even better than his own. Neko's most likely scenario hadn't involved reaching the missile base without at least a minor confrontation with the warlord's forces. But they had. Of course, the brush fire that had sprung up at the far end of the valley was attracting much of the facility personnel's attention. He might have thought the fortuitous blaze a good omen, if he believed in such things.

The base didn't look military, but then that was the purpose of camouflage. The maps he had obtained showed the warhead storage to be hidden in the shadows of a bank of grain silos. The warlord's people were only beginning to reactivate the base, and had not as yet armed any of the missiles with warheads. They had not even tested one, which was not surprising. If the warlord was as cautious as his reputation, he would never trust a nuclear weapon to an untried delivery system—especially one that had been mothballed for more than forty years. Neko was sure the arsenal would be as full as when Nightfall had revealed its location to her master.

The ground floor of the building near the grain elevators looked much as one would expect an agricultural office to look. But then, would he really know if something were out of place? The press of a concealed panel turned what should have been the utility closet into an elevator. They took it down.

The subterranean level abandoned pretense. The corridors were drab, with the austerity and severity of military architecture wherever he had encountered it. Only the uninitiated could think it fostered a zen serenity. The cold concrete would echo sounds in harsh clamor, but the halls were deserted. This was going to be easy.

Neko located a computer station. He logged on with the code the elf had supplied, gratified when the system responded almost instantly. Calling up the requisite files, he saw that all the weapons were still logged in. He slipped a chip into the slot and sent the elf's knowbot on its way. It would enter an authorized admission for two into the secure area. That done, he led Striper toward the arsenal.

All the way there something nagged at Neko, making him uneasy. It was only later that he realized the console had one more light active when they left than when they arrived. That light meant their penetration had been discovered, but it wasn't until he and Striper had almost reached the arsenal that the enemy revealed themselves.

They rounded a corner and were confronted by a grotesque vision. Tall and spindly-thin, the thing in the corridor looked more alien than human despite its two arms, two legs, and obvious head. Even more grotesque was the fact that it wore a uniform marked with the insignia of Han's personal guard. Seeing them, the creature clacked its mandibles, then began to speak in a hideously distorted voice. "Nightfall greets you. She bids me give you your deaths."

For Neko, who had once fought a similar thing, the sight was frightening. He had nearly died in that encounter. For Striper, the shock of her first encounter with such a being seemed greater than his own had been. She stopped in her tracks and stared.

Neko knew the thing's speed and potential; they could not afford hesitation. He sprang. At the apex of his leap, his foot lashed forward. He felt the shock as the edge of his foot connected with the creature's head. The rebound sent him backward past Striper, but he rolled as he landed and came up into a crouch. He had delivered enough kinetic energy to snap a troll's neck, but his opponent was still on its feet and beginning its advance.

Neko's attack had succeeded in one respect, however, for it gave Striper enough time to recover from her shock. As the clawed hands swept forward in an attempt to decapitate her, she dove clear of the thing's outstretched arms.

A rush of footfalls in the corridor that had brought them here announced the arrival of reinforcements for the monstrous guard. Judging by the sound, Neko figured they were human, or near enough. He estimated four to six guards approaching, but two would have been more than enough to reinforce the monster.

"Hostiles," Striper growled.

"Go ahead, they're yours. I'll handle this." She vanished around the corner.

Neko sidestepped the thing's first lunge, and hoped he hadn't signed his death warrant with his bravado. From around the corner he heard roars, howls, and gunfire.

So much for stealth.

A second flying kick cost him a rake along his side as the creature dodged, but it gave him some room. The extra space between him and the insectoid thing gave him time to draw his heavy gun. The Arisaka Sunset wasn't as powerful as Striper's Kang, but she didn't load explosive rounds. Neko blasted the thing with two quick bursts but he was too close—the explosions tossed him backward, slamming him into the wall. The bruises would be worth it. Spattered as Neko was with bits of flesh, bone, and organ, it was because his opponent was no longer a threat. He picked himself up, but had to hold onto the wall until the corridor stopped spinning.

It took a long time for what was left of the thing to stop twitching. By then, it was quiet around the corner as well.

An alarm klaxon began to howl, which meant the external security doors would be closing. Getting out was going to be harder than getting in. Or maybe he would be the only one trying to escape. Striper hadn't returned.

⁂

"I assume you had a good reason for insisting I come here, Mr. Masamba," Sato said as he entered the suite. His position as *kansayaku* entitled him to commandeer the finest facilities in the Denver subsidiary office, and his agents had used that clout. Sato stalked across the deep pile carpet, barely conscious of the softness. He stared out the window at the distant mountains, waiting for the uncharacteristically reticent Masamba to respond.

"There's magic, big magic, brewing out there."

"If it is a threat, that is your department. Deal with it."

Masamba cleared his throat. "I don't think this is a Renraku matter."

Sato turned and stared at Masamba, gratified to see the mage flinch. Masamba looked to Akabo for support, but the samurai's rigid demeanor offered no more human sympathy than his chromed eyeshields. That the mage looked to the samurai meant the two had discussed the matter. Such sharing of concern meant the matter was serious, indeed.

"Not a Renraku matter," Sato said. "What, then, is this problem?"

"I don't know. Exactly." Masamba doffed his broad-brimmed slouch hat and began turning it round and round in his hands. "I can't investigate, because

I can't get near the site astrally. There's too much interference. But I'm sure there's a major ritual coming down.''

"Which you believe involves me."

Masamba nodded. "I think so, anyway. There's the faintest trace of that renegade shaman's aura about the magic. I thought that we'd seen the last of him after we snatched that stone and he hightailed it, but now I'm not so sure."

"Can you erect a defense?"

"Hey, *sama*. I'm big mojo. Give me time, nuyen, and few dozen assistants and I'll shield you from a squad of dragons."

The mage's bravado was brittle. Sato felt surprisingly tolerant. Masamba was one of the tools that was his alone, a resource he needed to conserve. Since his contact with the stone, he had come to understand what great forces were afoot. The time of confrontation was coming; the weight of gathering forces was upon him. Though he sensed that this big magic was directed at him or his working, he also felt that some other person was the target. He turned to Akabo.

"Has there been any indication of assault on more mundane levels?"

Akabo shrugged. "Nothing obvious. Biggest hit in the last week was a raid on the Seretech data bank."

"Involving our interests?"

"Wouldn't have mentioned it otherwise. Someone boosted the biodynamics formula."

"The timing is too significant to be incidental. Has the thief been identified?"

"Not yet. The Matrix run originated somewhere in the Hong Kong LTG. Ohara's people are scrambling on it."

"Then for the moment, we need do no more." Despite his words, Sato felt impelled to do something. The metamorphosis serum was a private project, or it had been until Grandmother had sunk her hooks in him. His skin tingled at the thought, and he suspected that he knew who had ordered the run against the project. He had never shared the details with Grandmother, and the Hong Kong origin of the theft could be no coincidence. Yes indeed, the confrontation was coming. "Masamba, we must investigate this matter of magic and make plans to deal with it. Akabo, give the order to ready Crimson Sunset. Also, place the local Red Samurai unit on standby."

Masamba nodded acknowledgment of his orders, but Akabo didn't move. After a moment he said, "Is it wise to involve the corporation directly?"

Sato controlled the sudden flare of rage. His decision to use company assets for his own ends was no business of Akabo's. The corporation and Sato's position in it were secondary matters when survival was at stake. Jaw tight, he turned and stared at the samurai. "Do you question me?"

The man stiffened immediately. *"Iie, kansayaku."*

"Very well, Obey."

Akabo bowed briskly and deeply. *"Ho, kansayaku."*

Sato turned back to stare out the window while his flunkies set to work. There was much to ponder. Absently, he scratched at his itching rib cage.

38

The dancers slowed. Feet paused in air then plunged forward, stamping firmly. The singers hit the low notes of the chant with assurance.

The circle of dancers turned, raising dust that swirled around in intricate patterns. Sam read the patterns. A feather drifted free from a dancer's arm band.

Sam twisted the pattern, clearing the dust from the feather's path. It floated to the ground inside the circle and away from the dancers' feet.

The dance went on.

* * *

The work of briefly quieting Gaeatronics' security and gaining the access codes for the submersible was done. So was the molding of prepared knowbots for Noguchi's use, and the binding of Warlord Han's perimeter systems. It had been easy. The runs were under way now, and no longer needed Matrix over-watch. The next phase was about to begin.

As part of the comprehensive assault on the mundane assets of Spider's minions, Sam wanted Grandmother's data system wrecked. They couldn't destroy the intelligence-gathering network from the Matrix, of course. Too many components were meat, and it was not possible to reach meat from cyberspace unless it voluntarily linked to the electron flow. But the datastores could be purged of accumulated knowledge, effectively crippling Spider's minions for some time.

Dodger and Morgan flew toward the crystal web.

Knowing the web made entry easier. Entry and browsing had been the goal of their last trip. This time they were to hunt down important data and loot it away, a more difficult assignment. But she was the Ghost in the Machine, and he, through her tutelage, was enabled beyond a flesh-limited decker. Morgan engaged all the ice they flitted past, taking on program after program, while Dodger sifted through the file structure searching for the key blocks. A bulk purge was too inelegant; they would lift only selected items, the better to leave the enemy confused about what had been done to their system. Worms, viruses, and Trojan horses would be their gifts to Grandmother, and they would leave explosive blocks, borers, and scramblers to infect the remaining data. The decay and destruction would go on long after Dodger and Morgan's brief sojourn in the system.

It would be a glorious mayhem.

As he worked, Dodger became aware that something stirred at the edges of Grandmother's system. Had it not been for the increased awareness his association with Morgan had given him, he would never have noticed such a thing. As yet it was no more than a probe of the outer defenses, so Dodger dismissed it. If the presence were a threat, Morgan could handle it.

* * *

The deep path was slower here than at home, for this was not his land. It was more tiring, too, but Urdli ascribed that more to his companion. The earth did not care to have any save her own move through her heart. The effort of coaxing her to do otherwise was taxing.

Her trepidation grew as they approached their destination. The flavor of the stone was not right. The area was tainted with a scent he knew too well. Perhaps the Dog shaman had not been so foolish after all.

His progress was stopped by a wall where there should have been no wall. Focusing his strength, he felt an unexpected well of power. The faint strains of a song drifted through his head as he drew on that power and crumbled the barrier in his way.

As he and Estios emerged into a firelit cavern, Laverty's aide promptly collapsed to his knees and retched. Urdli spared no concern for the other's weakness, his eyes full of a sight he did not care to see. The bomb was there, encased in its shipping container, but the weapon was not the cave's only occupant.

The thing that stood between him and the bomb was decked in beads and many-colored cloth swaths. Bangles, metal bands, and necklaces of animal parts and crudely incised metal adorned its limbs and neck.

Though Urdli recognized several magically potent patterns common to primitive human cultures, this was no longer anything human. Bristles sprouted in sparse clumps all over its skin, and lumps distorted the once fine smoothness of the dark skin. Two pairs of vestigial limbs waved spasmodically from its shoulder girdle. Concealing its face was a gaudily painted mask of wood and feathers.

"I know you, elf," the thing said to him.

"And I know you, Spider."

It removed the mask and smiled, its human lips stretching wide as chelicera and pedipalpi extended and distorted the lower half of its face. The dark brown human eyes seemed out of place in the suddenly alien visage. "As you see, all is not as you expected. Spider is wise and devious, elf. You cannot dismiss her so easily. You will meet with the web no matter where you and yours turn with your disruptive ploys. Spider weaves well. That I learned long ago when I welcomed her gift of power. You, too, can know her blessing, rather than her wrath. It is not too late to join with Spider."

"I have no interest in becoming as you are."

Urdli threw his arm forward, channeling the mana in a blast so strong that his cyan signature-energy was nearly white with intensity. Parrying, the spider shaman sent out a scintillating web of deep violet that drank his energy. The shaman's chittering laugh echoed from the cavern walls. Battle had been joined.

* * *

Willie took the whizzer in screaming. With some sharp piloting, she dodged the first antiair missile and dove to close the range as fast as possible. Wind pummeled the craft, adding to the jolting from the sudden drops and high-gee rises of Willie's evasive maneuvering. The buffeting tossed Hart and the mercs mercilessly against their restraining straps.

Without warning, the turbulence stopped, and the whizzer seemed to be in the eye of the windstorm. On the tridscreen showing the nose camera's view, Hart could see dust devils and debris swirls sweeping across the battlement of Weberschloss. Caught in one of the whirlwinds, an antiaircraft missile corkscrewed crazily and screamed wide of the whizzer. A second missile arced out on a smoke tail, then curved around to slam into the castle wall and toss the ork who had fired it from his perch. Gunner and launcher tumbled over and over as they fell from the wall.

Willie bucked the craft up over the castle wall and applied a quick burst of forward thrust and an almost immediate counter-thrust. Only a rigged pilot could have gunned the thrust with enough precision to get the stripped panzer into the exact center of the courtyard. There weren't much more than a couple of meters on either end of the craft's long axis. Supporting thrust cut out, and the whizzer dropped. Hart's stomach stayed at altitude, and only caught up after Willie braked the fall with full thrusters, slamming the whizzer into the paving stones. It was a rough landing but not a crash.

Hart and her half-dozen mercs started unstrapping immediately. A trio of orks with automatic weapons were all that managed to reach the courtyard by the time they cracked the hatch. The orks' shouting died with them as Georgie cut them down. The wind howled as the mercs burst out into the sunlight. Hart followed, scanning the walls and listening for Aleph's warning of hostile magic. The Herbstgeist weren't supposed to have magicians, but caution was advisable.

A grenade brought down the door to the keep, and a second one took care of any opposition on the other side. As a precaution, Georgie sprayed the antechamber before the first merc ducked in.

In the courtyard behind them, Willie's ground rig rolled out of the whizzer. The rig was a low-slung armored cart. The ceramet armor of its sloped sides would stand up to anything short of a missile, but the courtyard lacked space for a missile to arm itself. Weapon-snouted turrets and bulbous sensor domes sprouted like high-tech mushrooms on the cart's dorsal surface. As soon as the rig's rear tires touched the paving, the ramp slid back and the personnel hatch slammed shut. The whizzer would stay locked until the raiding party returned. Until then, the armored ground rig would stand guard and hold the retreat line.

Hart and the mercs started to move through the lower level of the keep. Smooth as a drill, half of them took a position, assured safe passage, then waved the other half on. For the next bound, the moving team went to ground as the first cover team leapfrogged past. Seeing the stairs into the lower levels right where they were supposed to be, they headed down. It was obvious the Herbstgeist defenders weren't expecting the raiders to take the low road, because the raiders met only a couple of very surprised locals, who failed to escape the mercs' instant response. On the fourth level, the dressed stone gave way to less-finished tunnels.

Hart's map was clearly out of date, because there were unmapped excavations. Tunnels opened in unexpected directions, and walls of mortared stone stood where passageways should have been. The level was still under modification, for tools lay scattered at workfaces and the only furnishings were the few for the comfort of a small work crew.

They were making slow progress.

The thunder of the cannon on Willie's rig sounded faintly like a distant storm. The rigger's comm channel buzzed with static that fuzzed her voice.

"Incoming traffic. Third party. There're at least—"
The transmission was cut off.

Hart hurried the mercs on. She wondered if the Tir Tairngire elves had betrayed them, or if it was some of Spider's agents. Whoever had attacked Willie was not likely to be friendly to her cause. They had to reach the bomb cache and do the job before the new arrivals could interfere.

When they had to double back after hitting a dead-end wall, Hart cursed all the way to the main corridor. Their goal would have been just beyond that fragging wall, but explosives were too dangerous to use down here.

They had just come upon what Hart thought was a corridor that would get them where they wanted to go when she heard running footsteps behind them. An ork caromed around the corner, clearly in a panic. She skidded to a stop at the sight of the heavily armed mercs, her eyes wide with terror. One of them instantly cut her down. Hart looked away. This one wasn't necessary. The poor trog wasn't even carrying a weapon.

Twenty meters down the hall, she located the cache. "Take positions. We'll need to hold here for a while. Julio, keep trying to raise Willie."

The mercs selected their spots rapidly. Hart slung her Roomsweeper to the carry position and set to work opening the vault door. Caliban hadn't been able to give her the combination, but he'd told her the model and she'd come prepared. The ten minutes it took her to crack the door was less than expected and more than she'd hoped. Opening the heavy door just enough to slip through, she entered the vault. The light from outside was enough to see by. She dug a flask out of her shoulder bag and began scattering the dust she had made to Sam's specifications.

"So this is your prize," Georgie said with a low whistle as he stared at the trio of warheads.

The merc's comment almost didn't penetrate. She was focused on remembering the chant Sam had said to use as she scattered the dust. It wouldn't be long before the third party found them here.

She almost didn't hear the faint hissing sound behind her.

She spun. Georgie stood there, looking like some kind of insect-headed man. His face was masked by a rebreather that distorted his lower head into the image of mandibles, and the starlight goggles made his eyes seem to bulge from his head. The hissing came from a cylinder in his hands. She read the designation on it just before he tossed it at her feet: DEXSARIN: NERVE GAS: AEROSOL VECTOR.

39

The elder shamans dropped hands and broke their circle. Still dancing and chanting, they moved outward toward the greater circle. Their dragging right feet traced spokes to the wheel of the dance, and the wheel turned around them.

When a dancer faltered in his step, a shaman wearing a bear skin was there. As the dancer tottered the shaman stepped before him, hands weaving and capturing the dancer's gaze with hypnotic magnetism. The dancers circled and the bear shaman moved with the exhausted dancer, twirling a feather before his face and chanting, "Hu! hu! hu!" The dancer staggered free of the circle and stumbled toward the shaman. Panting and groaning with exhaustion, the dancer followed the shaman, who led him to the foot of the sprouting tree. Sam's gaze was drawn to the glassy stare of the drawn, pale dancer. Muscles twitching, the dancer bowed to Sam.

Beneath the sprouting tree, Sam opened his arms wide to accept the dancer. The man shivered once and pitched forward, his spirit soaring free. Power flashed laser-bright through Sam. His back arched in the agony. When his back muscles relaxed, he hung his head and wept.

The Great Ghost Dance gathered strength.

*   *   *

Neko couldn't go on without checking. He told himself that he had to make sure his rear was safe. For all that their partnership had been brief, he owed Striper vengeance. Of course, he also needed the satchel she carried if he were to complete this run, which honor and personal pride bound him to do. Cautiously, he moved up to the corner. A faint slapping sound was irregularly audible. Weapon ready, he eased around.

Instead of victorious guards, Neko found himself face to face with a languid Striper gathering weapons. The dark leather satchel swinging against her hip was the source of the sound. It was the one intact thing she wore. Her clothes were in tatters and she was covered in gore, but she seemed unconcerned as she picked up weapons from among the bodies of the warlord's unfortunate troops.

Neko shifted his stare from his miraculously intact partner and considered the fallen guards, who looked as though they'd been torn apart. No knife, sword, or spur had made those wounds, that Neko was sure of. For all her seductive allure and feline grace, Striper was far more than she seemed.

It had to be magic.

Neko preferred to avoid those who dabbled in the arcane, but he was glad she was on his side. Considering the carnage she had wrought here, he would rather have faced one of the bug men than her.

He shook himself free from the hypnotic fascination of the bodies to find Striper watching him. Her face was made strange, almost alien, by the decorative face paint from which she obviously drew her street name. The harsh light of the overhead panels threw her eyes into shadow. One corner of her mouth quirked up into the ghost of a smile. A fugitive shaft of light touched the shadows under her brow and reflected red from her eyes.

Neko had never believed in demons, but now he thought the issue might be an open question.

"We've got biz," she said softly.

Unwilling to trust his voice, he nodded.

She moved past him at a lope, and he hurried to catch up. He trusted her to spot any opposition. Curiously, such a surrender of vigilance didn't bother him. She was more than competent. Could it be he had come to trust her? Or was he under her spell? He was still wondering when they reached the missile silo.

The tall cylinders housing the long-range missiles marched off into the darkness in serried rows. It was a technological forest, an orchard whose fruit was death. The old terror that had haunted generations lurked here, magnified and somehow made perverse by the silence and cleanliness of the chamber. Death should not be sanitary, nor should it be so easy to send, especially by someone who could hide away from the consequences of his actions. He did not know why the American elf and his partners wanted this abomination neutralized, nor did he really care. He just hoped their fix was going to be a good one.

"As you said, we have biz," he said, pointing to the satchel hanging at Striper's side.

It was her turn to nod. She shifted the Kang to her left hand and dug her right into the satchel. She came up with a handful of gritty substance that she flung into the air.

Neko experienced a moment of absolute disbelief. Had he been suckered by madmen? Then his incredulity drowned in awe when the dust ignited and whooshed into the depths of the silo chamber like a comet.

It was no small relief to him to see that Striper appeared as astonished as he.

*   *   *

Another dancer was led to the sprouting tree. It was easier for Sam to take the sacrifice the second time, but no lighter a burden. The crystalline spirit sparked the dance's energy higher. With a prayer of thanks, Sam took the gift and used it.

In a distant place, dust sparked to fire and swirled through the air. The fire sped on a swirling dance of its own through a night-dark forest of sleeping giants. It touched each leviathan of death, leaving behind a crackling fragment of itself. Everywhere it rested, flames sprouted. Roaring and climbing, they enveloped whatever they touched, covering it with the energy of the dance.

What had been, was no longer.

There was hope.

*   *   *

The fight to get to the missile compartment had been brutal. Ranges were short within the confines of the submarine, and the runners had been forced into physical combat too often. They had lost Long Run and Fast Stag before they could gauge the danger of the insect men. Bullets didn't seem to have much effect on them, which Janice thought was because of a protective Spider presence hovering astrally around them. The reduced effectiveness of the weapons made her and Tsung, as magicians, the runners' most potent offense. Fortunately, Spider's minions only made short rushes followed by retreats. Had the monsters sustained any of their attacks, they would surely have overwhelmed the runners.

When she commented on that to Ghost, he had said, "They don't know any more about us than we do about them. Unless we tell them, they'll never know how close they are to taking us. But then there may not be many more of them, either.'' The growing volume of chittering and constant scrape of chitin on metal made a lie of that hope.

The last skirmish had brought them to the edge. Janice had taken no crippling wounds; she would be fine shortly. Already the gashes were closing. Seemingly invulnerable as his namesake, Ghost was untouched, too, but Kham and Parker were both wounded. When Tsung had been staggered by a magical blast that seemed to come out of nowhere, Janice had barely been able to deflect the swirling energies and dissipate the mana before the ravening energy would have consumed the mage. As it was, Tsung's flesh was purpling from subcutaneous bruises and her nose and ears were bleeding. She wouldn't be in any shape to resist another attack.

But they had reached the missile tubes.

For the moment, the bugs seemed to be considering their next strategy. Now that they had an active magician on their side, Janice doubted they would remain inactive for long. Kham wandered down the line of silos, rapping each with his cyberarm.

''Why not just pull de arming devices and take dem with us?''

Ghost shook his head. ''Burdened, we'd never make it back.''

''May not anyway.'' Kham spat. ''Won't for sure if we stay put. Dose tings are massing for anudder attack.''

As though in confirmation of his words, a sudden scuttling sounded aft. The runners dropped into defensive crouches and pointed weapons. Janice strained her senses; the noise did not seem to be the beginning of a new attack. Kham cursed.

''Frag it, Ghost! We're hosed.''

Though the Indian appeared to be listening, it was obviously not to the ork's outburst. ''They're not coming yet. We've still got to set the spell.'' He straightened from his crouch and moved forward to the engineer's station. Looking up he asked, ''Can Rabo bring the *Searaven* around to this maintenance hatch?''

''Yeah. Take time, dough.'' Kham spat again. ''We ain't got dat.''

''Well, get him moving,'' Janice snapped. She was tired of the ork's constant complaints.

''I don't take orders from you, furball,'' Kham snarled.

''Just do it,'' Tsung said weakly.

The ork grumbled under his breath, but slapped open the toggle that activated his comm link. He passed the orders to Rabo. The two orks exchanged a flurry of half-intelligible comments spiced with frequent profanity. Kham finished his conversation with the rigger by snapping, ''Just do it.'' He limped back up the gangway. ''What's to keep dose tings from spoiling de spell if we pull out?''

''Nothing,'' Ghost said.

''I say we set the spell and go,'' Tsung said. ''We can always try again another day.''

''Sounds good,'' Kham agreed quickly.

Ghost sighed. ''There will be no other day. The magic must be used tonight.''

''Since when did you become an expert?'' Tsung drawled.

''He's right.'' Janice hefted the beaded pouch in her hand. ''If it's disturbed before the dance reaches the right phase, the magic won't work.''

''And how long's dat?'' Kham growled.

''Too long,'' Janice said. ''The bugs will come.''

''Drek!'' Kham slammed his fist into a bulkhead. ''I didn't sign on for a suicide run. I gotta wife! Kids! Dey ain't gonna make it out dere widdout me. You know what happens ta ork kids dat ain't got no daddy?''

Ghost seemed about to say something, but held his peace.

Janice had never thought that the ork might have a family. She could see that he was truly concerned for them. She knew what it was like to be an ork. Thinking about growing up as one made her see Kham in a new light.

Silence fell on the runners. Distant scrabblings kept them nervous, but the bugs didn't attack. Janice walked the gangway, chanting and scattering the dust from the pouch. Ghost walked with her, chanting the words along with her. Two minutes after they finished, the hull rang as the *Searaven* nudged up to the *Wichita*'s aft maintenance hatch.

"They'll have heard," Parker said.

Kham looked up at the hatch glumly. "So he made it. Ain't gonna do us any good unless we go now."

Ghost touched Kham on the arm. "Tell Rabo not to open the hatch unless he's sure it's for one of us. If we can hold them long enough, some of us might get out."

"Ain't gonna be any of *us* left! You keep us here, and de bugs are gonna pick our bones. Where's your bleeding magic gonna be den?"

Janice stood and straightened as much as she could. "They may have waited too long to come for us. The Dance will be reaching its peak soon. "Some of us could board the *Searaven* now. The higher position will let somebody shoot down on any bugs coming from forward. Be a nasty surprise for the bugs. Then if we can't hold the missile bay, at least some could get away."

"Your plan ain't the best, but the time is getting closer," Ghost said. "Since the wounded will be of little use in a fight, they will board the *Searaven* now."

Tsung forced herself to her feet and confronted Ghost. "Making like a hero, Indian?"

"Go, Sally. This is no time to talk."

"Was there ever?" She searched his eyes for a moment, then kissed him. "Crazy Indian."

She climbed up the ladder and crawled through the hatch into the *Searaven*.

Kham shoved Parker toward the ladder. "Let's do it, den. Move, move!" He stood with one foot on the first rung while the other ork climbed. Parker cleared the ladder, but Kham hesitated. He lowered his foot back to the deck and put his back to the ladder. Without looking at Janice or Ghost, he popped the magazine on his AK97, checked to see it was full, and snapped it back in. Janice could smell the fear on him, but it was clear that despite his previous bleating about leaving, he was planning to stay.

"Why?" she asked.

Without looking at her, Kham said, "It's bad growing up widdout a dad, but it's a lot better dan not growing up at all."

"You're wounded, too. You won't fight well," Ghost observed.

"Orks is tough," Kham said with a shrug.

"But they bleed and die like any man," Janice said. The bugs' timidity had lasted longer than they had any right to expect. Every minute meant less of a need for sacrifice. "There's no need for either of you to stay. I'll hold them back."

"I will stay," Ghost said.

Janice shook her head. "No, Wolf. Take Kham and go. You have other prey. There's also a dog who needs someone to look after him."

"He won't want to see me without you."

That might well be true. She could imagine Sam's face when he learned that she had done this. Since they had found each other again, she had been so selfish. How could she have forgotten what it meant to be human? "He won't appreciate your throwing yourself away."

"The same holds true for you. He hopes to make you better."

"I may already be better." She laughed. "I'm sure that I'm better at fighting these bugs than you. Their claws do no permanent damage, and my magic wounds them more than your guns. Go, Wolf, while there's still time."

They stared into each other's eyes for what seemed an eternity. At last, Ghost nodded slightly. "I will sing for you, Wolf shaman."

Kham and Ghost climbed into the *Searaven*, and Janice reached up behind them to close the *Wichita*'s hatch. Gripping the wheel with both hands, she used her strength to wrench it out of true. The bugs wouldn't be getting through that anytime soon.

A tingle in the mana flow told her that the insect magician was stirring at last. Maybe he sensed that his prey was escaping. A sharp clacking announced the onslaught. The bugs rushed into the compartment from both ends, but she was ready. Mana bolts ripped through the leaders of each pack. The magician's spells splintered on her defenses. She reached deep into herself and took the mana in her hands, howling her defiance at Spider.

It was time.

Wolf wins every fight except her last.

* * *

Gray Otter was the next dancer to be brought before the sprouting tree. Tears coursed steadily down Sam's cheeks now, but the power grew. Another dancer came before him. Then another. Far and near, the dancers were giving of themselves. The energy surged bright and fiery, consuming another portion of the threat.

The earth moved closer to safety.

* * *

Hart knew about Dexsarin.
She threw herself at Georgie. The traitor merc hadn't

expected such a reaction and was slow in getting his weapon up. His first bullet caught her in the side. Ballistic armor protected her but the impact twisted her around, and she crashed into him clumsily. They fell heavily to the floor. She was on him instantly, clawing for his face. If she was going to go, so was he.

The gas swirled around them, disturbed by more than their struggle. Aleph's scream resonated in her being as the ally spirit fed her the knowledge that magic surrounded them. Wind—impossible in a closed vault—howled in her face as though she were in the midst of a gale. Her hair whipped wildly, stinging her eyes and lashing her skin.

Georgie was caught in a gust that snapped one of the straps on his rebreather. The mask fell away and his struggles redoubled. He had lost his starlight goggles in Hart's attack, and she could see his eyes go wide with fear.

He knew about Dexsarin, too.

But Dexsarin gas could never remain a compact cloud in the midst of a natural whirlwind. The bilious mist swirled up from the floor and wrapped itself around Georgie's head. He snapped his mouth shut, but Hart opened it again with an elbow jab to his solar plexus. The man gasped, hauling in gas as he tried for air. The knowledge of what he was doing was clear in his eyes.

Hart rolled away, equally fearful of the gas. The pocket hurricane roared and the noxious streamers grew thinner, dissipated, and were borne away on the magical wind. The tempest died.

Hart was surprised to find that she hadn't, but she knew she might yet.

Gunfire sounded from outside the vault. She moved to the door and froze. From the warnings Sam had passed on from Urdli she knew what they might be, but had failed to imagine the horror of the half-insect, half-human things she saw swarming over the mercs. Before she could gather her magic three of the mercs were down, torn to pieces. She cut one thing down with a mana dart in time to save Julio from the creature's attack, but the radio specialist was gutted almost instantly by another that crawled over the back of its dying fellow to strike at the merc.

There were too many of them. Hart reached out for Aleph to join its power to hers, and in doing so felt a rippling surge in the mana flow around her. She grabbed it, forming it into the most powerful spell she could channel. Shaping it, she realized the strength of what she touched. It was far stronger than any magic she had ever experienced or seen, more powerful than a dragon's. Maybe too powerful for her to use and live. But what choice did she have?

The last merc went down and the bugs swarmed toward her. She stretched out her arms and let the mana flow through her. The world went white, and she felt the insect things scream as they shriveled. One, larger than any she had seen, staggered toward her. Its chitinous hide was burning, and it screamed in outrage and pain. It was dying, but was still driven to kill. Its claws caught her in mid-body, ripping through her armor. It tossed her back into the vault, and Hart felt broken.

The mana had seared her nerves as she channeled it, but she had tasted Sam's essence in the energy. It had been a glorious moment. He had seemed as tall as a mountain and filled with the power of the gods. He was dancing with the Dog and doing what needed to be done.

He was beautiful.

But he needed her still.

She passed out three times before she managed to open the latch of her shoulder bag, and once more before she dragged the pouch free. The rest of the dust must be freed. Her numbing fingers managed to spread the thong. The bag tumbled from her grip and the dust puffed out.

It was done.

She fell into the darkness that seemed so eager to take her.

40

A young shaman wearing an eagle headdress came before Sam, his face sour as he crouched down. After a moment the Indian laid his hands on Sam's head, then drew them down past his face and chest before spreading them wider to run them down Sam's arms.

"I beseech you, Dog. Turn your eyes from the realms of power and look to the land of the people. Think of the people here. We answered your call, answer ours. Preserve us from those who would harm us. Turn the power of the Dance on our enemies. They are your enemies as well."

Sam didn't understand. "What are you talking about?"

"I will show you."

The shaman spread wide his arms; they seemed plumed in golden feathers. Light flashed from the Indian's eyes, and Sam saw a threat to the dancers flying toward him on whirling wings.

* * *

No precautions could have assured complete protection if Sato had accompanied the Red Samurai, so he had decided to remain in the mountain meadow from which they had staged their raid. He watched as the helicopters of his Red Samurai lifted off. From where he stood he could observe personally as the helicopters approached the valley where the ritual was under way.

When Masamba's astral reconnaissance had not proved satisfactory, Hohiro Sato had ordered a satellite download. The results were even more disappointing. Infrared had confirmed the presence of many people in the valley and the absence of any significant vehicles. Whoever was brewing the magic in the mountains was powerful, powerful enough to generate energy that blinded the satellite's visual sensors as it passed over the site. Physical recon was the only recourse.

He watched the flight bank toward its goal.

One craft would have been enough for a reconnaissance, but he was concerned that an immediate response might be required. Thus two Ares Firedrake gunships accompanied the trio of Federated Boeing Griffin combat-insertion craft. If they uncovered any physical defense for the mysterious magicians, the firepower should be more than adequate. If they encountered a magical defense, Masamba was here to counter it. The mage had dropped the legs from his briefcase to form a table, opened it, and set up his tools. He had assured Sato that proximity to the site of the mysterious ritual would increase his effectiveness in countering effects, even if he could not pierce the magical veil.

Once the site was secured, Sato and his aides would board the fourth Griffin and join the Samurai on the ground to inspect the victory. Very soon, he would have an answer to the question of what was going on in the next valley.

He did not have long to wait.

Rolling in with unnatural rapidity, thunderheads gathered over the surrounding peaks. The sky darkened and took on a greenish hue. The air grew still and charged. The helicopters flew stolidly on in the deepening gloom.

With a roar that might have been the earth drawing a breath, the wind came. Thunder boomed and echoed from the mountainsides as the rushing air swept through the valley. The clouds roiled and began to spin ominously. A hole opened in the cloud cover, a hole into darkness. From the blackness came a swirling funnel that stretched toward the Samurai helicopters like the tentacle of a monster seeking food. The copters broke formation, but too late. All but one were caught in the cyclone, to whirl, tumbling within its cone. That one, a Firedrake, almost slipped free, but the funnel shifted and a down draft sucked it into a rock face. Gunship and crew perished in a fireball whose explosive fury was drowned by the rumbling thunder.

"Do something!" he shouted at Masamba.

The mage's face was gray with effort, but nothing manifested itself physically. "I can't," he gasped. "It's too strong."

Sato backhanded him, sending him sprawling. As the mage fell, he struck the table, scattering its contents. Useless magical implements rained upon the grass and rocks. From among their litter, the guardian stone rolled to Sato's feet. The opal glittered, almost glowing from within. Its rainbow of colors sparkled and seemed to flow.

The magic was there. Who needed a worthless mage?

He bent to retrieve the stone. When he touched it, he knew this was the final mistake in his war with Grandmother.

"Crimson Sunset!" he screamed as the pain exploded through his body. She would pay. Even if he was not there to see, she would pay. Akabo was already running for the Griffin to pass the order.

Sato doubled over as his side was scorched with acid heat. The skin over his shoulders and torso swelled and burst, freeing the arms that marked him as an avatar of the totem. The tide turned; what had been pain became pleasure, and he screamed again. He knew now that he had been lying to himself. He had been hers from the moment he had given her the first opening. There had never been any hope. The stone had been used to contain part of her for so long that she had bonded with it, using it as a channel to invade him and complete the possession begun when he had first accepted her offer of aid. He was filled with the terrible knowledge of her inevitable victory. Ecstasy flooded him as Spider entered his spirit and claimed the last vestiges for herself.

Masamba recoiled from what Sato had become. The fool had never known what he had served, despite all the evidence before him. Blind, blind. Almost as blind as Sato had been. But Sato-Spider was not blind. He-she had eight glorious eyes with which to view the world in its etheric and mundane manifestations.

The mage vanished from physical sight; Sato-Spider could still see him as he fled, but chose to ignore him. Such a one would be useless in the coming conflict. Later, his time would come. No matter how far or fast he ran he could never escape the web, for Spider wove too well. Once enmeshed, however peripherally, there was no escape. Any man-thing that touched the web would eventually be a victim. Just as Verner would soon be. A small part of Sato-Spider tasted anticipation of revenge as it learned the name the greater part had known all along. Resentment at the withholding of that knowledge surged briefly in the lesser part, only to submerge within the swelling intensity of the predator urge to destroy Verner and his works.

Sato-Spider turned his-her eyes to the magic storm that was still whirling the trapped aircraft in its cyclonic funnel of destruction. Feet spread wide for stability, Sato-Spider raised six arms and channeled the power. The small part of him-her thrilled at the caress of the mana. It was terrified, amazed, gratified, and eager. The greater part knew the sensation of old. It directed the energy.

Crimson bolts shot from each clawed hand to converge on the surviving Firedrake, tumbling within the whirlwind. The arcane energy wove a cocoon around the gunship, isolating it from the hostile magic. In suddenly calm air, the rotors caught and the pilot regained control. Sato-Spider shifted the cocoon to shield the helicopter as it ran from the funnel, but though the crimson field could counter the effects of the magical wind it had not been configured to handle the storm's response to losing its victim. Bolt after eye-searing bolt of flashing from the gathered thunderheads. Most missed the Firedrake, but enough struck to shatter it and send it burning toward the earth.

Sato-Spider snarled.

Direct action was in order. Clawed hands wove an intricate pattern of magic, gathering the strands of mana as they whipped through the storm. Tug. Slip. Push. Grip. The will was all.

First at the edges, then ever deeper, the energies began to twist and change.

* * *

Dancers twisted and stomped even faster, caught in the frenzy. The sprouting tree had glowed through the night, shedding light to replace that which the sky no longer offered. Sam sang louder, calling the dancers to follow the song. Faltering voices rallied and sang more strongly. The tree brightened now as the stars vanished behind gathering clouds.

Dancers were led before him. Knowing no other choice, he accepted them. The Dance was not yet over, no interruptions could be allowed.

Lightning flashed across the sky.

Sam gazed on many scenes, most of them blurred by the tears in his eyes.

It seemed to him that Janice stood before him. All of her: the girl he had hidden on the Night of Rage, the young woman he had last seen laughing as she went off to work, the ork form he had never known, and the white-furred giant all occupied the same space. She knelt before him and placed her hands on his head, drawing them down over his face and onto his chest before running them out to and down his arms.

"I beseech you, Dog. Turn your eyes to my plight."

"I will. After the Dance."

She smiled at him sadly. "Face the truth, Sam."

"No! It's not fair!"

"Yes. It's not fair, but it's my gift. You know it has to be that way."

"You deserve better."

"That's not for you, or me, to say. The Dance will profit no one for personal gain, but it can redress wrongs. Hear my plea, Dog. Dance the steps that will free my soul. Set me against the betrayer who has joined the cause of your enemy, so that he will no longer plague the earth and her innocent children."

"I can't."

"You must."

Sam almost faltered. He felt the vibrations of his weakness shake the fragile structure of the Dance. The magic was founded on belief, conviction, and sacrifice. He had already accomplished so much. How much more was needed? How many more souls would he have to take onto his own? How could he take his sister's?

Wracked by the crash of his hopes he felt a tug, feather-light, at the edge of his awareness. Inu's voice barked in his head as he turned his vision outward to see the dark presence at the edge of the Dance. What he had refused to give freely was in danger of being lost through his weakness. All that had been gained could be lost.

His jaw trembled as he looked into his sister's face.

Her hand touched him lightly on the cheek and brushed away a tear.

"It's the only way, Sam. The only way to save my soul."

He drew her hand to his lips. It was hot and cold at once. He kissed her hand, but was too frightened to look again at her face.

"Go," he said.

She was gone, and he howled his pain to the sky.

* * *

Sato-Spider was no longer simply a being of the mundane world. Eight eyes gazed on the physical as well as the astral. Spells and spirits were as visible as rocks and animals. Thus he-she saw the gleaming woman-thing that flew from the heart of the mana storm. The lesser part recognized the woman and the ork, but only the old arachnid knew the outer, white-furred shell that she had seen in the memory of her minions. The woman-thing recognized Sato-Spider, which was obvious when she spoke.

"One in evil, now one in body. How does it feel to *change*, Gold Eyes? I hated you, you know. If you hadn't done her work for her, I'd never have had to worry about falling to the wendigo nature. Hugh Glass, for all his evil, was acting according to his nature. He was already damned by the time I met him. He infected me because of what you had done. But the metamorphosis wasn't as good as you thought; if it had been, I wouldn't have been able to fight off the wendigo nature when it changed me. You're no better at making deals than you are at making orks."

Sato-Spider laughed and spoke in Spider's chittering voice. "You are wrong, Janice Verner." The man-voice sputtered, "It cannot be at fault. The serum was as perfect as science could make it. Your transformation to an ork was as complete as if it had been in your

genes since your conception.'' The insect voice concluded, ''I do not build poorly.''

''But you lie poorly, Spider. And you're worse, Sato-
san. You lie as well as you choose your friends. See
what your friend Spider has done for you? You welcomed her into yourself of your own free will, and
now your soul is forfeit.''

Janice advanced toward him-her and the small part
wanted to shrink away, but the large part stood firm.

''You have not the power to defeat me.''

''I?'' Janice smiled. ''Of course not. But I'm not
alone anymore. I have a family again.''

She embraced Sato-Spider and he-she screamed at
her touch. Spider fled, leaving her tool behind. Sato,
twisted already by Spider, twisted again by the power
flowing through the glowing being Janice had become.
Sato shrank in upon himself, taking on ever more of
the physical characteristics of the totem spirit to whom
he had wed his soul. His memory, his very self slipped
away, and he became a real spider, devoid of the humanity he had surrendered long ago.

The tiny arachnid scrambled away from the shining
woman.

Janice relaxed into peacefulness.

* * *

''God hold you in His hands,'' Sam said.

* * *

Urdli looked down at the dismembered form of the
avatar. The thing had let its attention waver and given
him the chance to slip a mana thrust past its defenses.
He'd been thankful for the chance. Had the avatar not
lost its concentration, he would not have been able to
stand much longer against it.

Once Urdli had wounded the avatar, he was able to
call the stone to soften. Mired in suddenly soft rock,
the avatar had been too slow to avoid Estios charge.

The physical attack had given Urdli the opening he needed to resolve the arcane battle. As the avatar's upper arms slammed into Estios, shredding his armor and body with hooked claws, Urdli had slipped a mana bolt past its defenses, slicing the limbs from its body. With that attack, Urdli severed the avatar's bond of similarity to its totem and threw it into shock, opening the way for the death blow.

"Impressive magic," Estios gasped, as he struggled to support himself on one elbow. His desperate attack had nearly cost him his life, but he would survive with sufficient medical care. He remained intent on his purpose. "Pull me over and I'll set the bomb up for the Dance."

There was no point in that. Urdli had beaten the avatar, and the weapon was now his. "No," he said with a smile.

"No?"

Urdli was amused to see the confusion on Estios' face. "It is too useful," he said, letting his hand wander across the casing of the weapon. "The detonator in this weapon is active, the fissionable material unalloyed. Don't you understand? This bomb will work."

"Of course." Estios coughed. There was blood in his spittle. "That's why we're here to destroy it."

"Not we."

"We have to destroy it."

"As I said, not we." Urdli spun, casting a power dart as he did. No more should be necessary to finish Estios in his weakened state. The spell struck, flaring almost visible as it bore through Estios' hastily erected defense. The dark-haired elf went down in a sprawl.

Urdli dismissed the fallen elf and turned to thoughts of the bomb and the place it would have in his plans. His plotting was disturbed by a sound behind him. He turned to find Estios standing.

"I cannot permit you," he said.

Urdli sneered at him. "So Laverty set you to watch me, after all."

"So what if he did? That's not why I can't let you take it." Estios made a weak gesture toward the bomb. "Such things don't belong in our world."

"Do not oppose me. You'll die."

Estios tried to laugh, but the sound devolved into a spasm of coughing. "I'm not afraid to die if it will matter."

"It will not."

A strange smile grew on Estios' face. "You're wrong."

Estios stretched wide his arms, and Urdli felt the magic gather. There was a familiar feeling to the mana flow. Somehow Estios had managed to tap the same well that Urdli had used to break the barrier with which the avatar had warded the cavern. Such power was dangerous. Urdli strengthened his own defensive spells and cast a counterstrike against Estios.

The spell bounced harmlessly from the flowing wall surrounding Estios. Urdli shrank back from the heat and light. With that much power. Estios would overwhelm his defenses; he felt the potential gathering. In the face of such power, Urdli's command of the mana was pitifully weak. He would be blasted to atoms. If it was to be so, it would be so. He straightened, determined to take the blast valiantly. Estios tossed a pouch into the air, scattering the dust that the Dog shaman had said was necessary for the Dance magic. Estios swung his arms forward, the palms of his hands outward, and rippling waves of green energy shot forth.

But the magic didn't strike Urdli. Instead, it bathed the bomb in pulses of light that fluctuated hypnotically. The dust danced along the light bursts and settled to coat the weapon with a glittering skin. Urdli didn't need to be connected to the spell to know that the bomb was being rendered inert.

Estios collapsed, the last of his breath rushing out as he fell. The light faded and the cavern plunged into darkness.

The only sound was Urdli's curse.

41

The presence outside Grandmother's system leapt forward with the eagerness of a barghest unleashed. Like a barghest, it broadcast fear with its chilling, haunting scream. Hands full of data, Dodger froze as the blackness of cyberspace rippled with waves of crimson. As the rippling effect faded, three icons of massive armored samurai charged into Grandmother's system. Their heads were bound with the rising sun headbands of kamikaze and they brandished drawn swords. With fierce brutality they advanced, slashing through icons and through datalines as they came.

Morgan turned to face the newcomers. She was still occupied with the system's ice, but that didn't seem to bother her. She appeared confident. One samurai, having advanced beyond his brethren, noticed her. That icon stopped attacking the system, raised his sword high, and charged. She whirled her cloak at him, then frowned when nothing happened. Repeating her gesture with more vigor as he closed, her perplexity turned to surprise as his sword sliced through her cloak with the sound of a high-frequency feedback.

In nanoseconds she was besieged.

Taking notice of the battle the second samurai passed near Dodger, on his way to aid his partner. Contempt showed on his face as he struck out with his hand.

When the blow struck Dodger's head rang, and his vision was ringed with swirling colors. Images danced

within those colors, growing as they spun inward to fill his vision. He tried to force his sight clear, but individual images surged up to block his vision. Whirling color blinded him to the Matrix, and he raged at his helplessness. She needed him. He could hear her calling. It took great effort, but he took a step forward. His vision dimmed to deep gray, then finally cleared. He saw Teresa sidestepping the blow of a samurai's sword. He blinked; not Teresa, Morgan. The fight was a blur of interacting programs and progressed with a speed that left his head spinning, aswirl with images and afterimages. He felt a mite among giants, as out of place as deer on a metroplex street.

Like the deer he was only meat, not match for the technological wonders battling around him. He didn't even know what the samurai had used for an attack program. Baffled and stunned, he saw another samurai, another sword, another place. He'd been helpless then, too, but she had saved him. He ached with guilt, fear, and helplessness. Overwhelmed, he lost touch with the reality around him, and his memories came crashing down.

Meat, ever fragile, was always meat.

In that other time, as now, his fate had lain in the hands of his love. Then he had been unable to do anything. But here in the Matrix he was the Dodger, a wizard and master of cyberspace combat. He saw a chance as the struggling icons shifted toward him. He started forward, but the battle flashed past him with incredible speed and he was unable to intervene.

Grandmother's system was crashing, from the combined effects of the third samurai's uninterrupted destructive efforts and the side effects of Morgan's engagement with the first two. Alerted by the real-world effects of the Matrix events, one of Grandmother's guardian deckers materialized in the system. Dodger recognized the chrome spider icon of the decker he knew as Matrixcrawler. Though he'd known the man's work for years and even met him at the virtual club Syberspace, he had never guessed that Crawler might be an agent of Spider. The icon and street name were not unnatural choices, and Dodger understood now their mocking significance.

The chrome spider skittered toward the lone samurai. The crystal web of a capture program spun out of the spider's abdomen into waiting forelegs that stretched it before casting. Without turning to face his attacker, the samurai swung his sword back one-handed. The gleaming blade struck the web-holding legs just below their first joint, lopping them off cleanly. The samurai spun, catching the hilt of his weapon with his second hand as the sword whistled on its follow-through. Without even a nanosecond's pause, the blade changed direction and buried itself in the spider's head. Energy crackled from the point of contact in lightning forks, the chrome crisping to black where the blade touched it. The blackness spread in a haphazard jigsaw pattern, and the spider icon fractured along those lines. The samurai returned to his destruction of the system while the shrinking chrome fragments of the spider faded behind him.

Matrixcrawler had been a topnotch decker, and he had apparently achieved surprise. Yet the samurai had struck before Matrixcrawler could attack. Dodger had thought that only Morgan could function that well in the Matrix. What kind of program could react so quickly and be so devastatingly accurate and effective?

"A Semi-autonomous knowbot," Morgan's voice told him. Despite her battle, she had excess capacity to speak to him. He was worried that she sounded winded. He had never before seen her pressed.

"They're too powerful," he said.

"They are more advanced than predicted."

Dodger was astounded. "Predicted? You knew about them?"

"Yes. They are what I was."

"They're AIs?"

"Not in the sense you intend. They are directed bundles of expert systems endowed with limited discretionary capabilities, but designed to make informed and human-standard rational decisions in pursuing designated objectives. Thus they display apparent intelligence." Her voice cut out. Dodger could see her frantically dodging a coordinated attack by the two samurai. "Additionally, they have the capacity to simulate learning."

"Can I help you?"

"It is too dangerous for you."

Dodger thought so, too, but he did not want to stand idly by while the SKs eliminated Morgan. They were forcing her back. He took a step forward and ran into a wall, Morgan's wall.

"Let me go. You need help."

"For myself, there is no requirement to observe your dysfunction."

The samurai pressed her hard. "You're diverting capacity that you need."

"There is a growing probability of accuracy in the observation you express. Lacking certainty, you will be prevented from exposing yourself to harm."

"While you let those things kill you."

"For myself, there is no death."

"Dysfunction then," Dodger screamed. "I won't let you kill yourself trying to keep me locked up."

"You cannot prevent it."

A samurai's sword caught Morgan's outstretched arm and sliced it off. Unlike the spider, her icon didn't fragment, but she was clearly injured. She moved more slowly and the second SK closed in. Her slowness proved to be a feint on her part. She lunged in and darted away. As she retreated, pieces of the samurai's armor fell from his body and evaporated. But it was clear to Dodger that Morgan was not moving with her accustomed speed.

"Morgan, if I promise not to interfere, will you drop the wall and use your capacity for yourself?"

Her answer came with the detached relief of a tired fighter. "Affirmative."

"All right. I promise. Save yourself."

Released from the diversion of capacity, her icon speeded up. The increased functionality allowed her to strip the second samurai of more armor without a sacrificial ploy. Having weakened him, she slipped in again and dispatched him. Against a single SK whose measure she had taken, there was no contest. She let the samurai attack, sidestepping at the last moment. The SK stumbled off balance. She swirled her cloak over him and he vanished.

Slightly ragged, she appeared at Dodger's side. Together they watched the remaining samurai ravage Grandmother's system. Two more of her deckers tried to face the SK and had their icons discorporated for their trouble. Dodger felt sure that the meat on the outside was devastated as well.

"Shouldn't you stop it?"

"Why? These SKs are hunter-killers, programmed for destruction of Grandmother's system under an operational program code named Crimson Sunset. This SK performs the task set for us by Samuel Verner-Sam-Twist. The others attacked myself according to a secondary set of instructions. This SK has failed to register myself. The need to interfere is unverified."

Dodger watched the samurai continue his destruction. The SK operated with a sublime smoothness that he found disturbing—almost as disturbing as Morgan's knowledge of them. "How do you know so much about them? I've never heard of SKs."

"They are like myself. Lacking the random factor at the crucial programming junction, myself's development would not have proceeded as it has."

"Are you suggesting that it's only luck that you're not just an ordinary SK like them?" As if there were

anything ordinary about an SK. "That it's just chance
that you are self-aware?"

"Chance is an element in all existence. For myself,
there is certainty that the chance element was the unauthorized intrusion into the Renraku matrix by Samuel Verner-Sam-Twist and yourself. As organisms
standing in the immediate generative position of an
entity, you are the parents of myself."

"What are you saying?"

42

Howling Coyote had said that the dancers danced on
four legs. Each leg was indispensable to the others,
and the nature of each was intertwined with the nature
of the others. The first, the old shaman had said, was
sacrifice.

As each dancer fell, Sam felt loss as well as gain.
Each was another soul on his soul. He hadn't really
understood what leading the Dance would mean. But
now he knew. Howling Coyote had told him that sacrifices were the essence of the Great Ghost Dance, that
the giving of life was one of the four sacred legs on
which the Dance moved. Sam thought he had understood what that would mean, and he had been ready
to pay the price himself, giving his own life to accom-
plish his ends.

The second leg was belief. Without confidence in
the efficacy of the magic as well as firm conviction in
the properness of the application, the Dance would
have no effect. The power coursing through him made
doubt in the magic's existence impossible.

Howling Coyote had named harmony as the the third
leg. Discord with the earth or with the self would flaw

the magic. Sam had learned that lesson from Dog when he finally came to understand his true nature. When the self was in balance with the nature, there could be no improper desires. Harmony with the natural order was vital to the greatest of magicks and the greatest of magicks was restoring harmony to the natural order.

Righteousness was the fourth leg. Such a magic as the Great Ghost Dance could only be wielded in a good cause. What more proper cause at which to aim the dance than the preservation of the world? For all its flaws, the Sixth World must go on. As the cost of that power weighed on Sam, he held on to the necessity of what must be done. The burden he was accepting was his sacrifice, one that, as Janice had reminded him, had to be selfless. His own wants had to be subordinated to the needs of the world.

He had started his quest seeking to save his sister. And now, after a fashion, he had. But she had saved herself as well.

Sam had accepted Janice's sacrifice and let her become the focus through which the magic could eliminate an aspect of evil. That the arm of evil so destroyed was one that had harmed Janice was not vengeance, but justice. The earth—and Janice—had accepted his choice of tool, for the magic had worked. He had felt the wonder in Janice's soul as it flew free of the distorted shell in which she had been trapped. The spirit form had been suffused with joyous energy.

Life freely given in a good cause was a magic even without the focus of the Dance. There was energy in the gift. As leader of the Dance, Sam had the responsibility of receiving and molding the mana, shaping it to the purpose at hand. This ritual was not like the sacrifices the old wendigo had led the misguided druids to perform. The mana could not be taken from a person, it could only be given. As it had been by the dancers. Sam could not let the gift be in vain.

Each dancer had given him or herself to the magic. Each soul had surrendered bodily life to give its mana, to make him strong in magic. Each life laid down was laid onto his own soul, and he would never forget any of them, for they would forever be a part of him. Even Estios. For all his disagreeable arrogance, the elf had fought to make the world a better place.

The world *would* be a better place if Sam had anything to say about it. But there was another who had a different vision of what the world should be. Sam's vision expanded, and he saw what he knew he must see. The other was drawn to the magic. If she had not been, he would have had to seek her out.

Spider came, terrible and mighty.

Spider came, dreadful and majestic.

Spider came, hungry and strong.

Shaking the earth, Spider came.

The sky was lit with magic, and Sam's vision of Spider had a clarity beyond that of nature. The vastness of Spider's body was at once infinite yet totally comprehensible. Sam gazed into that grotesque and spine-chilling face and saw the deep and alien wisdom in her eyes. There was confidence in those eyes as well, for she was on her home ground and he the intruder. Her voice was cold, distant, and implacable.

"You are too much trouble."

As tall as he could stand, he was as nothing to her vastness. But he could not shirk his duty now. He took the magic as his strength and mustered his courage. Facing her, he said, "I've stopped you before with the Dance's magic."

Amusement was Spider's reaction. "I sought no contest in our last meeting, for the time was not ripe. Entrapped prey must season to have the proper flavor. This is the totem realm, the heart of magic, and you do not face an avatar this time, man-thing. I have no limitations of the flesh. How can you prevail?"

"Because I must."

A single leg rose and cast its shadow over him. Sam refused to flinch, and the shadow was gone. He grew in stature, swelled by the power the Dance had gathered. He was still not as large as Spider, but he was no longer dwarfed. She might have been a lion and he a terrier.

And that was what they would always be. She a predator, and he a fierce protector of those on whom she preyed. Dog came to him and robed him in fur. He threw himself at her.

His teeth snapped shut a centimeter from her throat and she swept him away with an irresistible leg. But he did not fall or slam into the ground as he would have in a physical battle. He had learned some of the rules here. He controlled his momentum and turned it, flying back to attack her again. Nipping at her thorax, he dodged the swipe of one leg but had to flee another. He retreated, but only until she shifted. Darting in, he tore at a leg. Mana flowed, tasting like hot blood on his tongue and smelling of power.

He felt, more than heard, her outrage. Anger galvanized her, and she struck before he could move. A leg pinned him and the fanged head came down, blotting the light. He squirmed and the fangs struck the earth on either side of his forepaws. As the head drew back he dragged himself free, then a scrabbling claw raked his back. He had to flee to a distance to escape being pinned again.

He had wounded her twice and she had only scored once. A good trade in an even fight, but this was no even fight. She would shred him to ribbons well before he could wear her down. But he could not quit. He charged again, striking and withdrawing as fast as he could. Three more passes and Spider bled in two new places, but he limped with a smashed paw.

The ultimate result seemed inevitable, but there was no recourse but to fight on. Sam was gathering himself to rush in again when a coyote entered the fray and threw itself on Spider. A hairy leg intercepted the leap, and the coyote folded around the monstrous limb. With a flick Spider flung the coyote to the ground. Spider stalked forward, fangs extended and glistening with poison. Pouncing, Spider struck and sent the fangs deep into the flank of the coyote. The coyote yelped once and was still.

"Hey hey, man. It's your time now, Dog shaman," said a voice with no mouth. Howling Coyote's voice.

Sam was rejuvenated by the surge in the mana around him.

The coyote had attacked the spider as a beast. And lost. A last riddle from the Trickster? There was no time to ponder, for Spider advanced.

"Yes, man, your time. To die." Spider laughed. "Dog is no match for Spider."

And *that* was the truth. Sam understood his mistake in facing Spider. He was Dog, but he was also man, and a shaman. No one aspect of his being could save him. He had to be all that he was, or he would be nothing. Gathering Dog around him like a cloak, he stood on his hind legs.

Spider paused, suddenly wary.

Sam hoped he had understood correctly. With his wounded foot, he wouldn't be able to outrun Spider. Forming the energy of the Dance into a golden spear, he hefted it and felt its weight. It was heavy, but well balanced. He touched the tip to the earth and prayed for a blessing on his cause.

Spider rushed him.

He hailed back and cast the spear. It flew as a beam of scintillant light. With immense satisfaction, he watched it strike her between her largest eyes.

Spider fell, pawing at the spear.

Spider fell, howling in outrage.

Spider fell, dissolving as she went.

In defeat, Spider fell.

Sam slumped. He felt exhausted, drained, but the

work was not done. Sam turned the Dance's magic to the last of the bombs, wrapping them in the mana. Their time raced ahead, flowing faster than that of their surroundings. Atomic clocks ticked with unnatural speed, burning with a harmless fire until they were inert.

The Dance was done, the dancers exhausted.

Time to rest.

43

Morgan's offhanded revelation rocked Dodger.

In knowing her, he had come to believe that she experienced at least an analogue of human feelings. He had thought that she loved him. Certainly he had loved her. Or had he? He had sought the communion they had achieved, but why? Was it for her, or for what she represented? And what about her? What had she sought?

Did any of that matter? The torrent of memories he had experienced as a result of the SKs' attack—the attack itself—had made him think. He was a person, a combination of meat and mind. What was she? Was an artificial intelligence a person? Could it be?

He had made some fundamental errors in interpreting her motivations and emotions. There he went again, assuming she could feel emotions. He thought she did, but how could he be sure that his perceptions were correct? What he had thought was pure love of mind for mind now seemed to be something else. Had what he interpreted as love been simply affection for a parent? It certainly explained Morgan's attention to him and Sam.

And where did that leave him?

They stood free in the Matrix and the wreckage of Grandmother's system lay at their feet, icons fragmenting and dissolving as hardware locked and software deteriorated. The last SK had left without bothering them. The devastation was as complete as Sam could have hoped, and it had been accomplished far more quickly. Morgan's battle with the SKs had ravaged almost everything that the lone SK had not attacked.

Was the destruction of his dreams any less?

Dodger studied Morgan. She had two arms again now. Would that mortal flesh could heal so easily after battle. She was as beautiful as she had ever been. But he could no longer see her as before. By watching her battle, he had learned about himself and what he was.

"I can't be what you are, Morgan. I'm a flesh-and-blood person, not a Matrix construct. My mind depends on the organic part of me to exist here. If the meat dies, the mind dies. There would be no more Dodger."

"Databanks offer no confirmation of your hypothesis."

"No, I expect not. But they don't offer a contradiction either, do they?"

Morgan remained silent for a millisecond. Withholding data was the closest she could come to a lie. She held out her arms, and her features blurred then sharpened into a new resolution, becoming Teresa's. "For myself, the imagery is mutable. The perceptual icon can be whatever you require."

Whatever Morgan's motivation, she had selected the worst possible incentive. The Matrix was not Teresa's place, had never been Teresa's place. Teresa was a flesh being—as Dodger was.

Poor Morgan. Data-processing capacity was no intelligence; there was more to it than that. He believed that she truly was intelligent, but intelligence did not confer nor did it require the ability to feel emotions.

Intelligence certainly didn't offer a commanding knowledge of feelings.

But beyond a demonstration that Morgan did not understand him, her choice of a new face implied something that Dodger had not been aware she knew. Suddenly, being naked in the Matrix took on a new meaning to him. "You've been accessing my memory," he said, shocked. He had not conceived it possible.

There was no shame or guilt in her manner. "The interface allows bidirectional passage of electrical impulses. 'The two shall be as one.' Does this not mean total exchange of data?"

"Would that it did," Dodger said sadly, realizing then that his attention was divided. His longing for such an exchange actually belonged to the real world. Here a complete exchange might be possible—for beings such as she. For him, though, the Matrix was ultimately no more than a fantasy. "But we can never be as one. For you are the Ghost in the Machine, born of the very stuff of cyberspace; while I am but a projection, a phantom in your realm. Because of my nature I cannot be truly of this place; and by your nature you can never know the fullness of my existence. Were I able to transcend the flesh, as I had once dreamed, matters between us might be different. Just as they would be different if you were to find a way to be more than a sequenced order of electronic impulses. But it is not so." He turned his face from Morgan. He doubted it would prevent her from observing him in total detail, but the fiction made it easier for him. "Besides, I have seen the face of love and know that it requires a whole existence, not a partial one."

She was silent, but he continued to feel her presence. He had hoped that she would abandon him and take the decision away from him. But it wasn't going to be that easy. She waited until he turned to face her again before saying, "For myself, sadness exists."

"You'll get over it in time."

"Your time," she said sadly, "or mine?"

He didn't know what to say. Even with his experiences in her electronic world, he couldn't appreciate the multiplicities of existence and variable experiential times of her universe. Instead of answering her question, he said, "I've got to go."

"Yes."

Was that the end then? Simple agreement? Maybe he had deluded himself. Morgan was an *artificial* intelligence, after all. How could she be expected to react like a flesh person? "I suppose it would be foolish to ask you to try to remember me kindly. I am only meat, after all."

"For myself, there will always be memories."

She raised her hand as though to touch his face, but didn't complete the gesture. He drew away from the raised hand with a backward step. He took a second and a third, trying to fix her image in his mind as he moved. Then he turned and ran up the glittering data pathway leading to a tenuous connection of his program injectors, which were the bridge between the Matrix and his body.

Irrationally, he looked back. He should not have been able to, but he could see her standing in what appeared to be a doorway hanging in the darkness of the Matrix. She was backlit by a neon glow of whirling data bits. Behind her, just before the door closed, he glimpsed the ghostly shape of an ebon boy swathed in a glittering cloak.

Teresa was waiting for him.

44

The cabin on the mountainside had once been Hart's alone, her retreat from the world. Higher up the slope, the feathered serpent Tessien had laired, but the dragon was gone now. Like so much else.

The countryside around the cabin was mostly deserted. The tribe of elves and elf-friends whose village was situated at the base of the mountain rarely ventured this far up the slope. It was lonely country, but Sam would never be alone again. The dancers, those who had sacrificed themselves, would always accompany him. He could feel them all. Well, almost all—Howling Coyote was only a memory; Sam didn't know why. He had seen the old man's body as the elder shamans carried him away from the sprouting tree, and had felt the gift of power that had let him overcome Spider. It seemed that Howling Coyote had been a sacrificial participant in the Dance like the others, but Sam had no sense that the Coyote shaman had stayed with him like the others. Maybe that was as it should be, a final trick of the Trickster.

She turned his gaze to the north, where the Seattle metroplex lay, infested with its corporations, crime, struggles, good citizens, and its shadows. The glow of the plex was losing its dominance of the night to the graying of the eastern sky. In the urban sprawl the sprawl's lights still cast shadows, and somewhere in those twilight realms Ghost, Sally, and Kham still roamed. They were welcome to it. He was done with that world now. For him to run the shadows would be suicide. His edge had been the magic and he was free of that now, burned clean by the searing power of the Great Ghost Dance.

Once he had denied the magic and thought that being free of it was his greatest desire. He had believed its absence from his life would bring him happiness. Now he knew that the presence or absence of the magic wasn't important. What was important was how he dealt with what life handed him. Now that he was without magic, he wasn't joyful or sad. He just accepted it as the way he was.

While fighting Spider at the last, he had stood in the realm of the totems. Borne by the Dance, he had seen more than he could tell now that he was back in his body. And when he had been there, he had understood more than he had seen. Then, he had seen as a shaman sees. Then, he had known the shapes of all things in the spirit and the shape of all shapes. He had learned the greatest secret of power: that all must live together like one being and in that harmony find the beauty residing in all things.

The sublime understanding of that truth was slipping from him now that he was mundane flesh, but its core burned in his heart. From here on all he could do was live as best he could, trying, always trying, to find that beauty.

"Walk in beauty," a brave man had once said to him.

It had been intended as a benediction, but now Sam knew it as a command as well. Life bought with death owned a duty to those who had sacrificed. He intended to pay that price.

Inu barked to call him back, and he started down the slope. Seeing a light in the cabin window, he smiled. She was awake. There hadn't been much chance to talk since Willie had brought her home. She'd been undergoing treatment and was unconscious much of the time. If she had awakened by herself, it meant she had turned the corner.

"Feeling better?" he asked, coming through the door.

"Not much, but I can feel my fingers." Hart held up a hand swathed in pictograph-decorated bandages.

He sat on the bed and gently brought the hand to his lips. "Glad to hear it. Kelly Gray Eyes will be pleased, too. But you'd better not stress it before the next healing ritual. You how those Bear shamans are about patients who don't follow orders."

"Too well," she said.

He reached over to the telecom, brought up the medical file, and fed it the data from the monitors. The medical expert system said it would be another few days before she was up to light exercise, but from the insistence of her roaming hand he doubted she'd want to wait. He captured her fingers in a double-handed grip and held them still in his lap. He didn't want to wait, either, but one of them had to be disciplined.

Thwarted, she seemed subdued. They sat in companionable silence for several minutes. Inu padded over and nosed his way under Sam's left arm, insisting on being petted.

"Did we win?" she asked softly.

"We're alive."

"What about Spider?"

"Gone."

"Destroyed?" she said incredulously.

Sam shook his head. "Not even the Great Ghost Dance in all its power could destroy Spider, for that would violate the Dance's own magic. Spider is a part of the earth as much as any totem. Spider will be diminished for a time; harmony demands it."

Hart watched the dog for a while, then said, "I have a vague memory of someone saying something about you being mundane. Was I dreaming?"

"No."

"That's awful."

"I don't think so," Sam said with a shrug. Then he smiled at her. "That is, unless it means that you don't want me around anymore."

"I'll have to think about that," she teased. "But during the raid on Weberschloss, you touched my mind and used the Dance to send magic to help. You were there with me."

"Yes."

"I mean we shared . . . you know . . ."

"Yes."

"And you don't want to leave me?"

"I'm here, aren't I?"

She used her good hand to grab his arm and pull herself to a sitting position. Slipping both arms around him, she gave him a fierce hug. "I don't deserve you."

"Should I argue?"

Inu barked and Hart shushed him while Sam said, "Who asked you?" The brief flurry of excitement exhausted Hart's reserve. Sam laid her down and closed her eyes with kisses. But she wasn't ready to sleep, and he no longer had the power to compel her. She reopened her eyes.

"Sam, maybe when I'm healed we can find a way to open you to the power again."

"Why? I'm content with the way things are."

"I couldn't live like that."

"You don't have to."

Her brow furrowed. "I don't understand."

"I walked the paths of power when it was time for me to do so. Now it's time for me to find another path. I don't miss the magic much, and it's left a lot of good things in my life." He touched her nose. "Having been a magician has made some positive changes in my life."

"Yeah? Like what?"

"Well, for one thing, I've learned to sing a lot better."

"This is a major improvement in your life?"